LAURIE R. KING'S BESTSELLING NOVELS

OF SUSPENSE ARE...

"Rousing ... riveting ... suspenseful." —*Chicago Sun-Times*

"The great marvel of King's series is that she's managed to preserve the integrity of Holmes's character and yet somehow conjure up a woman astute, edgy and compelling enough to be the partner of his mind as well as his heart." —*The Washington Post Book World*

"The Mary Russell series is the most sustained feat of imagination in mystery fiction today." —Lee Child

PRAISE FOR LAURIE R. KING'S BESTSELLING MYSTERY

THE MURDER OF MARY RUSSELL

"A tantalizing tale of deception and misdirection for her readers' delight." —*LibraryReads* (a Top 10 pick)

"Readers are in for a treat. ... A triumph of plotting ... delightful." —*Booklist* (starred review)

"Touching, remarkable, and wholly absorbing ... a high point in King's long-running series ... a compelling demonstration of the ways inventive writers can continue to breathe new life into the Holmes-ian mythology." —*Kirkus Reviews* (starred review)

"Whip-smart, suspenseful and intricately plotted, *The Murder of Mary Russell* shines a brilliant light on an often overlooked aspect of the Sherlock Holmes universe." —*Shelf Awareness*

BY LAURIE R. KING

MARY RUSSELL

STUYVESANT & GREY

KATE MARTINELLI

AND

The
Murder
of
Mary Russell

The
Murder
of
Mary Russell

A novel of suspense featuring

Mary Russell and Sherlock Holmes

Laurie R. King

BANTAM BOOKS

NEW YORK

2017 Bantam Books Trade Paperback Edition

Copyright © 2016 by Laurie R. King
Excerpt from *Lockdown* by Laurie R. King copyright © 2017 by Laurie R. King

Published in the United States by Bantam Books, an imprint of Random House, a division of Penguin Random House LLC, New York.

BANTAM BOOKS and the HOUSE colophon are registered trademarks of Penguin Random House LLC.

Originally published in hardcover in the United States by Bantam Books, an imprint of Random House, a division of Penguin Random House LLC, in 2016.

This book contains an excerpt from the forthcoming book *Lockdown* by Laurie R. King. This excerpt has been set for this edition only and may not reflect the final content of the forthcoming edition.

ISBN 978-0-8041-7792-4
Ebook ISBN 978-0-8041-7791-7

Printed in the United States of America on acid-free paper

randomhousebooks.com

2 4 6 8 9 7 5 3 1

Book design by Caroline Cunningham

For my sister, Lynn Difley, who devotes her life to encouraging white-haired folk to find their strength.

... a young seaman of the name of Hudson ...

† † †

"Bless you, sir, I know where all my old friends are," said the fellow with a sinister smile.

† † †

"'The game is up. Hudson has told all. Fly for your life.'"

—"The Adventure of the *Gloria Scott*"
by Arthur Conan Doyle

I

13 MAY 1925
SUSSEX

CHAPTER ONE

9:15 a.m.

rony comes in many flavours, sweet to bitter. The harshest irony I ever tasted was this: when I was interrupted that spring morning, I felt only relief.

But then, tyres on wet gravel sound nothing like the crack of doom.

The noise caught me in the midst of an attack on the post overflowing my desk in Sussex. Since dawn, I'd been elbow-deep in five months' worth of pleas, adverts, requests for information now out of date, proposals of joint ventures similarly belated, legal and scholarly papers in need of review, and a thin handful of actual letters from friends near and far. I wanted nothing more than to haul the lot outside and set a match to it.

When I heard the noise, I assumed it was Mrs Hudson, returning for some forgotten element of her morning's trip to Eastbourne. However, the tyres sounded more tentative than Patrick's hand on the wheel (Patrick Mason was my farm manager and our housekeeper's occasional driver). Nor did the approaching engine sound familiar. A taxi bringing Holmes, perhaps, finished with his unspecified tasks for his brother, Mycroft? I hadn't seen my husband since he'd left Oxford, two weeks before.

But a glance through the library window showed an unfamiliar car with London number plates and a solitary figure considerably smaller than Sherlock Holmes. The driver circled counter-clockwise, coming to a halt before the house.

I headed to the door with a light heart: unarguable proof that Mary Russell had no talent for reading the future.

I stepped from the front door into the roofed portico beyond, stopping as the fickle morning sunshine gave way to another quick shower. The driver's door opened, but he hesitated, seeing not just the rain, but me. He'd expected someone else.

"May I help you?" I called.

"Er, the Holmeses?"

"This is the place," I confirmed. The shower grew stronger, spattering down the drive, and although the day was warm enough, I had no wish to change out of wet clothes. I turned to rummage through the odd population of canes, sticks, and tools in the corner of the entryway, but before I could locate an umbrella that functioned, the car door slammed and footsteps hurried across the stones. I let go the handle and gave the visitor some room under the shelter.

He was a short, stocky man in his forties, wearing a new black overcoat, an old brown suit, and a cloth driving cap that he now pulled off, snapping it clear of drops before arranging it back over his blond hair. His brief question had been insufficient to betray an accent, but it had to be either Australian or South African—his pale blue eyes positively blazed out of sun-darkened skin, and his suit had a distinctly colonial air to it. I had just chosen Australia when his greeting confirmed it.

"G'day, Ma'am. Nice place you got here."

With that greeting, I finally raised a mental eyebrow.

A person's first words can reveal a great deal more than the speaker's origins. The closer one sticks to the traditional forms—*Good day, Madam, terribly sorry to bother you but* . . . or a chatty variation such as, *Dreadful weather for May, Ma'am, please don't come any further into it, I just* . . . —the smoother the transition into a stranger's life. But *Nice place you got here,* coupled with a blithe spattering of drops across the entry tiles and

a grin that showed too many teeth? The man was out to sell me something.

Had I actually been working that morning—had I not been so grateful for any interruption at all—I might simply have taken another step back and shut the door in his face. Might not even have gone out at all, for that matter, thus setting events off in a very different direction. But with nothing more compelling than a stack of mail to draw me, that self-assured grin made for a nice little challenge.

Wouldn't one think that life with Sherlock Holmes would have taught me all about the perils of boredom? And overconfidence? But like a fool, I felt only relief at this holiday from envelopes. "My husband is not here at the moment."

Another young woman might have said those words apologetically, or perhaps nervously. I merely stated them as fact. He gave me a quick glance, head to toe, taking in my short but decidedly unfashionable haircut, my complete lack of makeup, the old shirt I wore (one of Holmes' with its sleeves rolled up), and the trousers on my legs. He reacted with a degree more sensitivity than I might have expected. His posture subsided, his bare grin gave way to something more polite, and he removed his hat again, this time a gesture of respect rather than convenience. Even his words reflected the change.

"Sorry, Ma'am, but it's not him I'm looking for. I wonder . . . does Mrs Hudson live here? Mrs Clari—Clara Hudson?"

"She does, but—"

His right hand shot out at me. "Then you must be the missus. Mary Russell? You look just like she described you!"

I stifled my arm's automatic impulse—to catch that outstretched hand and whirl him against the wall—and instead permitted him to grab me and pump away, grinning into my face. Still a salesman.

After four shakes I took back my hand. "Sir," I began.

"Is she here? My mother?"

If he'd squatted down to tip me head over heels, he could not have astonished me more. *Mother??*

He saw my reaction, and gave a sort of smacking-of-the-forehead

gesture. "What am I thinking? Guess I'm a little excited. My name is Samuel—Samuel Hudson. Great ta meetcha," and the hand came out again to seize mine.

Mother?

Of all the mysteries that are love, maternal love may be the most basic. My own mother had died when I was fourteen. A few months later, with the raw instincts of a barnyard chick imprinting its affections on the first available surrogate, my bereft heart had claimed Mrs Hudson for its own. I had known her for ten years now, lived with her for more than four, and she was as close to a mother as I would ever again have.

I knew of course that she had a son in Australia—or rather, she had a "nephew" whom her sister claimed as her own. Glimpses of an older person's complex and unspoken history can be startling, even when one's main source of comparison is a dedicated Bohemian like Sherlock Holmes. Perhaps especially in that case: Mrs Hudson had always been a point of solid dependability amidst the anarchy that surrounded Holmes.

Motherhood is more than a biological state. Yes, I knew—well, suspected—about her past, but I had never conducted the close investigation I might have with a stranger, and definitely never asked Holmes if Mrs Hudson had been married before giving over the child to be raised. I admit that a few weeks into our acquaintance, when it dawned on me that the nephew might in fact be a son, my first reaction was an adolescent giggle over the idea of Mrs Hudson as a fallen woman. My second reaction was curiosity. Oddly, Holmes refused to say anything about the matter. It took a while before I realised that his blatant unconcern was the only way he could grant his poor housekeeper (as if she wasn't so much more than housekeeper!) some degree of privacy.

Once I saw this, I followed his lead. I made no further attempts to rifle her possessions or read the letters from Australia—written largely by her sister (who had died, some nine months before this) although Mrs Hudson's interest clearly lay more in the news about their shared son. To judge by the sighs and a general air of distraction after each letter's arrival, it was not an easy relationship. In fact, her "nephew" seemed to be

something of a ne'er do well, but since she never asked for assistance or advice, we could only politely ignore her unspoken woes.

Until now, when he stood on our doorstep.

Assuming this *was* Samuel Hudson.

Would most young women accept such a claim without question? Perhaps. And perhaps most young women would be justified in their naïve acceptance. However, I was married to Sherlock Holmes, had known him only a few hours longer than I'd known Mrs Hudson, and the basic fact of life with Holmes was: the world is filled with enemies.

So, I would not permit this person to meet Mrs Hudson without a thorough vetting.

All of this reflection and decision took me approximately three of the fellow's hand-pumps. I bared my teeth to make a grin at least the equal of his, and drew back to welcome him inside (which had the added benefit of removing my hand from his).

"She's away for the morning," I told him, "I'm not sure exactly when she'll be back. However, I can probably manage to make you a cup of tea in her absence. Unless you'd rather have coffee?"

"A cuppa would go down a treat," he said, then to clarify: "Tea, thanks."

I closed the door against the cool air and led him into the main room, our idiosyncratic combination of sitting room, library, and dining room. The south wall, to my right, had a table in the bay window, where we took our meals; the east wall held laden bookshelves, and French doors to the terrace; on the north lay a wide fireplace with chairs and a settee, along with the entrance to the kitchen. Holmes' observation beehive, set into the wall beside the bay window, was behind its cover.

"Whadda great room," the visitor enthused.

I bit off my tart response—*I'm sorry, it's not for sale*—and instead turned the topic onto a more pertinent track. "Not to be rude, but I don't suppose you have any sort of identification? You don't look much like her." Mrs Hudson's grey hair had once been brown, not blonde, and her dark eyes were nothing like this man's bright blue. Even if the fellow had been born "Samuel Hudson," it was a common enough surname. He

might be some lunatic with a Sherlock Holmes mania built around a minor coincidence.

If so, this would not be the first fantasist to waltz into our lives, although the odds were mounting in his favour: he was certainly from Australia, and he knew not only our names, but where we lived. Still, the thought of that hand clamping down over Mrs Hudson's beloved palm . . .

(I recount these details to show that I was not entirely oblivious to the world around me. Just not attentive enough.)

"Nah, guess I don't," he said, running a hand over his visage. "That's probably why I never doubted who my mother was—Mum and I both have my granddad's looks, or so I'm told. Identification, is it? I didn't bring my passport, didn't expect—ah, what about these?" His fingers came out of an inner pocket with a photograph and a golden chain. He handed me the first.

It showed two women and an infant. The women sat in the formal pose required of a slow shutter speed, although it had been taken in a garden, not a studio—a private garden, most likely, since neither wore a hat. The infant was as unformed as any small human, little more than pale hair and layers of cloth. The woman holding him was blonde, with light-coloured eyes, and I thought—as I had from the first time I'd seen this photograph, years before—that there was something odd about the way the woman's hands clutched the baby, thrusting him at the camera rather than cuddling him to her. Her features, too, had some faint air of hidden meaning, a triumph almost, that made one very aware of the empty hands of the woman at her side.

The other woman, taller, straight of back and dark of hair and eye, looked into the camera with a gaze of sad acceptance. Even if I had not recognised this woman's features, I would have known her by that expression: *I see what you are up to,* it said, *but I love you anyway.*

Heaven knows she'd had plenty of opportunities to look at me that way, over the years.

I handed the photograph back to Samuel Hudson. "She has a copy of that." I did not add, *Hers is worn down to the paper from ten thousand*

touches of her finger. My mother had used that very gesture, on the mezu-
zah at our door.

"Well, that's me," he said. "With my mother and aunt—although until
just a few months ago, I thought the two went the other way around."

I glanced up sharply at the bitter edge in his voice, to see his other
piece of evidence dangling from thumb and forefinger: a gold chain
strung through a hole drilled in an old half sovereign coin.

"Does she still wear hers?" he asked.

The chain looked too bright and the gold of the pendant less worn
than I remembered, but the necklace definitely caught my attention. I'd
never seen it around Mrs Hudson's neck, but I recognised it as the flash
of gold I'd first spotted years before, tucked in the bottom of her incongruously large and ornate jewellery box. I might have taken no notice, at
the time, but for the casual haste with which she had flipped something
over it.

"No, she doesn't wear one like that," I told him.

"Well," he said, "I guess she'll remember it anyway." He gave it a polish on his coat-tails, held it up in admiration, then set off on a circuit of
the room, pausing on his way to drop the chain over the jack-knife
Holmes always left on the mantelpiece. I watched with increasing un-
ease as he surveyed the walls, peered at the books on the shelves, poked
an obtrusive finger through the clutter of papers and oddments on the
table under the window. I was sorry I'd invited him in. And I changed my
mind about letting him cool his heels here until she returned.

I would give him a polite cup of tea, and I would get rid of him. Let
Mrs Hudson meet him on her own terms.

"Tea," I said. "Just let me put on the kettle. How long have you been
in England? I hope your trip went well—that you weren't caught in those
storms I read about last month?"

As I moved in the direction of the kitchen, I became aware of two
things. First, I wanted badly to be alone, just for a minute, so I could try
to beat my thoughts into order. (*Mother? Mother! Though nothing like her.
Shouldn't I be pleased? Does that make him my sort-of . . . brother? But—*)
Second and even more peculiar, while my mouth was making conversa-

tion, my body wanted nothing to do with him. I was edging away towards the kitchen door because I did not want to turn my back on this man.

What was going on? I knew of no wrongdoing on his part, other than making his mother sigh. Still, I kept retreating backwards, making conversation as I went—too bad he'd hit a rainy day because the view from Beachy Head was glorious. Where did he live in Australia? Was he staying in Sussex or just down from London for the day?

Sydney, came the reply (which I knew) and only for the day (a relief, although he hadn't come far that morning: the car bonnet was shiny, not hot enough to steam away the rain). At that point, my heels touched wood, so I ducked through the door and let it close, to stand with my hands resting on the old, well-scrubbed wooden table. I took a deep breath, then another.

I, better than most, had reason to understand that when one does not face up to events, they return—with a vengeance. My mother's death and my desperate adoption of Mrs Hudson in her place might be facts of a distant past—but only until a situation came along to upend matters.

Well, that situation had arrived. Mrs Hudson was not my mother. Mrs Hudson was getting old, and deserved a full relationship with her son—her *actual* child—before she died. That he was a touch smarmy for my taste had nothing to do with matters.

After a moment, I scrubbed my damp palms down my shirt-front and picked up the kettle. (*The new whistling tea-kettle that* I *gave her for her birthday, just last—Oh, get a hold of yourself, Russell!*) I filled it, shoved the whistle in place, and set its broad bottom over the flame. I would not hurry. Samuel Hudson might push through the door at any moment, to invade his mother's private realm, but he had the right to invade. This was his mother's home. If she were here, she would permit him inside. Therefore, so would I.

But I was relieved when he did not follow me.

Kettle on, two cups on a tray, anything else a hostess ought to do? A plate of something hospitable, perhaps? I searched through the tins where she stored her baked goods, and found a startling array of biscuits,

sponges, and tea cakes—ah, yes: we were having a party on Saturday. I hesitated between her Sultana biscuits and a loaf with strips of lemon peel on the top. Which would an Australian salesman prefer? Perhaps I should ask.

"Mrs—your *mother* has made Sultana biscuits and a lemon loaf. Which would you—"

My voice strangled to a halt as I stepped into the sitting room and looked into the working end of a revolver.

Behind the gun stood a man with murder in his eyes.

Chapter Two

12:40 p.m.

Mrs Clara Hudson came home through the kitchen door, as always. She placed her laden basket on the scrubbed work-table, then paused to sniff the air, wondering—but an armful of parcels was struggling in the doorway behind her, and she hurried to take some of it.

"Thank you, Patrick," she said. "I'm glad you talked me into going this morning—the produce would have been picked over, and you were right, it cleared up beautifully. Would you put those in the pantry? Thank you, dear."

"Don't know why you needed to buy taters," he grumbled. "Ours'll be ready in a couple weeks."

"Yes, but I wanted to make my potato salad for Mary's garden party. Her friend Veronica is particularly fond of it."

"Weather should go fine by Saturday, at any rate."

"That's what the papers say. Well, thank—"

"Oh, Mrs Hudson," he said, in a different voice. "I'm sorry."

She turned and saw Patrick's muscular back in the doorway to her rooms, squatting to pick up something from the floor. She moved around the work-table, and saw that the final survivor of her mother's treasured porcelain had leapt from its little shelf and shattered against the slates. Fetching the hand-broom and scoop, she took the pieces from Patrick's broad hand and dropped them unceremoniously in.

"It could be fixed," he protested. "I know a man—"

"That saucer has been fixed once already, Patrick. Let's let it die a clean death this time." In truth, she hadn't much liked its first repair. She'd only put it on the shelf because Mary had gone to such trouble, and expense.

She swept the floor, surveying the area for stray shards. She found a couple under the writing desk, and absently pushed the drawer shut as she straightened from sweeping around the narrow legs.

"It's really fine, Patrick. Thank you again, for all your help, the marketing would have taken me all day. Give Tillie my love."

He watched her pour the bits of porcelain into the dust bin, then gave a brief tug at his hat and went out. Clara Hudson ran a damp cloth over the floor to remove their footprints, then walked back into her quarters, taking off her hat and coat, pulling on an apron. She owned four hats but a dozen or more aprons, each suiting a day's mood and tasks—the one she chose now was cheerful but practical, with bright flowers and few ruffles. She checked her reflection (*As if anyone cares what I look like!*) in the small portion of the looking glass not covered by photos and mementoes. As usual, her thumb came absently out to brush the one taken in Alicia's garden. Unlike usual, she paused there, rearranging the mementoes around the gap where the porcelain saucer had stood.

The collection looked like any old woman's shrine to ancient history. It was not. Oh, ancient, yes—nothing here had come into being later than 1880. But it was less a shrine than a series of voices, each one speaking words of admonition.

The saucer had been from her mother's favourite tea-cup, damaged survivor of a careless past; the chewed-up string dolly, to a stranger's eyes the whimsical reminder of a loving childhood, was the work of a dangerous drunk, while the rose-coloured dress it wore had been made from a stolen silk handkerchief. And the photograph—the only photograph she owned of her blood relations? That too bore a message that her eyes alone could see: Alicia holding Samuel like a trophy; Samuel, out of focus and unshaped, waiting to be given form; she herself, wishing she could feel happy for the two of them. And out of sight, the absent figure that explained ten thousand affectionate brushes of her thumb, Billy Mudd, all seven years of him, behind the lens, watching fascinated as the sweating photographer did his work in the Sydney garden. Billy, the photograph's secret presence . . .

Mrs Hudson caught herself, and made a *tsk* sound with her aged lips. She was secretly pleased to be rid of that dreadful saucer—the mends had haunted her. And she had no cause to feel uneasy, on a beautiful sunny Sussex afternoon with three nice busy days of party preparations before her. The past was dead, good riddance to it.

She tied her apron's strings and returned to work. Mary must have thought about making tea, she saw, and got as far as setting cups on a tray before something distracted her. Bad as her husband, the girl was. She would appear, once she'd come to a spot in her writing—or experiment, or what-have-you—where she could be interrupted.

Mrs Hudson smiled as she unpacked the tender strawberries that had rewarded her early arrival in Eastbourne that morning. Funny, the things one was proud of in life—this life. Potato salad on a spring day; perfect berries from Mr Brace's stall, served with the thick cream that Mrs Philpott promised to send over. Scrubbed kitchen work-tables, shelves without dust, the gleam of sun on fresh-polished floors.

Trust, upheld and unbroken.

When the baskets were empty, their contents stored away, Mrs Hudson wiped her hands on the cloth and looked around, conscious again of that vague sense of wrongness. A smell, one that didn't belong here. Leaking gas? Something going off in the pantry? She walked back and forth, but couldn't find it, and tried to dismiss the sensation.

Tea: that was what she needed. Mary must be even more intent on her work than usual, since she had not appeared to help put away the shopping. Not likely she'd gone off for a walk in the rain—even the papers had said the sky would clear by afternoon.

The housekeeper reached for the shiny copper whistling-kettle, only to discover that it was not only full of water, but slightly warm. She frowned. *Oh, don't tell me I walked out and left my new birthday present over the flame! Have I done this before? Is that why Mary gave me one with a whistle, so I don't burn down the house with being absent-minded?* She was not yet seventy: far too young to have her mind go soft.

She set the kettle down on the flame and stood, kneading her arthritic fingers, wondering how to find out if she'd been absent-minded without asking directly. Questions like that were difficult, with someone as sharp as Mary Russell.

She shook her head and took down the flowered teapot, laid out spoons and milk beside the cups on the tray, checked the kettle's whistle to make sure it was firmly seated, and finally went in search of the young woman around whom she had built the last decade of her life—her already much-rebuilt life.

She did not find her.

What she found was inexplicable: the beautiful little glass lamp, fallen from the table directly into the trash bin; what appeared to be muddy footprints, crossing the freshly polished wood towards the front door. Her shocked gaze flew upwards—only to snag against an even greater impossibility: a slim knife, stained with red, jutting from the plaster beside the bay window.

Her breath stopped. No. One of their experiments, it had to be. A jest, some thoughtless . . .

Mrs Hudson forced her legs to move into the room. Two steps, three, before an even more horrifying sight came into view.

A pool of blood in two halves, some eight inches apart: one thick and as long as her arm, the other shorter and much smeared about, both beginning to go brown at the edges. Drag marks leading towards the front door. A terrible amount of blood.

And with the sight, with that scream of red across her polished floor, Mrs Hudson abruptly knew what the faint odour was, the one that had picked around the edges of her mind since the moment she walked into her kitchen.

It was the smell of gunshot.

II

CLARISSA

CHAPTER THREE

Clara Hudson's dark hair had gone mostly grey before she realised that childhood was not intended to be a continuous stream of catastrophe and turmoil.

At the time, while she was living it, the constancy of hunger, discomfort, dirt, and uncertainty, with the occasional punctuation of death and fists, was simply the price of existence. One fought, one prevailed, and one hugged to oneself the rare days when an actual dinner was set upon a clean table, with a family around it. Trust was a snare, safety a delusion; together they led to blood drying upon the floor.

Clara Hudson was born Clarissa, a haughty name for a child who drew her first breath in a seedy Edinburgh room without so much as a washbasin in the corner. Her mother named her. Her father was not there to be consulted.

Clarissa's mother, the former Sally Rickets, was not haughty—

although neither had she been born in a lodgings-house. Sally had once Been Better. Sally had Come From Money, although not enough of it that she could turn her back on Society's demands. As a girl, she was both clear-sighted enough to recognise the deficiencies in the mirror, and romantic enough to feel that lack of beauty would not matter if only the right man came along.

Romance and realism make for a volatile mix. In Sally's case, the mix gave rise to a painful shyness, driving Sally to the shelves of the circulating library and turning her wit to blushing awkwardness at any social gathering. Wit she had, along with glossy brown hair, skill with the needle, and an odd gift for mimicry (witnessed by few outside her family), but as her twentieth birthday loomed, Sally's heart went unclaimed. Another girl might have sighed and put away romantic dreams in favour of some youth with sour breath but good prospects. Sally raised her chin and declared that she would seek employment.

In the best tradition of the novels she adored, she took a job as governess, hiding even from herself the secret conviction that she would thereby meet a mysterious and intended mate. Instead, she met Jimmy Hudson.

Sally's employers moved from Edinburgh to London in the autumn of 1852, to be close to the father's expanding business interests. It was a lonely position, that of governess: too grand for the servants, too low for the family. Some nights, Sally felt very far from home.

But Sally did her best by her two young charges, seven-year-old Albert and his little sister Faith. She taught them their lessons and manners, entertained them (and occasionally coaxed them into obedience) with improvised plays, and took them for walks in this vast, filthy, fascinating, and crowded city from which an empire was ruled. Twice in the spring of 1853, Victoria herself rode past in a grand carriage. The second time, the Queen gave the children a nod.

That summer, young Bertie (four years younger than his namesake, the Prince of Wales) was given a model sailboat for his birthday. Sally's walks with her charges grew more cumbersome, as the great wicker perambulator that she already had problems wrestling along the streets now had a boat perched across it. One scorching August day, the little boat came to grief on some weeds in the Round Pond. Bertie began to wail, his sister (who was working on a new tooth) threw in her screams, and with increasing desperation (Bertie's mother had made it clear that the young master was not to ruin any more clothing) Sally looked around for some urchin she could pay to fetch the craft. In vain.

Then out of nowhere, a young man appeared. He stripped off his jacket, kicked his shoes onto the path, and waded out for the diminutive yacht.

The figure that climbed from the water, trailing mud and water weeds from a pair of irretrievably soiled trousers, was no lady's idea of young Lochinvar. The man—boy, really—was small and wiry, with an odd amble to his walk that suggested a bad leg and rather less white to his teeth than a hero ought to have. But his straw-coloured hair was thick and his grin was friendly, and although the boldness in his cornflower-blue eyes would normally have alarmed her, the young man did no more than tug his hat at the governess before turning his attentions to her charge.

"Captain, sir, I believe your ship has come to grief. May I make a suggestion or two, to keep it from happening again?"

He and young Bertie bent over the ship, instantly deep in the arcane subtleties of jibs, mizzens, wind direction, and the placement of ballast. After a bit, Sally moved little Faith into the shade and got her settled with a hard biscuit.

Sally watched as the two males returned the boat to the water. It tipped for a moment, then found the wind and took off, neat as could be. Bertie ran along the pathway in pursuit. His rescuer watched for a moment, then retrieved his jacket and shoes, bringing them over to the bench where she sat.

"Thank ye," she said. "I couldna' think how I was going t'explain another set of spoilt trews to the lad's mother."

"Happy to help," he said. He sat at the other end of the bench to put on his shoes. He smelt, she noticed, of sun and baking linen, not of the tobacco that permeated the pores of most young men. Pleased, Sally allowed her eyes a surreptitious glance, noticing first the bracelet of intricately knotted string he wore around his wrist, then further down, the state of his stockings.

"Och, sir, but look at ye! I shall pay for the launderin'."

"Wouldn't think of it," he said.

"I insist."

"Then you'll have to strip them off me yourself," he said.

She went instantly scarlet. He laughed.

Now, another man with that same exchange, and Sally would have wrapped her dignity around her and taken her leave. But the laugh had been a nice one, neither cruel nor forward. The sort of tease a brother might have made. The stranger finished tying his laces, brushed ineffectually at his sodden trouser legs, and restored his hat to his head.

"Sir," she found herself saying, "I dinna even know your name. Whom shall I tell young Albert it was, that came to his rescue?"

He paused in the act of rising and swivelled on the wooden slats, as if seeing her for the first time. After a moment, he doffed his hat and smiled—and if she felt a pulse of alarm, it was small and far away, lost beneath the twinkle in his eyes. "James Hudson, at your service."

"Well, I thank ye, Mr Hudson. My name is Rickets. Sally Rickets."

"You're from Scotland, Miss Rickets?"

"That I am. Edinburgh." She made a noise like a clearing of the throat, then continued in accents considerably closer to those of London town. "It will take me a good long time to lose the accent, I fear."

"Oh, don't do that, the real you is charming." She blushed again, less furiously. Mr Hudson's head tipped to one side. "So tell me, Miss Rickets. Do you make it a habit to bring your young captain here?"

Up to then, she had not.

The rest of the afternoon passed in a flash. He bought the children a sherbet from a passing vender, and a lemonade for her. He told them stories, outrageous tales of sea creatures and exotic places; some of them might even have been true. At some point he absent-mindedly drew a tangle of waxed thread from a pocket and set about knotting it in patterns, as another man might fiddle with a pipe or gold watch. When Bertie came back to the bench, grubby though unruined and pleased with his skills, he demanded to know what his new hero was doing, and was shown the lower portion of a miniature lanyard. An hour later, the child had the finished object in his hand.

From that day on, Kensington Gardens became a regular part of the week. Often, Jim Hudson was there. And more often than not, Sunday afternoons, Sally's half day of freedom, were spent in his company.

Within the month, she wore a delicately knotted bracelet around her left wrist.

Hudson was a sailor who'd grown tired of the life. He'd gone to sea at the age of thirteen, sent by his father in part for the money, but also to get the lad away from a doting mother who petted and spoiled her only child. Seven years later, a docking in Portsmouth coincided with his twentieth birthday and a growing conviction that life might hold other, less arduous, possibilities for a man of brains and determination. He was full of himself, was Jimmy Hudson, quick of wit and of temper, a curly-haired, blue-eyed charmer who had learned to conceal from his fellows the sure belief of his superior nature. Critics might say James Hudson felt the world owed him life on a silver platter. Himself, he said that the world was there for the taking.

It never occurred to the innocent governess that a young sailor's natural habitat lay not in afternoons beside the Serpentine, idling amongst the idle classes. Even less did she pause to wonder what Jimmy Hudson saw in her, an unbeautiful woman two years older and an inch taller than he. If she'd been home, around friends and family, there might have been someone to ask the question—but by the time Sally had friends around her, it was too late. She had fallen for him, this rogue with the lovely hair and the careless, crooked grin, head over heels. And although there was some doubt in her own mind about whether her virtue would survive to a wedding, in the end—to her pride and his astonishment—it did. For the rogue had taken a tumble of his own, into the dark brown eyes of a shy and awkward Scottish girl, and he gave her a ring and a name before he gave her a baby.

What he did not give her was the full truth about how he earned a living.

Their son was born, early and ill-formed, on a cool spring morning five months and three days after their wedding vows. Mother and father held their tiny blue-skinned child, they heard its thin cries dwindle and cease, they watched the life leave it. Hudson went out and got drunk. Two days later, he came home to find his wife delirious with fever.

If James Hudson had been as hard-plated as he imagined, matters would have been simple. He'd have bathed his wife's face and held her hand and watched her die, before going on with his life. But Sally was his one weakness, his hidden truth, the one whose belief made him real.

He panicked.

London in 1854 was a city of gangs, from those in Parliament to those of the blackest rookeries. Jim Hudson's habitual gang was in the middle of those extremes, a wide-spread corporation of criminal activity under the absolute rule of a man known as The Bishop. The Bishop was ruthless, but fair—and smart. He knew that sometimes the fist was called for, but that sometimes a hand outstretched, especially if it had money in it, could be a powerful way to buy a man's loyalty.

The Bishop listened to his desperate underling. He thought about young Hudson's history, his past usefulness in matters related to shipping and the passage of valuables through the docks, and he considered the young man's future potential. In the end, he nodded. Agreement was reached. Doctors were sent—good doctors, not stinking blood-letters with gin on their breath and filth around their finger-nails. A nurse came. Sally walked the edges of life for a week, two . . . and then backed away from the eternal cliff.

By which time Hudson owed The Bishop a considerable debt.

In the spring of 1854, Britain went to war with Russia over the Crimean Peninsula. During the summer, ten thousand Londoners died from the cholera. In the autumn, James Hudson moved from a dockland informer into one of The Bishop's burglary gangs.

He was small, strong, and as a sailor, easy with heights even in the dark. His job was to enter the house through windows left unlatched by a paid-off servant, letting his partners inside. One of those partners was a man he'd known for months, a wiry, foul-mouthed, and cheerful cracksman in his forties. The other Hudson was less happy about: a lad of fourteen who was new to the job, although he had lived in crime all his life. The Bishop's son—his only son—was there to learn his father's trade from the inside, and a less compliant apprentice would have been difficult to find. Nobody who worked with the surly and self-important lad enjoyed the experience, but Jimmy and his cracksman learned how to make him feel important without risking the job. And the boy was bright enough, if one could talk him around his tendency to hit first and think later.

Hudson did not tell Sally what he was doing, or how much they owed The Bishop, merely that he'd need to work the occasional night. Sally could be disapproving, at times, and love her or not, that Scots righteousness of hers could wear on a man's nerves. How did she expect him to make a living? Would she rather he went to sea, to be gone for months on end?

By the spring of 1855, Hudson and his partners were entering two or three houses a month. The Season being fully under way meant that family jewels had been retrieved from bank vaults for the ladies' throats, and since maids knew well where the necklaces and tiaras were kept . . .

Still, even with The Bishop's iron fist in control, it was just a matter of time before someone got careless. On April 27, a lady's maid was arrested. She talked. The dominos of The Bishop's organisation began to tumble—not that the man himself was in danger of arrest: The Bishop owned enough policemen to deflect an armful of warrants, and to free his son from worse crimes than house-breaking. Still, the lower levels of his network began to file into Newgate Prison.

James Hudson was tucking into his dinner when news reached him that the cracksman had been taken. Within the hour, he was pulling Sally from their tiny house, pushing her and a pair of trunks into a hired cart, and hushing her protests, not with a fist (though he was tempted) but with a sharp word and a promise that he would tell her all, later.

London was too hot for this upper-storey man. Edinburgh would be a risk, since everyone knew where Hudson's wife hailed from. Plymouth or Southampton were tempting, but surely the first places anyone might look for a sailor. Instead, the young couple's flight continued west.

On the first of May, Sally and Jim came to Falmouth, a small but active port town on the coast of Cornwall. They stored their trunks and walked through the streets until they found rooms bright enough to bear and cheap enough to afford. There, on the straw mattress behind the closed door, Hudson sat down with his wife at last. He took Sally's hand, and told her exactly why they'd had to flee.

When she took back her hand and got to her feet, he thought she was about to leave him. Half of him wished she would. But the fact that her illness had driven them to this gave Sally pause.

She stood for a long time at the little window, her spine rigid and unreadable. However, the longer she stood, the better his chances, so he sat, waiting, until she called him daft and an idjit and a list of other names. But she was *there,* and so Hudson swallowed his pride and his retorts (*She'd* lost the baby; *she'd* gone and got sick!) to hang his head and agree that yes, he was a fool and yes, he should have told her. He said yes, too, when she laid down the law and said that he would have nought more to do with crime. That they would work like decent folk and pay back the debt by honest means, no matter how long it took.

Hudson knew the chances of buying their way back into The Bishop's good graces were nil. But he said nothing. She came to sit beside him on the rough bed. When she slipped her hand into his, it was enough to be going on.

They both found work, he in the docks, Sally at a busy coaching inn. May went, and June. As July wore on, Hudson began to breathe again. The waxed threads reappeared, and his clever fingers resumed their darting knots: a pair of earrings took shape, in a dark red that echoed the chestnut gleams in his wife's hair. In August, the Queen and Albert were entertained at Versailles. In September, Sebastopol fell to the British. Two weeks later, Sally told him shyly that she was pregnant again.

Ten days after that, on October the seventh, Hudson was walking down a street when he saw a familiar face: one of The Bishop's men from London.

He ducked into an alleyway, trotting rapidly away from the docks to weave a circuitous path home, glancing over his shoulder the entire way.

He hadn't been seen, he was pretty sure. And although Sally had left already for work, he reassured himself that the man had never met her, had no reason to know what she looked like, and they were even using different names, here . . . Nonetheless, he poured himself a generous level of gin, standing at the window behind the thin curtains, and spent the day in an agony of nerves, convinced that Sally had been seized.

When at last he heard her feet on the stairs, the gust of relief instantly converted his fear to blind rage.

Chapter Four

He managed not to hit Sally—she was pregnant, after all—but her hair tumbled down as he shook her, and the fear in her eyes made his anger flare all the hotter.

But only for an instant. He turned to splash the last of the spirits into his cup, dumping it down his throat like cold water across a fighting dog.

By the time she understood, confession had soured the gin in his gut and his fury had given way to exhaustion. He collapsed onto the side of the bed, head in hands.

"Ah, Sally, what're we going to do?" he groaned.

"Ye should go."

"Where? If I go back to London, I'll be arrested. Or worse. I'll have to let The Bishop know where he can find me. Maybe he can make use of me out here."

"Is . . ." Sally hesitated, then forced herself to ask. "Is what you did a . . . hanging offense?"

"No! Nobody got hurt. But it'd be transportation for sure. And what good will I do you and the baby for seven years in Australia?"

They sat listening to the silence. After a bit, Sally straightened on her chair and took a breath. "What about getting work on a ship? Just for a time."

"What, shipping out?"

"It needn't be for long, just to get you away. A month, say, then get off the ship at the next port and work another ship back. You write and tell me where to meet you. I could make my way to Liverpool, or Hull— York, even, to get away from ports. Jimmy, we could be together when our son is born."

He raised his head, fighting hope. "But what if you have to leave here? How would I ever find you again?"

"My sister." The only person from Sally's past who still wrote, who still loved her. The only person Sally knew she could trust, absolutely. "Write to Alice. She'll always know where I am."

They talked it up and down, but in truth, there was little choice. In the wee hours, he wrapped tender arms around her, his fingers apologising for the bruises on her shoulders. Before light, his sailor's bag was packed, his feet carrying him towards the docks.

That very day he set sail upon the barque *Gloria Scott*, a heavy old tub bound for Australia with, in addition to its crew, eighteen soldiers, four warders, a doctor, and a chaplain—because (the irony made him grin uncomfortably) the ship also carried thirty-eight felons wearing the chains of transportees.

Sally stood on the hill above town, wrapped in her thickest shawl, skirts tugged about by the chilly October wind, and watched her husband sail away. When the ship had faded into the Channel mists, she resolutely turned back towards the town and resumed her job at the inn.

A month later, a spurt of seven letters and a small parcel arrived all at once, posted from Gibraltar, addressed to the inn. Sally took them from the innkeeper in wonder, and carried them safely home.

The paper-wrapped parcel contained a lengthy letter, crumpled from the string, encircling an object that must have taken Jimmy every spare minute of the trip to that point. He'd made a dolly longer than her hand, with stubby extremities and a knob for a head, stuffed firm with kapok. Tens of thousands of tight little knots had gone into its making, and a great deal of thought: it even had a face of sorts, picked out in black thread, and a tuft of long black hair gathered into a plait. In a post-script, the letter said that, depending on whether the baby was a boy or a girl, Sally could cut the hair or leave it long, and sew the doll a dress or a sailor suit. She ran her fingers over the little figure's taut waxed-linen surface, feeling her husband's hands on every tiny bump. How many hours had this taken him? What had been going on all around him while he worked, what conversations, what kinds of men at his side? Holding it to her face, she could smell the sea and the smouldering lamps, and the tobacco the others had smoked while he worked. She could smell his life, far away.

She gave the manikin a kiss and sat it against her cup of cocoa while she sorted the envelopes by date, feeling the thickness of each, studying his writing on the outside. Then Sally Hudson dove into her husband's words like a starving thing.

The first two letters had little to say beyond the boredom of shipboard work, the tedium of the food, and how much he missed her. The two after that had clearly been written following a ration of rum, as his wandering hand transcribed an equally meandering stream of thoughts, plans, complaints, and sorrows. The next one picked up a bit, describing the odd behaviour of the chaplain and the willingness of some of the soldiers to lose money at cards. He added, as an afterthought at the bottom:

> PS. I don't suppose you'll approve of me playing cards but when time hangs heavy I can only tie so many knots. And anyway its savings for our future my lovey.

His next letter mentioned the chaplain again, then went on to describe a troublemaker among the prisoners, an extraordinarily tall minor aristocrat named Prendergast who had defrauded a wide selection of

City merchants of a stupendous amount of money. The police, it seemed, had not only been unable to find the money, they did not even know just how much it was. And Prendergast wasn't the only rich criminal on board the *Gloria Scott:* almost all the transportees were convicts of a financial nature—fraud, bank theft, forgery. Some of them were so clever, Hudson wrote admiringly, it was a wonder they'd been caught.

Hudson's final letter ended saying he planned to post the letters when the ship put into Gibraltar. However, he added, he had decided not to leave the ship himself until Cape Town. He would write her from there, to let her know when to expect him.

That letter did not come.

Weeks crawled by: Christmas, New Year's. Her belly grew, although to her great relief, where the first time she had been constantly ill and aching, this time went without problem. If only she would hear from Jimmy, all would surely be fine.

Then in January, Sally overheard two men talking. In an inn, rumours lay as thick underfoot as the wood chips absorbing the slops, but over the following days, she heard this one from too many directions to ignore.

The transport ship *Gloria Scott* was lost at sea.

Sally told herself that the old barque was just late. That Jimmy had slipped away in Cape Town, that the letter telling her had been lost. Surely he would appear soon. As for the ship herself being sunk, it was not due into Sydney until February: it had just put in elsewhere along the way for supplies, or repairs. Sally laid a hand on her belly, and closed her ears to the cruel whispers.

As the five-month mark crept up, Sally waited in dread for her womb to fall still, for early labour to start. But nothing of the sort happened. The baby kicked, her back ached, her belly grew.

And, she lost her job. The innkeeper said he would be pleased to have her back—she was a hard worker, a friendly face, and a step up in class from most serving maids—but the men came for a good time, not a reminder of home, so she'd have to take the next months off.

Without money, without Jimmy, the only person Sally had was her sister. So she left careful instructions with the innkeeper: what to do if someone came asking for her, and what to do if a letter arrived. She then went back to Edinburgh, her head over the heaving rails all the way. Once there, her hoarded savings bought her a few weeks in a tiny room a mile from her sister's trim, airy house. Alice had clean windows, a garden, and two servants; Sally had no carpets, a common standpipe in the yard, and a stinking lavatory at the back, two flights down.

Sally went into labour on a soft spring morning in early May. At the height of things, she chanted Jimmy's name, over and over, even though by this time, she was certain he was dead. Alice caught her small, red, perfectly formed niece with her own clean hands, having elbowed aside those of the midwife at the last minute.

Sally gave her daughter the haughty name of Clarissa, and nursed her and loved her and cried over the poor fatherless bairn.

Six days later, a letter arrived. Much travelled, stained by damp, bearing her sister's address.

Posted from Sydney.

There had been an uprising of the prisoners on board the *Gloria Scott,* Jimmy wrote, the ship taken over, some of the sailors joining in mutiny— a mutiny funded by the aristocratic rogue Jack Prendergast, who'd managed to smuggle a portion of his ill-gotten gains on board. Some of the sailors, dissatisfied with the captain and the conditions belowdecks, went along with the takeover; others drew the line at outright murder. The objectors were shoved onto a small boat with sailor's clothes, basic provisions, and a compass and chart—but before the *Gloria Scott* could get under way again, a powder-barrel deep in her bowels was set alight, either deliberately or from a stray spark. The ship's hull ripped into a million pieces, every porthole and hatch punched out, her mast uprooted. In minutes, where the barque had been was nothing but smoking wood and shredded canvas.

The row-boat, which had been set adrift little more than an hour before, turned back to the wreckage. There among the floating spars and ravaged bodies, they found a survivor clinging to some boards. (Sally frowned absently at her husband's emotional—one might almost say personal—description of this stunned, burned creature.) They rescued the sailor, took on board a few more still-sealed kegs of provisions, and turned again for the distant coastline.

The explosion's smoke-cloud rose high, however, and the coast of Africa was a well-travelled route. Sure enough, the following day another Australian-bound ship hove into view.

Nonetheless, Hudson wrote, some of the men in the boat had been participants in the initial hours of mutiny, up until murder began; others, the prisoners, had now been handed a chance at freedom. In those lonely dark hours, pulling slowly away from the drifting timbers, the survivors came to an agreement: they would say nothing of the name *Gloria Scott.* A new ship was conjured up from their imaginations, a story built around it. By the time the brig *Hotspur* plucked them from the waves, they were the survivors of the passenger ship *Amelia,* which had gone down with all hands apart from them.

Unlike the *Gloria Scott,* the *Hotspur* was a fast clipper, with no planned stops before Sydney Harbour. Hudson's chances of jumping ship in Cape Town vanished. Seventy-nine days later, the *Hotspur* dropped anchor. The survivors of the *Gloria Scott* took a last meal together, then quietly scattered: some for the gold fields, others to book passage back to England. And Jim Hudson ...

Sally, reading the letter four months later in Edinburgh, waited for him to say when he planned to return. She waited in vain. Instead, Hudson wrote, he had looked at Sydney, and wondered if it wouldn't do as well as a place to wait for London's heat to die down? In fact, Sydney would be a better hope for them both. He wanted her to come out. He had no money to send her, but surely she could borrow passage from her sister?

And by the way: had his son been born yet?

She folded the letter onto her lap, and she wept.

On Clarissa's three-month birthday, marked by a hot spell remarkable even for August, Sally loaded a pair of hessian bags with all their worldly goods and struggled through the baking streets of Edinburgh to her sister's house. She looked up as Alice opened the door.

"I need you to watch Clarissa for a while."

Alice eyed the bulging sacks and told the housemaid to put on the kettle. She took Sally and the baby into the drawing room, where the air smelt of baking horsehair. Even when Alice flung open the window, it was still stifling. Clarissa stirred, and Sally put her to the breast.

"I'm happy to have the bairn, ye know that, but what's in the bags?" Alice asked.

"It's everything we own. And ye'll be keeping her for more than the day. Might be weeks."

Alice sat down abruptly. "Why? Dearie, whatever's wrong?"

"Nothing's wrong yet, but I have to commit a felony."

"What?"

"Jimmy canna come back, it's too dangerous. I don't know when he'll be able to send me the money for passage. Papa won't even speak to me, Mama will nae cross Papa, you've nought to spare, and even if I convince the government to send me on an assisted fare, as a domestic, I don't have two pounds. It'd take me months of scrubbing floors to save up. The only way I can get to Australia is to be transported."

"I . . ." Alice said faintly. *"Transported?"*

"I have to commit a crime. And if I act rough, they'll want to be rid of me."

"But . . . what about Clarissa?"

"Oh, she'll come with me—they send bairns, too. Saves the cost of the workhouse. But it might take weeks, for the trial and all, and I'll not have my daughter in a gaol cell."

It was a mad scheme, suitable only for a desperate woman. Sally had asked around about the law, and general opinion was that the chances of a fresh-faced young governess being transported—a punishment designed to rid a nation of troublemakers—was minuscule. She would need to stand in court a reprobate, shameless and without principles. There was one crime admirably suitable to her purpose.

That afternoon, Sally knocked at the door of the house where she had been born. The maid who answered gave a scornful glance at Sally's dress and opened her mouth to tell her the trade entrance was at the back.

"Hello, Hazel," Sally interrupted. The maid paused for a closer look before stepping back in astonishment. Sally gathered her skirts and pushed past into the foyer. "Would you please tell my mother I'm here?"

After a moment of goggling, Hazel closed the door and fled up the stairs. The instant her black skirt disappeared, Sally darted down the hall to her father's office. Inside of three minutes, she had what she needed, and crossed back into the drawing room: her mother would want a formal setting when she confronted her wayward daughter.

Sally loosed her bonnet ties, but did not take it off. Nor did she sit, just stood with her hands clasped, listening to the silence overhead. After a time came the sound of a door opening.

She half expected the maid with a command to leave. But the tread was heavier, and approached with an air of determination.

Her mother had not paused to change clothes; the sight of her simple tea dress brought Sally a faint hope. "Hullo, Mama."

"What are you doing here?" At the frigid disapproval, hope died.

"I came to give you something, Mama." Sally pulled open her little bag and took out a cheap brooch. She worked the clasp, and opened it to show her mother what lay pressed behind the glass: the tiniest wisp of light brown hair, snipped from the back of Clarissa's head that morning. "You have a granddaughter. Her name is Clarissa, after Grandmamma. Clarissa Huds—"

"You need to go, before your father comes home."

Sally froze. Slowly, her hand curled around the locket. Her daughter's precious hair, for this.

"Leave, now."

"Yes, Mama." The little locket shut with a faint snap. She laid it onto the polished surface of the table at the end of the sofa, and said, "I am going away for a time, to be with my husb—yes, Mama, we are married, and I love him. Clarissa and I will be at Alice's house this evening, if you wish to meet your granddaughter."

And she left.

Three hours later, the police came to her sister's house. They arrested Sally for stealing two expensive necklaces from the safe in her father's office. Necklaces her grandmother had bequeathed to Sally, many years before.

They could not find the necklaces themselves: not on her, nor in Alice's house, and not in the room Sally had been living in, over in the bad part of town. No trace of either necklace was found—but she did not deny she had taken them. Sally Hudson stood before the judge and admitted her guilt—boasted about it, even, in an accent considerably lower class than her natural voice. She was condemned to seven years' transportation to Australia, her father's courtroom curses ringing in her ears.

When the ship sailed, the third week of November, little Clarissa sat on her mother's hip. Tied firmly to the child's pudgy wrist was a crude dolly made out of knotted string. A curiously heavy dolly, for beneath its stubby exterior nestled ten gold guinea coins, proceeds from a hasty visit to a pawn shop. In her valise, Sally had two additional pieces of treasure, a going-away present from her sister: a matched pair of French porcelain tea-cups that, like the necklaces, had belonged to their grandmother.

On a blistering February day in 1856, the ship dropped anchor in Fremantle. It had not been a bad trip, as these things went. Once free of Edinburgh, Sally had let surface her native demeanour and superior accents, confusing the ship's warders enough that they moved her into "general" class, allowing her to avoid the worst food and the hair-shaving shame of those marked with "crime." Still, she had heard terrible things of the conditions that awaited female transportees, and she joined the jostling queue coming onto the docks with her heart in her throat.

Sally was doubly cursed—or perhaps, in this case, blessed—by a plain face and a babe in arms. She passed safely through the gauntlet of officials gathered to pluck up the prettiest girls as "servants," only to find herself beneath the probing eyes of the next rank of would-be "employers": working men with fewer resources, yet similarly interested in slaveys and wives. At the end of the process lay a wing of the prison to which transportees were theoretically bound, but before she reached that, her husband's face appeared, looking older and gone dark with the Australian sun, but as charming as ever.

She drew her first deep and unimpeded breath in what felt like years. He *had* received her letter, sent by fast clipper before she left Edinburgh, and he had managed to get from Sydney across a continent to the last remaining dumping-ground of Britain's convicts.

She ran the last steps to fling one arm around him, startling a wail of protest out of the child she carried in the other. She was laughing through tears of joy as she introduced her husband to his small, dark-haired daughter.

Hudson bent over the child, marvelling as her little fingers wrapped shyly around his. The palm of his hand was scarred, Sally noticed— a burn, months old, that caused the hand to curl somewhat at rest. For a moment, she thought of the letter she had read a thousand times, his heartfelt description of that mutinous survivor dragged from the ship's burning wreckage ... But she shook the thought from her mind, and looked into his face instead.

"I called her Clarissa," Sally told him. "I hope that was all right?"

"Beautiful. She has your eyes."

"Poor thing, hope she doesn't have my looks."

"She'll be 'right," her husband said, an Australian-sounding expression that rather lacked the romance Sally might have wished. Still, she was here, and the family was together at last. It would, indeed, be right.

It took some weeks, sweltering in the tropical summer, but the contrast between Sally Hudson—a literate, married young mother—and a recent influx of Fenian convicts encouraged the overburdened warden to hand over a Conditional Pardon and a transfer of her person to Sydney.

There the Hudsons resumed their married life, bolstered by the golden inheritance she had claimed from her father's safe. And if she studied Jimmy's back sometimes, when he stood up from the tin bath or slept shirtless in the heat of summer, if her eyes traced the foot-long scar along his shoulder-blade and wondered if it had been made by a piece of burning ship's timber, she never said a word. Certainly he never did—mere mention of the event turned him first pale, then taciturn. Everyone who came to Australia had a past they were leaving behind, not the least

James Hudson. In any event, he'd hardened during their months apart, and his patience was short: it was not wise to venture remarks that could be taken as criticism.

A second daughter was born in 1859, a little blonde-haired, blue-eyed imp with whom Jimmy fell instantly in love. They named her Alicia, after Sally's one faithful Edinburgh relation, and Jimmy bought the infant a real doll, and a lacy dress, and a little painting of an English shepherd to go over her cot.

Jimmy's work on the docks, which half the time brought him home stinking of raw wool, also left him in a position to pocket tips when a shipment of some value was being loaded, on or off. He no longer hid what he was doing, and although Sally could not condone his criminal acts, neither could she claim that she did not know what James Hudson was. The fine balance between the husband's goals and the wife's disapproval sometimes came to a head, and Jimmy did not always stop at a shaking. Sally lost a tooth once. Another time she was left with a ringing in her ear for weeks. However, this was her bed, one that she had made herself, and he never hit the children—not with his fist anyway. A lot of wives couldn't say the same.

Jimmy did provide, give him that. Sally did not have to find work outside of the home. She hired a series of small, malnourished girls, some locals, others transported from England for stealing a loaf of bread or apples from a tree. She let them sleep in the kitchen while they learned a few basic skills and lost the gauntness of their faces, she taught them their alphabets, then freed them to work for some other wife with slightly greater resources.

Neither Hudson spoke of how they had come to Sydney, although between Jimmy's nightmares and his horror of the sea, over the years Sally had picked up most of the story. Their daughters learned not to play "shipwreck" in Papa's hearing, as Sally's tongue avoided the use of words such as "mutiny" or "explosion."

In the course of time, Sally was given her Certificate of Freedom. She could have returned to Britain, after that—and was tempted from time to time, when Jimmy was in a black temper. Twice he was arrested, once convicted: the four months he was gone were the hardest yet. The only thing that kept Sally from being thrown into the streets with two little girls and a growing belly was the last remaining gold guinea, the one she'd not told Jimmy about. The coin she'd kept against the day when she would want to return home ... but she didn't, quite.

When he came out and found her not starving, he accused her of having sold herself, of finding a pretty boy to pay her way. The split lip he gave her nearly sent her to the docks to beg for passage, but by that time, she was so heavily pregnant that even if she'd had the money, the thought of giving birth at sea was more than she could face.

In 1866, Sally Hudson went into labour for the fourth time. Thirty-four hours later, her second son was born. She held him, whispering love and welcome into his wet little scalp. Then the blood started to come. The haemorrhage poured into the rough bed in a scarlet tide. When it ebbed, with it went Sally's strength, her colour, and then her life.

Little Jamie lingered. Clarissa nurtured him desperately, day and night, teasing drops of milk and sugar-water between his pale lips, warming him against her childish chest, dropping only briefly into sleep before she jerked awake again to feed, change, and warm her brother. She talked to him, sang her mother's songs to him. Days passed. Clarissa was oblivious to her father, her sister, her mother's funeral, her own needs: nothing mattered but her tiny brother, that he continued to draw breath. And he did, his cries weak and his motions listless, but he kept living. Clarissa's hopes solidified, making her fiercely protective of the sickly scrap of humanity—and then the fever took him, and he was gone, too.

Clarissa Hudson was ten years old when this happy childhood ended.

CHAPTER FIVE

Without a wife, with his son taken, James Hudson fell into the bottle. For months, he managed to forget: his loss, his dignity, his two living daughters. He would stir himself in the morning to go buy them breakfast, then come home at midnight with Alicia's favourite sweets rather than bread, or a little straw bonnet to go with her threadbare dress. Once, he gave Alicia a rag doll crawling with fleas. More often, he came home with nothing at all. On the rare nights when he and food were there at the same time, they would eat, and he would sit with his arms around little Alicia telling her stories until she squirmed away from his smell. Clarissa wondered if it wasn't better when he ignored them.

He would weep, and revile himself for their neglect, for his wife's death, for the fact that her two beloved daughters spent their days playing on the streets with the prozzie's brats. ("What's a prozzie, Papa?" Alicia would ask, until Clarissa hushed her.) After a while, he would stagger out, and disappear until the wee hours.

Sometimes he failed to come home at all, leaving the girls shivering together in a dark room, Clarissa trying her best to distract her hungry sister with stories of her own.

Were it not for the nice ladies downstairs (who were friendly and generous so long as the girls played silently in the mornings, for the ladies did not wake until noon) and the oncoming summer, the girls would likely have followed their brother before Clarissa could figure out how to feed and clothe her sister and herself. But it was October, and the extra warmth of the days gave Clarissa just that little bit extra distance between the two of them and death. Courting couples watching the little sailing yachts along the waterfront would toss a child a coin to be rid of her hungry gaze. Market stalls were busy enough to hide a short thief. Clothing, drying on lines instead of before kitchen fires, called out for a nimble new owner. Even the nights were warm enough for comfort.

Alicia was not as easy to mother as little Jamie had been, being both demanding and unappreciative, but Clarissa found her sister's greed oddly reassuring after Jamie's faint interest. She threw herself into the task of giving her sister first survival, then comfort, and eventually the triumph of a childhood. She stole for Alicia: food, clothing, hair-ribbons, toys—even coins from the pockets of her father's trousers as he snored. She fought to keep her sister clean. She made sure Alicia continued with the school that had been so important to their mother, and turned a deaf ear when Alicia whined that she wanted to stay home like Clarrie. When all else failed—when the cold rain fell and they had no dinner—she summoned their mother's entertainments, inventing little plays about their neighbours, acting out the various parts on the stage of their cramped and dreary room.

However, Sydney was not a big city, and The Rocks a crowded neighbourhood. The police began to recognise the scrawny child with the brown hair. Five months after Sally's death, one of them was quick enough to lay hands on her.

The three Hudsons were living in a squalid room above an even more squalid grog shop, two streets from the docks where Hudson only occasionally worked. Still, it wasn't all bad. Allie had a pet rat—rather, she had taken a liking to one of the smaller rats that had a comical mark on its face like a moustache, and fed it scraps from the bread Clarissa brought her. Clarissa had taken care to earn the affections of the few men in the house, docks workers who watched over the two girls to some degree. And the door had a latch on the inside. Matters could have been worse.

The policeman, fingers clamped around Clarissa's bony wrist, used his other hand to rattle the doorknob. When it failed to open, a slap from a meaty palm sent a shudder down the entire hallway.

"Hudson!" he shouted.

His reply was silence—but a latched door meant someone was home. Before he could change the flat of his hand for the point of his shoulder and rip the flimsy door from its frame, Clarissa reached past him to tap on the wood with her fingernails.

"Allie?" she said, then corrected herself, in a voice that might have come from the other side of the globe. "Alicia? It's me. Open up."

Often, her sister didn't. If Allie had food, if Allie was annoyed or bored or in the middle of a game, she was quite capable of leaving Clarissa out in the hallway until their father's uneven tread rose up the stairs. But today the sound of motion came from within, followed by a small voice with native Sydney accents. "Clarrie? Who's that man?"

"Don't fret, Alicia, it's just the nice policeman checking to see we're all right."

After a moment, the latch slid aside. A tiny blonde girl with corn-flower eyes looked up at Constable Taylor, clutching to her chest a crudely-made doll in a dress amateurishly sewn from what looked like a man's silk handkerchief. The constable deposited Clarissa inside the room before letting go of her wrist and shutting the door behind him.

It was easy to see that the father was not there. But the sight that did meet his eyes had him pulling off his constabulary hat and running a hand over his hair.

The lodgings-house was one of those that had been born decrepit, and by now was held together by dirt, damp, and the stained news sheets that papered the wallboards. The bare floorboards were rough enough to draw blood from incautious feet, and the furniture amounted to one bed, two stools, four mismatched tea chests acting as storage, and a rickety table set with a single candle-stick in which rested a stub of cheap tallow candle.

But unlike most—unlike any other the policeman had seen in this district, come to that—the thin blanket on the room's bed was neatly pulled up; the smaller mattress in the room's corner similarly tidied. The tea crates held folded clothing, the family kitchen-ware (two plates, three mugs, and a few spoons), and some old toys. An attempt had been made to clean the floor. The spalled paint around the door was scrubbed to the wood beneath, and the sash window—the constable had to walk over for a closer examination. On the inside, the cracked panes were spotless; on the outside, the lower half of the window had been similarly scrubbed. He turned to measure the older girl's arm with his eyes: the end of the clean patch looked about the distance that Clarissa Hudson's arm could reach without her actually standing outside on the frame.

As he said to his wife over the dining table a few hours later, that half-clean swath of window was one of the rummest things he'd ever seen.

In front of his knees was the table, one leg broken and propped on a brick. The light from the half-cleaned window fell across another thing he didn't see much in these parts: books. Four of them, all but one looking as if they'd been kicked about on the cobblestones. Beside them was a slate with a painfully drawn series of ABCs on it, written with the morsels of pale chalk-stone gathered in a clam-shell.

He picked up the new-looking book, wondering who she'd stolen it from. "McGuffey, eh? Who's the schoolgirl?"

The two girls spoke simultaneously.

"Me," said the little tow-head.

"We both are," said Clarissa.

He turned his head to look a question at the brown-haired child he'd nabbed stealing apples.

She explained. "Alicia goes to school, then she comes home and learns me. Helps her remember."

And, he thought, helps the older one not to forget.

"You've had some learning yourself, I think."

The girl raised her chin. "My mother taught me. She died. I told her I'd take care of Allie—of Alicia. So I do."

"Where's your father?"

"He's at work," she said promptly. Her dark eyes were as open and honest as the sky. If he didn't know better—if he didn't know his patch as well as he did—he'd almost have believed her.

"Sure he is. Well, you tell your Pa to come find me. I want a word with him."

"Indeed I shall tell him." The policeman laid the book back on the table, hiding his smile at the girl's proper accents.

But the younger child was frowning up at her sister. "Clarrie, why're you talkin' so fun—"

"Hush, All—Alicia. And call me Clarissa."

"But, Clarrie—"

"Thank you, sir, for bringing me home."

"And don't you take what don't belong to you, hear?"

"Yes, sir."

A right lie, he thought.

His heavy tread across the room set the window to rattling. He turned at the door to look again at that hard-won arc of clear view, then at the table.

"I might shout you a couple of slate pencils and the odd book, if it helps you mind your *p*s and *q*s."

From the expression on the girl's face, he might have been tantalising her with the offer of a full Sunday roast.

That night when their father came back, Clarissa said nothing about the police. As soon as his snores began to change the next morning, she slipped out to beg a mug of tea from downstairs, setting it onto the table with yesterday's uneaten crust of bread.

When Hudson sat up, dropping his feet to the floorboards and his head to his hands, she scrambled up from the corner where she'd been helping her sister sound out words, and stood before him with cup and bread in hand.

He squinted at her. "What's this, then?"

"Mrs Murdy had the billy on, she gave me a cup."

"Good of the old bat. What'd you have to give her for it?"

"Just a smile."

"Little liar," he said, but not without affection.

He took a swallow of the powerful, tepid liquid, then tore off a corner of the tough bread with his stained teeth and washed it down with more tea. Alicia had come up to watch the bread disappear. When there was one bite left, he noticed her stare "Had your breakfast yet, Allie girl?"

"Yes, she did," Clarissa answered, but when Alicia shook her blonde head, he held out the bread. She snatched it and crammed it in her mouth. He rumpled her curls, ignoring her shift away from his hand, and looked at his other daughter. "You got more tucker for yourself?"

She had not. "I'll eat later, thank you, Papa."

He nodded and finished the last of the tea. "Thanks for that, child. We'll have our own kitchen again soon."

"Papa, Officer Taylor wants a word," she said.

His eyes narrowed. "Why? What'd you do?"

"Nothing! Nothing at all, he just . . . I was down the greengrocers, lookin' at apples, and he—"

"Were you stealing again?"

She eased back, one eye on his hand, but this time it was the younger sister who flung down an intervention.

"Clarrie did an act, Pa," she said. "For the copper."

The distraction worked. Hudson's gaze moved over to Alicia. "An act?"

Clarissa glared at her sister, but that just urged Allie on. "Yair, like she was flash 'n' all."

"What're you talking about, child?"

Alicia turned to her sister, all sweet innocence to hide her glee. "Show him, Clarrie! Talk like you did."

If Pa got into his head that Clarrie was sometimes acting on *him,* telling him things he wanted to hear instead of the truth, she'd suffer. She ought to get out now. Let Allie take the brunt of it for once. But she gave her sister's wide blue eyes a last glare, then turned to the man on the bed. "Papa, it's just a game I was playin' with the copper. Acting, like. If you sound more, well, quality, people sometimes leave you alone." He stared hard at her, and she grew uneasy: any threat to Papa's pride was a venture onto dangerous ground. Still, his frown did not seem to be one of anger, for once, so she held off leaping for the door.

"Show me," he said.

"Pa, it's just a—"

"I want to see. How you talked to Officer Taylor."

Papa's breath stank, his eyes were red pools, he hadn't shaved in a week, and she wanted, wanted, *so* wanted her real father back. But ten-year-old Clarissa Hudson took a deep breath and obediently summoned the personality she'd worn for the copper.

"Sir, I really don't know why you wish me to perform this task of—"

"Ha!" her father barked, shooting upright on the bed.

Clarissa flung herself backwards with Allie, but Papa didn't lunge at them, just sat with an astonished look on his once-dear features. "Do it again," he demanded.

So, keeping Allie firmly behind her, Clarissa rehearsed for a moment the accent and attitude of the women she heard going into the fancy shops. When she could feel their clothing on her skin—taste their words on her tongue—she took a breath, raised her chin, and stepped out onto her father's stage. This time, he did not interrupt, just let her go on, his eyes slowly losing their focus as he followed some thought into a distant place.

Eventually, she let her voice run down. Her body relaxed into the posture of a slum-child. Alicia peeked around her elbow. Their father sat motionless for a long time before he drew breath and focussed on his elder daughter as if he'd never seen her before. "Your Mum could do that. Change accents. Like a parrot, she was."

"I remember." A trip to the shops with Mama could be like going down the street with half a dozen different women, as she shifted from her natural brogue to the stretched-out sounds of the local shopkeepers and then into the clipped English of the hat-maker, dipping into the exoticisms of the Greek fishmonger and his Chinese wife. All so naturally, Clarissa wasn't even certain her mother had been aware of it.

"How do you do that?" he asked. "How do you learn what people sound like?"

"I dunno. I hear things, I guess. Fit my tongue around them."

He looked down at her thin body, seeing no sign of the raised chin and straight spine that had gone with the accent. "It's not just your tongue. You're a right little actress, that you are."

He dry-washed his face, grimacing at the sound of stubble, then leant to retrieve his trousers from the floor where he'd left them. He swayed a bit as he stood, but managed to work the buttons and pull on the braces without getting tangled.

Then he thrust his hand into a pocket, and frowned. Clarissa's breath stopped. Would he remember how much he'd had the night before? No: not this morning. The hand came out and laid a few coins on the table. "Get yourself some breakfast, you and your sister," he said, then paused to look at the younger one. "Why aren't you in school?"

"It's a Sattiday, Pa."

"So it is. Well, to celebrate, I'm going for a bath. See you two urchins later."

"You won't forget about Officer Taylor?"

"I won't forget."

He mussed Alicia's hair again, missing her look of annoyance, then picked up his hat and was gone the rest of that day. (Hudson did, in fact, go to see the burly policeman, who took credit, in later years, for having set the family back onto the straight and narrow. At least, until things began to come out.)

The coins Pa had left (added to those Clarissa had taken earlier) were plenty for a day's food, and even stretched for the luxury of an ice from the Italian man. Clarissa took one slow lick, then handed the rest over to

her sister. They sat in the last of the afternoon sun, Alicia greedily sucking in the cold sweetness and Clarissa smiling at her sister's pleasure.

She kept enough back to buy a candle—a real bees-wax one—and
that night after their Saturday bath (fourth-hand and near cold after
Mrs Murdy's family had finished, but still) they snuggled together in bed
while Clarissa sounded out the words of *Dombey and Son,* a satisfyingly
long time after darkness had fallen. The smell was so delicious, she could
practically taste the honey on her tongue, and she didn't even have to get
up every few minutes to trim the smoking wick.

Nearing the end of both chapter and voice, Clarissa broke off at the
sound of unfamiliar footsteps trotting up the stairway. Most of the other
residents were nice enough, but every so often a stranger came. When
that happened, Clarissa and Alicia took care for a day or two until they
were sure he was harmless: that flimsy door would come down to other
shoulders than a constable's.

So at these footsteps, Clarissa stopped reading. Allie was nearly asleep
anyway, and in a minute she'd close the book and blow out the candle, to
go to sleep with the simple warmth of a sleepy younger sister at her side.
But the stranger's feet did not continue down the hallway. Instead, they
stopped right outside the door, as if the man had noticed candlelight
leaking around its edges. Clarissa's heart began to race as she planned out
a defence—and then came Pa's voice, no more slurred by drink than the
footsteps had been.

"Open up, Clarrie."

Clarissa scrambled across the room to slide the bolt, then stared up at
the vision that entered: James Hudson, shaved, trimmed, smelling more
of soap than of gin, under his arm a paper-wrapped parcel, on his body a
suit of clothes she had never seen before. He even wore a new hat, tipped
at a rakish angle. He looked like ... what was Ma's word? A toff?

"Pa?" Alicia sounded none too certain.

"Yes indeedy, it's your Pa," he said, sounding more tipsy than he
looked. "And a sorry old bandicoot he's been, these months, neglecting
his two girls something awful. But I'm back, and I've brought you some
treasures for your pretty selves. Go ahead, take a look."

Alicia slipped out from under their blanket and pounced on the tantalising parcel that he tossed onto the foot of the bed. She gasped, and drew out a fistful of glory: hair-ribbons, dozens of them, every colour under the rainbow and then some. Clarissa was drawn over to them, reaching a wondering finger to the gleaming tangle of beauty.

But Alicia was already digging back into the paper, coming out with a pink frock—pink!—and a pair of stockings more delicate than anything either girl had seen before, and a hair-brush and—

Jim Hudson pulled a stool around and watched the girls go through his gifts. After a bit, he realised that he could not tell what colour the little shawl was, and he suggested to Clarissa that she light a second candle.

"I . . . we only have the one, Papa."

The room went still. Clarissa tensed at his expression, but in the end he laughed it off, and said that tomorrow he'd buy them a whole box. "Put the dress on, dearie," he suggested. "No, not you, Allie—it's for Clarrie."

Both girls gaped, first at him, then at each other. Alicia's little fists tightened on the pink fabric before, reluctantly, she let it go. In disbelief, Clarissa picked up the dress: presents and pretty things were for Allie, never her. But the universe soon righted itself when the dress turned out to be too small.

"This is Alicia's size, Papa," she told him. "She'll look better in it anyway."

"No, I—" He caught himself. "Right, well, we'll find one that fits you when the shops are open. Meanwhile, you can help yourself to the ribbons."

The ribbons, too, would be fine in Alicia's pale curls, the curls Clarissa battled so hard to keep combed and clean, but as for her own head . . . Maybe Pa thought she'd cut it by choice, instead of to get rid of the lice? Obediently, she picked up the least shiny of the colourful pile and tied it around her short-cropped head.

Her father's smile dipped a little at the effect, but again he rallied. "A bonnet," he said. "That'll be the thing. Now, my child, tell me again about those voices you do."

For some reason, the glorious colours on the bed instantly lost their gleam. "What about them?"

"Tell me why you do them, to start with."

"Just a lark, really."

"But it's not. You know the story about how your Ma acted the slattern to get herself shipped here on His Majesty's shilling, you've heard me tell it often enough. And remember how she'd put on a fancy manner if she wanted to impress the vicar's wife or something? Is that what you do?"

Clarissa didn't know what a slattern was, and she'd never met a vicar's wife, but she could guess, a little, what he meant.

"I s'pose so. People who talk like big bugs—rich, like—they get away with things. Even if their clothes don't match. When Officer Taylor caught—when he brought me home, I thought maybe he'd leave Allie and me be if he thought we were, I don't know, gentry down on our luck instead of . . ." Her voice trailed away: Papa's temper was never more uncertain than when he was coming out of a drunk.

"Instead of no-good brats," he filled in. But his hands stayed down and his eyes studied her face. "You used to talk like your Ma, more. Scottish."

"I suppose."

"Do it now."

"Talk like her? Why?"

"Because I want to hear it."

Clarissa didn't like to think about her mother, and had no wish to stir up all those empty feelings. On the other hand, this was the most attention she'd had from her father in a very long time—and, she really didn't want to make him angry. So without thinking about it much, she brought the *R* sound up onto her tongue, lengthened some of the sounds and softened others, and spoke. "Aye, faither, wall i's a fair way to town and the day wa' dreich, so I slid onta tha tram amongst a fat lady's bairns, but I dinna ken the right stop and—"

Her father's stool went over backwards as he jerked upright. Clarissa cringed away behind one raised arm, but again, he merely stared for what seemed a very long time. Then he wiped his mouth and reached around to set the stool aright. He sat.

"Pa, what is it? You're scarin' Allie."

"Am I? Sorry, little one. So, can you do that parroting with other accents?"

Clarissa could, although it wasn't just the accents, it was the attitudes: a Sydney boy, a girl from Queensland, a dark-skinned woman from the Outback who lived down the road, a wealthy American she'd followed for a few streets, hoping he might set down the packet he carried. She had no idea what Papa wanted, but this felt like the first time, ever, that her father had looked at her rather than Allie. The fact that her trick seemed actually to please him was enough to make the squalid room seem brighter.

He interrupted her impersonation of the sari-wearing Indian woman she'd seen in the park the week before. "Darlin', I think you have a skill. And I think you and me, we might be able to make something of it. You think you can teach yourself to cry?"

Clarissa looked at her father, plainly intent on cajoling her into something. Why did he think she was not going to like it?

CHAPTER SIX

The shock of the gun in Samuel Hudson's hand froze me like an electric current. The world stopped: sound, breath, heart, dust-motes in a moment of sunlight. My universe narrowed down to a pair of truths: a round black gunmetal hole at the end of Samuel Hudson's arm, and the too-sweet smell of his hair-oil. Absurd thoughts were the only thing that moved: *In my own sitting room?* flitted across my stunned brain, followed rapidly by, *God, what will Holmes say?*

Then my chest thumped and my thoughts jostled to assemble some kind of order. Moving with great deliberation, I spread out my hands from the shoulders down, to illustrate a complete lack of threat. "So," I said. "No tea and biscuits, then?"

CHAPTER SEVEN

There were, it seemed, any number of ways to get by in Sydney—
and more so, Melbourne—if one had the use of an innocent young
face. According to Pa, men with yellow fever—fresh from the
gold fields—were just aching to have someone take their coins from
their pockets and free them up to go find more. It was doing them a
kindness, really.

Clarissa knew this was a story, but playing along with it kept him
happy—and sober—for the first time since Mama died. More important, it allowed her to take care of Alicia. Proper care.

Two weeks after the policeman's visit, Clarissa stood on a busy street
before a big man with a high hat and a thick gold chain across his waistcoat, her heart thumping as she sobbed and stammered out an incoher-
ent tale about losing the shilling her mother had given her to buy milk
for the baby and how Mum would *beat* her . . .

It had taken her some time to decide on this man among all the others
bustling past, just as she'd hesitated over the pretty new frocks Papa had

bought, ending up in a once-pretty, now-faded dress and a pair of shoes that looked like the well-cared-for hand-me-downs they were. Pa grew impatient, waiting for her to pick her target, but when she saw this one, she'd gone right forward because he seemed . . . happier, somehow, in a way that made him feel even larger than he was. It was years before she learned a word for it: "expansive." Which sounded like "expensive," and that was right.

The man with the gold chain had spotted her sobbing and stopped; listened to her where another might have circled past; frowned in sympathy where most would have just frowned. In the end he held out not a replacement shilling, but an entire half sovereign—then laughed when her wet eyelashes opened wide. "Can you use that, then, little girl?"

"Oh, sir, I can, yes I can." Then she remembered her act, and was quick to add, "My little brother will eat so well, thanks to you!"

Her first lesson: no man in a good suit would turn away from a little girl with clean clothes, nice manners, and tears in her big dark eyes.

When she took the coin back to her father, waiting around the corner, he crowed in triumph. His praise flowed over her like water on a desert plant. And—was it magic, or a secret message?—the coin had been born the same year as she: it bore the date 1856 under Victoria's profile. It went into his pocket, as did the handful of smaller coins that same act won them during the day, and they ate well that night.

Then, two days later—magic upon magic—Papa gave her back that very coin, strung on a golden chain. In an instant, Clarissa's lingering hesitations fled. Her father loved her when she helped him, and that was all she needed to know.

Of course, Alicia spotted the necklace. Clarissa glumly undid the clasp to hand it over—but Papa said no, it was hers. Even when Allie threw a huge tantrum—even when she whined for days and days, playing with it around Clarissa's neck, begging and sulking—Papa held solid.

Allie's mood lasted for a week. Then, to Clarissa's surprise, it suddenly stopped. It was rare for Allie to let go a pet hurt, but after Papa took her out for a row in the harbour—by herself, leaving Clarrie at home—the younger sister's woebegone expression was replaced by smug satisfaction and the occasional cryptic and knowing remark.

Still, she was happy, and Clarissa had her necklace. From then on, whenever a doubt surfaced about the rightness of what she was doing, Clarissa Hudson only needed to grasp the coin around her neck to know that she would do anything, anything in the world, for her father.

There were other lessons, as the weeks went on. The second, rather more complicated lesson came about a month after the first.

They were working on what Pa called a "Job" (but she secretly thought of as "Cheats") near the railway station, in the early afternoon. The railway was important, because he had to catch a train. The time of day was, too, since there should have been a lot of people through the station not long before, but not too many people in now. And, there had to be a train coming very soon, but not one for a good while afterwards.

Papa went into the Refreshment Room for a cup of coffee while Clarissa waited across the way, in a corner where she could see him but no one would notice her. There was a small valise at her feet, so that if anyone asked, she was simply watching it while her mother went to care for her little brother, thank you very much. After a while, Papa looked at the clock over the counter, then stood up. She watched more closely now: he would want her in a minute.

Papa walked over to the man selling the coffees and ices and showed him something in his hand. The two men talked, then Papa turned to point at the table.

I just found this under the table, he was saying. *I don't know much about ladies' jewellery, but it looks pretty valuable.*

Half a minute later, Clarissa rushed in breathlessly. Ignoring Papa, she asked the Refreshment Room man, "Oh, sir, my mother lost her pearls! Did anyone report finding them? She said she'd give five pounds reward!"

The two men looked at each other, then Papa held out the necklace. "Are these them?"

Clarissa exclaimed and reached for the pearls, but her father's hand retracted, just a little. He and the other man consulted without saying anything, then Papa looked at the clock again.

"I've got to catch the train. You want to give me two pounds? I'll let you keep the rest."

"I don't have two pounds," the man said.

"Ah, too bad." Papa made as if to slip the pearls into his pocket, then stopped. "Think you could just borrow it from the till?" He turned to Clarissa, as bright-eyed and innocent as the sparrows pecking crumbs outside the door. "Is your mother far away?"

"She's just down at the bank, to see if they found it there."

The bank was about three minutes away. Mention of a bank also made this "Mama" sound like a woman well able to redeem her lost pearls.

Reluctantly, the man gave Papa his two pounds. The two men smiled after Clarissa, bouncing away to tell her mother the joyful news. Papa left. And at the end of the man's day, he owed the till two pounds, and had in his pocket a string of pearls already losing their paint.

As they made their way home, Clarissa asked her father if the man wouldn't have to replace the money in the till.

"A course he will, honey."

"He seemed nice."

"He was a Mark. If he'd thought of it first, he'd have done the same to us. Two pounds—you clever girl!"

Her father's jubilation left Clarissa feeling oddly empty, as if she'd taken more from the nice man's pockets than two pounds. Thus, the second lesson: a person felt clever, but not entirely clean, after a Cheat.

It was driven home a few days later, when her regret at taking a coin from a man who looked as though he needed it more than she did led to her handing back the coin—and her father slapped her so hard, he loosened a tooth. She did not try that again.

But for the occasional blow apart, their "Jobs" made Papa happy, which was a new and exhilarating experience for little Clarissa Hudson. She also relished being Another—a girl with clean skin and confidence, someone who knew she was going home to a mother and a shining house, someone who was . . . better. When she put off the Act, her tongue returning to its natural place in her mouth, her head dropping to its normal angle, she missed the Other Clarissa.

Still, if it kept Papa happy and Alicia fed and warm, what did her own feelings matter?

Over the following months, the Hudsons' Cheats grew more complicated. They took longer to plan, and they brought in more substantial sums. They moved from their room in The Rocks to a place with a less interesting night life but sweeter air. Clarissa learned to call the men "Marks"—which turned out to be not a name, but a description, as if they were nothing more than stains in need of a good scrubbing.

Clarissa's third lesson was one she discovered slowly, and on her own: it was best to leave the Mark with some taste of happiness: praise him, give a touch of self-satisfaction, leave him with a brush of humour. Doing so not only made the Mark less suspicious, it also felt more like an exchange than a bald theft. Like those birds that traded one shiny object for another.

This was a lesson she kept to herself.

There were others—even formal lessons, of a sort. That winter, while Alicia sulked off to school every morning, Clarissa attended a very different sort of classroom.

Pa called the weasel-faced old man an "Acting Professor," although to Clarissa he was the Cheat Teacher. The thin, intense, rather smelly creature her father found to educate her young and nimble hands reminded her of a wonderful story by Mr Dickens that she had read to Allie during the lonely nights. Unlike Fagin, the Professor was a solitary figure, not one who gathered a band of young thieves around his hearth.

Clarissa tried, hard, to make her father and teacher proud of her, but in the end, even though she'd practiced so many times that she woke at night with her fingers making the dip in Alicia's curls, both men reluctantly agreed that the straight picking of pockets was not her strong point. She was better at palming goods, since the key to that was diverting the Mark—and the distraction was where she shone: a little girl bent over a skinned knee, or weeping over a lost puppy, or holding up a found coin in wonder was the most compelling thing in the world, and if James

Hudson's own fingers had had more skill, the pair would not have needed to look further for their income.

However, Hudson had spent too much time at rough work to be a smooth pickpocket, and he refused to bring in another partner. Instead, they concentrated on the more involved realms of criminality, those resting on Clarissa's dual talents of mimicry and reading the Marks. Their most reliable Cheat was The Found Note-Case, akin to the pearl necklace, which began with her hesitating at the door of a grog shop with a note-case she had found, and ended with Hudson leaving that saloon a couple of bank notes richer.

Lesson four: greedy people made for the easiest Cheats. And, she found, those with the least guilt attached. For example:

A pretty Saturday afternoon in the late spring; a busy Melbourne street; a brown-haired girl who looked no older than fourteen (though she was) perched awkwardly on the edge of a bench amidst the unfamiliar bulk of a crinoline, her hair swept up and ringletted beneath a bonnet; clearly a young girl attempting to look older than she was. She sat a short distance away from a busy jewellery shop, shoulders hunched and head down, either fascinated by some small object in her hands, or fighting tears. People passed her by, as oblivious of her as she was of them, until a courting couple approached, hand on arm at a primly decorous distance.

When they were ten feet from Clarissa, she glanced up. The girl stopped, pulled from her springtime euphoria by those big, dark, brimming eyes. Her beau would have pressed on, perhaps even more briskly having spotted the tears, but his young lady's arm—and her concern—anchored him in place.

"What is the matter, dear?" the girl exclaimed.

Clarissa hastened to dash away the tears with a childish hand. "Oh nothing, it's nothing at all, not that you can help with. But thank you," she added politely, blinking a clear, wide-eyed signal of distress.

The pretty girl lowered herself to the bench with the automatic swing of hips that betrayed a recent abandonment of steel hoops in favour of horsehair bustle. She reached out a gloved hand for Clarissa's bare one, somehow catching one of her glove's tiny buttons in the object Clarissa was holding.

"Oh!" Clarissa grabbed for it, working its satin cord free. When she had succeeded, her two hands held it out for a moment. All three young people studied the small, black velvet draw-string bag, until, with a cry of loss, Clarissa's head bent down to cover it, her shoulders heaving.

The story soon came out: a dangerously ill mother, a father honourably dead, a family so reduced in circumstances that all Clarissa had to sell was the ring left by her beloved grandmother.

"Nanna—that's what we called her," Clarissa said with a brave smile. "Nanna wore it all her life. When Granddad bought it, the ring cost a year's pay. She always used to tell us the story, of how he came to her father with the ring and a solemn vow: that he would love her even when all the diamonds of the earth . . ." She had to choke out the next words over a sob. "When diamonds had crumbled to dust. And he did. They were *so* in love, like newlyweds even when they were old and grey. They died within days of each other, both in their nineties, and left me the ring. It's worth hundreds. If I sell it, I can save my mother's life. But . . ."

Her voice trailed off into her hands.

The young woman's arm went around Clarissa's shoulders, she bent close to hear the words. "What? Oh child, what is the problem?"

Clarissa sat upright, taking a sharp, steadying breath. "I thought perhaps Mr Barnaby—the jeweller—would buy it, since he's the one who told Mama it was worth two hundred guineas. But it seems he has plenty of the new diamonds just now—coming out of South Africa? And people want a *new* ring, instead of one with seventy years of love behind it. I need the money today, if—" Another sob, bravely stifled. "If Mother is to have her operation. I shall have to tell her doctor that she must come home, for a time. Until I can find someone who wants it."

Clarissa raised her hand, and the sun caught fire on her ring finger: the cluster of many diamonds set into rose-coloured gold sparkled, it danced, it threw the sun about as her hand turned this way and that.

Then the dazzle winked out like the death of promise as she slipped the ring back inside its pouch, prompting a faint protest from the girl at Clarissa's side.

The girl looked up at her beau. He eyed the small velvet bag uneasily. The silence grew electric—

To be broken from an unexpected direction.

A small man with hunched shoulders, worn tweeds, and a jeweller's loupe in his hand paused beside the trio.

"Hello, young lady. I am really terribly sorry we couldn't convince Mr Barnaby to purchase that lovely ring of yours. But you were right, it's worth a great deal more than the ten guineas he was offering."

The young man peered down at the fellow, taking in the magnifying lens he carried. "Er, you're a jeweller?"

"That I am, young man. Though unfortunately, a jeweller without much cash just at the moment. The races, you know?" He gave a rueful chuckle. "Otherwise I'd have offered this young lady eighty guineas for that shiny bauble she's got, and made a good bargain out of it. Well, I've missed my chance. I wish you luck, my dear."

He tipped his hat first to Clarissa, then to the couple, and walked on.

The young man watched him go. When he turned back, his face wore a very different expression. Speculative, perhaps. One might even say it held a touch of greed.

"Young lady," he purred. "I hate to see you in distress. Perhaps I might help you out, and take that ring off your hands. Now, how much is it your mother needs for her operation?"

Clarissa blinked up at him. The young man's lack of reaction when "the jeweller" said *ten guineas* told her there was more than that in his note-case. How much more? "The doctor said it would be thirty-five pounds altogether," she lamented. The eyes made a fractional retreat. "—but he said that if I could pay him twenty-five now, I could work the rest off over the coming year."

That speculation returned to his gaze.

The girl rose, laying one hand on her beau's manly arm. "Oh, Freddie, we could help this poor girl, and save a life! And ..." Her voice drifted away in a blush, indicating that Freddie had not actually spoken for her hand yet. Strictly speaking, a ring was premature. However, was this not a minor point when balanced against seventy years of deep and abiding love?

The girl's blush deepened when Freddie reached into his breast pocket. Clarissa and her father were long gone by the time Monday morning came along, and a real jeweller told Freddie that the paste diamond in his hand was worth, at most, five shillings.

CHAPTER EIGHT

As their success grew, as Clarissa matured, the Cheats became more sure, more complex, the partnership more seamless, their clothing more clearly of the upper classes—hers, at least. Her father never did look entirely comfortable in expensive clothing, even when his hands grew softer and he'd had his teeth attended to. Still, compared to visitors from Britain and Europe, rich Australians often had the hands of labourers, and Hudson had been in the country long enough to sound native. As their Cheats pushed up into Society, her accents and attitudes grew more assured, the amount of money each one brought in grew.

They also spent much of every year travelling, despite James Hudson's loathing of sea journeys. The very first year of their operations, 1867, they spent two weeks in Melbourne, nearly twice the size of Sydney, and found the change of scenery both a relief and a financial triumph. Alicia went along on some of these expeditions, but without making the younger Hudson girl a part of their Act—a thing neither of them even considered—it was not a success. Matters came to a head on Clarissa's twelfth birthday. In May of 1868, her father pronounced it time they bought a house, a real house with a kitchen and a garden. They could have a dog, even. Wouldn't Clarrie like that? Allie surely would.

Twelve-year-old Clarissa Hudson stared at her father, and put her foot down—something she never did, since overt protest threatened to bring his hand.

"Allie's almost nine," she said. "And you and I are always gone. She's been ducking school, Papa. She's up till all hours, and—"

"She's not going back up The Rocks to play with those prozzie brats, is she?"

"No!" Her father's horror of prostitution, enforced with profanity and violence, would have made her deny it even if Allie had moved in with one of their former neighbours. "Nothing like that, Papa. But she needs a proper upbringing, if . . . if she's not going to go wrong," she added slyly. "She needs a family."

"She has a family."

"We're never here. There's no one to make her do her schoolwork or come inside at dark. She's going to get into trouble, Papa."

Neither of them so much as noted in passing that it was the child who was leading this conversation.

"You want to quit?" Hudson asked.

It did not need the dangerous edge to his voice to make Clarissa see the bad in that idea. Without her, Papa's attempts at crime would lead first to the bottle, then to the police, and finally a return to rooms with peeling wallpaper and the stench of urine and cabbages. She shuddered, and brought out the idea that she had been aware of for weeks now: an idea both appealing and repugnant. "I'm sorry, Papa, but unless you want to get a regular job, I think we'll have to find a family that Allie can live with. Just until we get more settled."

She hoped her father would object harder than he did. She knew that she was being selfish, wanting him all to herself. But he did not. In the end, it was Alicia who cried and sulked and dragged her toes—up to the moment when the spinster teacher in need of income opened the door of her guest bedroom, and little Alicia's jaw dropped. Her eyes travelled across the frills on the bed, the crisp curtains on the window, the little painted bookshelf in the corner. There was even a brand-new dolly with a porcelain head and fluffy skirt, propped against the pillow.

After that, it was Clarissa who had the tears in her eyes, leaving her sister with Miss Constable. And even when she and Pa did move, to a proper flat with a kitchen and housekeeper (of sorts) to keep it running, Alicia only came for the occasional visit.

The following year, they had to buy a series of new frocks as the old ones became too short and too snug. Clarissa no longer looked like a child playing dress-up, when she wore bustled skirts. Once or twice that autumn, she caught an odd, thoughtful sort of look on her father's face. Not until the closing weeks of 1871 did she understand.

Clarissa Hudson was fifteen and a half years old. It took some work now for her to look like a child, but no effort at all to dress her as a young woman. They were in Ballarat, working their way through the booming mine towns, posing as the widowed owner of a large emporium looking to expand business into the hinterland. It was not entirely appropriate to take his shy young daughter into the meetings he held in restaurants and saloons, but his widowhood was recent, and surely it was all quite innocent . . .

A survey of the railway maps had given them their plan. Three towns: Echuca, Bendigo, Ballarat. Find a Mark, soften him up, lighten his wallet, slip away.

The first two went fine, the takings nice and rich. But Ballarat was a problem. For one thing, the town was in the midst of a slump, having over-extended in the madness of gold lying free on the ground. As a result, the people weren't . . . happy. Not one expansive face in the lot.

"I think we should go home," Clarissa said to her father that night. "It would be a nice surprise for Allie."

"She's not expecting us until Christmas," Hudson said. "We can spend a few more days."

"Pa, I don't like it here."

His face took on that hated expression of wheedling he got when he was either keeping something from her, or trying to convince her to do something she didn't want to. "The place is one step up from the Bush, yes, but the men here have money."

"I know that, Pa, but—"

"You losing your nerve, girl? Want to trade places with Allie for a while?"

"Of course not, Pa. It's just, I don't like it here."

"Oh, for Christ sake, Clarrie," he snapped. "I hope you're not going to get all dithery on me. There's gold here. We'll leave when we have our share."

The next day, coax her as he might, Clarissa would not settle on a Mark. That night, Hudson got drunk for the first time in weeks, and ended up slapping her across the face. At luncheon the following day, a man approached them in the busy hotel restaurant, gave her a polite tip of the hat, then turned to her father to ask about the shops he was thinking to build.

It was a surprise, but not unheard of, for a man to hear rumours of profit and approach about getting an early slice of the pie. More unusual was the man's willingness to ignore her: Clarissa Hudson was presenting herself to the world as a nubile innocent, a morsel few men could resist. None in her experience had entirely overlooked her.

Until Mr Bevins. She might have been Pa's elder sister, for all the interest he demonstrated.

With growing pique, she watched the man and Pa talk business. Twice she broke in with witty remarks; both times, he gave her a polite smile and returned to the topic.

Then he asked how far the plans had got. Hudson had an increasingly worn set of architectural drawings to pull out when the topic was approaching actual sums, but they were not the sort of thing he carried about with him to the luncheon table.

He laid his table napkin by his plate and said he would just be a minute. At last, Bevins turned to Clarissa—but still, with that absent politeness on his face. It was becoming vexing.

"Your father is quite the inspired businessman," he said.

"Isn't he, though?"

"Although a girl like you must find these conversations tedious. It's too bad—oh, drat," he said, and pulled his watch from his pocket. "I forgot all about a wire I promised to send my partner in Melbourne. Young lady, I don't suppose you know where I might find a telegraph office?"

She did, in fact. She started to explain, but he apologised that, being new to town, he was unfamiliar with the landmarks she was mentioning. So she offered to show him the way.

Stepping down into the street, he offered his arm. She took his assistance, and left her arm through his. If she could convince the fellow that she was not a child, she might work herself back into this Job: it would not be good to encourage Pa to think he could manage without her.

They strolled past the shops, Mr Bevins paying a degree more attention to her, although there was still something of the attitude of an uncle unfamiliar with the ways of children about the way he kept his head politely tipped to listen.

Until they stepped around a tall heap of builders' materials and, momentarily out of sight of the street, he picked her bodily up and carried her into the dark alleyway beyond. One hand was across her mouth, the other pulling at the thickness of her skirts. In seconds, all that separated their flesh was the thin cloth of her drawers—and already, those fingers were seeking out the dividing seam . . .

The nearness of his goal distracted him. The hand across Clarissa's mouth went slack, just a fraction—and Clarissa's teeth clamped for all she was worth into one thick finger. With a bellow of pain, he shook himself free. She drew breath for a scream, but it scarcely began when his unwounded hand slammed against the side of her face. In a fury, his fingers went around her throat—but her one brief moment of shriek had been enough. Bevins heard the shouts from the road, and ran.

Her father put his arm around her shoulders and hurried her to their rooms in the hotel. The instant they were inside their rooms, he pushed her away and slapped her so hard, she fell to the floor.

"What the hell were you up to, you damned hussy? You think I didn't see how you had your eyes on that bastard? Flirting and—"

"No, Papa!" Her voice was hoarse, coming out as little more than a whisper. "I never, I didn't want, I was just—"

"—flinging yourself on him. Jesus wept, what would your mother say?"

"No! I was only showing him where the telegraph—" She was weeping, cowering on the floor.

He hit her again, and kicked her thick skirts, and might have done her serious damage but for the banging that came on the door.

Since she'd been in a state of turmoil when she'd entered the hotel lobby, the manager could not claim that her father had been roughing her up. He had heard the angry shouts, though, and knew what had happened. He agreed to say no more—if they left his hotel.

The Hudsons fled Ballarat that afternoon. Once they were alone in their train compartment, she used the last threads of her voice to convince her father that she was not at fault. That she was, despite her profession and her history, an innocent victim. A child who had failed to see danger in a predatory male.

Her voice trickled away to nothing, but not before his wrath was set aside.

It took many months before Clarissa's front teeth felt sturdy enough for an apple. Her throat was hoarse for a week, her body—and her confidence—badly shaken. When she could talk again, she told her father that he absolutely had to let her choose their Mark, from now on. That never again would she work a Cheat on someone who felt smooth as a sheet of polished glass.

James Hudson agreed, vehemently. Once he'd heard her truth, he was almost as frightened as his daughter. He gave her another long lecture on the dangers of loose morals, and the need to live up to her mother's love—which might have seemed outright hypocrisy, but did in fact make sense to Clarissa. She promised him that she would never give herself to a man except for love, as her mother before her had. Hudson put his arms around her, and wept, and went out and got drunk.

Two weeks later, he gave her a Christmas present of more value than a lecture: he gave her a gun.

It was an ivory-handled, two-shot derringer, tiny enough for a lady's handbag, serious enough to damage. What's more, he took her out into the bush to practice with it, until she could hit two bottles out of three from twenty feet away, and every other one at twenty-five.

Hudson's thoughtful looks disappeared, replaced by a sort of knowing pride, the shared secret of her weapon, and her skill. As he told her, men don't expect a pretty girl to have a sting.

That, then, was the life of Clarissa Hudson. For nine years, 1867 to 1876, she and her father worked their way up and down the young, growing country, Brisbane to Adelaide, running their Cheats. Every few months they would cross to New Zealand for a few weeks (Hudson fortifying his nerves with drink) to take advantage of the fresher fields of Wellington and Auckland. They talked occasionally of going further afield, despite Hudson's horror of sea voyages, but neither of them wanted to be too far from Alicia—though in fact, that young lady seemed little interested in their presence when they were in Sydney, and rarely replied to the long letters her father wrote from distant cities.

Alicia was one reason for staying near to Sydney. Clarissa's other concern was that, outside the rough-and-tumble societies of Australia and New Zealand, her father would look like what he was: a working-class outsider.

Not so with Clarissa. During those years, she went from child to woman. As her bust developed and her face lost its childish lines, the Cheats changed, becoming darker, more dangerous, and ever more lucrative. She was good at what she did, capable of everything from the most complex and time-consuming Cheat to the slow, flirtatious glance in a street-car, distracting a man so her father, despite his rough hands, could slip away with the fellow's wallet. And even if the man discovered he had been robbed, he never suspected the girl with the pretty dark eyes.

Which was the final lesson in her education: a man was loth to press charges if he was aware that greed—or lust—had got him into that situation. A public declaration would not only reveal his stupidity, but let others know how fully he had participated in his own downfall. Clarissa's victims practically begged her to take their money.

Still, by Christmas of 1875, Clarissa was aware that Sydney was growing decidedly small for the Hudsons. It took ever longer to locate a victim, and the machination of the Cheats became increasingly elaborate as the wary attitudes of those they'd taken from began to penetrate even the thicker skulls of Society.

Shortly after Clarissa's twentieth birthday, in May, 1876, Jim Hudson told his daughter that they were going to London.

"Don't be ridiculous, Papa," she said absently, studying her reflection in the cheval glass. "You'd be arrested in an instant. And besides, you hate to travel." This year's fashion suited her, she thought—what version of fashion that reached the antipodes, at any rate. No more crinolettes, thank goodness, and the combination of frothy bustle and train at the back with the long polonaise bodice up front made even sparsely-endowed women resemble a ship's figurehead. Clarissa Hudson was by no means sparsely endowed.

She smoothed the long bodice that stretched down torso and hips, then turned face front, attempting a deep breath: the whalebone made it difficult, but doing so certainly pushed out the breasts in a way that would distract the Marks. Maybe a bit too much? Or were the soft violet satin and white tumble of lace sufficient to counteract the low neckline and naked shoulders? Lace was always reassuring, somehow, to the mothers.

"Girl," her father was saying, "I won't be arrested—it's been twenty years. Nobody remembers Jimmy Hudson. Certainly not the police."

Clarissa lifted her gaze at last to her father's reflection, sprawled across the chaise behind her. "You aren't really serious?"

"As a corpse." He swigged the last of his drink, and got up to pour another.

The silken layers whispered as she abandoned the looking glass. "Why London? Why not Macau, or—I don't know. San Francisco?"

"You noticed the number of invitations on the mantelpiece have gone down?"

"Papa, I did tell you that your manners are a touch . . . jarring." And had become more so in recent months. *He's bored,* she reflected. *Really bored, if he's considering a trip to England.*

"Manners? For Christ sake, girl, this is Australia!"

"All the more reason. Society here is so new, it can't afford to ignore the niceties."

"Well, whatever it is, I think they're on to us."

"I did warn you it was too soon to go after Mrs Pondworth's emeralds. Are we expecting another visit from the police, then?" It had happened twice before. Both times, although the detectives had eyed her father with suspicion, in the end Clarissa's unassailable wide-eyed naiveté had sent them on their way. She did not wish a third such experience. "And even if the London police have forgot you, what about your boss? You left England in the first place because of him."

"Oh, Clarrie, The Bishop's sure to be dead and gone by now. And if he isn't, well hell, it's only money. I can pay him back easy."

"I do wish you wouldn't call me that. You know, perhaps it's time for me to set out on my own."

He laughed. "And without a loving Pa in the picture, what do you suppose Society will make of you? You think any of your high-and-mighty ladies would let a solitary girl like you within shouting distance of their sons?"

Clarissa frowned at her image. It was true, the mothers had begun to bristle when she stood too near their darling boys. Plus, she'd met all the local lads, not a one of whom interested her beyond what she could take from his bank account. She was twenty years old, and the prospects in Sydney—for money or for marriage—were few and dull.

"You may be right. When would you want to leave?"

"The Season gets going after Christmas. We should be there before, so you have some invitations to be starting with."

"That doesn't give us much time," she protested. "Surely we can wait until Alicia finishes the school year?"

"I think we'll have to leave Allie here for the time being."

She whirled. "Pa, we can't leave her behind—we're a family!"

"You sure about that? Miss High-and-Mighty Constable counts more with her than you or me."

"I see Allie *every* week, I send her money, I take her to the theatre, I ..." Hudson got up to splash another dose of gin into his cut-glass tumbler.

"Yeah, maybe you're right," he said when her voice had run down. "I'm not even sure she'd want to go to London, come to that."

But as Clarissa turned back to study her reflection—the composed young woman with artfully constructed hair, wearing a dress that cost what Miss Constable earned in a year—she knew that her father was wrong: Allie would react to the city as she would to this dress: she'd claw her sister naked for a chance at England.

But once there, what? Alicia had none of the elder sister's chameleon tendencies. Her voice and manners were nicely suited to Miss Constable's schoolmarm household, but even in Sydney, grandees would smirk before she so much as opened her mouth. Plus that, Miss Constable had spoiled her a bit. Alicia would never admit the need to learn a new way, to change with a new society. Here, among the middle classes, she had a niche. But in London?

"Still, she'd have time to get used to the idea," Hudson was saying. "It'll take us a while to get ourselves situated, like. Next year, maybe. The year after. She'll be, what, eighteen? We can hold a dance for her. She could come out, even—ah, darlin', just think what your mother would make of that!"

The idea was as absurd as a dingo in a silk bonnet: even Papa didn't believe in the likelihood of his blonde-haired daughter, tiara on head, making a curtsey before the Queen. As if she'd said it aloud, he went on quickly. "Still, it's a long time to leave her here, halfway around the world, all on her own."

But at that, Clarissa laughed. "Pa, Allie has more friends than I do, and Miss Constable's like a mother to her. What's more, the woman manages to keep Allie in line. Without Miss Constable watching, it wouldn't be long before—"

"Before what?"

"Oh, nothing. I just worry. But Alicia won't be lonesome here, and I agree, eighteen would be a good age to give London a try."

He was diverted, fortunately. Because what Clarissa had caught herself about to say was, *How long before Allie meets a Mr Bevins?*

Miss Constable would keep her charge from trouble, Clarissa had no doubts about that. But in fact, a beau would be an ideal solution. Alicia Hudson at sixteen and a half had a graceful figure and a convincing sweetness of manner. However, along with her father's features, she had inherited some of his darker traits: a blithe assurance that the world was there for the taking, a fondness for secrets, and a boundless persistence when it came to getting what she wanted—what she felt she deserved.

Her childhood greediness would have flowered into something quite unattractive had it not been for the cajoling, the sweet-natured discipline, and the unceasing dedication of Miss Constable. Very soon, the woman would have her hands full with Miss Alicia Hudson. Yes, what they needed was a man.

Clarissa made a mental note to speak with her sister's guardian about an increased dress allowance, to permit Alicia a wider social circle. In Sydney, Alicia would have a chance to make a good match. Uprooted and turned loose in London, it would be a disaster.

"She won't be happy," Clarissa said.

"Best not to tell her where we're going, just yet."

Clarissa's eyes widened, picturing her headstrong little sister gathering up her skirts and boarding a London-bound clipper, all on her own.

"We can't say that we're off to Hong Kong," she said. "She'd want to come. Or America. What about Macau?" The Portuguese colony would be less attractive: they could always convince Alicia that no one spoke English.

"We've always wanted to go there," he agreed drily.

"And in any event," she added, filling in the story, "we should be back in a few months. Better let me tell her, she'll suspect something if you try."

"Fine. What about clothes? You need some before we go?" Clarissa's wardrobe was a constant and major expense, necessary for their line of work, and normally she'd have agreed. However, at a party the previous week she had caught a look of disdain on the face of one newly-arrived and very superior English girl, whose bustle was the smallest in the room.

"No," she replied. "Fashion is sure to have moved on in London. Anything I have made here will look out of date there."

"Good. And you might see if you can get your money back on that one," he said, taking up his hat to leave. "It's about a quarter inch from making you look like a whore."

Thus, London was decided. And one thing about her life, Clarissa reflected: most of what she owned could be quickly packed up. A person didn't indulge in country estates and race-horses if he might need to leave town in a hurry.

At the end of June, their trunks were despatched to the harbour, with the Hudsons following soon thereafter. Clarissa picked her way up the rain-soaked gangway, stopping twice to unhook portions of her train. She was given a cabin of her own, tiny but smelling reassuringly of cleaning fluid, with a window to make the heave and toss of the swells less trying.

She went back up onto the deck, bundled against the rain, and found a corner where she was out of the way of men running to and fro. Officers and sailors alike gave her pink cheeks an appreciative glance, but to none of them did she reply in kind: it would be a capital mistake to flirt before they docked in London.

After what seemed a very long time, the windlass began to raise the anchor. Men swarmed up the rigging to loose the sails. A steam tug threaded the clipper out of the crowded harbour. The moment the pilot was put off, huge canvas sheets billowed down to fill the sky, going taut and full as the ship found the wind. Soon, every board and bolt of her leant eagerly forward, and the passengers gave a cheer, waving their hats as Sydney fell away. Slowly, almost imperceptibly, Clarissa Hudson turned in the direction of her native country.

In a tiny corner of her heart lay a feeling of relief, that Alicia was no longer her responsibility. The portion of her heart occupied by guilt was considerably larger.

CHAPTER NINE

"Where are my mother's things?" Samuel Hudson demanded. His oily amiability was gone so completely, I wondered for a moment if I'd been imagining it. His calm voice betrayed no trace of panic. The gun in his hands was equally steady: this was a man for whom a revolver was a familiar tool, not three pounds of steel about to emit a scary noise.

This man was no amateur.

Which meant that his entire smarmy-salesman performance had been just that: an act.

I spared a brief second of self-recrimination (*What is wrong with me, it's the second time in a month I've misjudged*—) before kicking doubt away. If he'd got past my guard, he was dangerous, and the why of it—along with how the hell this person could be any blood relation to Mrs Hudson—would have to wait.

That awareness changed my response. To blink guileless eyes and respond, "What things?" would only invite a warning shot—possibly into some portion of my body. Instead, I gave a straightforward reply that lifted to a question: "In her rooms?"

The right choice: his forefinger did not tighten, nor did his face. "Show me."

Holmes always said there were advantages in dealing with the professional, and although I lacked his familiarity with dedicated criminals, I knew what he meant. This man might intend to remove me as a potential witness before he was finished, but first, he needed something that belonged to Mrs Hudson. So long as my assistance was of value, the bullets would remain in his gun.

Too, the criminal brotherhood tended to be precisely that: an exclusively male club. While this person might be aware that Mary Russell possessed skills the average English girl did not (*How much had Mrs Hudson written about me over the years, anyway?*), I could still encourage his male instincts. At some point, he would forget to treat me as a threat, and when he did so, I would take his gun.

Until then: I would appear helpful, I would make no quick motion, and I would get from him every bit of information possible.

So, as I led him out of the sitting room, I did not hurl the door back into his face. Walking past the stove, I did not seize the whispering kettle and drench him with scalding water. I did pause there, to say I wanted to turn off the gas—then waited until he gave me permission before I did so.

The kettle's voice subsided, and we continued on to Mrs Hudson's quarters.

But as we invaded her private world, I became aware of a growing sense of rage. I held it to myself, nurturing it as a weapon.

When time comes to break his nose, I reminded myself, *try not to get too much blood on Mrs Hudson's floor.*

CHAPTER TEN

Clarissa had been disappointed to learn that they would sail west rather than ride the infamous gales of the Roaring Forties, but after a squall their first week out that shredded the mainsail and left bruises down her arms, her wish for adventure faded. A week later, following three days of storm behind tight-sealed portholes while titanic waves crashed over the decks and water poured through the saloon lights, she was positively grateful.

She was even more grateful for her sturdy inner parts: when the entire ship was heaving into their respective pots, including many of the crew, Clarissa stumbled across the rolling decks, laughing at the impossibility of straightforward motion. Even her father kept to his bunk—although that was drink rather than illness: numbing himself against the remembered horrors of the open sea.

The first week of October, one hundred two days after leaving Sydney, the cloud-like shapes on the horizon grew firm and became land. The Channel breeze grew fitful, with a constant scramble up and down the ratlines and adjustments to the rigging first on one side, then the other.

Clarissa retreated to the least-occupied corner of the poop deck, her attention on the dark outline approaching with such agonising slowness. What would this unfamiliar country bring her, she wondered? And how much would it permit her to shape her own future?

Closer they crept. Night fell. In the morning, her father appeared, though the shore was no closer. But just as Clarissa was thinking that she would go mad with the waiting, a passing steam tug answered their hail, taking them in tow and delivering them to the harbour with no more fuss than that.

The Hudsons had chosen to disembark in Plymouth, rather than risk spending days tacking first up the Channel, then up the Thames. The wind (which had picked up as soon as they no longer needed it) offered the crew an exciting glimpse of Clarissa's ankles as they handed her into the small boat, but since they had been gentlemen (more or less) despite her being the only female passenger under the age of fifty, she took her time in smoothing down her skirts.

She then gave two of the sailors a further thrill by leaning heavily on their arms as she set foot on solid ground for the first time in over three months. Her merry laugh was joined by all within earshot, and she gingerly set off with outstretched hands up the rough boards towards land.

Clarissa and her father spent two nights in Plymouth, which gave him time to get over his hangover, her time to regain her balance, and them both a chance to retrieve garments unstained by travel and free of the sticky salt air. While her father struggled to write a blandly uninformative letter to Alicia (adding it to the dozen or more he'd written from the ship), Clarissa went walking. When she returned to the hotel, she dug out her smallest bustle and wrestled with its wire, flattening it even more until it approximated those she had observed on Plymouth's more fashionable ladies: silhouettes here were almost flat, compared to Sydney.

On the third day, when they boarded the train for London, Clarissa Hudson betrayed no vestige of Australia in voice, dress, or manner.

London was, she had to admit, the mother lode for a confidence man—or woman. Especially woman. Clarissa's passage through Paddington station, her travel through these incredibly narrow and crowded streets, the stroll across their hotel's lobby, all held promise that here, nuggets lay gleaming and ripe for the plucking, and would require but the most meagre of efforts. The gentry would simply beg to be swindled—and as for the foreign visitors . . .

But she kept her fingers to herself, and left her gaze down so as not to attract attention: there were bigger goals here than the odd purse or note-case.

The Season, when the Names and would-be Names of the British Empire would gather in London, ran from midwinter until midsummer—which in this topsy-turvy northern hemisphere was December through June. Parliament was in session then, but politics was only the excuse for an endless series of coming-out balls, intimate dinners for thirty, afternoon salons, improving lectures, and charity events that benefitted the sorts of people one hoped never actually to lay eyes upon. Once the hunting season ended in the spring, the whirl would really get under way.

Clarissa had known, before she so much as boarded the ship in Sydney, that her chief task in infiltrating London would be to find a position into which Society could put her. In England, her father's bad teeth and working-class manners would be of little use to the partnership, but even with Clarissa's skills, she would be an outsider, unknown to this small, tight, suspicious, and supercilious community. She could all too easily end up pressing her face to the bars, a laughing-stock behind the other ladies' fans.

The traditional solution here, she had discovered, was a sponsor: a woman with impeccable antecedents, accepted within this exclusive group, who as a girl had been presented at Court, whose family had held dinners and balls and all the panoply of coming-out, who might even have married—but who since then had fallen into a financial hole. The demands of keeping face made it impossible simply to sell one's possessions, fire one's servants, and move to a suburban villa. Better to starve to death in the family jewels.

Before leaving Sydney, Clarissa had come up with a name: a titled widow of sixty-three who, rumour had it, was less ill (as had been given out) than ill-supplied with the means of maintaining her wardrobe, cellars, and kitchen. Clarissa spent hours constructing the right sort of letter, on the correct kind of paper: one that demonstrated intelligence, means, good will, impeccable spelling, and decent penmanship, while trailing behind it a lack of sophistication that just begged for the firm hand of someone like Lady Penelope Breiford. She had posted it from Sydney by fast clipper, the week before she left, and made a search through the newspapers on arrival to confirm that the ship had docked, almost two weeks before.

Now, in London, the first thing Clarissa did was to have visiting cards printed, bearing the address of the hotel. As soon as they were ready, she hired a carriage to take her to Lady Breiford's home.

Clarissa sat in the carriage while the hired groom bore her card to the door. She looked straight ahead, chin up, face relaxed, only the grip of her hands on her bag betraying nerves. The groom had been instructed not to wait, merely to deposit the card on the butler's tray and come away. They returned to the hotel.

Now for the hard part: the waiting.

Her father, meanwhile, went off to address negotiations of his own; namely, those ancient and festering debts owed the crime boss known as The Bishop. Twenty-two years before, when a housemaid's confession led to many arrests and the flight of James and Sally Hudson to Falmouth and beyond, The Bishop had been nearly sixty. A man of great physical strength and unwavering vision (even now, at eighty), he had built a criminal fiefdom with a hard hand but an even one. Typical of him had been a willingness to extend a loan to a young man with a dangerously ill wife, buying his services thereby. Also typical of him was the way he greeted that Prodigal's long-delayed return: he allowed his son to beat some of the interest payments out of James Hudson's skin.

But he only allowed the beating to go so far—although the younger Bishop was more than willing to finish the job. The son had been the apprentice lad on Hudson's house-breaking gang, and nurtured bitter memories of the arrest, the hard interrogation, and the two decades of paternal blame that followed. When James Hudson was shown into The Bishop's throne room—a literal throne, with red velvet cushions—he found the son pacing back and forth behind the old man like a dog on a chain. And like a dog, he attacked the moment The Bishop loosed him.

It took the old man's Demander a while to pull the younger man off Hudson, but The Bishop was above all a practical man: the dead have trouble paying their debts.

The amount required to mollify The Bishop made Clarissa blanch even more than the state of her father's face. Still, the debts were paid, both monetary and in honour, leaving Hudson free (once his injuries had faded) to stroll the boulevards and befriend those nouveau members of Society who found him amusing: the sorts of targets he and Clarissa would require to build back their fortunes.

In the meantime, Clarissa waited. She was fitted for six gowns and three hats, finding an adequate tailor for her father as well. She arranged for a maid and a carriage, took many rides through Hyde Park, and fretted.

Lady Breiford's response came on the fifth day, in the form of a thin, elderly man in faded livery. He was standing at the corner of the lobby when Clarissa came in from a nerve-driven stroll around the busy streets. The instant she spotted him, she wanted to run up and throw her arms around him.

Naturally, she did nothing of the sort. She continued her stroll across the Axminster carpeting, waiting for one of the hotel staff to draw her attention to the messenger.

She permitted the liveried figure to approach, accepted the envelope he proffered, gave him a gracious nod, and swept on. But once in the privacy of her room, she closed her eyes, as near to prayer as Clarissa Hudson knew, before looking inside: there, in an ageing lady's perfect copperplate hand, was a date, with an invitation to call. The Australian in her nearly whooped in triumph: Clarissa Hudson had a toe inside the door of London Society.

The Sydney rumours proved correct, and—as with most people who claimed an utter disinterest in something as crude as money—Lady Breiford's eyes betrayed a gleam at the thick packet Clarissa laid absently on the table during her brief first visit. After much negotiation, all of it under the pretence of no negotiation at all, a sum was agreed upon, responsibilities made clear.

Lady Breiford could not get Clarissa presented in Court: that degree of respectability brought too great a risk of exposure, and in any event, Clarissa was a bit old. And because there was only so much Clarissa could do to turn Hudson into a gentleman, he would linger in the background as an "uncle," at least until Clarissa herself was established. In this first Season, Clarissa's position would be exotic-but-acceptable rather than strictly one-of-us: Lady Breiford's honorary niece, an Antipodean treasure. Beyond that, Clarissa's success would rest on her own ability to charm.

With Lady Breiford at her back, and occasionally at her side (dressed in "gifts" from her young protégée), Clarissa was seen at all the right places during the autumn: lectures at the Royal Academy, shops in exclusive districts, slow carriages through Hyde Park, drinking tea at certain milliners that were as much salon as sellers of hats. Outfits and accessories poured into her rooms, readying her for the task of four to six changes of clothing each day. When 1877 began and the Season got under way, she had a handful of invitations. Those rapidly expanded to fill the mantelpiece. Clarissa Hudson was ushered into Society without so much as a ripple.

That first Season was exhausting, invigorating, challenging—and ruinously expensive until its very end, when the Marks were distracted by preparations to leave Town for country estates or foreign lands, freeing the Hudsons to cut a methodical swath through their carefully chosen and prepared targets. It proved a good thing that Hudson had made good his old debts: in April, they had been forced to borrow money. But by late August, The Bishop was well repaid.

Clarissa's first London Season was a resounding success, if for rather different reasons than most girls would claim.

In September, the Hudsons adjourned to the Continent, working their way through Paris, Berlin, and Rome, moving ever on to fresh pastures. Venice proved surprisingly lucrative, there being a community of wealthy Americans in residence. From there, a flirtatious conversation in a railway car brought the new casino in Monaco to their attention. They spent Christmas in Monte Carlo, convincing three different men that she was a wealthy heiress who just needed a bit of financial assistance . . . and came home to London very happy indeed.

The second Season began much like the first, with the difference that Clarissa no longer required Lady Breiford's close attentions. When she dropped visiting cards at the doors of acquaintances, response came within a day, two at the most. The balls got under way, and she put together a few dinner parties of her own. Clarissa Hudson was now an accepted presence at social events. This year was much less exhausting, since she knew the rules and did not have to spend every moment absorbing the tiny gestures and expressions of those around her. Indeed, her hardest task was keeping herself clothed in the latest fashion.

That, and keeping her father under control.

Hudson was getting reckless. Something about walking around London in a silk hat and embroidered waistcoat filled him with the other kind of confidence, the risky kind. Clarissa tried to tell him that they had to lay low and watch for the big targets, not try and fleece every drunken baronet they came across. Once or twice, she had to stand up to him, always a tricky thing—but she was no longer a child, and since even when drunk he had the sense not to bruise her face, she could usually get him to listen to reason.

They had their first real argument in March.

"London may seem huge," she insisted, "but Society here is as small as Sydney's. There's just a handful of families, and those that aren't cousins went to school together. One whiff of Clarissa Hudson being a wrong 'un, and we might as well turn back to Australia."

"So what d'you expect to live off of, hey?" he demanded. "That last frock you bought would feed a family for a year."

"I know. Well, what about if we take a couple of days away and do some Ch—some Jobs? Just not in London?"

So, the Hudsons spread their field of interest, making full use of the country's magnificent new rail system: two days in Manchester or Liverpool could keep them going for weeks, with little risk of alarming London. They also planned an April trip to Paris, which would help with both the finances and with his boredom. They would have to borrow again from The Bishop, perhaps, but less than they would without these trips.

Clarissa found it delicate work, asserting her will over that of her father. He knew her tricks, her every expression, and his temper would flare at her first sign of revolt. Cajoling and flattery took her just so far, and reasoning worked only when he was both sober and content. Once, she only kept him from playing a Mark dangerously close to home ground by pointing out that without her, he might still be climbing through an unlatched upper window. That threat, it was clear, would only work once.

But as the 1878 Season went on, she became aware that this one was not as sparkling as the first. Perhaps it was that she had mastered the skills, or that she had become jaded by the whirl, but something of the edge, the excitement, was missing. It was not until their April trip to Paris that she realised what the problem was, and how urgent its solution had become.

It was their second morning in the hotel. Hudson would be sleeping in, after the excesses of the night before, but Clarissa had got into the habit of rising early. She'd had her tea, read the papers, had her bath, and finished the morning rituals of lemon juice and buffing leather on her hands and nails. She rubbed in a touch of almond oil, then stretched her hands into the unforgiving sun to check. Delicate bones, perfect oval nails, flawless skin, with none of the roughness and needle-pricks of work: let her seamstresses spoil their fingers from now on! Pleased, she reached for her hair-brush. The sun streaming through the window raised a gleam to her chestnut hair—and then she sat forward in growing horror: a grey hair, curling up among the brown.

Next month, she would be twenty-two. A third Season on her own would cast her as a permanent spinster, a woman who had something wrong with her. A woman to be passed over when the choicest of invitations were issued. An old woman, useful for filling a last-minute cancellation at a dinner party.

Here, now, on a silken bench in Paris, the path of her life dawned on her: to do nothing would lead to permanent insecurity and a continual—and ever-growing—risk of arrest, and scorn, and failure. She had independence and adventure, perhaps, but the game's challenges wore thin.

Clarissa Hudson wanted security. On her own, she might have set out to build the kind of comfortable nest egg—well, call it a small fortune—that could keep a careful woman for life, but her father would never be happy with that. Her father would always be a danger.

What she needed was a fortune that was both permanent and beyond his reach. Respectability, but with a degree of freedom. Something that would challenge her, but would not demand that she watch her every step against that betraying slip of the tongue.

What she needed was a husband.

Back in January, flushed with triumph at the invitations on the mantelpiece, her father had urged her towards the young men and women who were intimates of the Prince of Wales—air so refined as to require a pair of specially-adapted lungs from birth. However, the Marlborough House set demanded more than chameleon skills from its potential mates: like presentation at Court, membership required either a family name or (definitely second best) a huge amount of money, and it protected its interests with all the close scrutiny of a jeweller appraising a ring. Clarissa had even discussed this, in the usual oblique terms, with Lady Breiford, before deciding that too enthusiastic a climb up the social scale simply begged to be exposed and banished forever. So, although she did get invited to some parties where the Prince of Wales trolled for companionship, and she was on a first-name basis with more than one Duke, Clarissa had contented herself with the level of Society a step or two below that, where wit and sparkling eyes might overcome the vagueness of her antecedents.

And that level was where she would hunt a husband.

The Hudsons returned to London. By the first of May, she had narrowed her possibilities down to three: one baronet, one viscount, and the untitled eldest son of a wealthy manufacturer of porcelain goods. All three were polite, pleasing to the eye, wealthy as Croesus, and amiable even when in their cups. Best of all, they walked the fine line of intelligence: all were stupid enough to deceive, but not so dull that living with them would drive her to murder.

It all looked very hopeful. For the first time, Clarissa dared to consider a real future, one that permitted her a small corner of permanence and happiness. One that, as a side benefit, enforced a degree of separation from her father. It would have to be soon: the younger girls looked fresher and lovelier with every passing month. She began to play the three young men off on each other, claiming a previous engagement with one before being seen riding on Rotten Row with another, letting them spot their rivals' names on her dance cards. She learned as much as she could about their mothers, and shaped her polite conversation with those sharp-eyed ladies around that knowledge. By June, faint overtures had been ventured by two of the three, and she thought that perhaps, by September . . .

Then the roof fell in. Utter catastrophe, when she least expected it— and from a direction she had never suspected. All her plans, a lifetime of preparation, a decade spent wearing the skins of other women, piecing together a heart as cynical as any white-bearded politician's, and the unthinkable happened.

Miss Clarissa Hudson fell in love.

CHAPTER ELEVEN

I t happened at a ball like any other, at a Berkshire country house. Clarissa always took considerable pains at these affairs to befriend the other young women, or at least to disarm them. The most enjoyable part of these evenings lay in charming her rivals while surreptitiously enticing her targets out from under their noses. It was all in the subtle shifts of voice, body, and face: a group of girls would be left complacent, knowing that Clarissa was a touch stupid and clearly no threat to their own ambitions. And yet, with tiny adjustments to the tone of her voice and the droop of her eyelids, the young man she was dancing with would be convinced that he had his arms around the most fascinating girl in the room.

Yes, there was a goal to this, and soon, but in fact, the act of turning others to her will was what Clarissa relished most. Of course, the only person in any position to appreciate her true skills was her father—and even he persisted in believing that he was her superior. It would have been nice, just occasionally, to talk openly to another person, to have an equal, if not in wit, at least in ruthlessness.

But on that path lay madness. What she required was one big Cheat, single and permanent, to set her up for life. The rest of it, the entertainment and the exercise of intelligence, would simply have to fit in where it could.

Such was woman's lot.

Clarissa Hudson gave herself over to the Act of finding a husband—although as the weather warmed and the Season began to ebb, her enthusiasm for conversation with eighteen-year-old girls flagged, just a bit. Every so often she felt the urge to do something outrageous—which she instantly squelched. Time enough when she was married.

This Berkshire house party to celebrate Midsummer's Night had started off promising: a special train from Town, a queue of carriages waiting at the rural station, a torch-lit drive, the ballroom decorated like a fairyland forest. The dinner was sensibly light, the music not too bad, and Clarissa dipped and whirled and flirted through the sea of glowing skin and twinkling gemstones, her ears filled with laughter and music, the rustle of gowns and the clop of a hundred heels meeting wood. As the air grew heavy with the odours of perspiration and heated silk and bees-wax, she could not help feeling that the Season had gone on too long, and the weather had grown a little too warm. In any event, Clarissa's least-favoured beau was the only one of her chosen trio in attendance, and it was time to suggest that she might be irritated with him, that he might press his case all the more.

So when his name came up on her card, she ducked through the French doors away from the dancing. The terrace air was deliciously cool, the night clear, with a moon that was nearly full. Clarissa strolled along the stones, luxuriating in a moment of solitude. Then she noticed people in one of the other rooms opening off the terrace. A billiards room.

Had it been men alone, she would naturally have passed by, but it was a safely mixed group, half a dozen young men and three of the less empty-headed young women—one was all but officially engaged; another more interested in horses than in men (she intended to let her mother assign her a husband); and a third the eldest daughter of a good family around whom swirled a persistent and scandalous rumour, of being secretly married to the estate manager. Precisely the sorts of girls it was dangerous to be seen with, but at the same time, the only ones who had any appeal just now.

The horse-lover spotted her in the doorway and waved her in. A sweet young baronet with a penchant for boys handed her a glass of champagne. The second son of a wealthy railway man offered her a billiards cue, and with only a moment's hesitation, she stripped off her long gloves and gave herself over to the game.

Twenty minutes passed, a blissfully irresponsible period where, being among people who did not matter in the larger scheme of things, she did not have to Act anything for anyone—until, eventually, the nagging voice of responsibility became too loud to ignore. She sighed.

"I'll finish losing this game and then I must get back to the dance. The boys on my card will be wondering if I've fallen into the lake."

As she positioned herself over the table for a final shot, the protests of her friends . . . she supposed they were, merged with the greeting of a newcomer. She did not look up, although she did become more conscious of the graceful line of her pale arms, the stretch of bare shoulder alongside her gleaming curls, the profile of her waist and backside against the baize: men did find it so titillating when a woman was performing an act they considered their own.

She made a couple of trial strikes over her propped fingers, then let the cue jab forward—and to her amazement, the ball dropped neatly into its intended pocket. Flushed with pleasure, she straightened, looked across the table at the newcomer—and for a moment, forgot to breathe.

It was not that he was beautiful, really, or that he wore his evening suit as if the style had been invented for precisely this pair of shoulders, that breadth of chest: Clarissa met beautiful young men every week, all of whom spent a lot of money on tailors. Nor was it the slightly too-long hair that looked about to escape control, or the dashing upturn at the ends of his moustaches. If anything, it was the eyes: a blue so light as to be without colour, with humour at their corners and an attentive focus that told their target that *she* was all he was seeing.

Intelligent eyes, Clarissa thought in confusion, were one thing a man could not buy on Jermyn Street.

Everyone in the billiards room saw her reaction, and half of them laughed. The baronet made the introductions. "Clarissa, this is my reprobate cousin, home from the wars, the Right Honourable Hugh Viscount Edmunds. Hugh, this is Clarissa Hudson, who has laid claim to half this Season's men."

As he came forward, she saw that he was using a cane to support his left leg. One of the others exclaimed, "Hugh, whatever have you done to yourself?"

"Zulu blighter took a pot-shot at me with his granddaddy's musket, if you can believe that. Sheer bad luck, he'd have been more accurate with his spear. How d'you do, Miss Hudson."

She took herself firmly in hand with the order, *Do not simper.* His fingers met hers, and in the brief moment of clasping he ran his thumb along her naked knuckles in a manner that shivered down to her knees. His hand dropped, his gaze turned away, and she was left, still a bit breathless, aware of the danger of this man, yet also somewhat affronted by his willingness to drop her hand.

Go back to the ballroom, she ordered herself. *He's nothing to do with you.*

Her face composed, she took her leave of the billiards refugees and resumed her gloves, making her way back to the hot, crowded, noisy room. Her promised dance partners reclaimed her, accepted her pretty apologies, swung her out onto the floor with sweating enthusiasm. She kept up a stream of witty talk, flirted as sweetly as ever she did, permitted just enough proximity to tantalise but not enough to constitute a promise, and all the while, she seemed to feel the touch of a pair of ice-coloured eyes against the warm skin at the nape of her neck.

At the very end of the night, when the dancing was over and those heading to their homes were queuing to thank their hostess, he was there again, with a pair of laden champagne glasses expertly threaded into the fingers of his free hand. He leant the cane against his knee to hold a glass out to her. She accepted it. He lifted, and said, "To happy accidents."

Amused, she raised her glass to his toast, and took a sip. He, on the other hand, drained his own glass in four deep swallows, the smooth skin of his throat working across the muscles in a fashion that was oddly disconcerting. He set his empty glass on the balustrade, then took hers and set it next to his without asking if she was finished.

"If you would care for another happy accident," he said, "the doctors have commanded that I spend an hour walking, every day. I find that circuits through Hyde Park in the mornings are a pleasant way to carry out the orders."

"How nice for you, Lord Edmunds, although I do not know why you are telling me this."

"Merely to let you know that my inability to claim a lady for dances is a temporary state. And to mention that, were a lady to wish to serve her King by lightening the burdens of an out-of-action soldier, this would be one means of so doing."

She laughed aloud at the wicked twinkle in his eyes, and watched him collect coat and hat, saying something to the butler on his way out that brought a quick involuntary smile to the older man's face. When she turned away, she found the pretty baronet at her side. He, too, had been watching Hugh Edmunds leave.

"Ambitious sort of a chap, my cousin," he mused aloud. "Wouldn't think it, looking at him, but it's true. And has a knack for being in the right place when it matters. Wouldn't surprise me if he planned that Zulu bullet, to give him an edge when he runs for office."

He turned a vague twinkle on Clarissa and moved towards the door. She frowned, wondering at the oddly weighty tone of his remark. Warning, or promise?

Both, she decided. Because a young man like the baronet could little imagine that a woman might be ambitious, too.

That night, she dreamed of pale blue eyes.

And Tuesday morning, she rested her parasol on her shoulder and went for a stroll in Hyde Park.

CHAPTER TWELVE

S amuel Hudson gestured with the revolver. "Stand over there by the
window."

I crossed Mrs Hudson's little sitting room to the window overlooking her herb garden. The sun was behind the clouds again, permitting a reflection in the glass. I tried to see what he was doing; tried
harder to ignore the crawl of skin between my shoulder blades.

"Do you mind if I turn around?" I asked.

He seemed to be looking at the collection of mementoes by the door,
tucked into the mirror's frame and propped against its shelf. Chief
among them was Mrs Hudson's copy of the photograph, its surface
nearly worn through by years of touch. "Go ahead," he said, so I turned,
keeping my hands out and visible.

His eyes were on the photo, but the revolver had not moved from me.
As I said: a professional.

"Are you looking for something in particular?" I asked. *Or just waiting
to murder your mother?*

"Papers," he said, and turned to look at me. "Contracts. Deeds. Old letters. A . . . passbook."

A tiny hesitation put the emphasis on that last item, and I nearly blurted out my reaction—*This is about stealing the life savings of a housekeeper?* "This . . . these rooms are hers. I don't know for sure, but she may keep that kind of thing in the desk."

The ornate little writing desk was an incongruous landmark in a room furnished otherwise for comfort. I had wondered over it—along with her equally expensive jewellery box—and eventually discovered that Holmes had given her the desk when the two of them had retired to Sussex following years in London. The generous gift said much about the unspoken depths of their rather formal relationship.

Mrs Hudson's son now flipped down the desk's front writing surface, causing me to wince at the hard bounce of its hinges. The pigeon-holes along its back were neatly arranged: writing implements, stationery, paper, glue, and the like along the left, correspondence on the right. He flicked the letters across the desk's writing surface, but saw nothing that interested him.

He banged the front shut and pulled open the drawer underneath, finding Mrs Hudson's personal and financial history. He glanced over at me. "Sit down in that chair."

It was her chair: the chair she sat in with a book or her needlework, brightly lit even on a cloudy day. She'd sat me here to arrange my hair up on my head for the first time; had sat there showing me how to sew on a button. The cushions were deep enough to delay any attempt at springing across the room at him. Reluctantly, I pushed back the little pillow and sat, spreading my hands over the antimacassars. With me trapped, he laid the gun atop the filed papers and tried to pull the drawer off its runners, but only succeeded in jerking the entire desk away from the wall. Desks often had a block on drawers, to prevent them from flying out. Had he asked me how to circumvent the safety latches, I might have told him. He did not. I watched as he pulled up the wooden chair and began to sort rapidly through the filed bills, receipts, and letters. Anything in an envelope, he picked it up to look inside.

At the front of the second row, he made a noise, and snatched up the passbook from Mrs Hudson's Eastbourne bank. His reaction to its contents was an odd mix of disappointment and surprise. He turned to its beginnings, then went through it more methodically before tossing it back in the drawer. Whatever the sum he was looking for, this was both not it, and a sum greater than he'd expected.

It proved to be the drawer's only item of interest. When he had reached the end of the filed papers, he thrust his hand in to feel the underside of the writing surface, then did the same with the bottom of the drawer itself. He even stood to wrestle with it again, but when the drawer did not come free, he retrieved his gun and made to push it shut—then stopped, picked up the passbook, and dropped it into his pocket. When he banged the drawer shut, it bounced out a fraction, but the force also returned the desk to its place against the wall.

He looked at me then. My heart began to thump. If I shoved my legs hard, the chair would fall and his first bullet would hit the window. His second, though . . . My hand would reach the knife on my ankle before his had corrected, but could my steel reach him before his lead reached me?

It could not.

Before the speculation in his eyes could change to decision, I hastened to lay an alternative before him.

"I do know Mrs Hudson fairly well. Perhaps if you told me what sort of old papers you're looking for, I could guess where she might have put them."

I looked into his pale eyes, the bones of my chest cringing away from thirteen grams of leaden death.

Chapter Thirteen

Had Clarissa Hudson allowed herself any actual friends among her many London acquaintances, if she had ventured closeness to any but a handful of fringe-dwellers, they might have urged her towards second thoughts. Or indeed, if she had met Hugh earlier in the year, while the Season was fully under way and before the young people scattered for country and Continent, amused murmurs and knowing glances might have made themselves known.

As it was, the loudest protest came from her father, and her father was precisely the last person she wanted to hear. Hugh was her chance for freedom, and she would not let her father take that from her.

He mistrusted Hugh Edmunds even without knowing who this "friend" was that took up her every free hour. *You're ashamed of him,* he'd tell his daughter. *I'll bet he's a bad 'un. Why else wouldn't you want me to meet him? I can see you're in over your head, girl,* he declared, on and on, until Clarissa stamped her foot and told him that she would not hear it.

The Season had been ruinously expensive, yet summer's takings were low. Normally, their solution would have been a trip to the Continent—but Clarissa did not dare leave London.

Distance continued to open between her and James Hudson.

In early September, the loans Hudson had taken to buy her dresses came due, and he could not pay. In late September, she found that her father had emptied the bank account they had agreed was hers. The first Saturday in October, he broke the lock on her jewellery box and helped himself to the most expensive pieces. It was the final straw. When he came to see her that night, she threw him out of her rooms, and demanded that he leave the hotel, and her life.

In desperation, with The Bishop's men on his coat-tails, Hudson set up a number of one-man Jobs. None of them were anywhere near as effective as when Clarissa was with him, and all were a greater risk: a man might hesitate to admit he'd been fleeced by a woman, but would have no such qualms against a man.

In late October, Hudson was caught with his hand in a proverbial till. He escaped out of the club's back door, but he was known, and report was made. Well after dark, he crept through the back door of Clarissa's hotel and made his way to her rooms.

She refused to let him in. When she saw his state, she refused even to speak with him, and started to shut the door in his face.

Hudson stuck his boot between jamb and wood, and was about to add his shoulder when a man's voice came from within.

"Who the deuces is that, at this hour?"

Hudson stepped back in astonishment. "Clarrie! Have you got a *man* in—"

Clarissa's reply to the voice was airy and amused, but pitched to carry back into the room. "Oh, it's just the old drunk who lives down the hall. He gets confused, poor old dear." And leaning out, she hissed at her father, "I said, you *have* to leave me alone."

The door slammed, the lock turned.

Hudson stood in the hallway, torn between the desire to raise his fist against the wood (and then the people inside) and the fear of creating a row that could get him arrested. Clarrie was running a Job, he told himself: that was all. She'd grown up. She was a woman now, and this was what a woman did.

She'd share the takings, after. The girl always did.

But she did not. For two days, Hudson made a series of increasingly desperate bids to reach Clarissa, and failed. On the third day, the hotel doorman saw him lingering across the street and threatened to send for the police.

That afternoon, penniless, half-frozen, and out of ideas, James Hudson was driven to the same escape he'd used twenty-three years before—only this time he was no longer young, and no longer unafraid. The ship he signed on to was in even worse shape than the *Gloria Scott* had been: an eight-knot tramp steamer shuttling cargo wherever it could find work. He agreed to a two-year stint, loathing the idea of all that water under his feet without the insulation of gin, but knowing he would jump ship at the first half-promising port. In the first week of November, 1878, Hudson vanished from London, and from his daughter's life.

Not that Clarissa knew he was gone. As the days went by, she listened for another knock on the door, watched the streets warily, braced for her father to step out from some nearby doorway. She was in love, Hugh was a perfect darling, all was going spectacularly—but she was also a daughter whose father could bring it all tumbling down. And in truth, she was becoming just a bit worried, when he did not make another appearance, and no letter arrived.

Anticipation's end did not come as she expected, nor did it take the form of her father's shambling figure or meandering letter. Instead, a big, heavily-muscled, loudly-dressed man with ginger hair and a face to match came to a halt before her as she climbed down from a carriage in front of her hotel.

"You Clarissa Hudson?"

She gathered her skirts and took a step back, glad for the watchful presence of the hotel's doorman. "Sir, do I know you?"

"You Jim Hudson's daughter?"

She did not need to ask what the problem was here: someone with that nose, those well-used fists, could only mean that Papa's loan-shark had sent his Demander. She had to get rid of this one, fast: any respectable hotel would ask a resident to leave if trouble followed. Particularly a resident who had become a little erratic with her payments.

"I do not know what business it is of yours, but yes, I am Clarissa Hudson." She held up a gloved hand to stay the approaching doorman, who obediently stopped, but who also did not take his eyes off the potential threat to one of the guests.

"You tell your father that unless he—"

"I am not in touch with my father."

The Demander reconsidered only briefly. "Your father owes my boss a lot of money. The loan's gone overdue. He's left town without makin' a payment."

The man's confident statement came as something of a relief: someone in a position to know things believed that her father was not dead, simply missing. With luck, he was making his way back to Australia. Let his darling Allie deal with him from now on.

However, there was the current situation to be smoothed away. Clarissa widened her eyes and stepped forward to place gloved fingers on the man's meaty forearm. "Oh, I am *so* sorry! I was *afraid* Papa had got himself into some kind of trouble when last I saw him, but that was weeks and *weeks* ago, and he and I had, well, something of a final falling-out. I told him I did not wish to know what sort of trouble it was that he was in, and that he was not to come back until he had settled it. Was I wrong, to send him away?"

The ginger-man was taken aback by the approach. He scowled, first at her hand, then at the sorrow-filled eyes with their hint of unshed tears. He cleared his throat. "We wants our money, we does."

"And certainly you should have it," she pronounced stoutly. She took a step away and set her shoulders in a gesture of resolve. "If my father has entered into a contract and gone back on his word, it is nothing short of shameful. I for one shall have nothing to do with him until he has repaid your employer. And you have *my* word on that."

He very nearly thanked her, but managed to catch himself in time. "Er, yes."

She tugged at her gloves, to mark the matter settled, and said, "I wish your employer Godspeed in his endeavour to reclaim his goods. Thank you for informing me of the matter."

"I—Miss!" She had been on the verge of stepping around his large form, as he had been on the verge of allowing it. She paused with a pretty frown on her brow. "Miss, if your father turns up, let us know."

"Very well. Have you a visiting card?"

He had not, and his face assumed another degree of ruddiness at the admission. "Just ask around, down the East End, for The Bishop."

"The *Bishop*?" she exclaimed.

He went even pinker. "Not a real bishop. Just what he's called, see?"

"Ah, that is a relief." She gave a little laugh. "The idea of a Church of England prelate lending money! Very well, if my father returns—if he comes to *me*—I shall send word to Mr Bishop in the East End. Thank you, Mr . . . ?"

"Smith," he provided.

"Well," she said, showing him a dimple, "it's a good thing I don't need to get word to *you*, as I imagine there might be some degree of confusion."

As indeed there was on the thug's face, as she walked up the steps and into the hotel.

Clarissa knew The Bishop would come back to her eventually, but her convincing display of innocence should put him off the scent for a time. In any event, the encounter had been worth it, for the information that her father had not been tipped off a bridge by the moneylender's men. When she let herself into the rooms, Hugh was sprawled across the settee reading one of her novels. He tossed it aside and got to his feet.

"Hullo, darling," he said, "you're looking very chipper. Hope you don't mind that I let myself in?"

"I gave you a key, dear thing, of course I don't mind." She presented her cheek for his kiss, divesting herself of hat and coat. (Clarissa had let go her personal maid—because of finances, yes, but also due to Hugh's presence: maids talked. The hotel's staff was perfectly adequate to assist her with hair and clothes.) She'd given Hugh a key the previous week. His club was some distance away, and when he'd complained (gently but pointedly) about the amount of time he spent travelling back and forth, and how wet he'd got waiting for a cab the other night, she had to agree, it was a bit silly for two grown people to worry about the strictest of proprieties, particularly when there was already very nearly an understanding between them. So she'd had her key copied, not mentioning it to the management, because after all, Hugh had generously contributed to the hotel bill after she had let him know that her "uncle's" absence had left her a little . . . temporarily embarrassed for funds. The hotel was, fortunately, large enough to ensure a degree of anonymity. In any event, he didn't mind using the side door.

She worried a bit, at first, that he might take advantage, but Hugh was a gentleman, and never did more than nuzzle into the nape of her neck. Not much more. And she had to agree, it was a thrill to come in and find him waiting. Almost like being married already.

"Have you thought any more about Christmas?" she asked, unpinning her hat.

"I have to go up on Saturday. I'll talk to the parents then." Hugh's father, the Earl of Steadworth, had financial interests in the City. As aristocrats went, he had some oddly *nouveau riche* ideas about business: first, that he ran one at all, and second, he expected Hugh to learn the family business from the inside. Since that business was one of the oldest banks in England, Clarissa could hardly object. Even Hugh, though he grumbled, was ambitious enough (his baronet cousin had been right about that) not to protest too loudly.

"Saturday? But you're away so much! And we were going to that party of the Carvers. Oh, dearest, do pour me a little glass of something—the shops were most trying." She perched on the settee, arranging the lines of her skirt as he walked across to the drinks tray.

"Darling, I did warn you how often the bank needs me to travel," he said. "You'll just have to go to the Carvers' without me: the Mater commands. And we do want her on our side."

"I know your mother is unwell, but I don't know why your father doesn't come down to London occasionally like normal people do," she said with a slight pout. "All these months and I've never even met him."

"I know." He put the glasses on the table, then continued around the back of the settee, where he bent to lay his cheek against hers. His deft fingers helped ease off her kid gloves. When her hands were bare, his lingered, tracing the vulnerable skin of her wrists, tantalising a path along her arms to her shoulders. The line of her collarbones; the lace around her neck; the warm skin of her throat. Stroking, feather-soft and mesmerising, along the hollows of her jaw. Her head tilted back, eyes half-shut. He smiled down at her, then moved his right hand to lift a tendril of hair, that he might bend to kiss the fluttering pulse in her neck. Wrapped in whalebone, it was hard to breathe, especially when his lips closed around the little pearl earring she wore and his warm tongue teased at it. She gasped, and turned her face to his.

Only when his hands discovered the old gold chain beneath her clothing and began to ease it from her dress did she stand, laughing a touch breathlessly, to check her hair in the glass above the mantelpiece.

She was really very lucky. She'd found a man she could not only bear, but even love, and at the ripe old age of twenty-two and a half. The two of them would make a formidable pair, although he might not realise it yet. With Clarissa Hudson at his side, all his lusts would be satisfied, all of his needs met. In the meantime, her father was off her conscience. Yes, Mr Bishop's loan was not about to go away, but she had some time to think about how best to pay him. He must be a reasonable fellow—and did Hugh have to know, really?

So: that was November.

For six weeks, apart from a niggling concern about her father, Clarissa clasped happiness to her as only an orphan who'd known hunger could do. For six weeks, as the winter drew in and wool gave way to furs, as Christmas carols rang in the streets and decorated trees began to appear in fashionable windows, Hugh Edmunds courted her, his hands making gentle, insistent inroads on her defences. He spent more time in her hotel, less in his club, and although his bank seemed to be making no recognition of the holiday (or the weather) in its demands on his time, she kept herself busy.

Christmas this year was a Wednesday, and his parsimonious bank had not given Hugh leave until the day before—ridiculous, he agreed, considering who he was, but he would go along with it this year. Therefore, he and Clarissa would take the train to his family home in Shropshire on the morning of the twenty-fourth, then return to London—parental blessings firmly in hand—on St Stephen's Day. She thought long and hard about her wardrobe for these three days: conservative but lovely; well-made but not costly-looking; of sufficient variety so as not to elicit disdain, but not so profligate as to appear a threat to their son's household accounts.

Early Sunday morning, December the twenty-second, when every piece of furniture in her rooms was covered by the lengths of silk and fine wool under consideration, the key sounded in the door and in came Hugh, wild-eyed and unshaven. He had never come to her rooms that early before—she was still in her morning dress! But her protests died away when she saw his state.

"Hugh, dearest, whatever is the matter?"

"It's—" He took a crumpled telegraph flimsy from his pocket, then shoved it back. "My mother."

Clarissa opened her arms in pity, and the man, rendered a boy by the loss of a beloved mother, came to her with a sob. He dropped to his knees and pressed his face into the comfort of her embroidered taffeta. She was acutely aware of her lack of a corset, and the loose wrapper felt positively wanton in the situation—but it would be cruel to push him away, quite yet.

They remained there for what seemed a long, long time. Slowly, his body relaxed against hers; her hand caressed his hair. She was glad that she could provide him some comfort, and grateful (though she'd never have told him) that now she would not have to encounter the controlling old termagant in her sick-bed. She could also not stop her mind from speculating what this would mean for her and Hugh. The mourning period would be an irritation; on the other hand, Hugh's father would be far easier to swing to her side without a wife, and fortunately there were no other . . .

She became aware at this point that Hugh had been moving against her, a small burrowing sensation like an infant at its mother's shirt-front. At the same time, his arms had tightened around her, and seemed lower than they had begun. One hand was splayed, pressing against the folds of cloth that in a day dress would be the bustle. There was a fascination in the sensations, and nothing . . . indelicate. He and she were, after all, to be engaged. Were all but engaged.

When his other hand slipped up her body to her neck, tipping her mouth down to his, she did not resist. Not even when his gentle kisses became harder, when his breathing went rough and her own caught in her throat. Hugh needed her: needed *her*, Clarissa Hudson.

He stood, strong against her. One button parted. Another. His warm hand touched her skin, hesitantly, a request rather than a demand. And when his mouth teased at her nipple, she was lost.

The first time in bed was confusing, uncomfortable, awkward—and quick. Afterwards, he spoke of love, soothing her with hands and words, playing with the gold coin between her naked breasts. After a while, his caresses changed from comforting to urgent. This time it was easier, no longer distressing in body or mind. They slept, and the third time, as evening fell over the city, was slow, compelling, and deeply satisfying in all the ways she could imagine.

Their fourth time, as the windows began to grow light again, was initiated by Clarissa herself, reaching shyly for her lover in the rumpled sheets of the hotel bed.

When she woke to full daylight, he was gone.

Three days later, purring with contentment before the morning fire, she turned the page in the day's newspaper and his name leapt out at her: engaged, to the Hon Virginia Walthorpe-Vane, the eighteen-year-old only child of a wealthy manufacturer from Shropshire, over the Christmas holidays. His mother was among the four named parents. No mention was made of any recent bereavement.

A lie, all of it. Clarissa Hudson was alone and friendless, with a lot of

bills, no partner for her Cheats, and any dignity and self-respect shredded by the clever hands of Hugh Edmunds.

In February, Clarissa surreptitiously moved out of the hotel, leaving
her bill unpaid, and took a room in cheaper accommodations.

In March, she knew for certain that she was with child.

CHAPTER FOURTEEN

Clarissa spent precisely one hour weeping, before drawing around her shoulders the wrap of cold reason: when an upper-crust girl found herself in this situation, she could disappear for a tour of the Colonies and return once her figure had recovered, by which time her family would have arranged a quiet, brief courtship by some male who had not appealed to the marriage market. Or she could have the baby removed—but Clarissa had seen what happened to women who submitted to those butchers, and had no wish to end her days raving with the agony of a septic womb.

But if she was to have this child, how was she to live? It mattered not how many silk dresses a woman owned: in this unforgiving age of Victoria, ultimately the soup-kitchen and workhouse loomed. Her child would be taken, and Clarissa Hudson reduced to a grey drudge.

Which left ... what? Turn to Hugh Edmunds for support? The bastardy laws would force his contribution, but she would have to crawl for it—and, prove it, never an easy task when it came to the well-defended upper classes. She could forge a character, but what honest employment could she find with that? Her mother had been a governess, but no family would employ a pregnant governess—and in any event, Clarissa could do little more than read and write, since the actual schooling had been left to Alicia. Her skills with sewing needles and saucepans were similarly basic, which left work in a factory, where she would spend every daylight hour spinning thread or making matches, giving her child's care over to the old witches who numbed their charges with a gruel of bread mashed with gin.

The coldly expected recourse for a woman in her position was prostitution. And yes, she possessed the wardrobe—and the demeanour—that would lift her above the poor diseased street-corner wretches. But she had met courtesans over the years, and had never failed to feel their self-loathing. The possibility of giving her body for profit had been the ghost at her shoulders since the day she'd donned a corset and put up her hair at the age of thirteen. Her father had (thank God) never countenanced anything beyond the flirtatious gesture. Indeed, he'd made it perfectly clear that using herself in that way would have caused him, and worse, her mother, to turn away in shame.

The idea of losing herself so thoroughly, of submitting to the hands and grunts of strangers, made Clarissa shudder with horror—although even with a belly that scarcely pushed at her skirts, she suspected that pride was a thing she could no longer afford.

Fortunately, she had other options, and easier skills. She needed only go back to her previous life, the life she had led before the Viscount Hugh Edmunds had made her his Mark.

The baby was due in September. If the child was to be born, and born healthy, Clarissa had to eat, and she had to be dry and warm. The thought of cursing her child with a criminal for a mother made her despair, but if she could not afford pride, still less could she afford scruples. The world cheated women like her, stacked the odds against them in so many ways. The only response was to Cheat in return.

By then she'd sold most of her jewels—those her father had not taken, back in September—and all of the furs. Dresses went next, to the second-hand dealers, although slipping out of the hotel bill had forced her to abandon the rest of her wardrobe. She kept a few good things, dresses that would not show much as she changed the bodices and let out the waistlines. Those few dresses, and a return to the basic skills the Cheat Teacher had given her fingers long ago, enabled her to raise the money for rent and food: an hour in Debenham and Freebody's, a few circuits through the Metropolitan Railway during crowded periods, and the contents of various pockets and bags were hers.

Spring refused to come, and the lingering winter was brutal. Palming goods from a shop was tough with gloves on. And some days, it took half an hour on the Metropolitan to warm her fingers enough for a dip. At times, she left with empty hands, when she'd felt the gaze of one of the more attentive guards. In the same way, she took care not to re-visit shops too often, as the guards got to know the customers—and their clothing. She rang all the possible changes on her appearance, adding lace or feathers to her hats, draping a shawl she'd lifted from a lady's shoulders, replacing the buttons: she could only move freely among her targets if she looked as if she belonged among them.

It was the gloves that made for a losing battle. One need only glance at a lady's hands to know her status, and keeping a soft kid surface clean, its stitches firm, and its knuckles snug were hard enough in good weather. Pawn shops sold gloves, although for not much less than the second-hand dealers. Only once did she manage to lift an unattended pair that came anywhere close to fitting.

It became harder and harder to make the rent for her ill-heated, ill-furnished room, even when the weather began to relent. For some reason, her hands became more clumsy as her belly expanded, and her self-assurance in slipping from one rôle to another became less reliable. Desperation proved no substitute for confidence, and a hesitant confidence-trickster was flirting with danger. Clarissa even missed her father. Without a partner, she felt very exposed.

Then in April, the baby moved for the first time. Clarissa was sitting on the Underground behind a tall man in a vicuña coat that would have set her up nicely for half a year. The car was crowded, and he had stood up so she could sit. She was rehearsing her move—make as if to rise, drop her bag, let him reach to the floor while sliding her hand into his coat—when suddenly, picking pockets was the last thing on her mind. The man heard her gasp and turned, his face—a nice face, a friendly broad face—going first questioning then, when he saw her hand resting on her belly, concerned.

"Are you quite well, Madam?" he asked.

"Yes, I—" She caught herself before she blurted out some intimate detail. "Quite well, thank you. Pardon me, this seems to be my stop."

It was not, but he had seen her, would remember her face.

Besides which, she needed to be alone, to consider things a bit more closely.

A baby. A real, living, kicking baby.

She could not go on like this. She was good at what she did, and scruples or no, she had to feed this kicking thing inside her. However, she needed a partner, someone to help work her Cheats, someone with even fewer hesitations than she had.

And as it happened, she knew where to find one.

CHAPTER FIFTEEN

had no clear idea how long it had been since I had looked up from my mail at the sound of a motorcar's tyres in the drive—ten minutes? hours?—but sitting in Mrs Hudson's armchair, waiting for her son to murder me, felt like longer yet.

"Papers are papers," he said at last. "Where would she put them if not in her desk?"

I eased out my long-held breath. "An old house like ours, it could be a dozen places. A knitting pattern might go in that hassock. A personal letter could go into storage. Something she didn't want people to see might be tucked behind her spice cabinet. Legal papers, well, she may have given Holmes something to put in the safe."

To my disappointment, he bypassed my offer of the safe—one of the house revolvers lay within reach of its door. "Let's start with storage."

"Would this be something she's had for a long time?"

"Could be. Or ..."

I waited, trying to look eager to help. For some reason, this question created a sticking point, for several very long seconds. I could see him come to a decision: his face relaxed, and he might as well have said aloud, *Sure, why not tell her? She's not going to live long anyway.* "I sent a crate of, well, things. Just odds and ends, really, after Mum—after her sister died. Did they get here?"

"I think so."

"Good! Good."

It was a fervent reaction, considering that the crate he was talking about had held little more than rubbish—and certainly no passbooks. Its contents had been so badly packed as to have been a deliberate message: granted, the child's string doll must have been tired to begin with, and the once-pretty beaded ladies' evening bag was the victim of time as much as abuse. But half a dozen photographs came out crumpled and gouged beyond redemption; a copy of *The Old Curiosity Shop* was missing the entire first section; several old letters—not even entire, but single pages from different correspondents—had been thrust in to fend for themselves. Three lovely doll costumes might have survived had they not been tumbled against broken porcelain during the long sea voyage. One of these miniature frocks, a full-skirted Victorian costume made out of violet silk with a million unbelievably tiny stitches, had been reduced to shreds.

I had thought, watching Mrs Hudson pick sadly through the mess last November, that this tiny dress was the source of her mourning, until she picked up one of the larger porcelain shards. A pair of tea-cups, she told me: her mother's only possession. Unshed tears quivered in her eyes when she swept the shards into the waste-bin. Afterwards, I rescued the pieces and took them to a porcelain mender. He managed to reconstruct a single saucer, although it showed the myriad lines of his work, and she had looked at it without much enthusiasm. Still, it was given a place on her shelf of mementoes near the door.

Her son now followed my eyes to the saucer. "That's the thing. Looks like it got a bit cracked in shipping." He put his finger behind it, and tipped it off the shelf. Bits skittered in all directions.

"Let's go look in that storage room," he said.

CHAPTER SIXTEEN

F acing The Bishop was the toughest Cheat that Clarissa had ever
talked herself into. She remembered all too clearly her father's
condition when he'd returned from negotiating old debts, and
while she did not imagine the man would do such a thing to her, she
knew full well that he would have an alternative for wayward women.
And as for his son, straining at his tethers . . .

In the end, as with any Cheat, the person she had to convince was
herself. The crime boss was just a man, and Clarissa Hudson was his
match. The Bishop's demonstrated brutality was less madness than a
ruthless dedication to business: nothing like throwing a thieving underling out of a high window to make the man's colleagues think twice
about cheating the boss.

Or so she told herself, over and over during the night. Her heart
counted off the seconds with dull thuds, her bed resisted any attempt at
finding comfort. Even the tiny fish in her belly was restless, protesting
her turmoil.

For half her life, Clarissa Hudson's ability to read people and reflect what they wanted had kept her family warm, fed, and clothed in silk. Her audience with The Bishop would be no different. *Follow his lead,* she told herself. *He's only a man. Read the clues he'll give you, then be what he wants.* A hundred times, she repeated, *You don't need forgiveness. You only need to convince him that he's better off using Clarissa Hudson than punishing her for her father's sins.*

But all she could think of, that endless night, that frigid morning, were the times her skills had failed. The smooth and impenetrable Mr Bevins, his choking hands in the Ballarat darkness. One or two others like him over the years, when only memory of that glassy façade had raised her suspicions.

Hugh Edmunds, who had somehow got under her guard.

Yes, she was capable, but Clarissa's hands were icy and her body damp as she rode the omnibus across town to The Bishop's palace.

And going against a lifetime of habit, she left the tiny ivory-handled revolver in her room. She might as well place it against her own temple, as use it against The Bishop.

"Yes, Mr Bishop, I am aware that when my father left London last autumn, he owed you money. He owes me as well, for that matter, although I imagine I have even less of a chance at seeing repayment than you."

The Bishop was in his throne room, a still-big man in a big decorative chair, with a desk before it to make clear that this was the centre of a business establishment, however criminal. The clerkish man who had been sitting there when she was brought in was dismissed. With him gone, every man in the room looked like a bare-knuckles fighter.

Surrounded by large, violent men, Clarissa sat, a demure figure with gloved hands lying across the beaded bag in her lap—a bag that had been pawed through at the door, by the first in a series of men whose rough handling had made their boss's attitude towards her crystal clear. Her voice was reasonable; the position of her back and shoulders politely upright; there was no trace of tension in her eyes or jaw. This young woman's apparent oblivion to the threat that radiated from The Bishop like a hot stove was making everyone in the room uneasy.

Everyone except the two people talking.

To Clarissa's immense relief, The Bishop's face had proved neither smooth nor impenetrable. The Bishop was angry and fed up and would take a great deal of convincing, but The Bishop was a man, and Clarissa Hudson had been shaping men her whole life.

The son, on the other hand . . .

Her father had called him a mad dog, and she had no doubt that if The Bishop decided to turn his son loose, her life would be over. The old man had already called him to heel twice. The younger man, in his late thirties and with the build of a docks worker, paced back and forth behind his father's throne—where he seemed about equally torn between throwing himself on her, and on the aged father under whose rule he was clearly chafing.

They all expected—Bishop and son, Demander and the others in the room—for her to babble and beg. Instead, she said her piece and closed her mouth, waiting in all apparent peace for his reply. And indeed, she was no longer sweating. Her stomach had settled. Committing to a Cheat was like going off a cliff: the first step was hard; the rest was merely waiting.

Seconds passed, the silence grew profound. One could hear the ticking of two pocket watches, a gurgle from someone's gut, and the holding of breath.

Clarissa permitted one of her eyebrows to rise in a gracious question, but said nothing. Her hands remained loosely clasped, her breasts rose and fell in a slow, even rhythm.

The sudden creak of wood nearly startled a twitch out of her, as The Bishop sat back, dropping one elbow over the throne's arm and resting a foot on his knee. He'd been a big man, once, and was still a physical presence in the room despite his eight decades. The cold rage that greeted her entrance had faded, to be replaced by an expression of interest, even (was it possible?) amusement. For the first time since walking into the room, Clarissa became aware that her lungs were drawing in air.

"So if you're not here to pay what your father owes," the old man asked, "what's your game?"

She smiled—not as triumph, but an acknowledgement that they had entered the next stage of business.

"As I told this gentleman"—she nodded towards the ginger-haired Demander, sitting to The Bishop's left—"Mr . . . 'Smith,' I believe, whom you sent to speak with me last October, I neither know where my father is, nor do I have the resources to pay off his debt to you . . . directly." She let him listen to that last word for a moment before she continued. "As you may have noticed, I have fallen on hard times. In my current condition, I find myself vulnerable to all the obstacles life sets before a woman, and more. Not the least of those being that as an independent . . . agent, as it were, I would be setting myself up in some degree of competition with you.

"Therefore, I should like to make a business proposition: my skills, which are considerable, in exchange for one of your employees as a partner. I would give you a percentage of my takings. In return, you would offer me your protection among your associates here in London."

The amusement on his face was clearer now, although it contained more than a little cruelty. "There's lots of houses need cats, Miss Hudson. Some men like a touch of what you got at the moment."

She was prepared for threats, and managed to hide her revulsion and terror by lifting the lumpy beaded bag from her knees and placing it on the desk between them. She pulled open its cord and laid out a series of objects on the polished wood: two knives, a gold watch, a silver propelling pencil, and a silver-and-ivory comb with a tooth missing.

At the last, an exclamation came from behind the throne, and the son lunged forward to snatch up the comb. "This is mine! How—Christ, the bloody tail knocked into me when she come in, and . . . Oh, I'm gonna—"

"That's enough," the great man said.

"But Pops, the bitch—"

"Shut it."

"Jesus, wan't it bad enough that 'er father—"

The old villain raised his eyes. "Want Jesse to throw you in the cellar?" The threat was quiet but the effect immediate and profound. The son's mouth snapped shut, and every other man there gave a sort of shudder. The son's gaze fell, and The Bishop returned his attention to the objects on the table before him.

One of them was a mechanical pencil. It had rested on the desk blotter when Clarissa Hudson sat down.

"You're a fly dolly, give you that," he said. "Clever fingers, the dive and the pinch."

"In fact," she replied, "what I am good at is the diversion. If you remember, as I started to sit, my back gave a sudden twinge and I was forced to lean on your desk. Each of these gentlemen had a similar distraction that enabled my fingers to remove something he prized from a pocket. My fingers are adequate, but I'm a better actress than a pickpocket. My father and I paid for a week in Paris with three sessions of the Found Note-Case routine. I have been blessed with a remarkably sympathetic face. Would you not agree?" she asked, a veritable study in angelic virtue.

The Bishop's own face was undergoing a challenge, the muscles working as if a small creature were caught beneath the skin. Finally he gave way to a cough of grudging laughter. "Missy, you ain't what I expected."

Clarissa permitted a bit of her satisfaction to show. After that, it was just a matter of negotiation.

His first offer of a partner was old enough to be her grandfather, a decrepit old stork with shaking hands.

"Most amusing, I'm sure," she told The Bishop with a cool smile. "Am I right in thinking you must have a number of apprentices in the trade? Boys young enough to be quick on their feet?"

"Not girls?" he asked, still amused.

"I do better with lads," she told him.

Before the day was out, she'd had a dozen boys paraded in front of her, aged thirteen to seventeen. Each one was either so shifty-eyed any constable with a speck of brains would have him up by his heels to see what fell out of his pockets, or so blatantly righteous as to raise the suspicions of a saint.

The Bishop's patience was wearing thin; Clarissa's ankles were swelling. "Are these all you have?" she asked at last.

"There's more. Come back tamarrah."

But on her way out of The Bishop's palace, a small child was coming in. His clothing was sparse and his brown skin had gone a peculiar colour with the cold, but he had about him a cheeky air that caught her attention. "What does that one do?"

The gang leader had to ask his ginger-haired Demander—Jesse—for information.

"Billy? He's look-out for Three-Card Louis."

"Is he Greek?" Clarissa had problems once with a Greek lad.

"Don't think so. African, more like. He granddad was a street-sweeper."

"That's fine, then. Let me talk to him."

Ginger dragged the lad from his bread-and-dripping and set him down in front of Clarissa.

Three-Card Louis must have been working the lower reaches of the city if this was the lad who watched for coppers. The boy wore a variety of hand-me-downs, none of which actually fit his thin frame, all of which had seen long use before coming to him. Despite that, he'd made an attempt at tidiness, with all his buttons fastened, oversized cap at a rakish angle on his tight curls, and a bright orange scarf hiding the dirt around his neck. He even wore stockings, although he did not seem to have learned to darn yet. His delicate fingers were surprisingly clean, and his skin, out of the bitter air, had taken on a warm colour, like coffee richly treated with milk.

"How old are you?" she asked.

"I'm seven, and you?" he retorted.

"Can you read and write?"

"Oi c'n read a 'Keep Out' sign and write me naim 'senough to be goin' on."

"If I buy a quartern loaf, a tuppence worth of apples, and tuppence of sweets, what's my change from a bob?"

"Why'd'ya buy any of dem fings? They're easy enough to nick."

"I said 'if.'"

"Though maybe not if you're old 'n' slow, loik you."

"You don't know the answer, do you?"

"Thruppence."

"Good. But you're not seven years old. I doubt you're much more than five. And with hands like yours, you've been practicing the dip. If you want to work with me, you're what I need. But I can't have a partner who lies to me: Can. Not. You either tell me the truth or you keep mum, those are your choices. Your first lie, I hand you back to The Bishop. And I'm very good at catching lies."

Most of the time, an inner voice added. As if he'd heard, the lad's black gaze darted down to her belly, then up to her earrings, before returning down to contemplate the toes of her shoes. And he nodded. "Oi'm six. Oi fink."

"Do you have a family?"

His eyes went sideways to the big man, who said, "'Is Mum's not interested in much but the bottle. His old man's off on a job for me."

Either in prison or hanged, she thought. "Then there's no one to object if the lad comes with me. We'll be back in two or three days."

"What, you want to make off with one of me lads?"

"Mr Bishop, you offered me a partner, I've chosen one. If you're not pleased by what we bring you, take him away again. But I need him clean and fed in order to do his job. He's coming with me. Come, boy," she said, and walked off.

After a time, the child followed.

On the street outside, she spoke over her shoulder. "What's your name?"

"Billy."

"Is there more?"

"William," he said. "Mudd. Dey call me Wiggins."

"Very well, William Mudd, you may call me Mrs Hudson. Our first order of business is to find you something to eat." *And immediately there-after,* she added to herself, *burn your clothes and scrub you raw.*

Billy Mudd was an impulse, but one that worked out—short term and long—beyond Clarissa's wildest imaginings. During the remainder of spring and into the summer, he proved a most efficient partner in relieving London's streets of excess cash. Scrubbed up and dressed in a white-and-blue sailor suit and straw boater (both of which came from a Sunday morning trip through Petticoat Lane, and both of which he despised) and high-buttoned boots (which he polished daily) he could act the concerned young son of a pregnant mother, or slip in among an Oxford Street crowd assisting a woman overcome by heat, dipping into pockets all the while.

The Bishop counted himself satisfied, and let it be generally known that Clarissa and the boy were under his protection.

Clarissa took scrupulous care in dividing the proceeds, which proved generous enough to put some away for the coming weeks when work would be difficult. She even took out a cut for the boy—only some of which went into his hand—and hid away her share in a growing stash of coins and a few pieces of jewellery. A small gold ring would do to pay the midwife: she did not want to be alone at the birth. She even put on her dignity and returned to the hotel, to make pretty apologies and, more to the point, a first payment towards the sizeable bill she'd left behind. The hotel had treated her well, and besides, if things went as she hoped, she would be returning to that level of society before long. Also, she was hoping they might have letters for her, but the only one was from Alicia, posted in November. It was addressed (naturally) to their father, to say that she was betrothed to the young law clerk mentioned in previous letters. She and Raymond McKenna would be wed on April 12: no suggestion that the bride might delay it so her family could be there.

There was nothing at all from her father. On reflection, Clarissa decided that was not a bad thing. It was now May. Having nothing further from Alicia could mean that her sister knew their father had left England. (Heaven forbid Allie would deign to write a mere sister, Clarissa thought sadly.) Clarissa invested in some good paper and penned a congratulatory letter, enclosing a bank note by way of present. After that, she tried to push her sister from her mind.

She moved again, to a pair of rooms in a worn but clean lodgings-house. The establishment was in a less-desirable corner of a decent neighbourhood, thus safe but cheap. The air smelt of baking and laundry rather than pig and neglected cesspits. Clarissa found it a great relief to have a proper bed, and a separate room for the rest of life. She bought a cot for Billy, two comfortable chairs, and a small table. The noises that came through the window were less the voices of children playing street football or games of cat and more the grinding of wheels or the cries of costermongers, but with the racket came peace of mind. Lamp-lighters arrived morning and night, her skirt-hems stayed clean thanks to the crossings-sweepers, and the wares of the muffin-men and the Italian ice-man were fresh and wholesome.

She could go days without being wakened by the sound of a police rattle and the shouts of a chase.

Billy was less enthusiastic. This new neighbourhood was for him a place of strange accents and too-broad streets, although he was immensely impressed by having a flowered basin with running water in the corner of the bedroom, the services of both chambermaid and cook, and a bath just down the hall. He'd never seen a hot-water geyser before. Nor had he seen such things as a slate and schoolbooks.

"When the school year starts," she told him, "you'll be going."

He objected mightily, that classrooms were for nancy boys and The Bishop wouldn't like it, but she stood firm. "You've grown too much to look like a baby," she explained. "If you're not in school, people will ask why. And you wouldn't want me to get in trouble with the law, would you? Besides, education is never wasted."

He grumbled, at the demands of book-learning and of bathing, but she also noticed that he used more than his share of soap, and spent more hours than she required bent over the tasks of literacy. She enjoyed having him there as she sewed by the lamp-light from his table. She took pleasure watching the gauntness fade from his bones, now that bread had butter again and dinner had meat.

By June, she and Billy had achieved a little comfort in their lives and, with The Bishop's authority behind them, even a degree of security. The boy was bright, he wasn't too careless, he listened. Some days, their odd partnership even felt like a family.

She should have known it couldn't last.

She should have known her father would be the end of it.

CHAPTER SEVENTEEN

"How the *devil* did you find me?"

But James Hudson was just staring at Clarissa's swollen belly. After a minute, his gaze went to her left hand, seeking out the thin gold ring she wore there. "You're married."

"No," she said irritably. "The ring's for idjits like you who think it makes a difference. Papa, how did you find me? Have you been here in London all this time?"

"You're not married?" He sounded horrified, which Clarissa rather thought took a prize, especially for a man in his derelict condition. James Hudson had obviously been putting in hard physical labour—on a ship, by the looks of him. He stank, his remaining teeth were yellow, and his hair looked like a home for lice. He seemed to have shrunk with the sudden onset of age, and the crooked smile that had once charmed the ladies in Monte Carlo now just looked crooked.

"It's none of your business if I'm wed or no. What are you doing here? And why did you not write, so I knew you were alive?"

He looked puzzled. "Write? I dunno, I guess I've never written to you, just to Allie. She's married, can you believe that? Little Allie."

"So I heard. You are aware that The Bishop is hot for you?"

That name finally got his attention. "You know The Bishop?"

"It would be hard not to, Papa, with his ginger-haired Demander accosting me on the street. You owe him money. A lot of money."

"*I* owe him? It was for *your* dresses!"

"And your card games and suits and horses."

"Anyway, I paid him. Some."

"He wants the rest. I had a time convincing him not to take it out of my skin. If we're seen together, I'll be in for it. You have to go."

"Clarrie, you can't—"

"Don't call me that! And don't come back until The Bishop is paid."

"Clarrie—Clarissa, child, I used my last bob finding you."

"Yes, how did you do that, exactly?"

"The hotel."

"Oh . . . *damn*!" she cursed. No good deed went unpunished, no responsible payments of debts failed to turn around and bite. It wasn't as if Alicia ever wrote her anyway. "How much do you need?" she asked, turning her back so he couldn't see into her beaded reticule.

"I don't want your money, dearie. I thought maybe we could, you know . . ."

She turned around, in her outstretched hand two five-pound bank notes. It was more than half her worldly goods, but she did not hesitate. Her father did, but only for a moment.

"I shouldn't—"

"Go."

"You don't mean that, my—"

"I do. I will not work with you again. I don't want to see you again until you have repaid Mr Bishop. I can't afford it, Papa. I have responsibilities now. I want you to go."

Dark fury stirred in the depths of his bloodshot eyes. For an instant, Clarissa was huddled on her childhood mat while drunken feet came up the stairs.

"Clarrie, my back's against a wall, here." He was trying to cajole, but they both heard the menace in his voice.

"Papa, I cannot help you."

She braced herself for the rising fist, but in the end, faced with a grown woman nearly as tall as he, James Hudson deflated with a foul-smelling sigh. "Right. Well, I got one last card up my sleeve—I was just hopin' to rest up a bit before playin' it. Get back on my feet, like. There's an old friend in Norfolk will help me out—though he don't think of himself that way. But if you won't have your old Pa, you won't."

He lingered, offering her a last chance to back down, then his shoulders slumped and he turned away, her bank notes vanishing into his noxious garments. She watched him shamble off. Then she took a shaky breath and closed the door.

The waiting began again. Clarissa fully expected her father to reappear on her doorstep, but days passed, and he did not. She could only imagine the reaction of the "old friend" when confronted by James Hudson in his current condition, but the man seemed to have relented enough to take her father in. She did not like thinking of Papa sleeping rough in a door-way—or beaten to death by The Bishop's thugs.

The summer wore on, turning wet, and so dreary that street-surface Cheats became all but impossible. The alternative was moving inside to shops and museums, but tight quarters increased the risk: fleet-footed Billy might dart away from the hard hand of the law, but she most defi-nitely could not. A number of days, she and Billy remained at home, her with swollen ankles raised, him bent over his books. Even when the wet relented, she did not last for long before exhaustion claimed her.

The Bishop was not pleased. Nor did she manage to send the hotel anything that month other than a note of apology, in hopes of staying the manager's wrath.

On August 20, her back ached dully, and the child within drummed merry heels on her bladder. The third time she clambered awkwardly up from her chair, warm water gushed down her thighs. She was appalled at the loss of control—until she realised what it meant: the baby was coming early.

She gave Billy every pence she could spare and sent him to The Bishop, telling the lad to fetch the midwife on his way.

Nine and a half hours later, Clarissa's son came squalling into the world, a small, crumpled, red-faced creature with wisps of pale hair, who bellowed his outrage at being shoved from a dim and comfortable home. She called him Samuel, a name held by no man in her acquaintance, but which shared three letters with that of her mother.

Samuel proved an irritable child, easily upset by unchanged napkins, infuriated with any delay in a meal. He woke often at night, with rashes and twitches and periods of inconsolable wailing that she feared would have them evicted.

When Samuel was a month old, Billy returned—or rather, was returned, with Jesse's hand heavy on his shoulder. The Bishop's ginger-haired Demander told her in no uncertain terms that baby or no, The Bishop expected her to resume work the next day.

Ill-fed and ill-slept, the following morning they were out on the streets. Samuel stretched his blue eyes at the brightness, then objected to everything. Billy had no need to feign the scorn of an older brother. The only advantage was, a wailing infant made men all the more eager to be clear of her, and less likely to check their pockets when they'd made their escape.

The first week out passed in a daze of forgetfulness and exhaustion. School was set aside for the time—without Billy, she'd have been arrested for sure. Even with him, they had a couple of close calls, and their working days were short.

If only the accursed rain would stop! Everything was damp, foreign visitors hurried on to warmer climes, museum crowds became so sparse the guards had time to meditate on the oddity of this trio and wonder why a mother this new was not at home.

At last, towards the end of September, came a Saturday that dawned clear. Clarissa took extra care with her clothing and hair, fed Samuel and wrapped him in his good blanket, and they set off for Regent's Park.

Even before noon, the crowds proved that London was eager for the sun. Boys ran past with balls; women in summer dresses strolled the paths on the arms of men in straw hats. Billy had brought his hoop-and-stick, the sort of camouflage that doubled as actual boyish fun (little enough of that in his life, she thought), and she smiled as he wobbled away down the path from her, his oversized shoes churning, a boy with nothing more pressing on his mind than where to spend the tuppence in his pocket.

She let him race about for twenty minutes while she enjoyed the simple sensations of a walk in the sun. Then fleeting time drew back the reins on her pleasure and moved her feet towards the Zoological Gardens. On Sundays, when the zoo was reserved for Members, this would be a realm of bright parasols and silk hats, but even on a Saturday there were few cloth caps inside the gates. The afternoon proved lucrative, the zoo-goers both amiable and distracted, an ideal combination for Clarissa and her young partner (partners plural, in fact, since the blond curl atop little Samuel's head proved to have a remarkably softening effect on the women). Every twenty minutes to half hour she slid another handful of coins, silk handkerchiefs, watches, and even a couple of notes into her reticule, and when she stopped a little before three to retreat to the Conveniences to feed Samuel, she transferred a satisfying quantity into the dress's larger inside pocket.

Once Samuel was fed and asleep, Clarissa took Billy for a restorative cup of tea and some sticky cakes. She was profoundly grateful for the chance to sit, and when Billy had scraped his plate down to its glaze, she gave him permission to wander off and look at the hippopotamus. The sun warmed her in more ways than the mere physical. This past month had been hard, but the tide, she thought, had turned: she would find her feet again, pay off her debts, and figure some kind of life for herself and her son. If it meant being a part of The Bishop's criminal empire, so be it. There were worse things than being a swindler. Being an irresponsible mother, for one.

Clarissa ran a lace-covered finger across her son's downy scalp. Soon, she would have to turn him over to a nurse, since a babe in arms was as clear a sign of the working class as dirt, a bare head, or an apron covering one's skirts—any of which would make her stand out in the moneyed crowds. Still, she promised herself, she would take care of him. Always.

A child screeched, somewhere in the distance. As Clarissa automatically raised her head to look, something caught at the edge of her gaze. She searched, not sure what had snagged her attention, but saw only a figure in the act of turning away into a group of people. Her impression was that it had been a young man—quite young—and that he had been watching her.

Not all that unusual. A mother and small infant drew the attention of half the world, even young men. No, this was merely a curious lad—turning away in embarrassment, perhaps, at his inner musings over the process by which a babe in arms had come into being. Still, the impression of an intent gaze stayed with her, although she'd seen little of his face. All she was certain of was the tilt of his silk hat and the exaggerated degree of white cuff at his wrist, as if his limbs were outgrowing his jacket.

Still, it might be best to take a break for a while. It was near to feeding time at the lion cage. If she had not seen that lad again after the big cats were finished, she would risk a few more turns at the swells.

By the time the lions had dragged their gory dinners off, Clarissa was about to drop. She'd kept a surreptitious watch on all sides, alert for young men with protruding cuffs, but though the nape of her neck crawled with imagined eyes, no one seemed to be interested in her. Still, the watch had taken the last of her energies. When she told Billy it was time to go home, he did not object much, either.

At the park exit, Billy turned automatically in the direction of the omnibus, but at the thought of that packed and sweltering box on wheels, Clarissa stopped him. "Let's take a cab," she said, then modified it to, "a hansom."

He was as astonished as he was thrilled—less for the rare luxury than for the sheer adventure of the thing. She handed Samuel up to him as she manoeuvred her skirts up the step, and settled inside—a snug fit, the little doors barely shutting across her knees, but the air was fresh. As the high carriage swerved and cornered down the crowded streets, Clarissa peered through its side window at the weaving tapestry of identical cabs. Billy asked what she was looking for.

"Nothing," she told him. "Just—see how funny the horses look, all trotting head-on like that?"

He was distracted. They spent the remainder of the ride with her hand clenched through the back of his trousers while he stood, leaning over the side and staring backwards, a wide grin on his face.

She really did like this young lad quite a lot.

CHAPTER EIGHTEEN

I t was a mistake, I told myself, to think of Samuel Hudson as human.

Samuel was the sort of creature who learns emotions as a mask, whose true empathy is precisely nil, whose only interest lies in his own comfort and preservation. Some of his sort make no attempt to hide their contempt for the human race, and end their days in prison or a noose. Others manage to learn early the lessons of survival, that even prey can have teeth, and become expert at hiding their contempt until the act can be set aside.

Samuel Hudson had set his act aside. Seeing his face, I felt the same visceral reaction of any normal person: run, fast and far.

I had seen men in India charming cobras, not by music or mesmerism, but by a cautious teasing: the snake feels threatened enough not to let down its defences and slither away, yet safe enough not to strike. There is a precise balance between threat and reassurance, distance and presence, while the charmer waits—either for a partner, or an opportunity.

God only knew where Holmes was. It would have to be an opportunity.

I led Samuel through the kitchen and sitting room to the front entranceway, where cupboards filled the space beneath the stairs. I started pulling open doors, trying to sound helpful yet puzzled.

"This is where we tend to put all manner of whatnot," I said, my voice muffled by a stack of aged blankets. "Your crate shouldn't be too buried. It came only a few months ago." I closed that door, and opened the next, every inch of me unhappy about having my back turned on this man.

He was waiting for me to pull out a weapon: I could feel the tension in his finger. And indeed, one might expect that in a household such as ours, this storage area would be just the spot to conceal a gun—were it not for two problems: Mrs Hudson, and Holmes himself.

Mrs Hudson simply detested guns, and refused to dust any shelf or clear any cupboard when she knew there was one stored there. (I had long ago decided that the tiny, ivory-handled derringer I had once seen in the depths of her wardrobe—a place where I had absolutely no business to have gone—was a decorative little fake.) Holmes, on the other hand, though not fond of guns for reasons I could understand, did acknowledge them as a necessary evil. However, he insisted on knowing *precisely* where each was, that he could lay a hand on it, instantly, blindfolded, on a black night.

A storage cupboard where things were forever being shovelled about made a poor place, therefore, for a loaded weapon. The most lethal things here were a crossbow with a broken string and a weighty set of bocce balls.

I dropped to my heels for the last door, pulling out three pairs of rubber boots, a stack of books headed for my library in Oxford, and a repair kit for bicycle tyres. Behind them was a wooden shape, just where I remembered it.

With my left hand resting casually on the topmost book of the pile, a history of the Punjab rendered satisfyingly dense by many glossy illustrated pages, I turned an eager and virtuous face up at him, to ask, "Is this your crate?"

CHAPTER NINETEEN

The next day, Clarissa was feeling the effects of long hours of walking followed by the slams and sway of a hansom—she should have spent the extra for a growler. Childbirth, it seemed, took some time to get over, like pleurisy and broken legs. A solid night's sleep would help—although last night had been better than most. Samuel seemed to have been tired out by the day, and only woke every couple of hours instead of every twenty minutes. Such luxury!

Sunday was Clarissa's usual day to give The Bishop his week's tribute. Since August, she had been sending what little there was with Billy. Once, the boy had set off with nothing more in hand than a note from Clarissa concerning her health and the weather. He had returned with a bruised face and a threat from the man that she should hurry up and birth her brat.

Today being Sunday, normally she would have roused herself for the trip to Whitechapel. However, Billy had paid the price for her failures: it was only fair that he should get credit for their success.

"Billy, you think you can carry our takings to The Bishop without losing them?" she asked.

He turned on her a look of infinite scorn. He'd been carrying coins and notes around the city for half his life: being known as one of The Bishop's lads meant the thugs tended to let you be.

So she laboriously penned a list of what they had taken and what she had kept, along with a polite note thanking The Bishop for his patience. (She had to check the spelling with Billy, since words that came freely from her tongue proved slippery on paper.) She bundled the silk handkerchiefs, a ladies' looking glass, two hair-pins, and a watch-fob into a tight bundle. She slipped it and the note into a bag, added The Bishop's cut of the coins, and tugged the strings shut. Billy, dressed in his loosest trousers, threaded his belt through the strings and dropped the bag inside. She pressed a coin into his palm and told him to buy himself some bread and coffee on the way.

Samuel stirred, fed, and actually went back to sleep. She took advantage of the respite to tidy the room and mend a pair of Billy's trousers, sitting at the window where the grind of iron wheels and the cries of street vendors drowned out Samuel's wheeze. Might she feel more . . . maternal about the infant if she wasn't so flattened by exhaustion? Shouldn't a mother and child make more of a partnership? Instead, he felt like a whirlpool, one more thing sucking her down into the dark.

Ah well. She had Billy. And Samuel would get easier.

Thinking of Billy, she'd neglected his schooling this past week: where had they got to, anyway? He'd been reading aloud to her, sounding out the words of a copy of *The Old Curiosity Shop* that she'd bought from a vender's barrow. It was missing its first few pages, but they'd soon caught up with the story. When she came to an end of her slit seam, she put down her needle and picked up the book, opening it to the green ribbon he'd left to mark their place. She tried always to review material before giving it to him, lest he think the teacher knew less than her student.

She read now under her breath, wondering why Mr Dickens felt it necessary to use so many long words. Still, once she'd picked through the individual words and got their shape, she could usually string them to-gether to get their meaning, almost like speech. *Through this* ... *de.lir.i.ous* ... (Delirious? What was that?) *scene, the child, fri—frightened and re.pell—repelled by all she saw, led on her be.wil.der—bewildered charge* ... And so on.

It was both exhausting and exhilarating to tease a story from endless and identical rows of black marks on the page. She had just reached the part where Nell was comforting her grandfather under the noses of two sleeping men (the illustrations helped, a lot) when a knock came on the door. She dropped the book with a bang, scrambling upright.

Samuel peeped, but did not wake. She stared at the door, heart in mouth, waiting for the Demander to bash it down, but the thin wood remained shut. She swallowed, and tip-toed over to put her ear to the crack.

Either her shadow betrayed her, or her visitor's hearing was very sharp. "Miss Hudson? I'd like a word, if you please."

Not one of The Bishop's men—not with that accent. She placed her hand against the cold iron, turned the knob—and the door pushed in, gently but firmly. She stepped back in surprise as a gangling, smooth-faced figure came through her door, eyes darting around as if making an inventory of the room, her clothing, and the books on the shelf.

He was little more than a lad, despite his six feet and more of height, all bones and a beak that made him (in a never-forgotten phrase from her mother) "look laik he was bein' led about ba his nose." His hair appeared to have been trimmed by three impatient snips from a pair of dull shears, his hands were dotted with odd stains and what looked like burns, and his overcoat, although of an excellent cut and jet-black cloth, had been made for a smaller man. He seemed to be leaning into a strong breeze as he swept past, almost sniffing with that absurd nose as he surveyed the room.

One long hand came up to remove the silk hat that rested upon his ears, a hand-me-down from some larger head. As his sleeve went up, her eyes followed the cuffs, also dotted with stains, that protruded from the too-short sleeves of his jacket. At that, she recognised him.

"You!" she exclaimed.

"I," he replied. He cocked his head to read the title of the book splayed across the floor.

"You were in the zoo yesterday. Watching me."

"Yes." He picked up the Dickens story and laid it upon her chair, a gesture less of tidiness than of masculine claim. Clarissa's self-possession stirred: so this lad imagined himself a man, did he? He'd seen a woman burdened by two small children, a woman not entirely without looks, a woman with little cash (a hansom, instead of a growler) and no man in sight: a woman whose vulnerability he could exploit? Well, this stripling was in for a surprise.

She drew herself up, summoning the kind of amused womanliness that reduced young men like this to quivering infancy.

"My dear boy," she began—except that he then turned to look directly at her, and she was rooted to the floor, rendered speechless by a pair of cold, vivid, steel-grey eyes.

His were the eyes of an old man, and did not belong above cheeks that scarcely knew a razor. That gaze had seen everything, knew everyone, would be surprised at nothing, and it flicked through Clarissa Hudson's layers like a scalpel through flesh, getting to the bone of her in nothing flat. Her crimes, her catastrophic love affair, her father's rule, the responsibility for a sister, a mother's leaving her—down to the person that was little Clarissa Hudson, Australian transportee.

And then a whimper came from the corner, and the grey eyes went wide as they searched for the source of the noise. They found the corner where Samuel lay, then returned to Clarissa. For the first time, he looked young.

"I need to—" she began.

"Yes," he said, and gave a wave of those long fingers.

Loosed at last, she retrieved the infant. When she turned, the intruder was running that penetrating gaze along the buckling wallpaper, the shawl she'd draped over a worn place on the chair, the polished silver frame around Alicia's face, and the bowl of apples on the table. He moved over to the bedroom doorway, to survey those contents: three frocks of incongruously rich fabric, hanging high off the floor: neatly tucked bed-clothes; tidy stacks of baby things; smaller piles of garments belonging to her and to Billy. His gaze came to rest on the window that looked out onto the bricks of the next house.

The glass was spotless.

With a nod, he retreated to the small table with Billy's schoolbooks on it. Clarissa became aware that she was holding Samuel like a shield; aware, too, that she was tempted to brazenly settle her infant to the breast, in hopes of driving the lad away.

But no: he would not leave. She doubted he would even turn his back.

The boy spoke at last, his voice high, biting, and of the upper classes. "You are the daughter of James Hudson?"

Whatever she'd expected, it was not this.

"I . . . he . . ." She stopped. "What has Pa done now?"

He bounced the silk hat against his leg a few times, his eyes icy with condemnation. "Your father is a blackmailer. His threats killed a man, the father of a friend of mine. I shall make him answer for it."

The declaration should have sounded absurd, coming from one so young. Instead, Clarissa felt the lad could have given The Bishop lessons in fury. Blackmail—Pa? Well, maybe, if he was desperate—but, *killing* the man in the process? A man with a social connexion to this terrifying invader—worse, a connexion that, judging by the emphatic way he spat the word "blackmailer," was very personal.

"I . . . I don't, I'm sorry. Do you—" But at that point, Samuel decided to join the conversation, less from hunger than to protest her squeezing arms. She'd never been so glad to hear his cry. Maybe she could drive the lad out, at least long enough to gather her thoughts. "I need to feed him," she said faintly.

"By all means," he said, sounding more irritated than distressed. Rather than retreat into the hallway, he merely took up a position at the window, staring at the street below.

She, however, did fall back to the bedroom before putting Samuel to her breast, leaving the door ajar. The moment the infant cries subsided, the young man spoke up.

"I can see that your father does not live here. Do you know where he is?"

"I last saw him in the summer, and—"

"When, exactly?"

"June, I think? Perhaps early July. It was the first time I'd seen him since November. We had an argument. He . . . shall we say, he had not made friends in London. At the time, I had no idea where he'd gone, but when he came back, in early summer, he said he'd been signed on as a sailor. He looked much the worse for wear, almost haggard, with—"

"Tar on his sleeve?"

"Well, yes. How did you know?"

"I saw him soon after. What did he want from you?"

"He assumed I would be glad to resume the . . . arrangement he and I had, an Act we put on in order to earn—"

He was suddenly standing in the bedroom doorway. "Miss Hudson, you and your father are a pair of scoundrels, bilking the wealthy from Manchester to Monte Carlo."

She stared. "You seem remarkably"—*well informed*—"sure of yourself, young man."

"I make it a point to know what other people do not."

Samuel stirred, as if the flow of his meal had been cut off. She shifted him to the other side, briefly exposing herself to the young man, but he did not react—rather, he reacted internally, but seemed somehow both to notice his own discomfort and set it aside.

"Very well," she said. "Since you know what we did, it will not surprise you to learn that he was looking to resume our partnership. However, as I said, he looked too decrepit. Even if I'd been willing, it would have taken a lot of time and effort to clean him up. In any event, I had recently made an arrangement—a financial arrangement—with a gentleman here in London."

"You went to work for The Bishop."

"You *know* him?" This young man looked nothing like The Bishop's usual clientèle—far less a partner.

"We have met." The flat statement did not suggest a social event.

"I was a bit desperate, back in April. Mr Bishop offered me a degree of protection—and one of his young charges as a partner. Since my father owed him a great deal of money—still does, so far as I know—I was not about to cross the man by going back into partnership with my father. So I sent Papa away."

"What did he say when you did so?"

"Something about having another card to play. A friend, in Norfolk, I believe. Although I didn't know my father had any actual friends. I presumed he had some kind of dodge in mind, although he said nothing about blackmail. I am sorry about your friend's fa—"

"No!" Those icy grey eyes stifled her words before they were born. Samuel whimpered; this time, the young man took no note. "Do not bleat an apology at me. Blackmail is wickedness incarnate. It destroys entire families. And you were your father's partner for too long to make any claim to innocence. Where would he go, if not to you?"

She could only shake her head. "I never had anything to do with blackmail. He may have, without me, but I always found the idea . . . unsavoury. At any rate, as I told you, my father has no friends that I know of. He and Mother lived in Cornwall before I was born. Falmouth, I believe."

"His parents?"

"Died long ago. He was the only child."

"Your mother's people? From Scotland?"

"How did you know *that*?"

"She left traces in your voice. Edinburgh?"

He had to have found out somehow about her grandparents: no one had heard a trace of Scotland in her voice since she was ten years old. "Edinburgh, yes. But he wouldn't go there. They'd have him arrested on sight. Or shot."

One eyebrow quirked upward, and she explained, "My mother stole some jewellery—her own, mind, left to her by her grandmother—from her father's safe. She had no money, and needed to get to Australia to join father."

"She stole her inheritance to pay for a ticket?"

"Well, not quite. She knew if she did that, they'd just cash back her fare and stop her from going. So instead, she stole it in order to get transported."

The other eyebrow climbed to match the first—then something astonishing: the young man laughed.

Even more amazing to Clarissa was the grin she found on her own face in response.

It was gone in a moment, but the air in the room had changed in some ineffable way—charged, almost, but with a kind of electricity she could not identify. Not attraction, and not quite fear, but somewhere between the two poles. The threat of it made her uneasy.

"Who *are* you?" she asked abruptly.

"A student, of life," he answered. "A friend of Victor Trevor, whose bull terrier took a liking to my ankle one Sunday morning last winter. And, a person in a position to bring a killer to justice."

"Do you have a name?"

"I do, although you will not have heard of it. The name is Holmes. Sherlock Holmes."

CHAPTER TWENTY

The young man departed, the latch rattling behind him like a cell door. Clarissa did not for a moment imagine that she was rid of him. She sat with her arms around Samuel, taking comfort from this small mite in a way she'd not have expected before this morning.

Young Mr Holmes (strange Christian name, that: *Sherlock?*) was going to be a problem, of that she had no doubt. Had her father been here, she'd have poured every coin she had into his hands to send the old man far away, because he hadn't a hope if that grey-eyed devil seized onto his trail. She had no wish to ally herself again with James Hudson—would not even have minded terribly if she did not set eyes on him again in this life—yet she did not wish him ill. His crimes had, for the most part, been committed on those whose own greed acted against them, and who in any event could afford the loss. He had been a reasonable enough father by his own lights. She would not want his fate hanging on her conscience.

She was still in the chair when Billy returned, filled with the virtues of responsibility. He set out upon a tale of crossing the city on his own, of his conversation with The Bishop, of . . . He stopped, head cocked to one side.

"Is summat wrong with yer?"

"No, Billy, I'm fine, although I am a bit tired from yesterday. How would you like to go to Kensington Gardens this afternoon? Not to work, just to hire a row-boat so you can paddle me and Samuel about?" The boy deserved a treat—and if Lord Hugh Edmunds happened to be there, strolling about with his bride, she would spit at his bloody feet.

Billy scowled in disapproval. "The Bishop said we're behind."

"Well, we can row first, then do a few Jobs."

But at the Park entrance, Billy spotted a boy who had once worked for The Bishop, which made him too anxious for fun. So Clarissa agreed to work first, and they turned back to work their way up the Kensington Road.

After that, they hired the boat.

A row-boat on open water was an ideal place to detect someone watching them: as a passenger, Clarissa's only task was to dandle her hand over the side and keep her eyes on the bank. She was looking for a young man with protruding cuffs—indeed, a tall young man in any shape—but saw no sign. There were a lot of children, but since Billy was occupied with keeping the ends of his oars in the water, his mind could not invent any more of The Bishop's spies.

An hour later they turned in the boat, indulged in an ice cream, and made their way home, working four more Jobs on the way.

The Bishop would be happy with them, and Billy went to his cot that night both tired out and relieved.

Samuel slept relatively well, too. The child clearly liked days in the sun, which would be fine if this were Australia. In England, the mite was in for a hard life.

To make up for their Sunday leisure hours, Clarissa's trio rose early. Monday mornings were lucrative, the streets and tram lines filled with men tired from their week-end excesses and often running late, so that a woman with a squalling child was even more of a distraction than usual. When the rain started again, tempers frayed and made things that much easier.

They worked their way through town and into the shops, where Clarissa had not ventured since the summer. She took care, wary of her lagging energies and attention, but found that the occasional stop for tea or a sandwich kept her from flagging too badly. Perhaps there would be life following childbirth after all.

Only once did Sunday's visitor come to mind, when she noticed a slim back that reminded her of young Mr Holmes. She did not catch sight of his face, and the hat was of a different shape, but she cut the day short anyway. If she was imagining things, she must be tired.

So the week went: work when the streets were crowded, sleep when she could, find time for Billy's schooling whenever Samuel permitted. There was satisfaction in the accumulated coins in the purse beneath her skirts—and considerable relief: The Bishop was not a patient man, and a month's holiday for birthing a child was all he was prepared to accept.

The first Friday in October, the tenuous peace crashed at her feet like a dropped jug when the landlady's clogs paused in the hallway and an envelope appeared beneath the door—slowly, it being unusually thick.

Billy leapt to snatch it from the boards, trotting over with it to the window where Clarissa was sewing.

"Who is it from?" he demanded. "Can I read it? What does it say?"

Post was all but unheard of in their lives. In the four months they had lived in these rooms, she'd had precisely two pieces of mail, both from Alicia. The first was a telegram, to say that a "blessed event" was anticipated the following February. The second had come just the previous week, a polite and uninformative thank-you for Clarissa's wedding present.

This was not from Alicia. Clarissa's heart turned over when she saw the handwriting, and she snapped at Billy's continuing demands. "This one's none of your business. Go on with your maths problems."

She ran her thumb under the glued flap. When she pulled out the letter, a flat blue shape the size of Samuel's palm fell out of it. She picked it up: one of Pa's thread decorations. She hadn't seen one in years, but when she was little—back when Mama was still alive—his hands were often busy shaping bits of coloured string into pretty little objects. Rings or bracelets, pull knobs for switches, once a hat decoration. The most elaborate of these had been the doll he'd made before she was born, later claimed by Alicia—a doll that had more clothing than both girls together. This one was not a doll, but a bird.

She laid it on the windowsill and unfolded the letter.

Dearest Clarrie,

Your old man is in a spot of trouble. Nothing I cant get out of, but I need your help, just for a day or two. Then I'm away, out of your life for good if you want. If you don't help me, it'll be even odds if the Bishop or the police find me first. My life's in your hands, girl. I didn't come to see you, even though I been threw London, cause you said you didn't want to see me. But Clarrie, this thing that's come up, I need your help, need it bad, and then I swear on your sisters head, I'll never ask for anything again. Honest, I wont need to—none of us will!

Come to the town of Fordingham, in Hampshire, as soon as ever you can. About a mile up the lane past the White Hart there's a falling-down rock wall with a tree growing through it on the left, with a path you follow up into the trees. Up that path there's a little house. I'll wait for you there.

I made this for the baby, Clarrie, a bluebird to hang over the wee one's cot. Somebody told me it was a sign of happiness. And happiness is whats coming, as soon as you come and just help me with this thing.

No date. No signature. No faint trace of apology or thanks. And he hadn't come to see her because she'd have refused whatever this was, in person. It was harder to say no without a return address.

Bloody man. *I swear on your sisters head.* Thank you, Pa. Did he imagine that she was going to set off into the wilds of Hampshire with an infant in arms? What had he ever done to deserve that extreme a loyalty? She'd told him she had other responsibilities. And, what was this about the police? Surely they couldn't be interested in his youthful crimes. What the devil had he done now? It couldn't be over that blackmail of Mr Holmes, could it? That had been up in Norfolk.

Whatever it was, he'd have to get out of it on his own. She was finished. And she had no intention of hanging his happiness bird over Samuel's head.

And in any event, she had no idea how to get to Hampshire.

But within the hour, she was packing a bag with Billy under her feet.

"What is this, Ma'am?"

Were there sufficient napkins for Samuel? Better add a few more. "What is what?" she asked absently.

"This bird." He had found her father's string creation on the windowsill.

"It's something my father made for Samuel." Cloak, umbrella, or both?

"You have a *father*?"

Damnation. "I suppose I do."

"Can I meet him?"

"No! Oh, Billy, sorry. I haven't seen him in a long time, and he's not a terribly nice man. So no, you probably won't meet him." *Ever, if I have my way,* she thought. "Would you like that bluebird? He says it's a charm for happiness."

"But he made it for Samuel."

"Sam would just chew it to bits. It's yours." To her relief, it distracted him from questions about its maker. She wrestled the valise shut, and picked up her cloak.

"You're not to go out working on your own, boy, you hear me? If I come back and find you nibbed, I swear I'll leave you in gaol. You just have a nice few days of rest, and catch up on that maths of yours. I'll post this letter to The Bishop telling him I've been called away, but I'll be back. He'll not mind." She hoped. On the other hand, the old criminal might just decide he'd had enough of her sass and draw a line through her name.

"But where're you going?"

"You don't need to know that. I'll be back in two or three days. A week at the most. There's money in the caddy for your meals, you'll be fine."

"Can't you leave Samuel here?"

At that she laughed. "I'm not sure which of us'd have the hardest time of it if I did—him, me, or you." Then she relented, dropping to her knees to grasp the lad's shoulders. "Billy, I promise you, even though I'm taking Samuel, I will come back. *We* will come back. This is to do with my father, and I'm hoping that at the end of it, he'll be out of my hair for good, and you and I can go on as we have been. You're my partner, William Mudd. Are you not?"

She feared for a moment that the hard little face would collapse into tears, but he regained control and just gave her a sharp nod. Still, she gathered him in for a quick hug, kissing his tight curls before briskly standing away to finish tucking the baby's clothing into the valise. She gave him a few more coins, repeated her commandments, and left, feeling his eyes on her back as she descended the stairs.

She bought a stamp from the agents' down the road, where she also confirmed her suspicion that the station for Hampshire was Waterloo. The Bishop's letter safely in a post-box, herself heavily encumbered with infant, valise, and a large umbrella, Clarissa Hudson set off to rescue her father from whatever stupidity he'd got himself into.

Merely crossing London took her most of the morning. Figuring out the confusion of Waterloo station with its multiple entrances, tracks, and ticketing offices took the remainder. There was, it appeared, a train to Fordingham, or there might be, if she could first locate a train to Salisbury . . .

She did not have to feign her womanly tears of despair, none of the three times she made use of them to gain the assistance of officials that very long day. She spent the night in a town she never knew the name of, and the following day, tears came even before she summoned them.

Modern transportation was nothing but one delay after another! She'd have been better off in a post coach. More bounced about perhaps, but no less exhausted—or filthy, her clothing dotted with black smuts and grime from the seats.

She did not reach Fordingham until late the following afternoon. Samuel, perverse child, seemed quite pleased with the tumult of the stations, the boredom of the trains, and the frustrations of his mother. He only woke to feed, such as when she stepped off the train at long last. She looked around the deserted station. A man and his son got off the other end of the train, and hurried away in the opposite direction: the man's coat and the magazine the child was clutching both whirled in the freshening breeze. The sky looked like rain.

Clarissa would have given a great deal for a cup of tea, but neither food nor drink was on offer. She did pause to fill Samuel's belly before continuing through to the little village beyond. The White Hart lay immediately across a minuscule triangle of grass. She settled Samuel more firmly inside her shawl, and crossed the village green to the road that ran past the public house.

CHAPTER TWENTY-ONE

B efore I had led Samuel Hudson out of his mother's rooms, I was ready.

The matter of his gun changed little. The longer I kept him occupied, the greater the likelihood of his guard slipping: when that happened, I would move.

Until then, I would appear a powerless young woman who might have something he wanted—who probably *did* have it, if only she knew what it was.

But, he did not bend down to look into the depths of the cupboard, merely ordered me to pull out the crate. Disappointed, I removed my hand from the pile of heavy books. "Take it into the sitting room and dump it out on the table," he said.

I carried the box through and upended its neatly sorted contents onto the polished wood. He gestured with the gun for me to move back, then paused to eye the pretty lamp that lived on the corner of the table—a fixture that made me nervous with its blown-glass delicacy, although I admitted its loveliness when the sun came through it.

"That belongs to her, doesn't it?" he asked.

"Mrs Hudson? I . . . don't think so."

"Yeah, it does. She sent Mum a picture of it, she loved it so much." His stress on the verb prepared me for his next act: he backhanded it straight into the waste-bin beside the table. The noise seemed to satisfy him. He gloated for a moment, then turned to the sad collection, thumbing through the packet of mismatched letters that Mrs Hudson had smoothed and folded together.

"My mother liked her secrets." He pulled a wry face. "*Both* mothers, come to that." He picked up one of the two surviving dolly costumes, this one of forest green velvet. "Who'd do that to a boy?" he mused. "Give him over to a woman who just loved to tease her son—the boy who *thought* he was her son. Letting him know he'd never be anything, never make her happy, never figure out that there was a hole in his life. She used to say that. 'Boy, you got a hole in your life and you don't even see it.' Like it was my fault I couldn't figure out something they'd hidden from me." He tossed the doll into the crate, then reached down to flip through the Dickens novel, as if looking for a bookmark left behind; some of the loose pages spilled out.

"You know what she used to do, my dear old Mum?"

His decision to talk, back in Mrs Hudson's rooms, had certainly loosened his tongue; now, if the gun would only sag, just a little more . . .

"What did she used to do?" I responded.

"She'd keep back the last episode of a magazine serial. Have you ever heard anything more idiotic than that? Used to open her big blue eyes and say she had no idea, why did I think *she'd* taken it? Bitch. My whole life was hints about secrets and these knowing remarks. She kept on right to the end, too, setting it up so I'd only learn the truth when she was gone. Took her two years to die, and all that time I wondered why she had that damned gloating smile on her face."

He caught up the book and threw it on top of the doll. Next came a cheap paste brooch. "Two years of gloating over what I'd find in her papers."

His eyes came to mine, startling me with a glimpse of very real pain. "What kind of a choice is that, huh? A mother who makes a boy's life miserable, or a mother who makes it possible, pretending she doesn't know what's going on? She used to send me money for my birthday out of her housekeeper's pay. Sweet old thing made *your* life pretty comfortable, didn't she? You and Mr Sherlock bloody Holmes. Funny thing is, I almost burned all those letters, the ones Mum left for me to find. I had this feeling there'd be something there I didn't want to see. Why else would the old witch have left them for me? Wasn't until New Year's Day that I thought, maybe reading them would make for a clean start. So I did. And that's when I found I'd been living a pack of lies, my whole bloody life.

"First thing I did was go piss on her grave. Then I sat down with all those letters—endless things, drive you mental with all that nothing—and think about what they meant. Not just what Mum wanted me to see, what she left there to make the rest of my life a mess. But something else that she didn't see. And I did.

"So I came here, for a couple of reasons. Business, and personal. One is a bit of punishment. My mother—my actual mother—left me with a hole in my life, so I decided it was time to make holes in a few other lives. Time to stop letting her make other people comfortable."

He tossed the brooch up and down in his hand; it glittered in the sunshine.

"One thing about travel, you got plenty of time to think things over. On the way here, I decided that the best thing, once I'd found what I needed about my piece of business, was just kill her outright and make it look like you two had done it. But then you walked out the door instead of her, and I thought, this is even better. I can give her and him a story missing its ending. You're going to be the hole, young lady—for the rest of their lives. I'm only sorry they're both so old."

I had been wrong, so very wrong, to assume that this man's only emotions were masks he donned. Hate was a thing Samuel Hudson knew all about: hot and cold, the urgent and the long-drawn-out. Hate ran through his veins as love did not. And much as he lusted after that mythic passbook, any moment now he would decide it mattered less than just letting the hatred spill over.

I held my eyes to his, but I was only half listening to his building rant. All my attention was on the gun: muscles set, feet balanced, knees ready to launch myself at him. Waiting for the moment . . .

"Yes, I can leave a big hole in those comfortable lives. As for business, well, who needs the bloody money, really? I'll make my own way, like I always have, other than—well, we'll see about him. Yeah, I got my secrets, too, don't I? One thing I learned from that bitch Mum of mine, how to enjoy secrets. Nobody'll ever never know what happened to you but me. Just like when I give the coppers my information, nobody but me will know where it came from. Oh yes: when the rope goes around her neck, and that high-and-mighty detective Sherlock Holmes is left all alone in this big old house, I'll be the one who knows why."

I was right on the edge, my muscles anticipating his momentary glance at the crate as he launched the brooch at it—and then his words reached me, and I became aware of a sudden internal tilt, as if I'd been building steam up a dead straight track, only to find myself careering off into a spur line. Wait: What information? Which police? What *him* was there to see about? And which *her* was meeting a rope? Who—

My muscles actually spasmed with my brain's sharp countermanding of orders.

"What *are* you talking about?" I demanded.

He whooped at the reaction he'd startled out of me. "Yes—there! There you have a little sample of what I went through when I read Mum's letters. I just know she died with that evil smile of hers across her face. Like *I* will when I look back on this, a long, long time from now. You got no idea, do you?"

I shrugged, wide-handed, to suggest not only ignorance, but disinterest—and as I'd hoped, he rose to the challenge of besting me.

"Hah! Clarissa Hudson. Butter wouldn't melt in the old lady's mouth. How many years has she been washing your dishes and tidying your messes, and you without a clue what's under your nose? Not like that husband of yours. *He* knows. Some of it anyway. And he hasn't told you a thing, has he?"

"About what?"

"Nah, that's all you get. Let it eat at you. I'll just say this: when I'm finished with her, Miss Clarissa Hudson will have a date with the executioner."

"Her name isn't Clarissa," I said automatically.

"It was."

I looked at his face, his stance, searching for delusion.

All I saw there was the truth.

CHAPTER TWENTY-TWO

Clarissa walked, baby Samuel a warm and contented bundle against her ribs, as the village of Fordingham fell behind her. The rolling countryside looked much like those areas she'd gone to with friends during her so-distant past, eighteen months ago, when she would pack her trunk with silk and wool for a Friday-to-Monday at someone's country house. The attractions there had been the shooting of birds during the day, the playing of cards in the evenings, and the slipping in and out of bedrooms during the night.

When did the shooting season end, she wondered? She hoped no one mistook her for a partridge.

She walked, and walked some more, watching for a tree in the low dry-stone wall, but saw nothing larger than bramble. Once she heard voices behind her, but saw nothing: only countryside, cows, and an endless wall.

The lowering sky took on shades of purple dusk. Farm labourers were no doubt settled before their hearths, tucking into their laden plates and steaming mugs. She, on the other hand, would find no train out of here before the morning. And the White Hart did not appear to be an inn.

She cursed her father under her breath, and walked the faster, twice turning to look back at imagined footsteps in the gloom.

Finally, up ahead, she glimpsed the outline of a tree growing out of the wall. Not that the line of depressed vegetation running off towards a distant copse was anything more emphatic than a rabbit track. Still, this was a tree, and that was a track. As she wavered, caught between the faint appeal of turning back and a grim determination to finish this business, she became aware of a source of light back among the trees.

With another glance down the empty lane, Clarissa heaved her valise and umbrella over the wall, then gingerly hitched her backside onto the stones and worked her legs over, an awkward process that did the back of her skirts no good at all. Once inside the wall, she squinted upward, then off at the trees. They weren't far, surely? And Pa could always come back for her things. So she tucked in the edges of her shawl, pulled her cloak over Samuel, and set off along the vague track.

The last light faded quickly, leaving her all but blind, picking her way along, stopping to loose her cloak from grasping thorns. She stumbled, nearly going to her knees. After that, she inched along, venturing her boot forward in search of rocks and hollows. Her cloak caught, time and again, invisible fingers tugging at the wool. She fought a building panic, cursing the sharp little ripping sounds, swearing aloud at the flicker of light, never any closer.

Then the rain began.

By the time she reached the clearing among the trees, she was wild with frustration and pain. A branch had whipped her bonnet into the night, leaving her wet hair tumbling across her face. She was limping from a wrenched ankle. Her sodden clothing weighed a ton, and her arms and face stung from the tiny assaults of invisible blades as she bent over her armful of child. The dim light became a line, then clearer: lamp-glow through a crack in heavy curtains. Some vestigial recognition that one did not knock on windows drove her around the side of the lonely little house: a faint dark rectangle suggested a door.

She nearly fell when her toe hit a stone step. Once on the step, she did not even try feeling for a bell-pull, merely pounded the wood with a gloved fist, ignoring the pain.

No one came. Oh God, she thought. The house was deserted, with nothing but a lantern left to burn in the dark. Her hand fumbled and found the latch, but it stood firm. She gave a sob, her knees going weak in despair—and then came a pale glow along the bottom of the door. It brightened, outlining all four sides, then stopped.

"Papa?" she called.

A muffled exclamation came, and the scrape of a bolt. Her father, his face stretched with some emotion that looked like fear, pulled the door open—tentatively at first, then with a yank that had her tumbling in. Never had she been so grateful for the solidity of a man's hand on her elbow.

It was a gamekeeper's cottage, designed for a solitary man. Rough stairs—a ladder, really—led up from one corner, but the ground floor was a single room: two small windows, one of which had the ill-fitting curtains, the other with a long table resting beneath it. The kitchen was nothing but a dry-sink and some shelves with plates and pans, along with a perforated tin food-safe and two large jugs to bring water from an outside pump. The broad fireplace, laid with a roasting jack and hanging kettle, stood behind two greasy armchairs, a foot-stool, and an ancient, burn-spotted carpet. A moth-chewed Tartan travelling rug on one chair and a tin mug on the three-legged stool beside it showed where Hudson had been sitting. A stack of dry wood was arranged on the stone hearth. The air inside was so icy, Clarissa could see her breath. She began to shudder.

"Do light the fire, Papa, I'm freezing. And I hope you have something to eat here."

Instead of either food or fire, he moved to a bottle sitting on the long table and splashed some unidentifiable liquid into a tin cup, holding it out to her. It stank of raw whisky.

"I don't like to raise a smoke when people are about," he said. "The place is supposed to be empty."

"Then you should pull the curtains together," she told him. "Anyway, who would there be? We're in the back of beyond, and it's pouring." She took a swallow, stifled a choke, and downed another gulp.

He hastened to overlap the curtain edges, then relented, setting a match to a handful of dry kindling. When her numb skin began to feel warmth, she took off her heavy cloak, hanging it on a fireside peg to drip.

Hudson turned with a plate holding a slab of cheese and dry biscuits he'd fetched from the food-safe, and nearly dropped it. "What's *that*?"

"'That' is your grandson," she snapped. "What did you think, I'd come away and leave him with some London childminder?"

"A son? I didn't know . . ."

"You thought maybe I'd lost the brat? Always the caring Pa, weren't you?"

"Let me see him." She wanted to snatch Samuel away, but he was stretching in her arms, yawning and blinking in the light. "Hello, little man," the proud grandfather cooed. "Why, Clarrie, he looks like me!"

She turned away, dropping to the edge of the chair to settle the infant defiantly to her breast, forcing her father to retreat.

Lots of infants had blue eyes. And Samuel's hair would darken with time, it was sure to.

Hudson lowered himself into the other chair, the taut lines of his face going soft as he stole glances at the maternal scene. He had put on weight since June, she saw, and was wearing a new suit, with a shirt of excellent linen. However, his collar was decidedly grubby, and his hair was in need of a trim. Something had kicked him from a position of—if not luxury, at least comfort, in the past couple of weeks. So much for old friends.

She washed down the last biscuit with a swallow of raw alcohol, and drew breath. "All right. Tell me what's happened."

He frowned into his cup. "Well, Clarrie, it's complicated."

"Papa, I'm not about to walk back to Fordingham in the dark, so we have till morning. When I saw you last, you were heading off to talk to a friend. Or, not a friend. He's turned you out?"

"Oh, a little more than that. Seems he's died."

Mr Holmes was right, then. "Oh, Papa, what have you done?"

"Not a thing! I swear, not to him, he just ... died. Weak heart, I'd guess."

"But you were there."

"Not even that. I was long gone."

"Papa, please, just start at the beginning. Where did you go, after I ...'"

"Turned your father out onto the streets?"

"After I told you I couldn't work with you until you repaid Mr Bishop," she corrected him.

His face took on an old, familiar expression, the one that said he wanted to talk her into something without telling her what it was. And as if that wasn't enough of a breath from childhood, he reached into his pocket and pulled out a tangle of waxed cord in a bilious colour of green. His deft fingers teased the ends free and began to form knots, as if under their own volition, a thing she'd seen him do a thousand times in her childhood, when he was thinking—but not, she realised, since they'd come to England.

"I been in a place called Donnithorpe, up in Norfolk. Bloke I knew, back before you were born. We were—well, let's say we were on the same boat together, out to Australia. He'd turned things around for himself, him and this other cove name of Evans—Beddoes, he is now. The two of them made their fortune in the gold fields, came back here to England, set up like rich colonials—one of 'em, him in Norfolk who called himself Mr Trevor, got himself made magistrate, if you can believe that! A man who'd sailed off to Botany Bay in chains."

"He was transported?"

"That he was. And he called *me* the criminal!" His laugh was a harsh noise in the small room. Clarissa unconsciously pulled Samuel closer to her chest.

"So, what? You went up to Norfolk threatening to turn him in, this Trevor? Surely he'd paid his debt?"

"Not to me he hadn't. And his high-and-mighty neighbours might not be so keen on old Trevor if they knew how he'd got his start. So I invited him to give me a berth for a time. First he wanted to make me a gardener—you can imagine how that turned out. I let him make me butler instead, which meant I could sit in front of the fire and sample his port for him, bring down the odd bird for the supper table. It all went fine for a while, until the son got all high-and-mighty. Little Victor Trevor," he sneered. "Didn't like his papa's old shipmate, embarrassed him in front of his friends. Still took him all summer to nerve himself up to say anything."

"Oh, Pa," she said sadly.

"What? Trumped-up thief, has the nerve to treat me like dirt? Then when his son manhandles me out of the room and won't so much as apologise for it—well, I knew the time had come to push matters. I told old Trevor I was coming down to Hampshire to see his partner, Evans—Beddoes, he was calling himself, didn't want people wondering if he might be Evans the forger. I figured if I played the two off against each other, one or the other of 'em would break.

"But before I did, Trevor and I had a little talk about . . . well, things." He shot her a glance and went back to his knots. "Nothing important, just, information. We'll have to see how it pans out. Anyway, his son threw me out, and I came down here to tell Beddoes that if *he* didn't want the world to know about the old *Gloria Scott*, he needs to find me some ready cash." He stopped, concentrating on the work his fingers were doing.

An excited tale of information leading to treasure was by itself a familiar childhood ritual, but at her father's close focus on the work, her eyes narrowed. "Then what?"

"Well, Beddoes told me that Trevor dropped dead. He'd just heard."

"Oh, Papa."

"Nothing to do with me." He did not look up.

"Papa, what are you not telling me?"

His eyebrows rose in an utterly transparent act of innocence, belied by the gaze that stayed fixed on his knots. "Nothing at all, dearie."

"Papa, there's something."

He dropped the act, and turned on her a crooked smile. "Ah, Clarrie, you know me too well. You're right, something happened. I'm not going to tell you what, not until it's sure and done, but it changes things, all the way down the line. I got to get back to Sydney, and I can't do it by honest work—last year, on that stinking tramp steamer, it nearly broke me. Your old man's getting too tired for that. So I need a grubstake, that's all. Just the cost of getting to Australia, and I'm gone."

"If I had it, Papa, I'd give it to you."

He completely missed the grim edge to her promise, and gave her a proud look. "I know you would, honey, but honest, I can get it from Beddoes. I just need to get to him."

"He wasn't at home?"

"Oh, he was, and I told him what I needed. I gave him the warning, and then I went away—had to sleep rough, damn the man. Anyway, next day I went back to tighten the screws, but the bloody butler wouldn't let me in, can you believe it? That riled me mighty, as you can imagine. So I trotted around the house to where Beddoes had his library and shouted through the window that I'd told all, that the coppers were coming to get him, that he was ruined."

"Why on earth did you do that?" The most important rule of all when it came to Marks was not to push a man to the brink.

"Ah, Clarrie girl, I was angry. And hungry and my bones ached."

"But—"

"I wasn't being completely stupid, not your old Pa! I figured I'd give him the next day to get himself into a righteous stew over it, and then I'd go back at night and say, 'Just fooling, I didn't tell anyone, but now you see how you'd feel if it was for real. So unless you get out your wallet . . .'"

"What happened?"

"Guess the old bugger had more to be scared of than I thought. See, I hid out, then went back after dark, but instead of sitting there drinking himself into a funk, be damned if he hadn't cleared out his safe and vanished."

It sounded to Clarissa a remarkably sensible thing to do, although she wasn't about to say so to her father. "So why call me in? I honestly do not have that kind of money."

"I don't need your money, girlie. I need you."

"Pa, I told you, I can't go back to the Act, not till you're square with The Bishop."

"I'm not looking to do a Job with you, Clarrie. No: Beddoes only went far as Portsmouth. Seems to be as quick in his head as he is on his feet, because from what his servants were saying the other night—they leave the window open, you can hear them easy—Beddoes left orders with the butler to send a telegram if he caught word of any scandal. None of 'em know what *kind* of scandal, mind, just that they're to listen for it."

"So Mr Beddoes knows you may have been lying about telling the police, and is waiting to see."

"'S right. And then I found out where he is. The post still comes regular to the house, and the butler's been sending it on. Took me a week of sneaking around before I could get a hold of it, but I knew sooner or later the post bag would go unguarded. He's in Portsmouth, ready to jump on the first ship out when word comes. And Portsmouth is just a quick run from here on the train."

"Good. I can give you that much fare if you promise to leave me be after that."

"I told you, girl, it's *you* I need. As an escort, like. Seems the butler told the police I'd threatened Beddoes or something idiotic, and they're looking for me. *Me*, get it? A single man. But a man with a daughter—and even better, his sweet little grandson—why, he'd be safe as houses. All I need's for you to go with me to Portsmouth. You'd be back in London by bedtime, I'd be off to Sydney first ship. And if things go like I think they will, I'll send you money for the best berth to Sydney that cash can buy. We could set up in comfort, Clarrie. You, me, and the little one. Get a house near to Allie."

Clarissa's dismissal of her father's perennial dreams and schemes gave way to a wave of revulsion at the idea of life together. But as the wave retreated, it left behind two pieces of knowledge: first, that her father would like nothing better than to have the boy to raise, and second, she could not let that happen.

She bent over Samuel, thoughts racing. It was not possible to slip away tonight, but tomorrow—get away from him at the station? Or she could appear to go along with his plan and accompany him as far as the crowds of Portsmouth, then disappear? She had the skills to vanish into any crowded station, step onto a boat for anywhere. America, even.

Except: Billy. To abandon Billy would be to leave a part of herself behind. Plus, the lad would be the only target left for The Bishop's rage—and that of the man's son.

No. She would have to run a Cheat on her father, though he knew her every trick and gesture. Manipulate him as she did any other Mark: agree with him, flatter his pride, appear to support him, and then . . .

She looked up. "I'll not have my son's grandfather gaoled, or hanged. I'll go with you to Portsmouth, but when you go after Beddoes, you're on your own. If you're caught while I'm with you, it's Samuel who will pay. I'll go back to London." *And then slip away—far, far away,* she did not add. "When you're ready, let me know and we'll join you. But if you're caught, I expect you to say nothing about me, ever."

"Fair enough."

"You swear?"

"On your mother's sacred memory."

"All right. You'll need to bathe, and I hope you brought a razor. As for that shirt, I'll see if—"

She broke off at a sound from behind her. Hudson had leapt to his feet and was staring at the door. *"You?"* he said. "What the devil . . ."

She spun around—and saw the very last thing she'd have expected: Billy. At his back, hat in hand, was the young man with the funny name.

Sherlock Holmes.

CHAPTER TWENTY-THREE

T *he father and son at the station—they hurried off the other way—so I couldn't see them*—but the tumble of thoughts broke off as her father's words registered. Papa *knew* this fellow? Puzzled, she looked back—then she was on her feet, too. "Papa—no!"

He was standing by the long table. Its drawer stood open; the massive pistol in his hand looked suitable for battering down doors. Her mind threw out another wayward thought—*a gamekeeper's revolver if ever I saw one*—then her body was in motion, swinging Samuel down to the chair behind her, snatching at the ties of her beaded bag.

"Papa," she warned. "If you shoot, it'll be your last act."

Hudson's gaze flicked sideways—then fixed on the little ivory-handled revolver in his daughter's hand.

"You wouldn't shoot your old man, Clarrie."

"Do not try me."

She watched him wrestle with the possibility that his own daughter might in fact pull the trigger. The heavy weapon sagged a fraction. She took a quick glance at the doorway—then wondered for an instant what she was seeing. An amorphous black shape, where two people had been standing, but no: it was the back of an overcoat. The tall young man was bent over Billy, hiding him completely. After a long moment, his ill-shaven face appeared, those remarkable grey eyes analysing the room over his shoulder. "Go!" he said, and the ridiculous cuffs flashed as he pushed Billy in her direction. He continued with the turn, slowly, hands empty and outstretched. When he was upright, he tore his eyes from the big pistol, to face James Hudson.

Billy hit Clarissa's skirts like an infant monkey thrown at a tree. Her free hand pulled him close but her gaze lingered on the figure in the doorway, that white, composed face.

Most men, she thought, *facing a gun, would snatch any available shield: this young toff turned his back to protect Billy.*

When Holmes spoke, his voice was no higher than its usual pitch. "Good evening, Mr Hudson."

"I know you," Hudson said. "You were in Norfolk, at old Trevor's place."

"We met in Donnithorpe, yes. When you arrived to blackmail my friend's father." His voice was calm—except for the word "blackmail," which he mouthed as if tasting something foul.

"Him and me, we were old friends," Hudson protested. "I was on hard times, knew he'd want to help out."

"You hounded him to death with your threats."

"Man with a heart so weak he can't take a little pressure, he'd have died of something anyway."

"It was murder. And now you aim to do the same with Mr Beddoes."

"I never!"

"You will come with me to the police."

Is he mad? Clarissa wondered. *Giving an order like that, armed with nothing more than a cut-glass accent.*

Hudson, predictably, laughed.

"Papa," she warned again, edging Billy behind her—and only when she'd done so did she realise what the gesture meant. *Just what I used to do with Allie—but this is a gun, not a fist. Papa wouldn't shoot towards a child. Would he?*

Although he might shoot at me . . .

The thought staggered her, more than anything else that had happened that night. *Papa?*

She tightened her hand on the ivory handle and spoke over her shoulder. "You need to go, Mr Holmes. Take Billy with you. There's nothing more you can do here."

"I will not leave without James Hudson."

"Then you won't leave at all," snapped Hudson, and with no more warning than that, the room exploded.

Two gunshots, nearly simultaneous; two high shouts of protest; two harsh cries of pain.

Smoke whirled through a silent room for a count of two, until Samuel's indrawn breath gave way to full-lunged screams of terror. Clarissa dropped the little gun to scramble towards her father, leaving Billy to snatch up the infant, holding him close to chant wordless reassurances over Hudson's gasps and Clarissa's desperate voice.

Then with an appalling, wet convulsion, the old man went limp. As Clarissa bent over her father, infant wails mingled with the keening sounds of her own abandonment.

CHAPTER TWENTY-FOUR

A date with the executioner—Mrs *Hudson*? Absurd. Obscene.

So why did I not dismiss it as the ravings of a madman? Samuel Hudson was clearly unhinged, this oily salesman who had slithered his way into my home, held a gun on me, and threatened all I held dear. Nonetheless, I could not doubt the ring of truth in what he said—what he clearly believed. Impossible, to dismiss it out of hand.

I drew in one deliberate breath, let it out slowly, then drew another. On the third breath, all my confusion and ambiguity drifted away.

They say that when a soldier flings himself onto a grenade, when a mother drowns in rescuing her child, a greater need has overridden the urge to self-preservation. Until that moment, I would have said those were moments of insanity, when impulse overcame rationality. Accidents, almost, of self-deception.

They are not.

Those are moments of grace. Uncertainty is removed. Mind, heart, and body fuse together, and decisions are made without pause for reflection.

In that moment, standing with the sunlight refracting off the artificial facets in his hand, my past and my future became a simple thing.

This creature could not be permitted to touch Mrs Hudson.

The world slowed. I watched his pale eyelashes blink closed, and part again; saw him remember the brooch in his palm. His torso prepared to shift, his left hand to rise, that it might toss away the piece of jewellery. He was speaking again—something about having to see if I'd do—but I was no longer listening. His left shoulder shifted a millimetre forward. I began to move.

Some minutes earlier, as I squatted before the storage cupboards, my left hand had rested suggestively on a nice heavy book—but my right hand had not been idle. The tips of my fingers had nudged the knife from its sheath on my ankle, holding it out of sight, then slipped it up my left sleeve as I stretched to pick up the crate.

Still, there had been a cost to holding a scalpel-sharp blade next to my skin. Any moment now, Samuel Hudson would notice the blood dripping off my fingertips. I was out of time, out of hope, out of any options but to move.

He would *not* touch Mrs Hudson.

With my final act, I chose death.

CHAPTER TWENTY-FIVE

Clarissa did not know how long she remained on the floor with her father before a hand pulled her back, urged her up, eased her into a chair, put a tin mug in her hand.

Brandy, this time. Body temperature. Samuel had gone quiet. Billy's eyes, peering at her over the baby's head, were wide with shock. Young Mr Holmes took a deep swig from his pocket flask, then picked up the gamekeeper's gun, laying it gingerly in the table's drawer, pushing it firmly shut. He then retrieved Clarissa's smaller weapon and placed that behind the run-down clock on the mantelpiece.

He swiped his hand hard across the front of his coat, then took the Tartan rug from the chair, draping it over the body of James Hudson. He pulled a stool from under the table, and dropped onto it like a puppet with cut strings.

"Billy," he said, his voice oddly hoarse, "if the child is sleeping, set him down and add a log to the fire. Then look around and see if you can find any bandages. Clean rags will do."

Clarissa lifted her head to make bitter protest, that her father was beyond need of bandages—then saw his arm. "You're hurt."

"I was prepared for his final declaration before he fired, but I didn't move quite fast enough."

"My father is a good shot." *Was.*

Billy returned with a wooden box containing a variety of medicaments, implements, and bandages, suitable for a man who made a living in the out of doors. He laid it on the table before Mr Holmes, who then asked the boy to take a pan out to the pump for water. Face rigid with pain, he shed his coat and jacket to the floor. His left shirt-sleeve was crimson down to the cuff.

Using a pair of scissors from the wooden box, he chewed at the bloodied sleeve, ripping the last portions of it free, then sat at the table with the pan of water. The fire crackled, water splashed, and the wound came into view: long but shallow, avoiding the meat of his arm entirely. If he'd moved a split second faster, the only hole would be in his overcoat. Had he been any slower . . .

The bloody swath was precisely the level of his heart.

The young man winced at the bite of iodine, then attempted to get the bandage wrapping started. At his third try, Clarissa rose, to take the roll from his hand, circling it round and round his surprisingly muscular upper arm. When she had tied it off, she carried the pan and lantern outside, finding the pump under a roof around one side of the cottage. She hung the lantern from a hook, and got to work on her father's blood.

She scrubbed at her bloodstained hands until they were numb, then reached to unfasten the tiny buttons down the front of her bodice. Since Samuel's birth, she had done this a dozen or more times a day, but tonight these were endless, tiny, impossible—and revoltingly sticky. Her hands wanted to seize the neckline and rip. She was weeping with frustration before the last button gave way and she could fight free of the clammy, stained garment. She let it fall—it was that, or fling it away into the dark for the rain to purge of stains—and stood, head down, fighting for control.

It was the thought of Billy that brought her back: left in the cottage with an infant, a corpse, and a wounded stranger. Billy needed her. She forced herself to bend over the pump and work methodical fingers down the bodice's front and left sleeve, where the worst of it lay. The fabric was dark: once the actual … substance was gone, only she would see the stains.

That was not the case with what lay beneath. The white cotton of her corset cover bore vivid stains. Fortunately, its buttons were few and larger, its fabric light enough to scrub mostly clean. The corset itself was another matter—and as for the chemise beneath …

Strip down to her drawers, out here in the gamekeeper's yard? Clarissa shook her head. If she ever made it back to London, she would burn the lot of it; in the meantime, her skin would just have to crawl.

She blotted the chest of the chemise as best she could, along with the top of the corset—it was a short nursing corset, so only its upper edges had caught the blood. Pulling the sodden cotton back over it turned her shivers to shudders, and she looked with loathing at the bodice: too heavy to wring out, so wet that putting it on would leave her skirts damp to the knees. *I'll catch pneumonia.* She looked at her bare arms. *I'd show more skin in an evening dress.* The lad would just have to blush and be damned.

The young man's eyes came up at her entrance, only to fall rapidly to the side. "Sorry," she said. "It needs to dry in front of the fire." She covered herself with the shawl, then arranged the bodice over a stool before the fire, hoping the wood did not spit too many sparks onto it.

"The boys are upstairs?" she asked.

"I suggested it."

Climbing the ladder-like stairs in long skirts required all the concentration she could summon. At the top, she found the boys asleep on a bed beneath sloping eaves. Billy was curled on his side under a thick blanket; the top of Samuel's scalp showed within the older boy's arms.

She pulled the shawl around her, leaning against the door jamb. Two boys softly breathing; the crackle of fire from below. *Papa should have had a son, instead of me. A son would have understood him, gone with him. A son would not have—*

She drew a ragged breath. Why in *hell* had that boy downstairs risked his life for a child he barely knew? Her father had not hesitated to pull the trigger. Would he have done so if Billy were still in the doorway? Clarissa's inner eye kept seeing that black expanse of overcoat, covering the boy like a shield.

She pushed off from the door frame and went to tug the covers a little farther over Billy's shoulders, then took her ancient bones down the ladder. The kettle was now bubbling over the flame. She walked warily towards the tin food-safe, bracing for the sight of her father's body, but he was not there. Only the burn-spotted little carpet lay on the spot where James Hudson had died.

The gamekeeper's pantry contained a packet of tea, two kinds of stale biscuits, and—luxury item, pushed to the back—a tin of condensed milk. What had happened to the man whose provisions these were? Had Beddoes fired him before taking off for Portsmouth? Given the man a holiday? In any event, she was grateful beyond words that he'd left his tea behind.

She put a steaming mug on the three-legged stool beside Mr Holmes, and lowered herself into the chair across from him. He eyed the drink for a moment, then picked it up, took a formal swallow, and laid it down again.

"It wasn't murder, you know," she said. "Your friend's father."

"Blackmail is despicable."

"But it's not murder. My father would not have hanged for it."

"He should have done," the lad snarled.

Another night, Clarissa might have laughed at the perennial complaint of youth at the unfairness of life. "Wanting a thing doesn't make it so. He'd have died in prison, or in Australia, but not from a noose."

The thin face worked; he looked away.

"It's personal, isn't it?" she realised abruptly. "You know someone, or knew them. Someone whose life was ruined by blackmail."

A year or two older, and he wouldn't have replied, but he was still boy enough to crave understanding. "My mother. When I was eleven."

"She—" Clarissa caught herself. The lad's marked distaste for guns might have nothing to do with someone blackmailing his mother. And really, she did not wish to know.

But why did she persist in thinking of him as a lad? He could not be that much younger than she, no more than five or six years. Truth to tell, he looked less like a boy today than a young man in ill-fitting clothes. Perhaps that was an effect of the stubble.

She pushed away these random thoughts. "What happens now?"

"Perhaps you should tell me that."

His tone of voice had not been that of a boy asking an adult for instruction. "I'm sorry?" she asked.

"Miss Hudson, with your father dead, do you intend to finish his work? Go to Portsmouth and see what you can shake out of this Beddoes fellow?"

The brutal accusation was like a slap. "Shake out—oh. You heard the conversation? Before you walked in?"

"Enough of it."

"I was not—I had no . . . Look, Mr Holmes: agreeing with my father was the only way to be rid of him. I had no intention to join him, either in his plans or in his return to Australia. All I wanted was to get back to London for Billy. After that, well, any place where Papa wasn't."

"You did not plan to blackmail Beddoes—or shoot him outright for whatever he's fled with?"

"For pity's sake, Mr Holmes, I'm not a—"

But before the word could leave her mouth, her hand rose to cover it.

"A killer? It would appear that is precisely what you are, Miss Hudson. A thief, a cheat, and now a murderess."

"But, Papa . . . He'd have killed you!"

"And instead, you killed him."

How had she ever thought those grey eyes young?

Clarissa sat against the slimy chair-back. Even in the early weeks with

Samuel, she had not felt this tired, this empty. Not since … since her mother had died.

After a long time, she spoke. "Very well. I will do whatever you want. Go with you, talk to the police, tell them everything. All I ask is a promise from you. If they hang me, you'll see that Billy and Samuel don't end up in the workhouse."

She stood without waiting for his response, and climbed up to join the boys on the gamekeeper's bed. She woke twice during the night to feed Samuel. Both times the smell of a pipe drifted up from below, an unexpectedly mature odour—and oddly comforting, considering that it came from her judge and jury, guarding the exit. When she woke for the third time, a tiny pale rectangle in the darkness, an unnoticed window, heralded the approach of dawn.

The air smelt of coffee instead of tobacco. And she heard a noise— from *outside*.

She pushed upright, cold dread washing away the sleep. So, Mr Holmes had sent for the police. Either that or servants had come from the house to investigate the smoke. Against her wrist, she could feel Samuel's tiny ribs pulling air in and out, in and out as she awaited the tramp of boots and loud voices demanding a murderess. Instead, the noise continued. There was a rhythm to it, with the occasional pause. Almost as if …

She eased out of bed, tip-toeing over to the window, but could see only trees. She looked uncertainly at the sleeping boys, and wiped sweaty palms against her skirts.

The creaks of her descent down the ladder did not wake the sleepers. The ground floor was empty, but for a valise on the long table. Her bodice had been shifted during the night, and was nearly dry. She buttoned it on, then straightened her hair-pins as best she could before pulling on her cloak. Outside, she followed the noise through morning mists to the woods behind the house.

The young man had stripped down to his vest. The lower half of him was enveloped in a pair of filthy brown trousers that could only have come from the gamekeeper's store, its waist held up by a length of twine. He stood past his knees in a rectangular hole that was slightly shorter, but a little wider, than he. A rising mound of dirt stood to one side.

He glanced up as he rested the spade against the side wall and reached for a hatchet. When he had parted a root with it, he resumed the spade. After a moment, Clarissa went back into the house, returning with a pot of coffee, a plate of hard biscuits, and the apple she'd been saving for her breakfast. He stopped digging then, to sit on the edge of the grave with an ill-stifled groan. The bandage on his arm dripped scarlet.

Clarissa took a pair of heavy gloves from under her arm, spotted the night before on a shelf near the pump. She tied up her skirts with a length of the same twine he had found, and shoved her hands into the stiff gloves. Mr Holmes swung his legs heavily out of the way, and Clarissa hopped down into the hole to take up the spade.

The gloves softened; the hole deepened. Not a word was spoken.

After an hour, shoulders burning and stomach clenched with hunger, Clarissa heard a thin wail from the house. She crawled from the hole and staggered off.

The sound of the spade resumed before she rounded the side of the cottage.

She fed Samuel, found something to fill Billy's stomach, and was pushing a few tasteless biscuits into her own protesting maw when Mr Holmes came in. He was wearing his own trousers now, his hands and face more or less clean.

"There's hot water in the kettle," she told him, "if you can find a razor. I've let the fire go out. My . . . my father seemed to think there might be people about."

"I'll shave after. Billy, take the baby upstairs, would you please?"

Without argument, the boy scrambled up the ladder, Samuel under his arm like a football. When he was out of hearing, Mr Holmes indicated the valise on the table. "Do you wish to keep any of that?" he asked. "I burned his passport, and two or three garments that had laundry-marks. What's left will not identify him."

The valise was an expensive leather case with the initials HWT:

Trevor, no doubt. Beside it lay the paltry remains of a life ill-spent: some coins, an empty note-case, a used train ticket from London, a folding knife, and a cabinet photograph of her mother so worn that, if she hadn't owned one of her own, she would not have recognised the subject. She picked up the tangle of green thread her father had been knotting just before his death, a small version of Alicia's—of *her*—childhood dolly, this one barely two inches tall. One leg was incomplete, its threads wrapped around the body.

"What is that thing?" Mr Holmes asked.

"My father was a sailor. He made objects out of string. Instead of smoking, I suppose." She dropped the partially-completed doll on top of the other things. "No, there's nothing here I want."

Mr Holmes removed his jacket, gathered up the things, and went out of the door. Clarissa followed.

James Hudson lay on the ground just beyond the front steps, wrapped in the thick Tartan blanket. Beside him stood a sturdy wheelbarrow. Mr Holmes dropped to his heels and distributed the handful of possessions back inside the dead man's pockets. He replaced the rug over the man's head and torso, then stepped around and started to slide his hands beneath the dead man's shoulders.

He froze, his face looking alarmed until his mind found an explanation for the sensations. "Rigor mortis," he muttered. He looked up at her. Clarissa bent to grasp her father's ankles, and in unison, they swung the dead man into the barrow. Mr Holmes put the stolen valise on top.

Fresh blood welled into the wrapping on his arm.

Within half an hour, James Hudson was in his grave. Another ten minutes, and the excess soil had disappeared into the woods, replaced by a natural litter of leaves, twigs, and a convenient fallen branch.

By tomorrow, the difference would be hard to see. In a week, the site would be invisible.

They stood, held there by a vague sense of incompleteness.

In the end, Clarissa spoke. "He tried to be a good father," she said. "He taught me . . . a great deal."

She waited, but if she expected Mr Holmes to summon a eulogy, she was disappointed. Instead, he looked critically at the ground, then up at the surrounding trees whose roots they had savaged. "The smiling countryside," he said bitterly. "Its potential for sin has always filled me with horror. Now I have added to its lonely secrets."

Back in the house, she pushed Mr Holmes into the chair. She made coffee with the still-warm water, and while he mechanically conveyed food and drink to his mouth with his good hand, she attended to his arm. When the bandages were tied off and his jacket drawn over his missing shirt-sleeve, she opened the gamekeeper's pot of salve, rubbing it into the angry, dirt-caked blisters that were rising all over his soft palms.

This, at last, made him uncomfortable—not from pain, she thought, but from the intimacy of touch. He pulled his hand away, under the excuse of reaching for the plate.

"What will you do with me?" she asked.

He frowned at the biscuit. "What family have you?"

"A sister, in Australia. And there may be family still in Scotland, but after my aunt died, I doubt any of them would acknowledge me."

"Friends?"

"None that I would wish to burden."

He nodded, then rose.

"I will shave now, then we must set off for the station. We can leave our débris in the woods," he said, gesturing at the bloodstained dressings and empty tins. "It will quickly disappear. You clean the dishes and get the boys ready."

"I don't think I can get rid of . . ." Clarissa gestured at the place her father had died. The stain was not large, and Mr Holmes had wiped much of it away when he dragged the body outside, but still, even a scrub-brush would not conquer it entirely.

"This is a gamekeeper's home," he pointed out. "Who is to say what manner of work he got up to inside?" So saying, he spilled the dregs of his coffee on the floor, rubbing vigorously with a bit more of the bandage (using, she was relieved to see, his good arm). When he was finished, he swept some ashes back and forth across the boards. At the end, it looked no worse, and no fresher, than any of the floor's other marks.

Watching his slim figure bent over the stain, Clarissa reflected on how easy it would be to knock him out and take the boys—or indeed, to use her little pistol to lock him in the gamekeeper's shed.

At that reminder, she retrieved her gun from where the young man had left it, and went to do his bidding.

CHAPTER TWENTY-SIX

They made it to London that same day. Afterwards, Clarissa could recall few details from the journey. She was cold, she remembered that, although she could not have said whether from the temperature of the compartment or from her own inner thermometer. She sat stunned most of the way, rousing only to feed Samuel and, occasionally, to put her arms around Billy. Once, while waiting for one train or another, she realised that her silk-hatted guard was missing. She had started to wonder if this was some kind of a test when he returned . . . from the direction of a telegraph office. Nausea joined the clamminess of her skin, but in truth, there was little she could do.

The long, silent train journey was shattered by the chaos of Waterloo, but young Mr Holmes seemed quite familiar with the challenge, and in a brief time he was handing her into a growler. The driver objected to their destination, but since they were already in, there was little he could do but slap the horse into motion.

Two other things she remembered from that evening—or, thought she did. The first was fairly definite, a picture of Mr Holmes jerking Billy back inside the cab, to keep the boy from losing his head at the close passage of a brewer's wagon. The second she was not so sure about: could that young man have actually put her into bed, removing her outer garments and shoes? Or was that fuzzy memory merely part of the dreams that haunted her that night?

She started awake a dozen times at the report of the small pistol, only to find a silent room with two sleeping boys. At some point, Billy crept into her bed. She slowly warmed, and slept at last.

She woke the next morning, first to the thought of that telegraph office, then to the question of mourning. To dress in normal clothes, as if nothing had happened, was unthinkable—yet to acknowledge this particular death was impossible. She could not even write to Alicia without also telling how their father had died. Slowly, she rose, and dressed, waiting all the while for a fist on her door.

It rained. Billy raised no great objection at being kept at his books, although Samuel complained at the lack of movement. Clarissa fidgeted the day away, snapping at Billy, exclaiming at yet another dirty diaper, ready to bite someone. The police would arrive, or that young man would: either way, the end would present itself with a rap on the door.

By evening, she had exhausted both her expectations and herself. She lay awake most of the night, waiting for the pounding fist.

At ten o'clock the next morning, with dull yellow fog pressing against the glass, the knock came. But only a knock. And only Mr Holmes.

It was, however, a new Mr Holmes. He had shed the protruding shirt cuffs and handed-down hat for a superbly tailored set of clothing, head to foot. When he took off the silk hat (one that did not ride down on his ears) to duck inside, she could see he'd had his hair properly trimmed, too.

Well, well.

She was not altogether surprised when he gave Billy a coin and told him to take the baby off for a time, perhaps an hour. The door closed. Her visitor looked in vain for a hat-stand, then deposited his top-hat and overcoat on Billy's little table, his movements betraying discomfort, but no worse, in his injured arm. He ran a hand over his hair before turning to face her.

She'd had days, now, to think about this moment. The lad would want something from her, and although Clarissa Hudson had never given away more than a kiss or two in the course of a Cheat, this was a different situation altogether. She was in his debt, for actions both past and future, and had little to repay him with apart from herself.

And in any event, it might be an interesting experience.

She stretched out a hand to his pristine new lapel—only to cringe away as he seized her wrist and twisted hard. Mewling in pain, she retreated, backing obediently until her skirt touched the chair before the fire. Just as she was sinking down, at the instant when pain was joined by fear—*Oh my God, he's one of those men who like to*—he let her go.

She cradled her injured arm, blinking up at his steely expression. "That *hurt!*"

"I am sorry, Miss Hudson. I needed you to understand that certain acts will not occur between us. Not now. Not ever."

She felt remarkably small. And dirty.

He pulled over Billy's stool to sit, his knees brushing her skirt. Even though it put his head slightly below hers, there was no doubt in her mind who was in charge here.

"You killed your father. Yes," he interrupted her protest, "you were attempting to save my life at the time, but the fact remains that you killed him, with your own gun. My testimony would see you hanged."

A black-draped judge pronouncing sentence could sound no more final. Clarissa gave a tiny nod.

"Even short of that, my testimony alone, with no word at all from your many victims, would see you imprisoned for a list of previous crimes. I believe you will agree that I hold your future, as well as those of your son and William Mudd, in my hands."

She began to tremble: what horror, what blithely unanticipated monstrosity was this person about to inflict upon her? Whatever it might be, she was without recourse: she was a mother now, banned even the escape of self-murder. As the lad went on, the bleakness of her situation made her wish for even the temporary retreat of a swoon: this creature promised to be a far worse taskmaster than The Bishop, whose only interest was money.

"I believe that putting you in prison would be a waste," he was saying. "Just as I have begun to suspect that there are certain crimes the law cannot touch without creating even greater havoc. Such a one is yours. Traditional punishment for you, Miss Hudson, would turn one child into a confirmed criminal and the other into a workhouse boy, farmed out to those who would starve and beat him to an early death. I have spent today, while waiting for my tailor to rid me of the cuffs that have so distracted you, meditating on how best to make use of your talents."

He paused, his eyes going to the window. He muttered something under his breath—it sounded like, *And of my own.* Then he rose to fetch a tobacco pouch from his overcoat. He filled the pipe, wandering over to examine the street below, while Clarissa dug her finger-nails into her palms to keep from screaming at him.

The oblivious young man put out his left forefinger to swipe down her window, then looked at the flesh. She could have told him there would be no stain: coal smoke or no, Clarissa Hudson kept her view of the world unimpeded.

"What, I was forced to ask, would be served by perpetuating this circle of misery and violence? How would the traditional forms of punishment repay the fear engendered on a blackmailer's victims? Was there another form of service that might suffice?"

He was now speaking to his pipe, or to himself: certainly not to her. His musings were an agony, but she did not break in, feeling that to do so would be to push him from a path whose direction he was feeling his way along, half-blind.

"Many things would have to change," he muttered. "University, for one."

University?

"But does one need all that . . . that lumber? Life is so brief, so appallingly brief, and other minds so inadequate. Might it not be best to make a break of it now, and start furnishing the storage rooms with what I might actually need, rather than continue to collect the detritus of the academic world? And if that be the case, does this situation bring opportunity, or ambush? If the former, I cannot afford to turn my back on it. But if the latter . . ."

Clarissa was startled to find his eyes on her, that cold grey gaze drilling into her very soul. "If one eliminates the impossible, then whatever remains must be the way forward. And the only way to prove an hypothesis is through experiment. Miss Hudson, I believe you have considerable talents as an actress?"

She was confused, more by the abrupt shift in address than by the question itself. "I, no—well, I suppose . . ."

He made an impatient gesture. "I have watched you at work. You are extremely clever. But it appears to me the element of the task you most relish is not the actual thieving, but the change of nature that it requires. For example, in the zoological gardens I watched you pass before a trio of nursemaids with their charges, and you might have been one of them, dull and bored. Thirty feet further on you walked in front of two young men with their legs outstretched on the grass, and without so much as a glance in their direction, you changed, becoming not only attractive and flirtatious, but a person of their own class. Further on, when you came under the purview of a disapproving older married pair, your steps grew heavy, your shoulders slumped, giving the impression that you, at least, understood the burden of life. Have you ever been on the stage?"

"Not really. I tried, when I was very young, but it was, I don't know . . . hard. Because the other actors weren't real, and nothing came to life. Of course, stage-acting also means a lot of reading—of the scripts? I'm not too fast at reading."

"Yes. Tell me about your sister."

This rapid-fire change of direction was making her dizzy. "Alicia? She's three years younger than I, pretty. Married. Last I heard, they were expecting a child."

"What does the husband do?"

A discussion of the husband's reliability and social standing led to questions about how Alicia had been raised, and ended up giving away rather more about her own past than Clarissa intended: Mother's death, a father's fists, a local constable who brought them pencils and books.

Finally, his questions came to an end. The pipe had gone out, so he filled it again, lighting it with a spill from the fire. As he puffed, he seemed to be looking through the resultant smoke at the street below.

At last, he turned to deliver his judgment.

"This is what I propose. There is a clipper sailing with the tide, the day after tomorrow, bound for Sydney. You, Samuel, and young Mr Mudd will be on it. Your ticket and expenses will be paid. If you choose to remain in Australia, or indeed any place outside of the British Isles, I wash my hands of you. However . . ."

He walked back to the stool and sat, knee to knee, his gaze locking her in place. "If you wish to come back to England, you will do so within one year's time. You will come without your son. And it will be under the agreement that you abandon, completely and utterly, your former way of life. If you return to this country, you will be under my parole, but apart from that, you will be a woman without a past. Neither you nor I will ever mention what has happened these last few days. Nor will either of us ever forget it, for so much as a moment.

"Miss Hudson, I give you my word, here and now: if you return, you will always be aware of your past, but I for one will never bring it up."

This was not the vow of a boy, Clarissa could feel that down to her bones. This was a promise Sherlock Holmes would keep to his grave.

"The choice," he continued, "is yours, absolutely. I will only add that, should you choose to come back, I may be in a position to offer you a life of considerable interest, and more acting than you could dream of."

She goggled at him. The words he'd said were so far removed from the threat and condemnation she had anticipated, they seemed to whirl through the room like a dust demon. Her brain spun about, her breath seemed caught in her throat. Her final awareness was his curse, as she slumped into a faint.

CHAPTER TWENTY-SEVEN

Two days later, the *Lady of the Seas* shook off the last reaches of Gravesend and turned her slim prow to the south. Sails grew over their heads as Mrs Clarissa Hudson, a young widow lady travelling to Australia, bade her two sons (the dark and the light) to wave good-bye to England. Letting go of the baby's tiny wrist, her own hand brushed against the hidden purse beneath her skirts, a motion she'd performed a hundred times since that morning: yes, the fat little Morocco leather folder with the letter of credit was still there, along with its handful of gold coins.

Despite that weight, she'd never felt so light—light-hearted, light-headed, as buoyant as the graceful ship beneath her shoes, pulled into the future by the filling sails above her feathered hat. She laughed aloud at the thought. When Billy looked up in surprise, she laughed all the more. She had no idea why that mad young man with the grey eyes had set her up so thoroughly, with tickets bought, money provided, even a quick trip along Oxford Street to fill in the gaps of their wardrobes. She and the boys had all they would need for a year—more, with care.

This irrational largesse would have made her uneasy had Mr Holmes not made it so abundantly clear that she was under no obligation to return. That so long as she stayed in the antipodes, she owed him nothing.

It must be remorse, she'd decided: his way to acknowledge that she'd pulled the trigger for him, and that the stigma she felt for having killed her father was best dealt with by getting her out of his sight, for good.

And for good it would be. Clarissa Hudson had no intention of coming back to England, never planned on seeing The Bishop, the city, or that lad with the piercing grey eyes, ever again. She could not help worrying a little about this fluke of freedom. She also knew that the dark events of Hampshire were far from over, that the hundred or more empty days that stretched out before her would be haunted by her father's death. But for the moment—for this hour, on this ship, she would neither mourn her father nor argue with good fortune. Today, she would be a mother, and choose life. She would seize it and run, never to return from what Australia had to offer: freedom to make another life.

She lifted her face to the sun, and laughed aloud again.

Three hundred fifty-one days later, in the third week of October, 1880, Clarissa Hudson leant over the rails of the steamer *Ben Jonson* and watched the Thames close in, turning the water around their hull from sea to sewer. She was not laughing this time as they churned methodically past Gravesend. Nor was she travelling as the widowed mother of two sons.

Billy leant into her side, making himself small against the cold wind. She rubbed his shoulder, wondering yet again if she should have made him stay behind.

Not that it was easy to persuade the boy into something he did not want. Eight-year-old William Mudd had a mind of his own.

"Will Mr Holmes meet us?" he asked.

"He doesn't know we're coming. When we left, he said I should place a message in the newspapers to say I had returned." *If I returned. Which, for some completely mad reason, it would seem I have done.*

She did not laugh with a light heart, nor did she reach down to touch the purse beneath her skirts. That reassurance was gone: the gold spent, the letter of credit dwindled to a mere breath of its beginnings. Most of it she had transferred to Alicia, Samuel's new mother, that the boy would not be a burden on his adoptive family.

Of course, if she and Billy had worked some Cheats, in Sydney . . .

But they had not. She had lived a life of virtue, squeezing every farthing and ha'penny before it went out of the door. It would have been easy, to choose comfort instead, but for some reason, the memory of a pair of grey eyes got in the way.

That strange, and strangely innocent, young man, Sherlock Holmes. The only person who had ever looked at her and seen beneath the surface. Not that she loved him—the very thought of romance was ridiculous. Yet she had given up her son and her freedom to return here, to the life he offered.

And—a truth she would whisper to none but herself? Leaving Samuel had been less devastating than she had anticipated. Nowhere near as hard as it should have been.

In part, it was the situation. Alicia's own son had died in June, and Allie, whose doctors said she would have no more children, responded to the loss with a deep and abiding bitterness. She would not be comforted, by husband or sister. Clarissa's apparent success in life only made matters worse. Clarissa had jewels, travel, a healthy son—everything but a husband; Alicia's jewels were paste and opals; she had travelled no further than her husband's family in Melbourne; her son was nothing more than aching breasts and a black-bordered photograph.

So Clarissa gave her Samuel.

It was hardly an impulsive gesture. The possibility had been in her mind since . . . well, since young Mr Holmes had told her that she would not be returning if she had Samuel. She had come to Australia fully intending to make her future there—school for Billy, a family for Samuel, a new life unencumbered by a past.

That had not worked out. Billy never fit in, no more than she did. He came home from school with blackened eyes. As for her, well, Australia was never the right size for her, somehow, both too big and too small at once. She had spent most of her life as an Australian girl, but she longed for London, for *home*. Still, she would not have left Samuel—until Alicia's need was greater than hers.

Truth to tell, Samuel had never seemed to like his mother, much—but he took to Alicia the moment he saw her, settled right into her arms. Even when Alicia's son was alive, she and Samuel had been a match, as akin in personality as they were in looks. Not that Allie was the most maternal of women. Clarissa had even wondered if there wasn't something missing in her sister, who had never outgrown her childhood tendency towards selfishness and secrets.

However, Alicia had married a gem. Raymond McKenna was a good man, a solid man, who would raise a son as strong as he. Clarissa liked Ray. She admired him. When he understood that Clarissa was offering him a son—she spoke with him about it first, before Alicia—he broke down and sobbed. He already loved his nephew, and now he would love him as a son. With Raymond to guide his family, the arrangement would be as good for Alicia as it was for Samuel.

Giving up a baby, Clarissa thought, should have been harder. Perhaps she'd never been meant to be anyone's mother. If so, things had been set aright: she had Billy now, and that would be enough.

Clarissa had once dreamed, back when she was waltzing through her Seasons, of having a person she could speak with openly—someone her equal, if not in wit, then at least in ruthlessness. At the time, she had pictured that person as a husband, or at least a friend. Instead, she looked to have the grey-eyed enigma of London.

There was enough in her purse to eke out ten days in the city. If young Mr Holmes had not laid claim to her by then, Clarissa would have little choice but to go, hat in hand, to The Bishop.

The next morning, her notice appeared in the agony columns of several newspapers:

Lady Clarissa to Mr Holmes—I have come
home and await your news at the Dragon.

On the third day, he came.

"You've grown," she told him. The gawky boy was nowhere to be seen in this sleek, confident man who waited in the threadbare yard of the Dragon Inn. No protruding cuffs on this one.

"As have you, I think. Are you free to come with me?"

"Now?" He gave an eloquent glance at the warm cloak over her shoulders, hardly necessary for an indoor meeting, and put on his hat by way of reply. She hastened to follow. "I thought you might want to talk, so I told Billy to stay in the room."

He stopped. "Billy has returned?"

"He insisted."

"But not the infant."

"Samuel . . . no. My sister's own son died last June. She was happy to have Samuel."

"I see."

Clarissa gave him a sad smile. "They will raise him as their own. He even looks like her." Although his eyes, she suspected, would be considerably lighter than Alicia's cornflower blue.

Mr Holmes gave a quick nod, blithe dismissal of a mother's pain, and threw up an arm to hail a passing cab—a hansom.

He held out a supporting hand, but she hesitated: a hansom was a rather . . . intimate container, for a man and a woman who were unrelated.

"We haven't all day," he said. She gathered her skirts, and folded herself inside.

The cab bumped along the stones of Southwark to the river, then across, making in the direction of Regent's Park. The interior was remarkably full, what with her skirts and the silk hat upon his knees. The hat juddered up and down—not, she noticed, in time with the wheels. No: his left leg was jumping a rapid rhythm. She glanced at his face. He did not look in the least nervous, merely impatient. She'd seen that kind of jitter in neighbours over the years, men and women who indulged in certain chemicals. Were his pupils perhaps larger than usual?

He turned, feeling her gaze. "Is something the matter?"

"No, no, I was just wondering—"

"Yes?"

It was too dark to tell, inside the cab. "Are you still in University, then?"

He turned his face forward. "Not anymore."

"What do you do?" Gentlemen tended not to "do" much, but this one was hardly of the usual run of gentlemen.

His narrow mouth twitched. "One might say I have been finding my vocation."

"How nice. And what vocation have you found?"

"Detective."

She recoiled, as far as possible in their crowded confines. "You're a *policeman?*"

He gave a scornful swipe of the hand. "Certainly not—the limitations would stifle. I shall turn my skills to those problems the police are baffled by, or unable to address."

"A private enquiry agent, then?"

"Of a sort."

To spend one's days investigating cases of fraud, missing children, and illicit love affairs did not sound appealing to her. Perhaps his was a *Boy's Own* sort of romance. "Like Mr Poe's stories?"

"Dupin!" he scoffed. "Showy tales, lacking in substance."

In fact, when she'd read the orang-utan story to Billy, they had agreed that M. Dupin's abilities were remarkable—but she would not argue the point with a man of such conviction as Mr Sherlock Holmes.

Instead, she nodded thoughtfully. "A sort of . . . consulting detective, then. Are there many of those?"

"So far as I know, I am unique."

Thank the heavens for that, she thought fervently, and let the rest of the ride pass in silence.

After a time, the horse turned along a row of terrace buildings, the upper storeys brick with shop-fronts or stone faces on the street level. The hooves clopped to a halt before the number 221.

Holmes tossed the driver a coin and helped Clarissa down from the cab, fishing in his pocket as he trotted up the front steps. The house was clearly empty—had been for some time, to judge by the condition of the paint around its windows—but the lock mechanism worked smoothly.

Inside lay cracked floor tiles, dusty cobwebs, and buckling wallpaper that had known the touch of many greasy hands. A half-windowed door missing its glass was tucked behind the stairs. On its upper rail, a tarnished brass *A* dangled from a surviving screw. Mr Holmes stepped forward to open the door to apartment A, pressing his back against the wall as invitation. She gathered her skirts and pushed around him, but rather than follow, he retreated to continue up the stairs. She watched his polished boots disappear, then turned her jaundiced eye to the rooms that composed 221A Baker Street.

Every inch of it wanted carbolic, plaster, paint, and fresh paper. Any attempt to kindle heat would burn the place down. However, once the surface decay had been banished and the flues entirely rebuilt, she imagined the kitchen, pantry, and small sitting area would be comfortable enough.

At which time, the only way she could afford the rent would be to go back to work for The Bishop.

She closed the door on flat A and started up the stairs, testing each before committing her weight to it. The carpet was frayed and filthy and the carpet rods were either missing or loose, but the wood beneath seemed in good shape.

On the next floor up, flat B did not even have its letter, merely two holes in a door that was leaning against the wall. Through the empty door frame lay a potentially comfortable suite consisting of two spacious bedrooms at the back and a large sitting room at the front. In this latter, a pair of stingy windows looked ready to dive onto the street. The floorboards were bare, apart from the dust and droppings of vermin, the wood so badly gouged and scraped, it looked as if a pony with loose shoe-nails had been stabled here. The sound of pigeons came from above—and not, she thought uneasily, from out of doors.

Clarissa studied a twisted length of gas pipe protruding from the wall, wondering how much force was required to break a light fixture away like that. "Is the house yours?"

"No. I have no wish to take on the burdens of householder." His voice echoed from the next room, followed by the ominous thumps and trickle of falling plaster.

"Good thing," she said, relieved that he was not proposing that she let a room from him.

"Don't you want to see the rest of it? Go ahead up."

"No, that's quite all right." She did not want to see what the birds had done to the upper level. "The next flight of stairs looks about to fall in."

He came back into the sitting room, slapping off bits of plaster from his shoulders. "I shouldn't think the place has got quite that bad."

"Whose is it?" she asked, meaning, *Why show it to me?*

His reply startled a yelp out of her: he grasped her hand, pressing it fervently between both of his. She stepped smartly back, her mind awhirl—*But he said*—*Is this some mad declaration of affection? His face says nothing of the*—only to realise that what he had been pressing was not his suit, but a physical object. She looked down at her gloved palm.

A key.

"The lease has been purchased in your name," he told her. "Assuming, that is, you are willing to take on the burden of Sherlock Holmes as a tenant. I intend to live here, although I shall make certain demands as to the rooms. These windows, for one thing, will prove meagrely in winter."

He was squinting at the window putty, peeling out bits with his finger-nail. "Also, one year ago, I gave you my word that neither of us need mention your previous life. Concerning that agreement, let me say three things. First: your debt to the man known as 'The Bishop' has been paid in full. Second, lest you wonder, no: you do not actually have a choice as to this arrangement. That is due to my third and final point." He turned to pin her down with those eyes. "Never, ever, even *begin* to think that your crimes and your father's death have faded in my memory. They will always stand between us. They will echo through every conversation we have, every request I make, my every month's payment of rent. If this is not acceptable to you, I shall put you on the next ship to Sydney. Is that understood?"

A nod was the only motion she could venture, until his cold grey gaze finally let go its hold. She drew a shaky breath, while he frowned up at the twisted gas pipe, shaking his head. "Very well. Although I fear, Mrs Hudson, that you will find me a most troublesome tenant. Also, if I might suggest, concerning your given name? 'Clarissa' seems a touch frivolous for a Baker Street landlady. 'Clara' might make the rôle more—oh, for God's sake, woman, don't faint on me again!"

The house renovations were fast—suspiciously fast, particularly when one considered the work-men's preference for night-time deliveries in anonymous carts as they supplied tiles from mixed sources, paint of various shades, and furniture that did not quite match. On the twenty-third of December, Mrs Clara Hudson and her young houseboy, Billy, moved into their near-empty ground-floor rooms, that Billy might have his first, tiny, honest-to-goodness Christmas tree. Four days later, furniture began to arrive. Three weeks after that, Mr Holmes brought home a potential house-mate for 221B, a nervy, limping medical man recently out of the Army who twitched at every shout and crash from the street outside. Dr Watson seemed expressly designed to be Holmes' exact opposite: tidy, Spartan, and (once his nerves calmed somewhat) interested in his fellow man.

And his fellow woman.

The first thing "Mrs Hudson" did upon meeting him was to glare at Billy, forcing him to slip the doctor's watch back into its pocket. The second was to drop into the pace and posture of a woman a decade or more older, lest Dr Watson's appreciative eye come to rest on his new landlady.

And from thenceforth, a landlady she was. Clara Hudson settled into the twenty-four-hour-a-day stage-play with deep misgivings, fearing the closing-in of walls, but in fact, the walls proved generous, and opportunities for escape—temporary and sanctioned escape—came surprisingly often. For her . . . what was Mr Holmes, anyway? Tenant? Employer? Gaoler? At any rate, his romantic plans to become a detective did in fact come to fruition, and he did indeed work beyond the limitations imposed on the official police. His associates were often members of the criminal underworld, while his clients were as apt to be unconcerned with legality as the detective was.

As Acts went, this one kept her interest.

Clara Hudson never doubted that righteousness was required of her and transgressions would be instantly catastrophic. Nonetheless, as time went by, Mr Holmes relaxed his standards just a little. She was granted brief holidays from virtue ("The seaside" was what they called a trip to Paris; "Mrs Turner" was both a friend and occasional stand-in, as well as a code for Monte Carlo). Even in Baker Street, her special skills found occasional employment: when Mr Holmes needed a woman to provide surveillance or to follow someone on the streets—or into places men were forbidden—he called upon her. She also supervised Billy's army of street urchins that Mr Holmes called his "Irregulars."

The others—police, clients, even Dr Watson—knew none of this. As far as they were concerned, Mrs Hudson was the landlady, ready with the tea tray and a substantial breakfast at any hour, her stately tread climbing at night past her tenants' door to the spotless rooms where pigeons had once reigned. In the same way, Billy was the page, whose inappropriate friendship with young street Arabs distressed Mrs Hudson down to the bones. She spoke with her mother's native accent, she put on weight, she watched her hair go grey.

And deep in the back of a bedroom drawer, nestled into a threadbare little bag that had once been rich with beads, lay a small, ivory-handled ladies' revolver and its box of tiny bullets.

III

CLARA HUDSON

CHAPTER TWENTY-EIGHT

Clara Hudson, née Clarissa, occasionally reflected on the number of sharp turns her life had taken. Born ten thousand miles from her father. A transportee before she could walk. At her mother's death, first a surrogate parent, then junior partner in a firm of confidence thieves. Two triumphant Seasons; a foolish love; an arrangement with a crime baron; a finger on a trigger. Then: Baker Street.

Two other sharp turns remained to her. The first came when the Queen died and Sherlock Holmes retired from London. Not that he retired from work: merely, he left Baker Street for rural Sussex.

To her own astonishment, his landlady decided to accompany him.

Once, long ago, during the strange and lonely pair of years when Mr Holmes was presumed dead in the Reichenbach Falls, Billy—a strapping young lad of eighteen by then, and off to University—had come by to read aloud with her in front of the fire, to help obscure the creaking of the empty house.

Dickens had always been a favourite with them. That night it was

Great Expectations. Billy was reading—his schooling was more solid than hers, his reading smooth—and had come to the following passage:

> Put the case, Pip, that passion and the terror of death had a little shaken the woman's intellects, and that when she was set at liberty, she was scared out of the ways of the world and went to him to be sheltered. Put the case that he took her in, and that he kept down the old wild violent nature, whenever he saw an inkling of its breaking out, by asserting his power over her in the old way.

The words sent a chill down her spine, of truth and recognition. *She went to him to be sheltered* . . .

Clarissa Hudson—Clara, now, that dull and dependable name—had hated the grey-eyed young man who took hold of her freedom. For him and his damnable honesty, she had given up her son, taken sharp scissors to her own wings, exchanged her silks for a landlady's drab, allowed her hair to go grey and unadorned. Her world had shrunk to the supervision of housemaids and the carrying of tea trays. More than once, she had eyed the tin of rat poison, wondering . . .

And yet, under that iron control, she came to feel strangely free. Clara Hudson acted a lie from the time her feet hit the floorboards in the morning to the moment she blew out her bed-side candle or turned out the electric lamp, but that lie grew increasingly comfortable. A rôle more real, more *her*, than the flirtatious girl at the billiards table ever was. Her few attempts at inhabiting the stage had failed because her partners rang false: here, under the Baker Street roof, every person played his part without lapse.

Well, that was not entirely true: Billy, at first, had chafed and questioned. But Billy was young. When all around him held up their sides, when even she failed to respond to his suggestions of independent fund-raising trips through the city streets or his queries about Mr Bishop, the boy's memories faded. In any event, school rooms and Mr Holmes' band of Irregulars soon took the place of his former excitements.

As for "Mrs Hudson," the old part of her (that *old wild violent nature*)

withered as its sustenance was withheld. At the same time, the new ca-
maraderie, the partnership she found with Mr Holmes and the good
doctor—a man who came to share a flat and ended up sharing a life—
poured nourishment on a long-forgotten side of Clarissa Hudson.

The process was slow, and uneven, but inexorable. Ten years and four
months after pressing the Baker Street key into her hand, her gaoler
vanished down the Reichenbach Falls. All the world mourned him.
Strangers wore black armbands. The now-married Dr Watson eulogised
Holmes as "the best and wisest man" he had ever known.

A week after the death was reported, Billy came to see her, and asked
what she intended to do. She knew what he was asking.

"Ah, lad, I'll stay on here for the present. Mr Holmes' brother wants
the rooms kept. A sort of memorial."

"He'll pay?" Billy asked in surprise.

"Apparently so."

"Funny, he didn't strike me as the soft-hearted type."

"His way of grieving, I suppose."

"If you say so. But will that give you . . . enough?"

"To live on? Certainly," she answered firmly. It was not the money that
she would miss, it was the excitement. But the thought of returning to a
life of Cheats after the years of enforced rectitude proved not as enticing
as she would have expected. Maybe she was just getting old, but she had
come to like feeling a part of something larger than herself. It was satisfying to use her skills in the service of Mr Holmes and his clients. Mad
as it sounded, she enjoyed doing good. And if it came right down to it,
she could not imagine betraying Mr Holmes' trust.

In any event, she wasn't convinced he was dead.

If her tenant's brother had permitted her to let out the now-empty
rooms in a normal fashion, she might have believed. But Mycroft Holmes
was one of the most powerful, unreadable, and frankly terrifying men
she had ever encountered: the polar opposite of sentimental.

So she kept her peace, and kept the rooms, and she and Billy remained (doing, if truth be told, the occasional Job for a few of Mr
Holmes' older clients). When Mr Holmes dropped out of a blue sky one

April day in 1894, she managed not to clobber him with some household implement, or to faint dead. She did permit herself a course of hysterics.

He even thanked her the next day for crawling about the floor in Baker Street, adjusting the position of his wax bust, set up to tempt an assassin's bullet. (She was not well pleased when Billy's replacement, a wise little urchin also called Billy, was called upon to perform the same function in the course of a different case. Holmes, somewhat belatedly, was made to question the wisdom of permitting a child to stick his head into danger.)

A new century began, an old Queen died, and something of the heart went out of London. Mr Holmes' announcement that he would retire to Sussex, there to pursue the philosophical occupation of beekeeping, brought about a second course of hysterics, this one as much laughter as astonishment. This most London of gentlemen—moreover, a gentleman who was only forty-two years of age—wandering about the sheep-clotted South Downs with silk hat and ebony cane?

However, he was both adamant and close-mouthed when it came to any explanation, and again, she wondered: Did London have too many eyes, perhaps, for the work he had begun to do for his older brother? Was the anonymity of the city working against him, making a train journey to London the price to pay for the security of open countryside?

He never said, not in so many words. And he made it quite clear that he meant what he'd told her all those years before: 221 Baker Street belonged to her, to do with as she liked.

In the end, what she liked was to sell what remained of the lease. She closed the house and sold most of the furniture. Half her profits went to William Mudd, thirty now and with a family and investigation business of his own. Clara Hudson dropped her key through the Baker Street mail slot and turned her back on twenty-two years, exchanging a landlady's authority and independence for the rôle of housekeeper.

The things she did for this man never ceased to amaze her.

On the even rails of rural Sussex, her life ran for the next twelve years. Her grey hair edged towards white, her step grew stately in fact. In 1914, the Kaiser's war that had been so long a-building finally broke out.

When 1915 turned on her calendar, not even the sound of guns across the Channel made her anticipate much more excitement in her own life. She would turn fifty-nine in May. The previous year had brought what felt like a final grand adventure in a long and tumultuous life, when she had acted an aged servant to a German spy with such finesse, even Dr Watson had failed to recognise her. With that, she was satisfied. Apart from the occasional disruptions that Mr Holmes would bring, she was content that her life would now drift softly towards its final stages.

That was before she met Mary Russell, and her life took one more abrupt turn.

April 8, 1915. Mr Holmes had been in a dreary state for weeks—months—and his housekeeper practically shoved him out of the door that morning into the fresh spring air. "Bees," she'd ordered. "Go look to your bees."

To her astonishment, he had.

To her dismay, he did not come back. Hours went by. The sun crept lower, the clock slowed, every tick marking an eternity. She cleaned and scrubbed and tried not to think about how morose the man had been of late, how black his moods, how heavily he had been maltreating his body by starving it and drugging it.

The wave of relief that washed over her on hearing his hand on the latch made her dizzy. The jolt of surprise at seeing his companion made her change.

"Mrs Hudson," he declared loudly, before even he had cleared the kitchen door, "I've brought one of our neighbours home for tea. I trust you have something to put before her?"

Into her kitchen stepped a child, a girl of no more than fifteen years, thin and tall and peculiarly dressed in a man's hand-me-downs. Her hair was a rich blonde colour beside his grey, her eyes blue instead of his steel, but were one to judge only by posture, the set of the head, and the gaze of the person within, the two might have been blood relations.

To her own astonishment, Mrs Hudson responded as she had not done in years: an Act rose up to claim her, strengthening her vestigial Scots accent, hunching her shoulders into those of a woman well accustomed to a scrub-brush, squinting slightly as if she'd left her glasses somewhere . . .

Miss Mary Russell walked into their lives, and made them both young again.

Mary Russell, whose blood lay drying across the freshly polished boards of Mrs Hudson's floor.

IV

MARY RUSSELL

Chapter Twenty-nine

Chief Inspector Lestrade walked into the kitchen and held out the knife with the dried blood on it. "Mrs Hudson, are you certain this is Miss Russell's?"

"Chief Inspector, I told you: it looks like hers, but I do not know that sort of weapon intimately enough to tell one from another. And with the blood . . ."

"Yes. But when you say—"

Mrs Hudson stood up sharply and began to clatter the delicate cups onto the tray. "Enough. I can say no more until Mr Holmes comes."

"Why won't you help me?" he demanded.

"I have helped you, as much as I may without consulting Mr Holmes."

"Mrs Hudson! There's a young woman gone, perhaps dead, and you—"

She slammed a cup against the table and it shattered in all directions. "You think I don't *know* that? You think I saw the floor and thought, *Oh, mercy me, someone has dropped a bottle of preserves?*"

Lestrade hastened to retreat before the old woman's climbing voice broke into sobs. "No, no, I understand, he's your boss. But he's not here, is he, and . . . Mrs Hudson? What have you—oh dear, watch out for—"

He snatched up a tea-towel to catch the blood welling from her finger. She wrapped the wound, then began to gather the porcelain shards.

"I'll get those," he said. "Please. Do you have a plaster?"

Without answering, she turned and left the kitchen. As she hunted through the little medical kit for the scissors, she could hear the sounds of porcelain shards dropping into the bin.

When she came back, eyes dry and gauze snugly wrapped around the offending finger (plasters being a bit newfangled for the Holmes household), a different sound drew her attention.

"What is—oh dear Lord, no!" Mrs Hudson bolted towards the sloshing noise in disbelief, to find one of Lestrade's constables with a bucket, wiping bloody footsteps off the sitting-room floor. Fear and heartache took welcome relief in fury as she stormed across the room to snatch the rag from his hand. "What are you *doing*?"

The man scrambled to his feet. "I thought—he said . . ."

She whirled on Lestrade. "Did you order this?"

He eyed the dripping cloth. "I didn't want—"

"Sir, I—" said the constable.

Mrs Hudson overrode them both. "Did you order this man to clean up the evidence, Chief Inspector? Or did the fool come up with that idea on his own?"

"Mrs Hudson, we have our evidence." His voice was that of a man well experienced with soothing irrational old women. "We have many photographs."

"Oh, for God's sake. Take your men and leave." She looked down at the mess on the floor: all those footprints, all that evidence that Mr Holmes would have flung himself on like a dog on a scent, reduced to a smear. She had not wept at seeing the blood on the floor, but the thought of having failed him brought her near to collapse.

Lestrade nodded at the constable, who went in search of a dry cloth for his hands.

"Mrs Hudson, you really must—"

"Chief Inspector, are you going to arrest me?"

"*What?*"

"Your father would have," she said bitterly.

"I think my father would have had more sense than that," he protested.

"Then you don't think I . . . did *this*?" she demanded, her voice breaking at the last word.

"Of course not!"

"Then go. Please."

"Mrs Hudson, I need to ask—"

"Sir, I have told you what I know: I came home, I saw this, I telephoned to the police. When Patrick and I left for market this morning, I expected no visitors. So far as I know, neither did Mary. I thought she would be here working when I returned. Your associates have been here for hours and found nothing. Shouldn't you be out asking the neighbours what they saw?"

"The local men are doing just that. But—Mrs Hudson, what is it you're not telling me?"

"Oh, Chief Inspector. There are so many things I cannot tell you."

The small man's pinched features took on an expression of mingled dread and outrage. "Oh, no. This isn't something to do with Mr *Mycroft* Holmes, is it? State secrets and the rest?"

She raised startled eyes. "How on earth should I know that?"

"Well, if it's not those kinds of secrets you're keeping, then what?"

"The kind Mr Sherlock Holmes will need to give you himself. Now, please, may I be alone for a while?"

Chief Inspector Lestrade, hauled down from London over the disappearance and possible murder of the wife of Sherlock Holmes, stared at the old lady. The perfect image of the housekeeper, with her trim white hair and her work-worn hands, innocence shouting out from those dark eyes. He might as well arrest Queen Mary.

Lestrade gave up, and grabbed his hat from the rack. "You ring me as soon as Holmes gets here," he ordered.

"After he and I have spoken," she corrected.

No point in protesting: the woman had too long a history in the life of Sherlock Holmes to be pushed around. But as he yanked open the front door, her voice came, oddly hesitant. "Sir, once Mr Holmes has seen . . . You are finished with the room, aren't you? I can clean, after . . ."

He looked back at her. Lestrade had known this woman most of his life, as had his father before him. Nearing seventy, must be, but the kind of woman who'd keep her backbone until she was tucked in her coffin. Mrs Clara Hudson was not one to display her grief, not one whose face would show what it felt like to scrub up the blood of a woman she'd raised like a daughter.

For a man who claimed not to care much for women, Mr Holmes sure found some strong ones.

"Yes," he said gently. "I think we're finished. I'm leaving a constable here. Ask him to help you when you're ready."

"That won't be necessary, Chief Inspector. My knees are quite up to the task."

And your spirit, Lestrade did not say. "As you like. In any case, there'll be a man here. Oh, and we'll be placing a tap on the telephone line, in case a ransom demand comes. That means the exchange will be watching your calls," he explained, "and we'll listen to anything of interest. We might be able to trace its source."

Well, she thought as she locked the door behind him, *it's a good thing I already talked to Billy.*

Outside on the gravel drive, Lestrade had a word with the men, dispatching some of them back to Eastbourne, giving orders to the one who would keep watch. Before climbing into his car, he glanced back at the house and saw Mrs Hudson's figure just inside the bay window, her back to him. The aged shoulders were clenched, the white head bent to study the sitting-room floor. A motion from higher up caught his eye: the breeze tugging a dust-cloth, left hanging from an upstairs windowsill. Sure sign of the proud housekeeper's distraction, that she'd laid it there to dry in the sun, and forgot.

The Chief Inspector climbed into his motorcar and told the driver to take him to Eastbourne.

When the police detective had left, Mrs Hudson stood for a long time, staring down at the two pools of blood. The smaller one was completely dry now; the larger one, crimson at first sight, had gone a sickly red-brown. The second time in her life she'd stood over a loved one's drying blood and known herself responsible.

For if this was not Mary's, then where was the girl?

And if it was not the fault of Clara Hudson, whose was it?

Clara Hudson: a woman with a history of failure and crime, dragged from her moral gutters and shown how to stand upright—and *this* was how she repaid him? First bringing her past to his door, then being away when it arrived? *My fault.*

She picked up the constable's bucket and filled it with fresh water, then got on her knees to finish the destruction of the footprints. She worked numbly, keeping thoughts at bay by an intense focus on the work: wiping and rubbing with the rag, emptying the bucket whenever the water took on a trace of pink, using a tooth-brush to scrub the last traces from the cracks in the floorboards.

It took hours. Every time she thought of Mary—Dead? Dying? Bound and gagged in a cellar somewhere?—she scrubbed the harder. *My fault,* whispered the brush. *My fault my fault my fault my—*

The telephone blared through the silent house. She dropped the brush and tried to rise, gasping at the bolt of pain. At the second ring, she managed to get to her feet, and picked up the earpiece on the third.

Her voice was none too certain.

"Clara, dear, is that you?" the earpiece asked.

She sat down, hard, on the little bench beside the door. Her head was spinning.

"Clara?"

Her arm moved to lay the receiver back on its stand, but she caught herself. Clearing her throat, she summoned Mrs Hudson's voice. "Hello, Ivy, I was dusting, and must have breathed some in. I'd love to have a chat, but I was just ... look, my hands are a bit full just at the moment, can I ring you back in a day or two? Good, take care."

She hung up, silencing Ivy's voice from the earpiece. She rested for a moment, but when her thoughts resumed their downward spiral, she got stiffly up and went to change the water in the bucket.

She stopped cleaning at the very edge of the dull, dry blood. Arms, shoulders, spine, hips: all on fire, all grating and stiff. She had to use the settee to pull herself upright like someone in her nineties, and wondered if she was going to cry again.

No: perhaps not.

She retreated to the kitchen, closing the door to the sitting room, wishing she could close the door on her own thoughts as easily.

(*myfaultmyfaultmyfaultmy*—)

Would it be hours, or days, before help arrived? She could scrub no more, not on her knees, but there were other ways to keep busy.

Through that night and into the next morning, she employed most of those ways. She polished the old house down to the bone, leaving her so exhausted, she even managed a little sleep in Thursday's pre-dawn hours.

The house was so damned silent.

She cleaned: stove, tiles, windows, ceiling.

She cleared: pantry, spice cabinet, the backs of her cupboards, the depths of her wardrobe and chest of drawers, ending up with two boxes and three pillow-cases of items for the church sales.

She baked: six loaves of bread, three pies, and several batches of short-bread to pack up and send to Dr Watson, currently in ... New York, was it? She ate none of it, forcing down half an egg and some dry toast.

She mended everything she could find, laundered all she could lay hands on, polished the silver and the crystal.

Three times, she approached the garden-party strawberries, intending to cook them into preserves, and three times she let the cloth drop over them again, unable to accept the finality of it.

Thursday morning, twenty-two hours after she had come home to blood on her floor, the waiting ended. She was at the front door, reassuring the bored constable that his superiors were certain to call him home soon, when she heard the small tick of the kitchen door closing. She ended the conversation quickly, telling the young man that she would bring him a sandwich later on, and hurried through the sitting room to the kitchen.

It was empty, but the door to her quarters was ajar.

She paused long enough to light a low flame under the kettle: one thing Clara Hudson had learned from the past forty-five years was that any catastrophe could be softened by tea.

Mr Holmes stood in the centre of her private sitting room, his body braced like a soldier awaiting the over-the-top whistle.

"Mrs Hudson, what is it?"

The question told her how he'd heard: if Billy had found him, he'd know already.

"You saw the notice in the papers?" she asked.

"The agony column, yes. And then your dusting cloth signal at the upstairs window. What has happened?"

There was no softening it. "It's Mary."

A person who did not know him would have seen no reaction. Certainly his face revealed nothing. But Clara Hudson had known Sherlock Holmes, man and boy, for forty-six years. She had lived with him, nursed his wounds, cooked his meals, worked at his side: she felt the man's shock as if his bones were her own. His long, rigid body seemed to falter, like the moment before a sawn-through tree began to teeter, and she hastened to prop him up with what little information she had. "When Patrick and I came home from market yesterday, she was missing. There was blood on the sitting-room floor, and her little knife—a knife that looks like hers—was sticking out of the wall next to the bay window. Lestrade was here within a few hours, and he's left a man to watch the place. I didn't know if you'd want it known that you'd returned, so I left the cloth as warning. His men took the knife, and dozens of photographs."

At the words "sitting-room floor," Sherlock Holmes had started to move. She followed him out of her rooms and through the kitchen, throwing facts in his direction as one would throw floating things to a drowning man. "There were footprints," she said at his back, "but one of

Inspector Lestrade's men mopped across them before I could stop him. I'm sorry. I did manage to preserve the . . . well, this."

He was looking down at the ominous barrier she had left on the floor, an Indian carpet that normally lay before the fireplace. Another man would have sunk to his knees, or thrown a chair through the window; with Sherlock Holmes, reaction lay in acts of the mind.

"I couldn't bear to see it," she admitted. "So I laid the rug across it. I hope that was all right?"

Without reply, he bent to seize two of the rug's corners, glancing a command at her. She hastened to take hold of the other two, and at his nod, lifted.

The light carpet stuck sickeningly on what lay beneath, the blood not having been as dry as she'd thought. However, even with a few missing patches, the stains were clear. Too clear.

He tossed the rug to one side and squatted down.

The larger of the two blood puddles, on the side nearer the window, was mostly intact. The other was smeared about, where a blanket had been laid down and the body rolled onto it.

"There were drag marks and footprints going towards the door," she told him. "I did take—"

"What kind of drag marks?" His voice was crisp, even, utterly focussed—what would have sounded cold to someone who did not know him. Clara Hudson heard the panic around the edges.

"Bloody."

"What *made* them?" he snapped. "Heels? Chair legs? A wheelbarrow?"

"I think it was a blanket. There's one missing, that heavy one I keep in the cupboard beneath the stairs, for picnics and such. I put it there after Mary . . . she said it was too scratchy to—"

He had lowered his face to the floor, as if to breathe in the stain. "The footprints," he interrupted. "What were they?"

"Shoes, rather than heavy boots. And none of them were complete footprints, only partial marks, to the side of the dragging blanket. As if someone had stepped around to readjust the . . . body. By the time everything reached the door, it was barely visible."

He nodded curtly, then shifted to see the stain from another angle. She went on.

"I took some photographs, with your camera, before the police got here, although I don't imagine they're as good as Mr Lestrade's. I also made a sort of drawing, what I could remember of the prints before they got cleaned away."

He held out his hand for the page she took from her apron pocket, sitting back on his heels to look at it: a crude map of the room, two long ovals to indicate the blood pools, x-marks showing where the footprints had been.

"It's as best as I could remember." He raised his eyes to the pristine boards, and she flushed. "Perhaps I should have left the smears, even though . . ."

That steely grey gaze hadn't changed since it first stabbed into her in the autumn of 1879. It had rooted her in place then; it did so now.

"I am sorry," she repeated miserably.

But to her astonishment, he gave a brief nod. "I understand." He turned back to the stain.

She closed her eyes, fighting for control. "There's something else," she started to say, but he was already speaking.

"Was anyone seen, in the area?" he demanded. "I assume the police have performed that much of their function? The Rootley brothers were released a few weeks ago—"

"Mr Holmes—"

"The two of them swore in 1902 that I would pay for their little brother's death. Benny Rootley certainly would have attracted notice—"

"Mr—"

"—being bald and taller than I. Or, this case I was consulted about last week, there's some nasty business brewing there that might have—"

"Mr Holmes! It's not you."

His eyes snapped up, more at her tone than her words, then followed her gaze towards the fireplace. He rose, more rapidly than most 64-year-old knees could manage, and strode across to see.

When Sherlock Holmes had moved to Sussex, twenty and more years ago, he'd left behind most of his London possessions and many of the habits. One that had persisted, to the irritation of both women in the house, was his habit of fixing any correspondence he deemed important (which, granted, was not much) to the mantelpiece with a jack-knife, lest a stray breeze carry it into the flames. From that knife now hung an object that she had seen the previous morning, the moment she walked back from making the telephone calls. An object she had not drawn to Lestrade's attention.

An old half-sovereign coin on a golden chain.

CHAPTER THIRTY

"Yours?" Holmes had his nose inches from the coin pendant.

"No. It's almost identical—it's even from the Sydney mint—but it's the wrong year."

"Where is yours?"

She pulled its twin from the neck of her shirtwaist. His eyes narrowed. "Am I wrong in thinking you haven't worn that in a very long time?"

"No, you're right. I keep it in my jewellery box. But before . . ." *Before death; before Baker Street . . .* "When I was young, I used to wear it all the time." So much so, the hole had elongated and Victoria's youthful face was barely visible. "It can only be a message. To say that whatever has happened is because of me."

She waited for him to stoutly deny the link as coincidence, to issue a blanket reassurance. However, Sherlock Holmes may have kept from her any number of things over the years, but had never lied to her, so far as she knew. He did not start now.

One hand plucked the chain from its resting place, the other yanking out the jack-knife. "Clean paper, Mrs Hudson."

Commands were a refuge and a relief, for them both. She scurried away for some pristine sheets of typing paper, and came back to find him lying on his belly with a magnifying glass, examining the blood. The necklace and jack-knife lay on a clean patch of floorboard to his side. When the paper appeared, he picked up the knife and used its tip to prick something invisible out of the blood, looking at it under the strong glass.

"What colour was the blanket?"

"Several colours, mostly blue."

"Is any twine missing?"

"Twine?"

"You heard me, Mrs Hudson."

"There's a roll of twine—I'll go look."

It was a large roll, and far from new. When she came back she had to admit she could not be sure. "It's possible there's more gone than when I last used it."

"What about that dent beneath the edge of the table?"

At last, a question she could answer. "That is new. Lulu and I polished the floor on Tuesday, and it was done after that. Although after I left Wednesday morning, Mary could have—"

"Yes. The drag marks crossed here?"

"They did. I cleaned nothing that the constable hadn't already, er, obscured."

Holmes set the magnifying glass to one side. He scraped the tip of the knife through the stain, then wiped the resulting gobbet onto the white surface. He cleaned the blade on his handkerchief, then repeated the act in a different place.

Six times altogether. He discarded the handkerchief atop the Indian rug, then rose, glass in hand again as he stepped to the section of wounded plaster. "This is where the knife was?" he asked.

"Yes."

He lifted the glass to the gouge, tilted his head in preparation of telling her to bring the lamp, and then looked at the table where it had stood.

"I'll get a torch," she said.

She shone its light onto the plaster hole, trying to anticipate his needs. She succeeded in doing so, enough that his next words were not a command. "The lamp could not have caused the dent in the floor?"

"It fell directly into the trash bin. The few bits of it that flew out seemed to be where you—where *I* would have expected to find them. I took photographs of that, too."

The bright light revealed a clean divot out of the plaster with a quarter-inch slice at its base. Holmes peered into this so thoroughly, it looked as if he were about to climb inside. Then he stepped back and looked at the floor, seeing one piece of evidence she had managed to preserve: the bits of fallen plaster.

He swept them onto another piece of the paper, twisting it around the pieces.

Then he stood back and studied the three: blood, plaster, dent. He stepped to the far side of the blood and looked over the wall and the floor, his hands unconsciously tracing motions on the air. Dissatisfied, he ran his fingertips over the dent, several inches back from the edge of the table, then picked up the torch for another close look at the hole the knife point had left behind.

His frown grew deeper: nothing was making sense. Back around the bloodstain again, toes at its beginning, he looked behind him at the tiny dent.

He grabbed the torch and jack-knife and dove under the table, working his way along the window to the corner bookshelf—where he gave a grunt of satisfaction.

His arm swept the lowest shelf clear of books, twisting around to peer into the depths of it. Mrs Hudson hurried to take the torch, freeing his hands to dig with the knife.

He emerged with a flat grey lump between finger and thumb.

"A bullet!" she exclaimed.

It went into another screw of typing paper.

However, its presence only seemed to trouble him further. He stepped around the table, trading positions, bending down, his fingers playing the air as he tried to envision what had taken place in this spot.

In the end, he made an impatient gesture, and turned away from speculation. "I shall consider the evidence," he said, and gathered his bits of paper to take up the stairs.

Mrs Hudson put away the unused paper and the big magnifying glass. She thoroughly wiped the table, where he had casually laid the jack-knife. She waited twenty minutes, then followed him up to the laboratory with a laden tray.

He was on a stool at the long table, shirt-sleeves rolled back on his forearms. The accusing necklace lay at his right hand, covered with fine, black powder. She set down the tray beside it. "Did you find any fingerprints?"

"Even schoolboys know to wipe away evidence," he snarled.

Mrs Hudson poured her employer a cup of tea. She added milk as he liked and sugar as he needed (he would have neither eaten nor drunk since seeing her message in the morning paper) then placed it at his elbow, where he would notice it eventually. As she withdrew her hand, she noticed first that the glass vessel he was staring at so intently contained an alarming quantity of very-liquid blood, and second, that his left wrist was crudely wrapped with a blood-soaked handkerchief, like a suicide whose resolve had failed at the last instant.

"What have you done to yourself?" she exclaimed.

"Testing a theory."

"What, that Sherlock Holmes doesn't require blood in his veins like a mere mortal?" She took his hand and stretched it onto the high table, wincing as she loosened the sodden cloth.

"Don't move that," she ordered, and went for the medical kit, stocked for any emergency short of replacing an organ. She cleaned the arm of blood, and was relieved to find that his blade had missed major vessels and tendons. "This should have stitches," she told him.

"Go ahead," he said.

But the wound seemed to be clotting already, and she had no wish to sew through her employer's flesh. Instead, she took out the narrow adhesive. "What on earth were you thinking?" she asked.

He glanced at the wrist, and seemed surprised at what he saw there. "I needed blood. Fresh blood. Or rather, its serum."

"And you couldn't wait to do it properly?"

She had once assisted in drawing blood for some experiment or other, and told him in no uncertain terms that she did not wish to do so again. After that, he'd learned to do it himself.

"I was in a hurry."

"And if you'd gone light-headed from—" All the talk about blood was making her feel queasy. "Never mind. Let me bind it, and see if it'll hold."

He allowed her to clean and tape his arm, all his attention divided between the clock on the wall and the flask before him. The muscles beneath her fingers felt so taut, she imagined his very bones were creaking. Adhesive drew together the lips of the wound. As she waited to see if it would suffice, she could not help wondering if she would end up drugging his supper, to force his body to take relief from his mind's demands. She'd done so twice before over the years, when she and Dr Watson had feared for the man's health.

She wished the Doctor were here, or even Billy. But Dr Watson was away for another month, and she had already told Billy that she needed him less than she needed the information he could get.

Which left her with her time-tested means of distracting the man: permit him the release of words.

"What is this you're doing?" she asked.

Predictably, his face twitched in irritation, but the pressure was great enough that a lecture began to spill out. "I am waiting for the blood to clot. When it has, I shall extract its serum. Just an hypothesis, you understand, although I believe that dry blood can be restored to some degree . . ."

The adhesive seemed to be holding. She laid down gauze and then bound the arm, letting him explain, understanding only that he was doing the one thing he could think of, the thing he had spent his life doing: searching for the truth among facts.

After a time, his words ran down. She tied off the ends of the bandage, hoping it wasn't too tight. When the clock's minute hand made a tick forward, Holmes reached for the small flask. He tipped it gently. The substance quivered but held, like tomato aspic that is almost set—and with that, Mrs Hudson's normally phlegmatic stomach tipped along with the beaker. She took a quick step back from the table; reminded of her presence, he shot her a glance like a dagger.

"I'll go," she told him. "Drink your tea, Mr Holmes. Just not . . . that other."

She picked up his coat, discarded on the floor at the base of the laboratory table, then stopped at the sound of his voice.

"Mrs Hudson, are you . . . Is there anything you need?"

She stared at him in astonishment.

"It could not have been easy," he said. "Coming in to find . . . what you did."

Slowly, she shook her head. "The only thing either of us needs is for you to find Mary," she told him, and left him to his work.

There was no cleaning left to be done. When the choice came down to tears, strong drink, or potatoes, one chooses potatoes.

She was gouging the eyes out of a heap of the vegetables, bought for the garden party, when a bellow came that began with her name and went rapidly indistinguishable. The mangled lump dropped from her hands and she bolted up the stairs.

"What is it?" she asked, somewhat breathless.

"Your hearing is going, Mrs Hudson," he snapped, eyes glued to his microscope. "I said, tell Lestrade I need Russell's knife. And ask if it had any fingerprints. I can only hope their laboratory didn't ruin the evidence."

"You don't mind if he knows you are here, then?"

"No."

"Very well. But, sir, that blood. Is it . . . is it hers?"

He made her wait until he'd finished dripping some liquid onto a slide. He looked up, noticing the untouched cup of tea. The milk lay in a skin across the top, but he picked it up anyway.

"Oh, don't drink that," she exclaimed, "I'll make a fresh pot."

He swallowed, then he set down the cup with a grimace and reached for the glass pipette. "I've only processed one sample. That one is type B. Russell's blood type."

After a moment, she said, "Someone's been through my desk."

His eyes rose.

"It wasn't Mary: whoever it was took my bank passbook. And something I forgot to mention, since it seemed to have nothing to do with matters, but when Patrick and I returned from market yesterday, the saucer from my mother's tea-cup that I kept near the mirror was on the floor. I thought it had just fallen."

"Nothing else missing?"

"Not that I've noticed."

"Go and search," he said.

She left him to his work.

Unusually, when he came down the stairs an hour later, he brought the tea tray with him. She was at the sink, drying a batch of glasses that had not needed washing, and listened to the approaching rattle. Tidiness was rarely a good sign with Mr Holmes: it indicated a determination to do for himself. Was she about to be fired? Arrested?

"The Chief Inspector said he would come straightaway," she told him as he came in. She straightened the corners of the dish-towel on its rack, and turned to face him. "I also looked for other signs of disturbance. Someone may have sat in my chair, the one near the window; I think the throw-pillow was moved. And I found that among the papers on the sitting-room table."

That was a very battered page from *Dombey and Son*.

"It's from that box of my sister's things that Samuel sent me, after she died. I put it under the stairs months ago. November, it was. The contents were tidy when I left them, but they're now somewhat at odds. That could have happened at any time, if the box fell over when someone moved it around. Nothing else appears to be missing."

He studied the page, and recited, "Blanket, passbook, twine, saucer. Necklace."

"What have you learned?" she asked.

His jaw worked. "My theory that one might reinvigorate dried blood with fresh serum proved—"

"Is it Mary's?"

He shifted the cup on the tray. "Nine or ten percent of the population—"

"Mr Holmes. Is it hers?"

He could not meet her eyes. "I do not know. All I can say for certain is that all six samples react as type B."

Mrs Hudson's hands had decided to brace themselves against the side of the table. "Sir, how much . . . Was there actually as much as it seemed? Spread all about like that, it's hard . . ."

"Without knowing how much blood might have been absorbed by clothing, one can only—" A retreat to the discourse mode had allowed his eyes to come up, but the look on her face stopped him. When he resumed, his voice was cold, precise. "Two or three pints. A person of Russell's mass has between eight and nine. With a thirty percent blood loss, a person goes into shock and requires urgent treatment. The patient would be extremely light-headed and possibly unconscious. However, one must also take into account the marked fading of the blood trail as this body was pulled across the floor. Even with a blanket beneath, it would have leaked considerably more if the wound had not been staunched in some manner. Which suggests that—Mrs Hudson, sit!"

She lowered herself into the chair, clutching the edges of the table as her vision faded. "Perhaps . . ." She swallowed, tried again. "Is there any of that tea left?"

A cup of tepid, too-sweet, tannin-rich tea later, the room became more solid. The word "staunched" stood front and centre in her mind. "You think she could be alive?"

"I . . ." he started. "If . . ." He cleared his throat. "Someone went to the effort of dragging his victim away instead of simply leaving a body for you to find. There could of course be any number of reasons why—"

"No," she broke in. "Don't tell me. Let me believe in a ransom demand. As you say, the blood might not even be hers."

He blinked. "It was the possibility that she is *alive* that caused you to faint?" he asked. "Why do women find relief a greater burden than fear?"

His exasperation made for a blessed note of normality, and Mrs Hudson responded in kind. "Perhaps because we have so little experience with relief." The tart reply was barely off her tongue when she thought, *Good Lord, could he have said that—in his current state—to stiffen my backbone?* Well, it worked. "You were saying: if her wound was treated?"

"I was about to say that your description of the trail leading to the door, half-dry footprints and indistinct drag marks, suggests that the wound was staunched in some manner."

"I thought . . ." No. She would not say it, no more than he would: the other reason for a person not bleeding was that their heart had stopped. "Could it in fact have been a kidnapping? It's only been a day: they could be waiting to send a demand?"

"Delay is a time-honoured means of building tension," he agreed, with a clear lack of conviction. He dropped into the chair across from her, taking out his tobacco pouch. For once, she raised no objection: smoke in the kitchen today would be a welcome thing. When the pipe was going, his interrogation began.

"The blanket. Who knew it was there?"

"Anyone who looked in the cupboard."

"Someone familiar with the house, then?"

"Not necessarily. Anyone might search under the stairs for a rug or tarpaulin."

"Your necklace. Who knew about that?"

"Anyone who knew me . . . then. Or someone who had poked about in my jewellery box. There was even a photograph, taken when I was perhaps twelve or thirteen, that showed me wearing it."

"Who among those people would be aware that it was significant to you?"

"It's only a good-luck charm."

"It's more than that. You have always treasured it above more valuable pieces of jewellery. You used to wear it as you have it now, beneath your clothing. And it is one of the few pieces you still have from . . . before."

It was the closest, in all these years, that Sherlock Holmes had come to talking about her life before Baker Street.

She sat for a time, digging through distant memories. "My father gave it to me when I was ten, as a memento of our first . . . Job. We had no money—really none—so a half sovereign meant the difference between eating and going hungry. But even that first day, we brought in enough for dinner without the coin. And since it was from the year I was born— 1856—it seemed like an omen. Papa surprised me with it strung on a chain, two or three days later.

"Alicia would have been seven. The minute she saw it, she wanted it. Well, she wanted anything I had—clothes, toys, food—and I usually gave it to her. But this time, Papa wouldn't let me. And dear heaven, the tantrum she threw! She moaned about it for days, until he took her out into the harbour for an outing. Because I didn't get to go, that seemed to satisfy her."

He plucked the key element out of her memories. "Your sister was born in 1859?"

"Yes, why—that other coin! That was the date of the one from the mantelpiece. You think she might have had one, too?"

"Wouldn't you have known, if your sister had one like yours?"

"No," she said. "Well, perhaps. It depended . . ."

"On?" His patience was wearing thin.

"My sister loved her secrets, and she was very good at keeping them. If she had a necklace like mine, especially if Father had given it to her—"

"On a day spent out in the Sydney Harbour, perhaps?"

He could see the answer on her face. "To repeat the question, who knows its true significance?"

"No one. If anyone noticed, I would just say it was a lucky charm."

"Your sister? Your . . . lover?"

The thought of Hugh Edmunds playing with the pendant between her breasts could still make her blush, after nearly fifty years. "Not him. But, my sister . . ."

"Yes?" Her pause made his voice sharp.

"I *think* that if Alicia knew my necklace had meaning, she'd have dropped hints about it. And, Papa would have hesitated to tell her, especially when she was small, because it would be revealing to her what he and I did. It is possible," she admitted, "that Papa wrote her about it after we'd left Australia. It's not the sort of thing he would normally commit to paper, but sometimes he wrote her when he'd been drinking."

"You would say that your sister knew the necklace had significance to you, but not why?"

"Yes."

"And anyone who saw that childhood photograph would notice it?"

"Yes, although I'm not sure you could tell what kind of a coin it is."

"Someone who found both photograph and necklace might think it had been yours?" he pressed. "Her son, for example?"

Not *your son:* that would violate his scrupulous adherence to the vow.

"He might."

"Your sister died last August, I believe?"

"Yes, some kind of infection in her lungs. And I know what you are thinking."

His sceptical glance stung.

"Mr Holmes, I am nowhere near as clever as Mary, but I have watched you at work for a very long time. When I found . . . that"—she made a gesture at the adjoining room—"my first telephone call was to Billy, before the police. I told him I had to find you, and asked him to place notices in all the papers. Then I asked him to make urgent enquiries in Sydney, to find out if Samuel is still there. Considering the time it would take for a response, I thought it best to begin matters immediately, rather than wait for you to give the order."

The grey eyes blinked. After a minute, he said, "Mrs Hudson, you have again managed to surprise me. Thank you for the tea. I shall be upstairs in the darkroom, developing your photographs."

"What shall I tell Mr Lestrade, when he arrives?"

"That if he comes into the darkroom and spoils the photographs, he will regret it. I shall speak with him when I finish."

"And may I . . . that is, are you finished with the . . . the bloodstain?"

He could not control the sideways glance of his eyes towards the sitting-room door, no more than he could control the dread that lay behind them. "I will deal with it," he said.

"No. This one is for me to clean."

In nearly half a century of life together, two people build a vocabulary of glances and tones, permitting entire conversations that go unspoken. In the end, he rose, and said only, "Yes, I am finished with it."

CHAPTER THIRTY-ONE

Mrs Hudson was relieved when the door-bell clattered, interrupting her attempts to get the last marks from the floorboards. She stifled a groan as she clambered to her feet, drying her hands on her apron.

"Come in, Chief Inspector Lestrade. I'll put the kettle on." Twenty-eight hours after she had returned from market, and every motion still caused the world to spin a little, every sound gave off an echo of the macabre. But when normality was impossible, one embraced pretence. "Or would you like something stronger?"

"Tea. Thank you." The policeman followed her through the house, his steps faltering near the wet spot on the floor. Miss Russell had not always made his life easy, but that had little to do with affection, or respect.

"Did you have any lunch?" The housekeeper reached for the clean towel she'd left across the tray of sandwiches she'd made for Mr Holmes to ignore.

"I told the wife I'd be home, thanks, so just the tea for now. Well, all right, I could probably . . ." He sat at the scrubbed deal table and reached for a thick triangle of bread and cheese. "Any word from Mr Holmes?"

Just then, the sound of a distant crash came from upstairs.

"What the—" He stopped at the touch of her hand. The two kept a tense silence for a full minute before Mrs Hudson eased back on her chair.

"He is upstairs—and by the sound of it, having no luck." She gave him a cheerless smile. "The last time he threw something across the laboratory was 1905. We had to call in the fire brigade."

Lestrade's mouth would have dropped, had it not been full of food. He swallowed hastily. "Mrs Hudson, I specifically told you to ring the Eastbourne station the moment he showed up."

"Yes. However, *he* wished to work without distraction. I imagine that he will be down shortly." When Lestrade made to set down his impromptu meal, she hardened her voice to a landlady's no-nonsense tones. "Mr Holmes said to permit no interruptions, even from you. And in any event," she added in more sympathetic tones, "if he's as furious as it sounds, you'll want to give him time to collect himself."

Lestrade had felt the edge of Holmes' cold wrath too many times over the years to ignore the warning, and permitted her to distract him with a question about his children. A few minutes later, as he showed signs of summoning the courage to beard a lion in his den, they heard the noise of feet on the stairs.

"Ah," she said unnecessarily, "here he comes."

Lestrade thrust out his hand when the older man came in. "Mr Holmes, how are you holding up? I was terribly—"

"Lestrade, your constables are a menace. Where's the knife? Mrs Hudson, have you no lights in this room?"

"They weren't *my* constables," Lestrade protested.

"Were my photographs any help?" she asked, switching on the electrical light over the table.

"Photographs? No." He snatched the envelope from Lestrade, ripping off the end and tipping the contents onto the wood. Someone had wrapped a piece of card stock around its blade.

"I'm sorry," she said. "I'm a terrible photographer."

"Yes." He reached for the magnifying glass, then paused. "Not your fault. I should buy a decent camera."

A reassuring lie—from the mouth of Sherlock Holmes? "What did I do wrong?"

He bent over the knife. "Your hands. They seem to have been somewhat . . . uncertain."

She had been trembling all over, after calling Billy and before the police arrived. She'd never stopped to consider the effect on photographic film.

He examined the knife minutely: the direction of the stains, the smeared tip, the side of the blade less marked with blood. He then raised his head to look through the doorway, his eyes tracking invisible motions.

After a time, Mrs Hudson ventured, "It does look like hers." Mary generally wore a slim little throwing knife, either strapped to her ankle or in the top of her boot.

"It is," Holmes said. "But how was the knife in two places?"

"What do you mean?" Lestrade asked.

"The blood, man. Look at that blood."

Mary Russell's knife lay across her husband's palm, no longer than his hand and wickedly sharp. A thick bead of dried blood marked one side. When he flipped it over, the line was considerably thinner. The last inch of its point showed a smear where it had hit the plaster.

"I agree it's odd," Lestrade told him, "but there's any number of blood vessels right under the surface."

"With no spray?"

"It could have got wiped off on clothing," he said.

"It was."

"I don't understand," Mrs Hudson said.

Impatiently, Holmes dropped the thing and snatched up the table knife, stabbing it into the butter pot with a suddenness that made Mrs Hudson jump and the little pot crack in two. He pulled out the smeared knife and wiped both sides on the tray's linen napkin. Paying no attention to her protests, he then took the sandwich from Lestrade's plate, parted its halves, and slapped it butter-side down on the table, peeling the bread away and tossing it back at the plate. He then scraped the table knife along the buttery deposit, and held it out for them to see: overall, the blade had an oily sheen, as the throwing knife was dull. One edge now had a thick bead of butter; its backside had but a trace. He made another fist around the knife's handle, but Mrs Hudson caught his wrist before he could conclude his demonstration by burying the point in her table.

"You think the knife was used, cleaned, then scraped through the blood on the floor?" Lestrade asked.

"Evidently."

"Why do that?"

"Chief Inspector, I try to form my hypotheses upon data, rather than shape the data to match my wishes."

And with that, he picked up his wife's throwing knife and walked out.

Lestrade made to follow, but Mrs Hudson stopped him. "There's little point in our watching him do his dribbles and drops, and he's cross enough as it is. Finish your tea and I'll do you a fresh sandwich, then we can go up and see what he has discovered."

The Chief Inspector knew Holmes well enough to see the sense in the suggestion. He watched the older woman move through her kitchen, her face giving away none of the distress she had to be feeling.

"How is he holding up?" he asked.

"How do you think?"

"Yes. Dr Watson is away, you said?"

"In America. I'd rather not try to contact him, until . . ." *Until we know, one way or the other.*

"What about his brother? Has he talked to Mycroft yet?"

"I don't believe so."

"You might want to telephone to him."

She gave Lestrade a glance. "You imagine Mycroft Holmes would be a source of comfort?"

"Not what you or I would think of as comfort, but . . ."

She considered what he had said, then nodded. "I'll suggest it to him."

"Well, he's sure to throw me out before too long. Let me know if you want me here. Anytime. Even if you just need someone to knock him unconscious for a while."

The similar path of their thoughts gave Mrs Hudson the first trace of a smile since she'd returned home from Eastbourne: both had worked with Sherlock Holmes long enough to know how relentless the man would be, unless an intervention was forced upon him.

Lestrade finished his tea. "Shall we go up now, and see what he's found?"

"Yes. And, Chief Inspector? Thank you."

What Holmes had found on the blade was more type B blood. Mrs Hudson's long experience allowed her to interpret the prodigious frown with which he was regarding the little weapon: there was as much confusion there as fury. He was feeling betrayed by science, and running out of things to grasp: if he didn't uncover some new facts, and soon, the man would turn upon himself. She broke into Lestrade's attempts at reassurance with a question for her employer.

"What does it mean?"

He gave an irritable shake of the head and pushed away from the laboratory bench. "There's some message in it, but the devil only knows what. Lestrade, I shall need—" He went rigid: a motorcar's tyres on the drive. He was the first at the window, and headed instantly for the stairs. The others looked out.

"It's Billy!" Mrs Hudson exclaimed.

"Who?" Lestrade asked.

"William Mudd. An old friend of Mr Holmes. He has an enquiry agency in London."

"Ah, that one," he said, with considerably less enthusiasm than she had shown, and followed her downstairs.

Holmes and Billy were already deep in conversation, an unlikely pair of confederates even without eleven years of difference in their ages: the tall, thin, grey-haired English gentleman, and the short, stout, dark-skinned Cockney with the first traces of salt in his tight black curls.

That skinny lad of The Bishop's is fifty-three, Mrs Hudson thought. *I must be truly ancient.*

"Billy, it's good to see you," she said, somewhat repressively. "I think you know Chief Inspector Lestrade? Chief Inspector, William Mudd."

The men's hand-clasp was brief, the air distinctly cool. "We've met," said Lestrade. Billy nodded, then turned to Holmes.

"I'll wait till you're finished here."

"I think we are through, yes, Chief Inspector? Your wife no doubt expects you at home."

It was as brusque a dismissal as Lestrade had ever received from the man, which was saying a lot. Still, he couldn't very well insist on remaining, not unless he was ready to declare Sherlock Holmes a suspect in his own wife's death. (*And God help me if that day ever comes,* he thought.) The policeman shook hands with the old detective, lifted his hat to Mrs Hudson, and climbed into the waiting motorcar. The motor began to move away, then jerked to a halt when Holmes stepped in front of it.

Holmes did not wait for Lestrade to lower his window. "I'll need the photographs your man took."

"Oh, you will, eh?" But by the time Lestrade had the window open, he was speaking to Holmes' retreating back, leaving only the driver to absorb his irritation. "Get on, man, I'll miss my train!"

Mr William Mudd, petty criminal turned respectable businessman, put his arms around his former partner. She clung to him. "Oh, Billy, Billy," she breathed.

"We'll get her back safe, Mrs H," he murmured against her hair. "This is Miss Russell we're talking about, never you worry. You should've let me come earlier. Oh, but that is a drive and a half, down here from London. I don't suppose there's any chance you have the kettle on?"

"Of course I do! Just give me two minutes."

The two men watched her hurry away. "How is She holding up, sir?" In Billy's mouth, Mrs Hudson's pronoun always bore a capital letter.

"Mrs Hudson is tough as nails," Holmes said automatically. "Billy, we need to find Russell, and fast. What have you for me that you couldn't give me over the telephone?"

"You think they've put a tap on the lines?"

"Police these days will do anything to interfere. Come inside, let's talk."

"Actually, sir . . ."

Holmes stopped. "Something you don't want Mrs Hudson to hear?"

"I think you'll want to hear it first. We can decide how much to tell her."

"Let's walk. I need to check my hives anyway."

But Mrs Hudson spotted them from the kitchen window, and came marching through the walled orchard with a laden tray. "You two want your privacy, I can see that, but Billy's had a long journey. Dinner's in the oven."

She set the tray onto the chopping block with a clatter, and gave her employer a close look. His jaw was not quite as clenched as it had been, his eyes not so haunted: Billy had always been reassuring, she thought. Mr Holmes might always find his culprit, but Billy had a way of making a person *feel* that the culprit was sure to be found. She gave Billy a look that, if not a smile, was at least warm. Then she turned and marched back to the house.

Not a protest, nary a question, just the tea. "Amazing woman, that," Billy said.

"She has been for years," the older man pointed out. "Fill your plate and tell me."

Obediently, Billy carried his refreshment over to the ancient weathered bench against the high garden wall. He balanced cup and plate on the arm, but before sitting, he fished an envelope from his breast pocket and handed it to Holmes.

"When I got her call, yesterday noon, asking me to put notices in all the papers, I was all set to come down here that very moment, but she said no, because the police were sure to be . . . underfoot. I would've come anyway—I've never heard her sound like that—but it seemed to me she was right, that if I held off, I might be able to help. Such as this."

The telegram read:

SAMUEL ALISTAIR MCKENNA LAST SEEN SYDNEY MARCH FIFTEEN
THIS YEAR STOP SOLD MOTHERS HOUSE SOLD FURNITURE PUT
CAR ETCETERA IN STORAGE STOP MARCH NINETEEN PASSENGER
NAME SAMUEL HUDSON BOARDED RMS NEFERTITI DESTINATION
LONDON STOP FINGERPRINTS OBTAINED AND SENDING VIA MAIL
STOP YOU OWE ME BIG COMMA MUDD BUT WATCH YOUR BACK
CHUM STOP WESLEY WARDER

"Warder's a bloke I met during the War, runs an agency in Sydney. We do each other favours, time to time. I told him this one was urgent."

"Hence you being in his debt."

"It's nothing. He's sure to find more on McKenna, but I thought you should see that. And actually, I've had Warder keeping his eye on Samuel McKenna for a long time now. Just from a distance, nothing pushy, wandering by to check on him every few months. If it'd been closer up, Wes might've noticed he was gone sooner. *She* doesn't know, of course. And she hasn't seen this, from a while ago. Not that it's worth much."

A photograph, taken in a non-English city, its target on the opposite side of the street. The man's face was both indistinct and half-shaded by a hat brim. Still, one could see that he had light-coloured hair, and that his body was compact, but muscular.

Plenty strong enough to lift a tall young woman into the back of a motorcar.

Holmes sat back on the bench, eyes on the bees but his mind clearly elsewhere. "Samuel Hudson," he said, his voice troubled. "So: Mrs Hudson's sister, Alicia McKenna, dies in August. In March, her son Samuel closes up the house and sails to England. In May, someone comes here and has a bloody fight with Russell, leaving behind an object with personal meaning to Mrs Hudson alone." He described the necklace. Billy nodded, remembering it. "We need to find Samuel McKenna."

"He's been staying at a third-rate hotel around the corner from Paddington, although he hasn't been there since Tuesday."

Holmes withdrew his gaze from the bees, eyebrows raised.

"I haven't been there," Billy told him. "I only found it this afternoon. But he's calling himself Samuel Hudson."

"Interesting."

"'Fraid the rest of it's more interesting yet."

"Tell me."

Billy folded the last of the bread-and-butter into his mouth. "Sorry, that was breakfast. I have a file-folder in the motor, left it there since I didn't want her to see it. The gist of it is, Sam McKenna runs some clubs in Sydney with what you might call 'dubious ties.' The sorts of clubs that have layers of ownership papers and back rooms for men who don't want to be seen together in public. McKenna's only spent one stretch of a few months behind bars, for selling liquor without a license, but he's been arrested a dozen or more times. Mostly for assault. Two of those involved guns."

The fragrant garden seemed to go still. The beekeeper stirred. "Hence your friend's warning to 'watch your back.'"

"Yes, our Samuel has a temper," Billy agreed. "There's also reports on the Mum, Alicia Hudson as was. Squeaky clean lady, nothing against her but being hard on her servants—none of 'em ever lasted more than a few months before she fired them. Lots of acquaintances, no close friends to speak of. No other children. Mrs McKenna was big on her position in the city—her husband died when Sam was four or five—and liked to put on an English accent. Took the English papers, bundled up, and shipped out weeks late."

"Why are you telling me all this? Even if her death was falsely reported, no woman in her sixties could have—"

"Hold on, I'm telling you because of the papers. You haven't caught up with yours yet, have you? From being away?"

"Only the last three months."

"This was earlier, around Christmas. It started . . ." He looked down at his hands, somewhat at a loss. "Well, we know when it started. You may not be aware, but I remember that night, in Hampshire. I was only—what, six? Seven? *She* thinks I forgot, and maybe you did, too, but I didn't. I don't know that I actually *saw* it, him getting shot, that is. I think I was standing behind her. But I remember the gun going off, and this old man lying there, all still and bleeding, and Sam wailing and she . . . Anyway, you sent me upstairs with Samuel. When I came down the next morning there was nothing but a carpet where he'd been, and blisters on your hands—both of you. I never told anyone about it—not even my wife. But I never forgot."

"I see."

"I owe Her everything. And I owe you all the rest. One of the first things I did when I started up my business—twelve years now, thanks to you—was set up a service that sends me clippings from a whole lot of regional papers. I gave 'em a list of names and places—most of them meaningless, just covers. But the ones that mattered were those I remembered from that night: Beddoes. Evans. Trevor. Fordingham. I had a few articles about Victor Trevor—your friend, that would be. He went to India to raise tea, and died a few years back."

"Yes."

"The name 'Beddoes' came up from time to time, but just as a place, not a person. The man himself seems to have left England about then, but his name stayed behind, and every so often there'd be a mention of the Beddoes Estate, near Fordingham. He didn't have family, so when he vanished, it took forever to sort out who owned it. Some third cousin or something. Anyway, a few months ago—October, I think it was—the land around the house was finally sold. A month after that, there was a small piece saying some builders would be putting in a lot of suburban villas—a couple factories had set up in Fordingham, which is on a nice convenient line to Southampton.

"When they were clearing ground, just after the first of the year, they turned up a skeleton."

"Oh."

"'Skeleton Found in Beddoes Estate, Near Gamekeeper's Cottage.' It made for a minor sensation, since estimate put the body as being buried more or less when Beddoes himself vanished, forty-five years ago. Though once they decided this wasn't him but some pauper with bad teeth, the papers lost interest."

"You kept well clear of it, I imagine?"

"You bet. Wouldn't want the police wondering why Billy Mudd was sniffin' around."

"Very good. And, Mr Mudd: was there a reason you came in your motor instead of the train? You'd have left approximately the same time, and got here slightly earlier."

Billy smiled a bit at this apparent non sequitur. "Not much gets past you, Mr Holmes. Yes, it did occur to me that you might want to do a little sniffing yourself. And that might be easier behind the wind-screens of my motorcar."

Holmes closed his eyes. He sat back against the bench.

"If a ransom call comes . . ."

The odour of hawthorn blossom drifted over the wall; sheep blatted at each other from down the lane. After a time, Billy asked, "If the call came, would you trust Mrs Hudson to handle it?"

"Yes." Not a speck of hesitation, Billy noticed. He waited some more, then said, "I can pop down to Fordingham, if you like. Ask around about the skeleton."

Holmes stayed motionless, legs outstretched and hands linked over his shirt-front, the late afternoon sun against his closed eyelids. A person might have thought him relaxed were it not for the raised tendons along the backs of his hands and the faint, rhythmic quiver of his right foot. There was an almost audible hum of tension from the man.

He broke the silence with a question. "Do you know the very worst kind of crime? The one that families never get over?"

Billy knew many such, but he replied obediently, "Which is that?"

"The unsolved disappearance. Murder is foul, but a loss with no answer is a wound that remains forever raw and bleeding."

Billy gaped, open-mouthed, at his mentor's devastating confession. Holmes sat forward, tugging his shirt cuff down over the gauze beneath. "Patrick Mason and Lestrade's man should be able to keep Mrs Hudson from harm. And if I sit and wait for a telephone call, I may in fact slit my wrists before it comes."

"Do we tell her about Samuel?"

"No," Holmes said, without hesitation.

"Which leaves another question. Which of us has to let her know we won't be here for dinner?"

CHAPTER THIRTY-TWO

t was a long drive, eighty miles across the lower end of England, most of it in the black of night. Mrs Hudson had raised mighty objections to their setting out without eating her roast and the scrubbed potatoes, but when Billy pointed out that Mr Holmes planned to leave with or without him, she subsided, tight-lipped, to fix a pile of sandwiches and a thermos flask of powerful coffee.

The two men waited until Patrick came, carrying his favourite shot-gun over his arm. While they waited, Holmes spoke to the constable outside their door, then talked with Mrs Hudson about what to do in case of a ransom demand. He did not tell her where they were going. Nor did he enlighten her during any of the telephone calls he placed to Sussex from call-boxes along the way.

Holmes pored over the file on Samuel McKenna until the light failed, then smoked two pipes, occasionally switching on the little map-reading torch mounted on the dashboard to check on some fact or other. Billy could think of nothing to say, since any comment on Samuel Hudson would be a comment on the danger to Mary Russell. He simply drove on. He expected to be told that they would sleep in the motorcar beside the Fordingham green, but to his bleary-eyed relief, as they neared Southampton, Holmes told him to watch for a travellers' hotel. The beds they took were not a great deal more comfortable than the seats of the motor would have been, and certainly not as quiet, but it did make for a change of position.

Holmes had a bed, but did not occupy it, any more than he had slept during the drive. He walked the dark streets. Every two hours, he returned to the hotel, flipping impatiently through old newspapers as he waited for his telephone call to go through. When he had spoken to his housekeeper, and listened to her lack of news, he resumed his pacing of the streets.

He let Billy sleep until dawn before dragging him to the breakfast room for a half gallon of coffee, and they got back on the road again.

Fordingham had changed in four and a half decades: the only thing Billy recognised was the White Hart. The small green across from it had been carved up to make room for a pair of converging roads. The village shops now boasted broad windows and garish signs, and houses with the occasional pebbledash front dared to raise their modern façades.

As they passed through the village, only a tea room showed any activity. The White Hart appeared to be following the 1921 Licensing Act as to its hours, and was shut tight. Billy circled the remains of the green and headed for the road beside the pub's spruced-up exterior.

The 1870s village had spread somewhat, but once away from the new houses, the countryside was little changed since that night an excited little boy and a young man in ill-fitting clothes had crept silently through the dusk behind Clarissa Hudson.

Both men now peered through the wind-screen, searching for landmarks. The lane was wider, its surface metalled. The rock wall remained, although it had been rebuilt and made taller. The copse of trees off in the distance had been plucked to a vestige of its former self, and the drive down which Holmes and Billy had walked that night, rather than beat their way along Clarissa Hudson's rough pathway, led not to the game-keeper's cottage but to an expanse of construction materials dotted by buildings in various stages, from bare foundations to snug slate roofs. A few early work-men were preparing for the day.

The cottage had vanished, along with most of the trees. "You want to take a look around?" Billy asked.

"Little point, I should think," Holmes replied. "Let us try the village tea room. It should be a lively source of gossip."

A couple of the labourers watched the motor turn around. A lorry laden with hessian bags paused to let them escape, and twice, Billy pulled into the narrow verge to let other lorries inch past. As they went by the restored wall, he said, "I can't believe you talked me into going with you, that night."

"I resorted to bribery. Once I'd got my pocket watch back."

"And that pretty little pen-knife. I'd forgot about the bribe. Ah, penny dreadfuls. That was the first Jack Harkaway I ever owned. Funny, my son discovered my collection of *Boys of England* just the other week."

"Beware of his taking Mr Harkaway's chivalrous lessons to heart. You came because I suggested your presence would offer her protection."

"You always were a sly one," Billy agreed.

The village tea room was open. This suggested an establishment that offered actual meals rather than afternoon social entertainments—and indeed, as the entry bell rang over their heads, all the smells of breakfast seized their senses. Billy thanked the stars, and turned to consult Holmes on a choice of table.

But his companion had changed. The man who climbed out of the motor two minutes earlier had been a tall, intense figure, vigorous beneath his haggard expression; this person who blinked beneath the tea room's lights was a vague, amiable, and absent-minded sort with narrow shoulders stooped by his years. The old dear smiled his encouragement at the waitress who bustled forward, and tottered forward with an uncertainty that made Billy's hand come out, until he caught himself.

They sat, a fiddly operation involving coats and adjustments and spectacles, then ordered—a full breakfast for Billy, milked coffee with toast for the old geezer across the table. By the time they were left to themselves, Billy, despite their reason here, was not far from a grin.

"As many times I've seen you do that, it still sets me back on my heels."

Holmes blinked, goggle-eyed through the magnifying spectacles. When their drinks came, he spilled the sugar (Sherlock Holmes did not take sugar) then dropped his table napkin (nor did he drop things) and apologised to the waitress half a dozen times in the space of two minutes (much less did he apologise) before explaining to her that he was an amateur archaeologist and someone had told him—was it in Salisbury, William? Or Wells? There was a cathedral, surely, or perhaps it was that abbey in Bath? "I am a retired vicar, you see, and my dear nephew here takes me about the countryside on his free days to look at old bones. And someone, somewhere—Little Malvern, was it?—told me that you had some bones down here. On the Beddoes Estate, it was. Do you know anything about those, my dear?"

She did, and she was happy to tell him what she knew, which was pretty much nothing. Although she was fairly certain the bones weren't all *that* old, not like fossils and such, since the man's suit—it had been a man, and he'd been wearing tweeds—his suit was almost intact, although there was nothing in his pockets beyond odds and ends. No, nothing that would identify him. Still, the skeleton was definitely not Beddoes himself—and did the vicar know about their other local mystery from the previous century, the disappearance of Mr Beddoes? No? Well . . .

Only the arrival of another set of customers kept them from hearing the entire adventure and thirteen sets of alternate explanations, but she told them enough to ensure that there were no secrets to be had here.

As they were paying—Holmes counting out coins from a little purse—she expressed regret that she hadn't been able to finish telling them all the details.

"It really was ever so interesting, the press came down from London, even, asking about. Mr Rathers, across the green—the White Hart, you know?—had quite a week of it, everyone wanting to come and see what he had. Even offered to buy some of the bits and bobs off him, but he figured he'd make more off selling beer to those who came to see them."

"Bits and bobs?" Holmes enquired, rather more sharply than a vicar might.

"Oh, Mr Rathers has some of what Constable Mackey found in the poor fellow's tweed rags. I wouldn't have them in my place, of course, disgusting things, but the White Hart patrons, well, they're not quite so particular, are they?"

Back out on the street, the two men eyed the public house, still resolutely shut. "William," said Holmes, "how long before opening time does a publican arrive to sweep the floor and polish his glasses?"

Billy had a hard time convincing Holmes that a wait would be worth it: fitting pick-locks to the back door might gain them access to the White Hart's trophies, but it was sure to hinder any investigation of what the publican might know about them.

Fortunately, only two cigarettes passed before the man himself appeared with the keys. He looked surprised at the early customers, and delivered the formal protest that opening time was at 11:00, but the click of a coin on the bar had him agreeing that a responsible publican needed to test his taps thoroughly, and in any event, the front door was still locked if the constable wandered past.

Holmes-the-vicar had given way to Holmes-the-rogue: loosened tie, hat on the back of his head, and nary a spectacle in sight. Five minutes of conversation on the Salisbury races established him as a betting man; two minutes of wrangling with Billy made it clear that he generally backed the losing side; another two minutes and the topic was local history, with the old man offering the publican a wager that nothing of interest ever happened in this little backwater. That he'd never seen its name in the newspapers, not even once.

The owner of the White Hart proudly challenged the claim, and in thirty more seconds, was displaying the framed article from the *Southampton Times*, along with the grubby mementos taken from the pockets (what had once been pockets) of their local celebrity, The Skeleton from the Gamekeeper's Cottage. Billy agreeably kept the fellow talking, about the problems of identifying the body. ("Wasn't Mr Beddoes himself, he was a fine figure of a man with good teeth, we all knew that. And it waren't the gamekeeper, neither, just a titch of a fellow. And—he'd a bullet in him! A titch of a bullet, for that matter, but big enough to do a man in. Obviously.")

But at this point, Billy was not listening to the man, either. Both he and Holmes fixed upon the noxious little blob the detective had unearthed in the publican's collection: a two-inch-tall figurine, one leg ending in a tangle of greenish linen cord. Holmes had seen the thing itself; Billy had seen its like: a faded happiness bluebird was pinned to a board over his desk.

"Funny," the publican said. "The other fellow was interested in that, too."

The man was gratified at their return of attention, and happy to tell them all about the other fellow, who had come through the door one warm afternoon, just the previous week.

Australian, he was, a tow-head with blue eyes. Yes, might be the man, he said, looking at Billy's photo. Better-looking than you'd think from that picture. Had a good smile, professional-like. No, not like a toothpaste model. More like someone who has a car he thinks you'd just love.

"Did he stay in the area?"

"I don't think so. Said he was just here for the day, had family that used to live around here. Funny, though, I can't remember the name. He must've told me, wouldn't you think? Anyway, some kind of family, but they moved away a long time ago, so I might not even know them. Nice fellow. Talkative once you got used to that accent of his. Wanted to know all about the place, and like I said, the gamekeeper's skeleton struck his fancy. What he was wearing, what he had in his pockets. Seemed a little disappointed that this was all I had, but I pointed out the police kept anything that might give a clue about who he was. Told him he could talk with the village constable about it, if he was interested."

"And did he?"

"I sort of got the idea he wasn't keen on talking to policemen, you know what I mean? But I had to tell him, there wasn't likely much the police knew that I hadn't heard about—village this size, we all know each other's business, and Constable Mackey isn't exactly close-lipped. So I could be pretty sure there wasn't anything in the skeleton's pockets with a name on it. No driver's license, no passport, no cheque-book. Not so much as a monogrammed handkerchief."

"Did that satisfy this Australian?" Billy asked.

"Well, not satisfied, since there weren't any answers, but he seemed happy enough to move on. Like I say, nice enough bloke, laughed like a drain when I told him about the robbery I once had here when the robber came and went in a taxi, of which we got two in the village."

Neither Holmes nor Billy corrected him to point out that this would make it a burglary, not a robbery, but merely gave him a dutiful laugh. Holmes then asked the publican for the thread figurine, by way of a souvenir.

Interest having died down considerably since the glory days of the London press—apart from passing Australians—the man sold Holmes the grubby object with barely a quibble.

Outside again, the two men looked at the object in Holmes' hand.

"I'm not what you might call fastidious," Billy said, "but I don't know that I want that thing rolling around my car."

Holmes not only allowed the younger man to bundle it away in a sheet of newspaper, he agreed that washing his hands might not be a bad idea.

"So," said Billy. "We're looking for Samuel."

"He is certainly a person of interest," Holmes agreed over a gush of water from the tap in the pub's yard.

"London, then?"

Holmes turned off the handle, frowning as he dried his skin with a clean handkerchief. "No," he said, putting the cloth in a pocket. "Let us see if we can find a working telephone."

This conversation with Mrs Hudson was slightly longer than the others, but no more rewarding. When Holmes had rung off, Billy peeled himself off the wall of the village shop. "A constable just went into the tea shop," he said. "In case you want a word."

The grey eyes concentrated on the frilly paint of the little shop as if attempting to drill a hole through its lace curtains.

When he made no move, Billy added, "You're Sherlock Holmes. He'd be flattered if you took an interest in his bones. He's not about to ask for your whereabouts that night."

Holmes nodded, and they went across to the tea shop, confusing the waitress somewhat with the transformation of her absent-minded vicar. One question led to a dozen more, and one police station led to another. Before the end of the day, they were shown the complete collection of materials found on or around the gamekeeper's skeleton. At the end of it, they knew little more than they had when they left the Fordingham pub.

The sun was low in the sky when they returned to Billy's motorcar, standing beside the Portsmouth police centre.

Holmes had telephoned to Sussex every two hours, all that long day. Billy was tired, but not unhappy at the lengthy drive before them: without the monotony of travel to encourage sleep, the older man might drop in his tracks.

"London, then?" he asked as he pulled onto the main road.

"No."

"But aren't we looking for Samuel?"

"To hell with Samuel Hudson—we need Russell. I was wrong to wait for a ransom demand. We should have set out looking for her from hour one. We've wasted an entire day."

"It wasn't a waste," Billy protested. "Unless you think it was a coincidence that Samuel Hudson shows up in Sussex a few months after his grandfather is found."

Holmes did not dignify that with a reply. "Samuel Hudson would not have taken Russell to a Paddington hotel. We must look closer to home."

He did not need to add, *We need to turn Sussex upside-down.* Billy could hear it in his voice.

CHAPTER THIRTY-THREE

Despite the purr of the engine and the hypnotic unwinding of tarmac, Holmes did not fall asleep. Darkness gathered, but he stared on through the wind-screen, his clouds of tobacco smoke streaming out from Billy's half-open window.

After an hour, the driver gave up: if the detective wasn't going to sleep, he might as well talk.

"You buried her father that night. You and her."

Holmes turned his attention to his pipe. "Mr Mudd, I gave my word that I would not speak of Mrs Hudson's past, ever again."

"You really think this is a time for niceties? And anyway, this is me. I was there."

The passenger sighed. "Yes. Burying him seemed the only way forward. Considering our resources at the time."

"What about Beddoes? Why didn't he ever return?"

"That was my doing. No," he said, feeling Billy's alarmed gaze, "I merely drove him away. After I escorted you and Mrs Hudson back to London, I took the train to Portsmouth and hunted him down. He was in the second hotel I tried—not that there are many first-rate hotels in the town, even now, and the man liked his little luxuries. He'd been a forger, once, by name of Evans. Another transportee on the *Gloria Scott*."

"That's the ship her father was on, that sank? I remember the story, but not the details."

"It was before she was born. Hudson had got into some trouble and signed on board the *Gloria Scott* to get out of England. It was a prison transport ship. I learned about it twenty-four years later, when a University friend by name of Trevor invited me to visit his home. His father, it later transpired, had been a transportee to Australia, along with Beddoes and thirty-six others. One of those was a fellow named Jack Prendergast who had defrauded a collection of City men out of an astounding sum of money. Prendergast seems to have bribed key officers and sailors into mutiny, which went bad when a cask of powder in the ship's hold blew up. Hudson, Beddoes, and Trevor were among the handful of survivors. They were rescued and taken to Australia. Beddoes and Trevor returned to England after a few years, rich—or so they claimed—from the gold fields.

"Trevor certainly spent time at hard labour, one could see it in his hands. However, when it came to Beddoes, the forger, I thought it likely that his return was less a matter of making money in the gold fields than making money, full stop. When I found him, he was spooked and poised to run, trunks packed and passport ready. According to Hudson, he'd told Beddoes some days earlier that the police knew all. The man's reaction, to flee England, seemed extreme to me. As if he were anticipating arrest, not merely humiliation before his neighbours."

"If he'd escaped before serving his seven years, wouldn't that be cause for arrest? To say nothing of whatever he might have done in the mutiny."

"The *Gloria Scott* simply disappeared: no one knew of her fate apart from the survivors. And it was unlikely that a country gentleman and magistrate would face arrest for a twenty-five-year-old crime. Embarrassment, yes, and no doubt a fine, but not enough to cause a man to pack his trunks and run for it."

"Had Hudson in fact told the police?"

"No, it was merely a threat, to extort money. I, however, informed Beddoes that Hudson was not the only man to know of his sins, and suggested that he make use of that ticket to America."

"It couldn't be him, could it? Who . . ."

"Came to Sussex on Wednesday? Beddoes himself would be in his nineties, if he's still alive. He had no legitimate children, hence the lack of a clear inheritance to the estate, but when I last looked, there was an American grandson who appeared to be following in the family tradition. In Chicago, I believe, where this experiment in the prohibition of liquor looks to be taking a very bad turn."

"What about the other family? The one you were friends with?"

"Ah yes, Victor Trevor's dog certainly seized on more than my ankle, that Sunday morning. Victor never got over the revelation of his father's history. He did manage to marry and beget a son before going off to India, but that was the extent of his sociability. The son is still alive, I believe."

The detective shifted around to retrieve his tobacco pouch, and switched on the little map-light. "Do you know, Billy, it's a good thing I never believed in omens, or the *Gloria Scott* case would have turned me against detecting before I started. It was a farce, that began with a dog bite and ended with failure: my client died and my friend lost his faith in humanity; I buried the villain and compounded my first felony by saying nothing. I drove away a man I suspected of forgery, rather than confronting that crime.

"The case ate at me for years. I even conducted a search for Jack Prendergast's missing fortune, thinking that some portion of it might have stayed in England. But everything I found pointed to his having taken the fortunes of six families with him to the ocean floor. And it's not over yet: I lacked the courage to dig that bullet out of Hudson, in 1879, so the police now have the thing. Utter failure, start to finish." He jabbed his cleaning tool at the pipe with irritation. "The only good things that came from it were you and Mrs Hudson."

Startled, Billy looked sideways, but Holmes was intent on his work. It took a minute before the younger man's thoughts could retrieve their direction. "Hudson killed Victor Trevor's father, is that right?"

"To be precise, he made threats that terrified the old man into an early grave. Hudson's true crime was blackmail, not murder."

"And, Hudson himself. Was it you, who . . ."

"No," Holmes said gently. "She shot him herself."

"I thought so. I was behind her, so I only heard the sounds. And afterwards, I was never really sure. It seemed like some kind of a fever-dream. Guns, the woods. You. And then later . . . I didn't make your promise, but I never wanted to ask her about it."

"She'd have answered if you had."

"I know. I suppose I was afraid."

"Of her?" Holmes sounded astonished.

"Of you."

Holmes gave a shake of the head, and began to press tobacco into the bowl.

"Because *she* was," Billy explained. "Afraid of you, that is. Not that she ever said, but she was always different when you were in the room. Formal. Careful, like you are around a loaded gun. Did you . . ." He stopped, trying to find a shape for the next question. The pipe was going at last, but Holmes did not help him, merely filled the car with smoke. In the end, Billy blurted it out. "Has she worked for you all these years because of some kind of . . . blackmail?"

A spray of burning tobacco flew into the air, followed by furious slaps and the stench of scorched wool. Once Holmes was sure he was not about to go up in flames, he turned to the driver in a fury. "*Blackmail!* Do you not know me *at all*, Mr Mudd? Could you *possibly* be unaware that of all the world's sins—"

That the car did not swerve off the road at Holmes' outburst was proof that Billy knew what the impact of his words would be. He kept his eyes on the road, although his knuckles had gone somewhat pale beneath the skin.

"Yes, sir, I am aware of that," he said evenly. "But you cannot deny that you have some kind of hold over her, and have done since the day she and I came back from Australia. If you say it's not blackmail, I accept that. But I can't help wondering just what it is."

Holmes let loose a bitter laugh. "And you imagine I set her up in Baker Street for my *convenience*? Because it made my life so carefree? Lad, it took years before I could feel at all certain that she wasn't going to lace my supper with poison."

"Then why?" Billy asked. "Why did you . . . why?"

After a minute, Holmes bent down to pat around the floorboards for his pipe. Billy surreptitiously flexed his hands on the wheel, and started to breathe again.

"Call it parole," Holmes answered, when he'd got the tobacco burning. "A French word indicating that a prisoner has given his pledge, that he would thenceforth walk a straight line. A prisoner is granted probation—a period of testing—to prove that he is not hopelessly corrupt, and that freedom under supervision might return him to a sense of morality.

"When I sent your . . . guardian to Australia, it was a clear and unfettered offer of freedom. She *chose* to return. She chose to enter into the agreement I had offered: that her past in all its specifics would be put behind her. Behind both of us, for that matter. I vowed that I would never mention it, never seek any form of punishment whatsoever, so long as she continued to walk that straight line. Your presence did complicate matters, but after a considerable negotiation, I agreed to extend her parole over you. I was not convinced that London would not tempt you, that the adventure and apparent ease of conquest offered by The Bishop and his ilk wouldn't pull you back in. But you never let her down. Or me."

At that, Billy did swerve a little before catching at the wheel. "I never knew. That she'd had to 'negotiate' for me to stay."

"I was young, and convinced of my rightness."

"But . . ."

"Yes?"

"The baby. Little Samuel. Leaving him behind hurt her. Bad."

Miles passed before Holmes responded. "I was young," he said again. "I thought a mother's child would be her weakness. I hoped to force her to stand alone. I may have been wrong.

"It also occurs to me that, having been responsible for their separation, I may be the one her son is out to punish."

Traffic along the coastal roads was heavy, causing Billy to curse day-trippers and inexpensive petrol. It was quite dark when they passed through East Dean, head-lamps lit against the wandering sheep—and, as they got closer, the house's two guards, first Lestrade's constable, then Patrick Mason with his bird gun. Mrs Hudson had the front door open before Billy had set the hand-brake, but one look at her posture told the two men that there had been no telephone call. No ransom demand. No news.

The house was redolent with all the comfort a housekeeper could summon: warmth and light and odours from the kitchen that, even in his bone-weary state, set Billy's mouth to watering. She pressed strong drink into their hands, demanded that both men get themselves around a bowl of thick soup and a slice of fresh bread, then marched them both to their beds. Billy she shoved into the guest room, telling him that she had already telephoned to his wife in London, who did not expect him back tonight. Then she did the same with Holmes: not trusting him to abstain from the temptations of the laboratory, she accompanied him to his bedroom door and saw it shut before she would go downstairs.

Such was Holmes' state that he permitted it.

Not so long ago, he reflected, *forty hours without sleep would have been nothing . . .* He eyed the bed (the empty bed) and decided that three hours of rest might restore some degree of wit, and energy.

Maybe four.

At 3:20 the following morning, Saturday the 16th of May—a day intended for garden parties with strawberries and cream—the silence of the old stone villa was shattered by a bellow from the top of the stairs.

"Mrs Hudson!"

The most long-suffering housekeeper in all of Sussex fought her way out of the bedclothes' confines, struggled into her dressing gown, flung open her door—to come face to face with Holmes, equally dishevelled and dishabille. "Why did you not give me these the instant I returned?" he demanded.

She pulled back to focus on the sheaf of pages beneath her nose. "What are those?"

"The photographs! What is wrong with you, woman?"

"Yes," said another voice. "What *is* wrong?"

Billy's brown cheek bore seams from the pillow, having apparently not moved since dropping face-down onto the guest-room bed.

"I don't know," Mrs Hudson said. "However, clearly this calls for tea and—"

"Tea!" Holmes' objection was very near to a shout, and he loomed above her.

Mrs Hudson drew herself up in all her six years of superior age, fixing him with one dark eye. "Mr Holmes, you are standing in *my* bedroom, at some unearthly hour, with what clearly is going to require some attention. Please leave. I shall come into the kitchen when I am decent."

He gaped at her. Then, to Billy's astonishment, Sherlock Holmes turned obediently and went out. He even ran water into the kettle and placed it over the flame before dropping the sheaf of photographs onto the work-table and splaying them along it like a deck of cards.

Billy went to look over his shoulder: the police photographs of the scene. His gaze dwelt on the sickening black stain on the floor, smeared and trodden about—but that was not where Holmes' interest lay. Instead, he had his magnifying glass over one that showed the knife protruding from the wall.

When Mrs Hudson came in—having donned clothing and combed her hair in something under three minutes, although her feet were in bed-slippers—Holmes snatched up the photograph to thrust at her. She ignored him in favour of the tea caddy and a couple of brisk orders to Billy that sped matters along.

When the drink was brewed and a symbolic first sip taken, she returned her cup to its saucer and accepted the photograph.

"That's Mary's knife, in the wall," she said.

"But look at it!"

"What am I not seeing?" she asked patiently.

"The angle. Don't go by the photograph, cameras lie. Is that what you saw? Actually *saw*?"

"A knife, sticking out of the wall? Yes."

"No! The *angle*, Mrs Hudson! It's all in the angles. From the start the evidence contradicted itself—the dent, the bullet, and the knife. Think, woman. You have seen Russell practice a thousand times: is there any way a thrown blade could come to rest at that angle?"

"I thought you had determined the knife was stabbed into the plaster, not thrown there?" She handed the photograph to Billy, craning over her shoulder.

"But the angle!"

"Mr Holmes—"

"Look: you are standing at the wall with the knife in your hand. The table is to your right, the hive's cover is at your knees. If you drive the knife into the wall, what is the resulting angle?"

"Why would she—"

"Never mind why—let us look at the facts, not speculate on motivation. What angle?"

Clara Hudson took another fortifying swallow from her cup, then laid her hands in her lap and meditated upon the photograph. After a minute, she pulled open the table's shallow drawer and took out a paring knife, carrying it over to the bit of wall between the back door and that of her rooms. She held the handle in her fist, mimicking the act of stabbing it into the plaster. The result left her dissatisfied. She turned her wrist this way and that—then shifted the knife into her left hand and held its point against the wood.

When she turned, her face had changed.

"Ha! Ha!" Holmes crowed—and then something he'd never done, in all the years of their acquaintance: he leapt to his feet, clapped his hands on either side of her head, and delivered a kiss smack to the centre of her forehead.

In a swirl of dressing-gown, he dashed away, shouting for Billy to dress, they were headed for London.

"What about questioning the neighbours?" Billy called, but to no reply. He looked at the woman he had known longest in the world. "What just happened?"

"Someone drove that knife into the wall with their left hand," she said.

"But, there's millions of left-handed people about!" he protested.

She merely shook her head. From upstairs, thuds gave evidence of a madman disrupting the contents of his wardrobe. "I'll do some egg sandwiches, but you'd best go and dress, lad. He'll set off for London without you."

Billy even had time to swallow coffee before Holmes came pounding down the steps—dressed and clean shaven, humming some complicated tune beneath his breath.

"You will ring me," Mrs Hudson said sternly as the two men went out of the door.

"Yes, Ma'am," called Holmes meekly.

The engine protested at the hour, but caught at the second try. Once they had left the village and hit the main road, with Holmes his captive for the next two hours, Billy set out for some answers. "Why would Miss Russell have put the knife in the wall? Why even assume it was her—there's hundreds of left-handed people around. Maybe Samuel is left-handed. Or maybe he didn't want to let go the gun in his right hand."

"Mr Mudd, you see but you do not observe."

"Now, that's just irritating, that is."

But the old detective said no more. Instead, he scrunched the travelling rug against the window and settled his head into it. In seconds, he was snoring, leaving Billy to wrestle with the conundrum of the knife in the wall, all the way to London.

The sun rose at four o'clock. It was full daylight when Holmes spoke, passing through Camberwell. "You remember how to find Mycroft's flat?"

"Is that where we're going?"

"It's either there or Oxford." He sat up. "You made good time."

"We've missed most of the traffic. Will your brother be awake?"

"If not, he soon will be." There came the rustle of paper, then: "I thought Mrs Hudson made us sandwiches?"

"I ate them."

"Yes?"

"And drank the coffee."

"Well. Good thing we're headed to Mycroft's."

Mycroft's doorman had little luck with stopping their invasion, or even delaying them much. Holmes strode through the entrance foyer to the lift, hauled the gate shut the instant Billy's heels had cleared it, and worked the controls without waiting for the lift-man. A pulse of the hand against his leg betrayed his impatience with the dignified ascent, and he slammed back the lift's gate before its rise was finished. Down the hallway, around the corner, fist up—and the door opened before he could pound.

About the last expression William Mudd might have expected on the face of a dead woman was one of exasperation. Even if the dead woman was Mary Russell.

Miss Russell in a dressing gown, hair awry, a bandage on one arm: very much not dead.

CHAPTER THIRTY-FOUR

I opened the door to my husband, much aggrieved at my days of waiting. "Where the *deuces* have you been?" I exclaimed. "I expected you—oomph!" then "Ouch!"

The embrace was as brief as it was emphatic, and left Billy open-mouthed as Holmes stepped away from me—one hand lingering on my shoulder.

I felt a bit open-mouthed myself at this unprecedented public display. I looked a question at Billy, saw his confusion, and returned my attention to my husband. "Holmes, what on earth is wrong? Did you—oh. Oh, dear Lord. You didn't see my message?"

"Not until a quarter after three this morning," he said.

I was appalled. "And you thought—what about Mrs Hudson?"

"I told her I would telephone. Patrick is with her, and a relatively competent constable."

A voice came from the depths of the flat. "Perhaps we might move this discussion behind the door? The neighbours do complain so."

I raised my voice to include my brother-in-law, who had been nearly as unwilling a participant as I in the three days of my residency. "Mycroft, they thought I was dead."

"Most inconvenient," said his voice from behind me. "Good day, Mr Mudd. Sherlock, do you require coffee, or strong drink?"

V

MARY RUSSELL

CHAPTER THIRTY-FIVE

I watched Holmes' growing impatience as his brother fiddled with his new patent coffee contraption (which, frankly, produced a beverage indistinguishable from the boiling-beaker-and-old-sock method we used over our laboratory's Bunsen burner) and carried the laden tray out to the sitting room, arranging it beside the platter full of sweets and savouries he had summoned from the depths of his pantry.

The big man stood back, decided the offering was sufficient, and brushed the labours from his hands. "If you will excuse me, I am expected at the Palace for breakfast. The *Gazette* goes to press in the afternoon."

Billy's eyes narrowed as he watched Mycroft leave. I explained, "The next issue of the *London Gazette* contains the King's birthday list—of honours? Mycroft is usually called upon to vet the names, to save the Palace any potential embarrassment. Would you like to pour the coffee, Billy? I'll have cream in mine."

"How much of that blood on the floor was yours?" Holmes asked.

"Not a lot. How much did you add to it?" I looked pointedly at his wrist: he had winced slightly as his arm came into contact with me at the door, and the edge of his cuff betrayed a dressing in need of attention.

"Two and a half ounces."

"A remarkably precise measurement."

"It went into a beaker."

I eyed the bloodstain: either something was interfering with his usual fast healing, or the blood-letting had taken place quite recently. Yet if he thought I had been abducted or murdered . . . "Seems a bit nonchalant, Holmes, to be conducting experiments while one's wife is missing."

"I was attempting to determine the blood type of the dried sample on the floor."

"Oh, how interesting," I said. "Were you trying to apply Schiff's work on serum—"

"I don't believe this," Billy growled. "Miss Russell, where the devil have you been?"

"Here, mostly. I thought I left a clear sign that I was well, and I figured that Holmes . . . but evidently not."

"Start at the beginning!"

Billy had never spoken to me in that tone before. I glanced at Holmes, who was sitting remarkably close to my side. He nodded. I settled my coffee onto my knee, and started at the beginning.

"I was in my study on Wednesday morning when I heard a car in the drive. At first I thought it might be Mrs Hudson and Patrick returning for something, but when I looked out of the window . . ."

I told them about seeing the strange motor, it pulling close to the door because of the rain showers, and my introduction to the man who called himself Samuel Hudson. I took some time describing his almost-impudent manner: strutting through the sitting room as if I were an estate agent and he the prospective buyer.

"Anyway, he'd seemed surprised to see me, which suggested at least a possibility of criminal intent. Then I found myself reacting to him as if I knew he was a threat. Very odd. At any rate, all indications were that he was, if not her actual son, at least a close relative. I decided to see what information I could get out of him. So I offered him tea, and went to put on the kettle. When I came out, intending to ask if he preferred Sultana biscuits or lemon loaf, I found myself looking into the working end of a revolver."

Holmes' disapproval verged on outrage. "You did not notice he was armed?"

"He was wearing a large overcoat, and it must have been in the right-hand pocket of his jacket. I was to his left."

"Yet despite your body's reaction to this man, you returned to the sitting room unprepared?"

"Surely you know me better than that, Holmes? However, if I'd gone in with a drawn revolver of my own, he'd have started shooting and then I'd have had to join in—window glass everywhere, furniture ruined, the panelling full of holes. Mrs Hudson would have been very cross." Billy's mouth had dropped again, so I amended my frivolous tone. "Besides, I'd have got no answers from him. He hadn't come just to shoot *me,* or I'd have been dead already. Presenting an apparently harmless face for a while longer might tell me what he wanted."

Holmes grunted, and reached for his tobacco.

"I'll confess it's an uncomfortable sensation to have a gun aimed in one's direction. But he did seem to be after something—some *thing*—and I didn't think he was going to shoot me if he thought I was helping. When he asked me where Mrs Hudson kept her possessions, I took him to her rooms. He sat me in the chair and went through her desk, but didn't find what he was after. Although he did take her passbook. And broke that saucer I had repaired for her last year, out of spite.

"I then suggested the storage under the stairs, so we went there and I took out the box of her sister's whatnot. By the way, Holmes, we really have to figure a way to store a weapon in there without offending Mrs Hudson's sensibilities."

"You did have your knife?"

"Yes, but—anyway, I took the box into the sitting room and dumped it onto the table, but it wasn't there, either. He was looking for something paper: a passbook, legal forms, a letter. He seemed to think he'd sent it accidentally from Australia last year, along with that other rubbish—it sounded as if he hadn't known at the time what it was. But whatever he was looking for wasn't in the box, and I couldn't remember seeing anything like that in it when it arrived last winter.

"So: failure. Which left him with two choices: shoot me then, or hold his gun on me and use me as a means of pressuring Mrs Hudson when she arrived. He became overwrought, describing how horrible his mother had been to him. Maybe he wanted me to understand why he had to kill me. I had just decided to get the drop on him when he said something that stopped me cold."

I fixed my gaze on Holmes. "You and I, we've never really talked about Mrs Hudson. Who she is, how she came to work for you. I know some of it, I've extrapolated more over the years"—(God forbid I should admit to guessing)—"but it's clear that you do not want to discuss it. Now, I don't mind that our housekeeper has a history, but I do think the time has come for you to explain it a bit more. Because the thing her son told me, waving that gun around in my face? He said he intended not just to ruin our lives, but to see Mrs Hudson hanged for murder."

Holmes knew what I was talking about, I could see that. Worse, Billy knew as well.

"So, he wasn't lying, then. Is her name actually Clarissa?"

"It used to be," Holmes conceded.

I appeared to be the only one required to start at the beginning here. "Anyway, I could tell that he believed she was guilty of some major crime, and I could also tell that he was working himself up to shoot me. So I waited until he was distracted, then went for him. With my knife. Although, just as I did so, when it was too late to stop, he was saying something about how I would have to do."

"His precise words?" Holmes demanded.

I'd had three days now to reconstruct Samuel Hudson's final words. "He said, 'I'll have to take *you* back and see if you'll do.'"

"'Do' for what?" Billy asked. "Back where?"

I could only shrug my ignorance. "Holmes, does that sound to you as if—"

"—he had a partner? Yes."

"Perhaps even a superior: there's a bit of the dog-bringing-home-a-bone air about the phrase—but that was all he got out before, well . . ."

"The knife."

"Yes."

"Your arm was cut, too."

I pushed back my left sleeve, revealing the bandages over the shallow, jagged slice that Mycroft's pet medico had stitched when I arrived; the arm hurt, but was healing. It would not be my first scar. "I had to put the knife up my sleeve when I was getting the box from the storage shelves. But I keep that blade extremely sharp, and what with carrying the box and keeping the tip of it away from the fabric so it wouldn't fall to the floor—well, flesh is soft."

Looking at their faces, I was glad the wound was concealed by a tidy bandage: even the doctor had been angry over how close I'd let the blade come to something vital.

As it was, Billy's chief concern was a different matter. "You went after a gunman with nothing but a three-inch-long blade?"

"Nearly four. And he wasn't expecting it."

"I'll bet."

"Also, Mrs Hudson had polished the floor."

"He dropped the gun," Holmes said, "and it went off."

"Right. The bullet's somewhere under the table."

"In the bookshelf, actually. The gun also left a dent in the floor where it landed."

"I imagine it did."

"When did the lamp fall?"

"Oh, that was before. He recognised it as belonging to Mrs Hudson, and tossed it in the bin."

"And some pages of *Dombey and Son* fell out."

"He flipped through it. Whatever he was after wasn't there."

"Well, that clarifies some of the more distracting details."

"I tidied up the box of Mrs Hudson's things a bit, and put them back under the stairs, but I was afraid to spend any more time cleaning. So I . . . left the rest."

I stared into the fire, caught up in those terrible minutes: gazing down at the figure on the floor, turning away to the only task my mind could come up with, that of neatly packing away Mrs Hudson's rifled possessions in the storage beneath the stairs. Taking my time with every page and piece of it, until the sounds had stopped.

I could feel the two men watching me. I knew there would be a frown of concentration between Holmes' eyebrows. I knew precisely when the penny dropped in his mind.

His question was gentle. "How long did it take Samuel Hudson to die?"

My throat closed up. "I couldn't . . . I had to . . ." *Breathe.* One deliberate breath: in, out. "I was afraid of what he might tell the police. About Mrs Hudson."

"How long?"

"Not long, really. It just felt like forever. He . . . His noises were . . ." Outside, London was waking, the day getting under way, but in that sitting room, the only sound was the settle of the dying fire. "Mycroft's doctor agreed, that even if I'd left the knife in place, he'd have died before reaching a hospital."

I felt Holmes' hand on my shoulder, his voice in my ear. "This was self-defence."

"It felt like murder."

Billy chimed in. "It was not."

But it was. "In any event, I took my time putting away Mrs Hudson's box, then went upstairs to wrap some gauze around my arm. By the time I came back down, he had . . . stopped. Of course, he'd bled all over, stupid of me not to think of that. And as I said, I was going to clean it up but I looked at the clock and I thought, *Which is worse: leaving blood for Mrs Hudson, or having her come in and find her son?*

"So, I took one of the old blankets and dragged him out to the car. Managed to fold him inside the boot. And I was about to drive away when it occurred to me—God, why does the brain just stop functioning in times of stress? It occurred to me that I should leave a message, so you would have some idea what happened. I couldn't very well leave a note saying, 'Gone to London with . . .'" *With the corpse of Mrs Hudson's son.* "For one thing, I couldn't imagine her keeping the police out of it. And for another, there was that statement he'd made about me 'having to do.' If I was his second-best target, it suggested either you or Mrs Hudson was the person he was after. So I left messages that you would read but no one else would notice. I just didn't imagine it would take you three days to read them. What happened?"

"A series of well-meaning unintended consequences, beginning with a constable's scrub-brush on the footprints—"

I winced.

"—and continuing when Mrs Hudson permitted Lestrade to take the knife down and away—"

"Good Lord."

"—then coming to a climax with the unfortunate coincidence that Samuel Hudson and Mary Russell share a blood type."

At that, I uttered an Anglo-Saxon phrase.

"Quite," he agreed. "Of course, once I saw the police photographs, I was set on the right track at last, but those only came into my hand a few hours ago."

Billy, who had been following this with growing agitation, broke in. "I don't see where these messages of yours lie. The footprints, sure—those might have shown that Miss Russell's shoes were doing the clearing up, but the knife?"

Sherlock Holmes with a look of disappointment on his face is a terrible thing. "Mr Mudd, if some ten percent of the population have type B blood, and some ten percent of the population are left-handed, what are the chances Russell's attacker shared both characteristics with her?"

"Like I said earlier—"

"The dent in the floor told us that he was *not* left-handed."

"Why?"

Holmes lifted an eyebrow at the poor man. "You saw the dent, beneath the table."

"Yeah. So?"

"And the blood?"

"Next to the table, yes."

"Its shape indicates he was lying on his . . ."

"Back. The blood ran down both sides of his chest. One side was smeared when he was rolled into the blanket."

"If the gun had been in his *left* hand, and it fell at the same time he did, to land beneath the table would require that he was standing . . . where? Given that he was not three feet tall?"

Frowning, Billy tried to re-create the place. Blood there. Gun there. Person standing . . .

Holmes saw comprehension dawn, and nodded. "He'd have been standing in the bookshelf, yes. Simple geometry. But it wasn't until I saw the photograph that I could be sure of the sequence. That someone left-handed had driven the knife into the wall—had first wiped off the knife, then scraped it through the blood, and driven it into the wall—could only be a message. Hence, the blood was not Russell's."

Billy was not entirely satisfied, but then, he seldom was when it came to the explanations of Sherlock Holmes. "I'm not sure you can keep all this from Mrs Hudson," he said. "Sooner or later, she'll have to know her son tried to kill you, or maybe her."

"Why?" Holmes asked.

"You can't honestly intend to—"

I did not think this was the time for that particular discussion: I interrupted. "Until we know exactly what *was* going on, I'm not sure we can make that decision. I just didn't want her coming back from market and . . . oh, damn. The strawberries. Today was supposed to be . . ."

"The party," Holmes said. "She has made the necessary telephone calls. She merely told your friends some important case had come up."

Crates of rotting strawberries, on top of everything else, I thought sadly.

Billy pushed us ruthlessly back on track. "You should at least have left her a note. So she knew you'd not been kidnapped. Or killed outright."

"I did leave a message—tried to—just not for her. I didn't think a note would be safe. Samuel's partner—or employer, whichever it is—could be anyone. He could break in and see the note, he could hear about it from the police, it could even end up in the newspapers. If there was a message that Holmes alone could read, it was secure. At the cost of some hours of grief for her, yes, but I could see no way around that."

"Why would it matter if everyone knew you were safe? You'd killed a man with a gun, in your own house. No one would call that wrong."

"Her *son*," I said. "Who had some terrible secret about her. Which he might have told a partner."

I let him think about that for a moment—Billy, who loved Mrs Hudson as much as I did. "If his partner knew that Samuel had failed, we were all vulnerable. But if Samuel just vanished, along with me, it would at least confuse matters for a few days. Long enough that we could set a trap for a second attempt at the passbook or letter or what-have-you."

"Which we could have done," Holmes remarked, "were it not for the helpfulness of the police."

"I didn't even know if Samuel had come alone, or if there were companions watching the place. I knew they wouldn't be able to see his motorcar, where he'd left it—not without me being able to see them. I thought that if I motored off with him, it would at least get him off the premises and away from Mrs Hudson, so we could decide what to do with him. But I also thought that if he did have companions in the area, and they spotted his car driving away, they might follow."

The two men raised identical eyebrows.

"I was armed, remember. With his gun. And I thought I could lead them for some distance before I tried to lose them. By that time, Mrs Hudson would have got home. I knew the first thing she would do would be to telephone the police. They and Patrick would stay with her until you arrived and deciphered my message."

The best-laid plans.

"In fact," Holmes said, "her first call was to Billy."

"Really? Ah, to have him locate you—I saw the message in the agony column. My own message demanding that the Beekeeper be in touch with his brother will appear in today's papers."

"Why on earth didn't you telephone me?" Billy asked.

"I did, twice. The first time you were out, the second time you had gone to Sussex, and I wasn't sure I wanted to leave a message with your secretary. But if you all thought I was dead, shouldn't one of *you* have 'phoned *here*? God knows Mycroft wanted me to 'phone you." I'd never have managed to keep my brother-in-law from interfering if he hadn't been so preoccupied with the Honours list.

"Had you gone missing in Paris or Macau, yes," Holmes said—and it was true, Mycroft's sources of information were strongest when it came to international affairs. "But Mycroft has been looking a bit . . . stretched. I thought that adding a burden about which he could do nothing would benefit no one. At any rate, it was only a few hours later that Billy provided me with a file on Samuel Hudson. I did not feel that Mycroft could improve on it."

I had not been talking about using Mycroft, but about telling him— still, I let it go for the time.

Billy started to ask another question. "So where's—"

But Holmes spoke over him. "Speaking of Mrs Hudson, I did promise to let her know you were safe. Billy, if you don't get home to your wife, she'll never permit you to come to Sussex again. I'll ring you later in the day when Russell and I have made our decisions."

Billy did not care for being dismissed. I could see him consider a pro-test, but as he watched Holmes go to the telephone and begin the busi-ness of putting a call through to Sussex, he subsided—not happily, but with a lifetime of experience.

Still: he turned to me. "She's spent three very frightened days."

"I imagine. I'm sorry."

"Tell her that."

"I will."

He cast a dark glance at Holmes, who was patiently arguing with the exchange, and picked up his hat.

I half expected Holmes to ring off the instant Billy left. Instead, he let the call go through, and said quite clearly, "Mrs Hudson, I shall be stay-ing in London for some days, with friends. Yes, friends. I do have them, you know. No, I don't know when I'll be back. Give my greetings to Lestrade." Abruptly, he returned the earpiece to its stand.

I was surprised. "That was an odd sort of conversation, even from you."

"A tapping of the telephone line, Russell. The police hope for a ransom demand. Mrs Hudson and I agreed on the code word 'friends.'"

Holmes had code words with Mrs Hudson? Well, at least that made for one tiny concern off my mind: Mrs Hudson could rest easy now.

Holmes placed his hands lightly on my shoulders. "It was not murder, you know."

He felt my shudder. "Yes, it was."

"Where is the body?"

"Mycroft had someone come for it, and the car. He said they would make it look like an accident, with a fire. He also told me that Hudson bought the thing just last week. He paid cash."

"I was not sure that you would bring the problem to Mycroft," he said. "You have not been terribly fond of my brother, in recent months."

"Even if there hadn't been a threat lying over Mrs Hudson, I couldn't let her walk in and find that. And I haven't changed my mind about Mycroft. He has too much power. But in the end, who else did I have?"

"That may, in fact, be the entire point of Mycroft Holmes. In any event, it was the right decision. You could not have anticipated the problems."

He drew me into a quick embrace, then turned towards the sitting room, grumbling as he went. "I have to say, Russell, haematology has proved a most irritating science, woefully slow to develop past a crude analysis of evidence."

It was his way of apologising, for his own perceived failure to summon a miracle. "Still, once you saw the photographs, you knew. Why did it take Lestrade so long to get them to you?"

"Ah. Well. That was not entirely his fault. More coffee?"

Holmes poured from the dregs of the pot. I arranged a pillow beneath my aching arm.

"Were you away?"

"In Hampshire," he replied. "With Billy."

"Hampshire? What was so urgent down there?"

"I needed confirmation of an identity."

"Holmes, don't make me pull teeth. Just tell me."

"It has to do with the *Gloria Scott* case."

"Who is she?"

"It, not she. A ship that went down following a mutiny, six years before I was born."

"Oh yes, I remember now. You had a friend. Talbert?"

"Trevor."

"That's right. His father was being blackmailed by a man named . . ." I stopped—and not because I could not recall the villain's name.

He nodded. "Hudson."

"Do you mean to say, *that* Hudson has something to do with this?"

"I am afraid so."

"What?"

"I can't tell you that."

"Why on earth not?" I knew more state secrets than half the men in the House of Lords: what could possibly be worse here?

"A promise made."

"A promise involving Mrs Hudson, who used to be called Clarissa, who had a son that the whole world assumed belonged to her sister? A son with clear criminal tendencies, who was related to a blackmailer, and who came to England to get something from his mother?"

Holmes did not comment.

"The *Gloria Scott* was one of your first cases," I continued. "I knew it was no coincidence that you came to rent rooms from her on Baker Street. I'm now suspecting that I didn't guess the half of it."

He cocked his head. "Are you saying that you knew Mrs Hudson was . . . not all that she appeared?"

"I've known that forever, more or less."

"How?"

"Simple mathematics. Dr Watson's readership might believe that the names are but an amusing coincidence, but what are the odds that two unrelated people, both of whom had a great impact on your personal history, should bear the same surname? There was another Hudson, too."

"Morse, who owned a statue shop. A distant cousin."

"Also," I admitted, "I searched her rooms." He blinked; I laughed. "I know, not a thing one does to one's housekeeper, but the first time I came back from Oxford, during the Christmas holidays, I noticed that her accent had slipped somewhat. She regained it quickly, but I started to reflect on some other behaviour of hers that didn't entirely fit with what I knew of her—what I *thought* I knew of her. You apparently had not noticed—certainly you'd never given me any indication that she might be other than she appeared. I had to be certain. That you did not have a traitor in your midst, I mean. So one day when you both were away, I conducted a search."

"You, were protecting me?" The look on his face was most peculiar.

"I suppose I was. She has a pistol, you know? A tiny little thing, but with bullets."

"Does she, now?" It did not seem to come as a surprise to him. He fiddled with his pipe, taken up with the image of seventeen-year-old Mary Russell, protecting an experienced grey-haired detective from his potentially homicidal housekeeper. "And what," he asked eventually, "did your search tell you? Apart from the gun?"

"That she had secrets, but nothing that seemed ominous. One thing was interesting: a birth certificate for a boy, with her as the mother, and no father's name. Nor was there a marriage license among her papers."

He picked up his pipe, and busied himself with its bowl.

"Since then, I've been aware that when letters came from Australia, they spoke of her nephew, but gave news of her son.

"So, Holmes, tell me: who is Samuel Hudson's father?"

His tobacco was giving him difficulties. "Holmes?" I said sharply.

He shook out the match and dropped it into the laden bowl. "I met Clarissa Hudson in the autumn of 1879, when Samuel was an infant. A year later, she returned from Australia without him. Three months after that, in January, 1881, Watson and I took rooms in her house. Outside of that," he said, "I made her a promise. That so long as her past remained behind her, I would make no further enquiries into her life, pursue no more investigation into any crimes and misdemeanours she might have committed. From that day, her slate was clean. I gave her my word," he reiterated.

"For forty-five years?"

"An excellent mental exercise, always to be upon one's guard."

"Always?" I exclaimed.

His grey eyes squinted at me through the smoke.

"And has that past remained behind her?" I asked. "Doesn't her son sticking a gun in my face call for a re-evaluation?"

"If she brought him deliberately to our doorstep, perhaps. Do you think that to be the case?"

"It could be argued that his presence alone was a statement, but no, he said nothing that directly suggested she knew he was coming. And," I added as a memory hit me, "the bonnet of the car wasn't hot. It hadn't come far."

"He'd been waiting for her to leave the house?"

"It's possible. He may have been at least roughly aware of her habits, and knew that she always goes to market on Wednesday. Years and years of letters, they must have contained a lot of casual information such as that."

"One must also consider Samuel's words, that you would 'do.' If she was his primary target, she was hardly a willing accomplice. It leaves my promise intact."

That did not mean *I* could not ask Mrs Hudson many pointed questions about her past.

And what a pleasant conversation that was going to be.

CHAPTER THIRTY-SIX

"**S**o if we're not off to, er, interrogate Mrs Hudson," I said, "where do you propose we begin?"

"Your arm requires rest."

I surreptitiously eased my elbow from its supporting pillow while glaring at my husband. "Holmes, I have been lounging about here for three days listening to Mycroft discuss whether or not the chairman of the electricity commission should be made a Knight Grand Cross or a Knight Commander, whether or not the Minister Plenipotentiary to His Majesty the Shah of Persia has served long enough for his KC, and whether a youthful indiscretion should keep the retiring head park-keeper at Holyrood from an OBE. If I have to stay here any longer, I shall vote Socialist in the next general election."

"We cannot have that. Very well, I propose to pay a visit to the hotel room of Mr Samuel Hudson."

"Good plan. Any idea where we might find it?" My heart sank a bit at the task: how many thousand hotels were there in London, anyway?

"A relatively specific idea, as it happens," he replied. "Mr Mudd located a guest by the name in an hotel near Paddington."

"He hasn't searched it?"

"He did not have the time before coming to Sussex."

I stood up. "With luck, they won't have cleaned the rooms yet. Let me just dress and run a comb through my hair."

But when we got downstairs, Mycroft's doorman greeted us with a tip of the head towards the street. "You have a friend."

Billy's car stood directly in front of the door. As we emerged, the legs that were stretched across the seat drew back. His head appeared at the window.

"Offer you two a ride?"

A lesser man than William Mudd would have gone straight to Hudson's hotel, that he might greet Holmes with a fait accomplis of evidence in hand. Billy just craned his neck up at us with an expectant look on his face. Accepting defeat, Holmes opened the front door for me, then climbed into the back.

"You'll want to see Hudson's rooms, I'd guess," Billy said.

"Billy, you've done enough," Holmes said.

The swarthy driver put his elbow on the seat back and met Holmes' eyes. "This is Mrs Hudson we're talking about. There are no other jobs on my books until she's in the clear."

When Holmes did not object further, Billy turned to reach for the starter—but before the motor ground into life, Holmes opened his door. "You two search Samuel's rooms. I shall meet you back here this afternoon." He stepped briskly out onto the pavement, and was already moving off when I got my own door open far enough to call at his back.

"Wait," I said. "Where are you going?" With armed men in the picture, it did not seem an unreasonable question—but he said something I only half heard, then waved a hand and was gone in the morning crowds.

"You think he knew I was still down here?" Billy asked as I shut my door again.

"Are you asking if Holmes deliberately planned this, what—division of labour?"

"I'm wondering if he's off to put his hand somewhere he doesn't want ours."

"He never looked out of Mycroft's window, after you left the apartment. Whether or not he noticed the lack of an engine starting up, I couldn't say."

"Want to go after him?"

The question was slightly moot, since Holmes was nowhere in sight. "No, let's go look at Samuel's room before some maid cleans everything away."

Billy pushed the starter button. "What did Mr Holmes say? When you asked where he was going?"

"It sounded like he was going to see a bishop, but I can't have heard him right."

Billy went still. When I looked over, his face was unreadable.

"What?" I demanded.

Slowly, he slipped the car into gear.

"Billy, what does a bishop have to do with anything?"

"Not *a* bishop," he said at last. "*The* Bishop. An old lowlife with more sins to his name than Lucifer."

"Oh, right. I've heard of him. Not for a while, though."

"He used to be a power in London, like his father before him. Inherited the position, you might say. The father and Mrs Hudson had an arrangement, when I was young."

I gaped at him: was he suggesting that the man was Samuel's father? "Mrs Hudson and an aged villain were . . . friends?"

"No!" he said, after he'd nearly ripped the stairway from an omnibus. "No, those two were never 'friends.'"

"What, then?"

"Business partners? Though that'd be stretching it."

"When was—"

"That's all I have to say on the matter."

"Oh, Lord, not you, too?" I was going to have to convince the Save Mrs Hudson League to accept my application for membership. "Can you at least tell me: Samuel Hudson is actually her son, rather than her nephew, correct?"

He nodded.

"Why did he think she'd killed someone?"

He took a long time to reply, and even then, it was no more answer than Holmes had given me. "Tell you the truth," he said, "I wouldn't know where to begin."

He parked down the street from an hotel of the sort favoured by commercial travellers, cheap but clean. As if to confirm my judgment, a man tugged to one side by a weighty sample case came down its front steps and made in the direction of the railway station.

"Do you know Samuel's room number?"

"No, just that he was here, and he's paid up till Monday."

"Good," I said. "Then there's a chance they haven't cleared out his things."

The woman at the desk looked as if she'd been up all night. On impulse, as we crossed the linoleum floor of the lobby, I tucked my arm through Billy's and murmured, "Follow my lead."

At the desk, I leant into my startled companion and fluttered my eyes at the raddled female with her elbows on the stained wood, asking in a tiny voice if she had any rooms that were ready to let out. I had to repeat it twice in progressively louder tones, then admit that my . . . *husband* and I would only require it for the week-end. At this point, two men in shiny suits came out of the breakfast room and stood in the lobby talking loudly about the difficulties involved in hauling about wallpaper samples. I gestured the woman towards the desk's far end to explain that we would not require cleaning services in the morning, that we would be gone by Sunday evening, and that our suitcases had inexplicably failed to arrive. She cast a knowing look down the desk at Billy, who was making a desperate attempt at nonchalance by glancing through the pages of the ledger. The giggle she loosed brought an interesting cast to his dark skin: a blush.

She and I returned to our original places across the desk from one another, and watched Billy sign the ledger: Mr and Mrs Smith.

She pushed the key across the desk and accepted Billy's money. With chins raised and cheeks warm, we walked arm in arm up the stairs.

"Room 307," Billy muttered. "He checked in on the fourth."

"Isn't it nice when hotels are thorough?" I murmured back. Not all hotels were thoughtful enough to note the guest's room number in their book.

The moment we were out of sight, we hastily drew apart, to walk down opposite sides of the corridor to our room. Billy clattered the key into the lock of room 204, opened the door wide, and slammed it shut. We then turned back on silent feet and continued up the next flight of stairs to room 307.

"Shall I?" he asked, gesturing at the door.

"You'll be faster," I told him. I could manage, with my arm, but it was sore.

He laid out a set of pick-locks somewhat more elaborate than my own. I took up a position that would hide the tools if some commercial traveller happened down the hallway, waiting in silence until the lock gave way. He gathered his tools, inviting me to step inside.

I hesitated, although I could not have said why. Perhaps I feared the cloying odour of his hair oil, that it might stir memories: the gun, that blood, those sounds . . .

But the air smelt only of cleaning fluid, cigarettes, and bacon from the kitchen downstairs. I let Billy shut the door, and we looked around us.

The bed had been made and the spatter from his shaving brush cleaned from the washbasin, but his possessions remained. Some of them, at any rate. There were Australian labels on the shaving soap and underpants, blond hair in the hair-brush.

"He didn't intend to be gone for more than the day," I commented, and opened the next drawer.

The drawers held nothing of importance.

"What did he have on him?" Billy asked.

"A photograph, some money. Not much more."

"Passport? Cheque-book?"

I put my hand into my pocket, and pulled out the ring of keys My-croft had handed me, after his man had returned from . . . what he had done. The car key was gone, of course—one didn't want the police to wonder why a burnt-out hulk lacked its means of ignition. Three keys remained.

We looked around us at the room's complete lack of locks, then embarked on a more thorough search: stripping the bed, overturning the mattress, prodding the pillows, taking out the drawers to check beneath them, seeing if the bed rails had hidden compartments, prising at the suitcase for false sides.

All we found was a single unused bullet, pushed into the corner of his sponge-bag.

I took out the keys again. One was a house key that had been manufactured in Australia. One bore the name of a brand of padlocks. The third key was small. I thought about the man we had seen leaving with a sample case. "Would a place like this have its own secure storage area?"

"We'd have to come back when that woman has gone off her shift," he pointed out. "I can't very well pretend that I'm a salesman, now."

"She could be here all day. We'll have to try something else."

We went back down to room 204, where an argument soon began, building so loud it was audible at the desk. When the door crashed open and the two combatants spilled out into the hallway, few residents could have been unaware of the noise. I stormed down the stairs, hat awry, hair flying, eyes red and swollen, my voice a shriek of almost unintelligible words.

"—don't know *what* you were thinking, I *told* you I'd come because I *loved* you and now you say you're not so sure, you want to *wait*—oh, how *could* you, you *beast*? I hate you, you—oh, *why* didn't I listen to Mother, she *warned* me, she took one look and she just *knew* that—"

And on, in that vein. I staggered blindly across the lobby with Billy at my back, weeping and agonising at him. Every male in the place stared in horror; the female staff watched in glee.

I came to a halt between the end of the desk and the door to the breakfast room. There I sank to my knees and cried out like a penitent in Rome.

Such was the uproar that no one noticed Billy's absence. I watched through my fingers until I saw a pair of familiar boots through the forest of suited knees, making for the door. With a final exclamation, I pulled myself upright on the arms of the two nearest men, settled my cloche, and thanked them with as much dignity as I could pull together.

Billy had the car moving before my door was fully shut.

I retrieved the metal box from the floor, and fitted in the key. Inside lay a trove of papers and letters.

Billy made a noise, and then he was laughing, pounding a fist against the wheel. "You—I got to say, Miss Russell, you're good. As good as—"

When he did not finish the sentence, I prompted him. "Yes?"

"As good as the best actress I've ever known."

Chapter Thirty-seven

Sherlock Holmes stepped away from wife, friend, and brother, heading east towards the underbelly of London. His knowledge of London was intimate, the foundations of soil and paving stone, accent and air quality laid down when Victoria was on the throne. His passage through its streets and alleys had once been as smooth as a tongue through teeth, but the past twenty years had seen a century's worth of change: what the Great War had not demolished, the massive growth of the city threatened to topple.

The past three days threatened the same to him.

Watson had once accused him of coldness, claiming that Holmes regarded any strong emotion as a distraction, akin to grit in a sensitive instrument. It was true, to an extent: he was uncomfortable around anger, terror, love, hatred—distractions and grit, one and all.

And yet, Watson's remark had been written before the doctor knew him well. True, rage could derail the mental processes, but Holmes had also found it a boundless source of energy, just as hate made for a powerful means of focussing the mind. And love? Love was the thing that kept a person going past exhaustion, beyond reason, after hope was at its end.

Grit, yes—but then, grit was what one used to hone steel.

Still, for three days he'd been sprinting flat-out with the hounds of hell behind him, and extricating himself from that state took a deliberate effort. With his immediate concerns laid to rest—Russell alive, Mrs Hudson safe—his next actions would require every bit of cold purpose he could summon, a mental shift best supported by physical effort. The mind was, after all, a machine, and even the one belonging to Sherlock Holmes had moving parts.

So, he would move. He would walk to Whitechapel instead of storming across Town on wheels. He would take his time, each crack of his boot-heels like a hammer on sheet-metal, rendering it smooth and hard. Each mile would pound composure into his nerves; each minute would harden his purpose.

Pall Mall; Charing Cross; Old Scotland Yard; the Embankment. He'd been seventeen the year he and Mycroft watched the bedevilled and ill-named Cleopatra's Needle rise between its supports—and fifty-six when a German bomb nearly flattened it. A curve came; a bridge. Here was the spot where John Openshaw was thrown into the Thames, back in 1887. That street marked the western boundary of the Great Fire. Up this road, Irene Adler's husband had lodgings. Over the long-buried River Fleet, and on.

Near the Billingsgate market (a stone's throw from Neville St Clair's favourite opium den) the incongruous odour of bacon teased the fishy air. Across the river lay the boatyard where the Aurora . . . but Holmes' steps slowed. Bacon? He was not hungry, nor thirsty, but he was willing to eat and drink for the sheer normality of the act—just as he would walk despite his hurry and, once at his destination, he would talk instead of launching straight into bloodshed.

The chop-house served porters and fishmongers from Billingsgate, substantial men with substantial appetites. Holmes ate, paid, and left, then continued along the river to the Sugar Quay. There he circled the

Tower—armoury, treasury, prison, symbol, nine hundred years of London's darkest history. At the beginning of the Ratcliffe Highway, along which two families had been slaughtered half a century before his birth, he spotted a newsagent.

Since his conversation with Billy amongst the hives, the time after Reichenbach had been on his mind. Not that Billy—or Mrs Hudson—had voiced any complaint about his long and unexplained absence, ever. Nonetheless, he'd been aware of their unspoken reproach, that he'd left them to wonder. Yes, he'd had his reasons to disappear, but to do so a second time would be unforgiveable.

Worse, he would not have Russell living with a wound forever raw.

He knew his concern was unjustified. Nonetheless, he stepped into the newsagent's to purchase a piece of stationery and envelope, to be handed a decorative card dating to the late Queen's reign. He quirked an eyebrow at its profusion of flowers, imagining his brother's reaction, and asked to borrow a pencil.

To the bearer: delivery of this card to Mycroft Holmes at the Diogenes Club, Pall Mall, London, will bring a reward of five pounds sterling.

—

Mycroft: I've gone to see The Bishop. If I fail to return

Here, his pencil faltered. *If I fail to return*—then what? Then I have failed.

Neither he nor Mycroft was in the habit of superfluity—far less, Russell. So he finished the sentence:

If I fail to return, I am sorry, to you all.

SH

He walked back to the desk. "Have you glue?" The man reached down and pulled out a pot, watching expressionless while Holmes wrestled it open and applied the brush. He pressed down the flap, then held the sealed envelope out to the newsagent. "Would you care to earn two pounds?"

The man eyed the card.

"I shall return by midday and retrieve this from you. If it is unopened, I will pay you two pounds for it. If one o'clock comes and I have not appeared, there is still money to be had. Simply open it and do what the card says."

The man turned to prop the envelope on the shelf behind his head. Holmes nodded and left.

Would that all life's transactions could be so seamless.

If London's buildings and roads had changed since the days of his youth, even more so had the architecture of crime. Walking through London forty years ago, he could have named every dip, broadsman, and palmer who went by—along with the mobsman who ran him and the beak who'd last sent him down.

It looked like a cleaner city now. The Ripper killings, that bloody spasm that took place seven years after he'd moved into Baker Street, would be difficult today under London's electric glare—though by no means impossible. And the average citizen was less likely to climb off an omnibus with empty pockets or wake up in an alley with a bloodied head—but it still happened. The dirt remained; it had just got pushed into the corners.

This street was one of those corners.

Professor Moriarty was by no means London's first organising criminal, nor its last. He had been the most efficient, having never looked out from behind bars—or even come to the attention of Scotland Yard until one consulting detective had pointed him out. This claim could not be made by the man Holmes was going to see—nor by the man's father, who had first come up against the hard knuckles of the law when policing was done by Bow Street runners.

He'd had brains, the older Bishop had. He might have given Moriarty a run for his money if he'd been born into a different class or time, but by the time Moriarty was building his organisation, the senior Bishop was dead and his son was taking over. The son, whose hold on what the father had compiled was based more on brutality than on finesse.

The Bishop's son assumed command in the summer of 1880, shortly after an absurdly young Sherlock Holmes managed to scrape together full payment of the Hudsons' debt. This younger Bishop was an old man now, in his eighties, and with no fresh blood in the wings, the enterprise had become so outdated as to be Dickensian. In this modern era of permissive morals and ever-expanding technology, it had also shrunk considerably—but only in numbers. The organisation's age and decrease in scope had, if anything, intensified its filth and viciousness. This was a dilemma for Scotland Yard: it might be an advantage to have all the snakes gathered in one basket, but was it right to leave that source of venom crawling about?

The Yard chose to keep a watching brief on The Bishop, with the occasional hard slap when he showed signs of reaching out. Holmes had gone along with their decision—until now.

If The Bishop had made a move against him, Sherlock Holmes would have no choice but to stamp his heel on the adder's head.

The Bishop retained his offices in Whitechapel, instead of moving into the shiny business blocks favoured by London's new breed of crook. Holmes had not set eyes on the man in six years, had not spoken with him in ten, but he did not imagine the methods of obtaining an audience had changed much.

Calm without and within, Sherlock Holmes took a seat on the ornate little bench across the street from the incongruous marble façade, and got out his pipe. The interlude was both a means of presenting his calling-card—one did not walk hastily up to a house filled with armed men—and a final summons of composure. Had he arrived here before seeing the photograph of Russell's knife, at three o'clock this morning, he'd have gone for the man's throat, without hesitation.

Long ago, Sherlock Holmes had come before The Bishop with a promise: that any venture in certain directions—Mary Russell, Mrs Hudson—would bring reprisals both swift and deadly. A treaty had been agreed. Holmes was here to see if it had been breached, and if so, why.

Ten minutes later, soul composed and tobacco burned, he knocked the pipe's dottle to the ground and spoke to the man attempting to loom over him. "I see your boss still hires his Demanders for brawn rather than brain." Standing as the fellow was, one sharp jab from an old lady's parasol would have done him in.

Holmes strolled across the marvellously untrafficked street (not one car had passed since he arrived) and up the steps to The Bishop's palace. He stood aside to let the big man open the door like a servant, then continued across the ornate tiles towards the throne room.

There was in fact a throne, a massive gilt and red-velvet construction that the father had installed as a jest and the son had taken seriously. A rumour had made the rounds, back in the 'nineties, that an underling who dared to explain the joke was later found in the river. True or not, the story held all the key elements of this Bishop's rule: a lack of humour, a ruthless hand, and a devotion to gaudy things.

The throne was still there. The man who filled it was even more grossly enormous than he had been six years ago, if that was possible. Certainly, his number of chins had increased. How was it the man's heart continued to push blood through all that mass? Holmes wondered.

Being prepared for the setup, his arm had reached out to snag the guard's wrought-iron chair from the foyer, dragging it through the door and across the tiles with a long and satisfying screech. He stopped before the throne, where a century of supplicants and penitents had stood (including, he suspected, one Clarissa Hudson) and took out his handkerchief. When the seat was dusted, he folded the linen back into his pocket and sat, to all appearances oblivious of the others in the room.

He was gratified to see uneasiness on the old criminal's face, under his habitual look of jovial menace. "Why, Mr Sherlock 'Olmes, wha' a pleasant s'prise. Certainly kept your figger, 'aven't you? I s'pose you've come to arsk a favour?"

His acolytes chuckled. Holmes said merely: "Samuel Hudson."

The Bishop reclined back into his throne, sausage-like fingers laced across his bulging stomach. "'Udson. 'Udson. Now, there's a naim from the past. I do recall a luscious young—"

"No." The monosyllable snapped through the room like a whip-crack, giving The Bishop pause, although the presence of lackeys made it impossible for him to back down entirely.

"I also 'member 'er old man, with less affection. 'E trimmed the Gov'ner, Jimmy 'Udson did—trimmed 'im right close. An' when we welcomed him back, 'e turned aroun' an' 'e did it again."

"Both times, your father was repaid his loan, with interest," Holmes pointed out in a bored voice. "And if you are now going to lay your arrest as a lad at James Hudson's feet, we both know that was someone's poor choice of a lady's maid to let your gang in. Have we finished this pleasant stroll down memory's lanes? Because I have more interesting things to occupy me than a conversation with you. Now, about James Hudson's grandson."

One pudgy finger described circles on the worn-through gilt at the end of the throne's arm. The man then tipped his head to speak over his shoulder. "Hook it, lads. This gennlemun and me, we needs to talk."

"But boss, wha'—"

"Naouw!"

The feet shuffled out, the door shut. When The Bishop spoke again, his words had fewer glottal stops and more syllables.

"Grandson, eh? Seems ta me young Samuel's a shade closer to . . . our mootchual friend than a 'nephew.'"

"I don't believe it matters one way or the other. It's Samuel McKenna I'm trying to trace."

"Lost him, 'ave ye?"

"You knew he was coming to see me?"

"'E seemed bent in that d'rection."

"Did you send him?"

"I never sent no one. We got an agreement, you and me."

"And you've never gone back on it?"

"Never needed to yet."

Holmes searched the man's face, checked his hands and posture. When someone like The Bishop lied, it was usually blatant: why pretend, when you could just crush the person you were talking to, instead? Which meant the man was unpractised at earnest deception—and at the moment, he appeared sincere.

"You did not aim Samuel Hudson at my household?"

"Bugger me, man, I got enough problems on me 'ands wifout that. I take it the lad come to your door and raised a stink, then?"

The first part of the statement rang true; the second revealed a trace of slyness.

"You did not send him, but you knew he was coming to see me."

"Not you, mate. Your 'ousekeeper. C'mon, Mr 'Olmes," he urged with an uncomfortable laugh, "you can't think *I* sent him? 'E knew all about you."

"So why did he come *here*?"

"'Ere to Lonnun, or 'ere to me?"

"Both."

"You really *don't* know nuffin, do ya? Anyways, it's the same thing. 'E come about 'is granddad's money."

"What money?"

"Well, that's the intrestin' question, innit?" Again, the knowing look.

"Why did he think James Hudson had money?"

"Ah, see, Jim wrote a letter to 'is daughter—the one in Synney? Summat about borrowin' gelt off a shady lender. Which ain't a nice way to talk about the Gov'ner, but I guess Sammy asked some friends a' his about who'd a' been 'ere, back in them days, to lend a man money, and 'e come up wif first the Gov'ner, then me."

"James Hudson wrote to his daughter about borrowing money from your father? When?"

"Not long afore he disappeared. And it waren't in so many words, I don' think. But yeah, enough to lay one end of a tread 'ere. So old Sam 'Udson could put two an' two togevver and follow it to my front door."

This conversation was not going as Holmes had anticipated. He'd come prepared to rip the lies out of The Bishop, confronting the man with the treaty violations and letting him know that the wrath of the gods was about to descend. But if Samuel Hudson already knew about his mother, and if The Bishop had *not* been co-conspirator in the attempted abduction, or murder . . .

Holmes realised that he had been on the brink of that perennial trap: theorising in advance of one's data. He took a mental step back, and picked up the last hint The Bishop had given him.

"Why would Samuel Hudson come looking for money his grandfather had borrowed from you?"

But the pause had been enough to give The Bishop a sense of change from his opponent, a drawing-in of threat. He ventured a question of his own. "Look, I done nuffin 'ere but tell you wat you wanted t' know. How 'bout you answerin' one for me? When old Sam come to see you, what did 'e want?"

There was tension behind the feigned nonchalance, Holmes thought. What was this hideous old villain after? He proceeded with caution. "Why should he have wanted anything, apart from seeing his . . . aunt?"

"'E dint ask you nuffin? No casual conversation, like? About old cases and such like?"

"Which old case might that be?"

The Bishop seemed torn between a desire for information and a reluctance to reveal his interests. In the end, need won out. "The 'Udson one. Jimmy 'Udson's money."

Holmes did not have to pretend his incomprehension, although he expected The Bishop would take it as pretence. "You'll have to give me more than that before I can answer you."

The rolls of flesh convulsed in a brief expression of fury. Then the man sat forward on his throne, his voice soft, as if his men might have their ears to the wall. "Jim Hudson wasn't the only bastid to run out on me. I think you'll know the name Prendergast?"

Holmes' head came sharply up.

"*Prenderga*—" he began to exclaim.

"Sst!" The Bishop hissed, cutting him off with a hard glance at the door.

Holmes did not lower his voice. "You're interested in *that*? Good Lord. The money Jack Prendergast stole went down with the *Gloria Scott*, seventy years ago."

"You know that for sure, d'ya? You were there to see it?"

"I looked at it very closely, I assure you. In any event, there were but a small handful of survivors. Did any of them behave as if they had a quarter million pounds to their name?"

"No. But they wouldn't of if they was smart."

Sherlock Holmes had to concede the point: the best way—the only way—to hide a fortune is to act as if it did not exist. He would not have expected the gross old man on the gilt throne to understand that. Still, it was hardly relevant here.

"The ship went down," he said. "There was nothing but the ship's boat with a few survivors."

"Prendergast made 'is money nice and portable, like."

"So?"

The grotesque expression that passed over the rolls of fat, Holmes decided after a moment, had been a wink.

"Am I to understand that you believe your father was linked to Jack Prendergast in some way? Bank fraud was not exactly The Bishop's métier." Prendergast's financial jiggery-pokery had been both extremely clever and set amongst the highest levels of the banking industry: what had either to do with an East End crime boss?

"Right you are," the old man's son replied. "Bit above the Gov'ner's station, like. But even bankers got what you might call outside interests. Any road, Prendergast knew the Gov'ner. The two of 'em talked in this very room. I was a kid—couldn't'a been more'n twelve—but it'd be around the time the job was runnin'. I 'member the argy-bargy when he got hisself nicked. Prendergast was here," he repeated firmly, emphasising the fact with a pronunciation of the *h*.

"Very well. But why do you think your father had anything to do with the fraud?"

"He dint. Like you said, not his mettyer. But once the money was in Prendergast's hands, what'd he do with it? And the Gov'ner knowed *somefing*, the old bastid, just on the fringes of the action, like. I dunno—'e mighta gave Prendergast some bright ideas, made some introductions, anyfing. But whatever, I know 'e hant a clue how bloody *big* the thing was until Prendergast got nicked. Jeez Mary, I thought the old man's heart was gonna stop then and there. An' all through the trial and after Prendergast was lagged off Down Under, the Gov'ner kept 'is ear to the ground. An' never stopped, even after that boat went down.

"'E allus swore that Prendergast 'ad put all that money into *some* form that'd travel light—passbook, bank notes, that kinda thing. Diamonds, maybe. Used ta talk about how the cove dint necess'rily have it on the boat with 'im—could of left it to be posted to him Down Under. And even if 'e did have it, summat like that could float, couldn't it? Dint need nuffin but a sharp eye to spot 'em and a quick hand to pluck 'em out the wreckage. Yes, Mr 'Olmes, the Gov'ner went to 'is grave believin' that Prendergast money was out there somewhere.

"And me? Well, I'm a sensible man. All them years and no breath of it, I more or less decided, like you, that it's sunk to the bottom of the briny, waitin' for some fella with one a them sub-marine boats ta go after it. And then be damned if Mr Sam 'Udson don't walk up, bold as brass, to say how his granddad'd got a serious amount of money, and did I have any idea where it might be?"

"I met James Hudson twenty-four years after the *Gloria Scott* went down," Holmes said carefully. "He had no money at all."

"Then 'e found it just after, 'cause 'cording to Samuel, 'is letter said 'e 'ad a ruddy fortune droppin' out of the sky. All 'e had to do was get back Down Under to cash it in."

Over the course of The Bishop's peroration, Sherlock Holmes had begun to feel decidedly ill at ease. He'd come here unarmed and unafraid, trusting in the fat old villain's self-interest to ensure that he would walk out again. But this was another matter entirely. This was compulsion, fantasy—madness. Like walking into a room and having it erupt into flames.

The obsession this Bishop had inherited—rendered dormant by the years—had been galvanised by the arrival of Samuel Hudson. The fat hands gripping the throne arms, those piggy eyes gleaming with passion: mania was building around him like an electric charge. Hair rose on Holmes' scalp.

Think, he commanded his brain: rage, hate, love—and fear. Strong emotions to stimulate the adrenal glands, weapons in the hand of a thoughtful man, a delusion in the mind of a criminal.

Think! The Bishop had found a kindred soul in Samuel Hudson, criminal to criminal. Had he dangled that mind-warping sum in front of the Australian, sparking the greed in both of them, and sent Hudson to Sussex in search of it?

Speak—now! "You think Prendergast converted his stolen fortune into a bank passbook or the like. Is that what Samuel Hudson came to me for?"

"'E dint tell you?"

"Our conversation was . . . limited."

"Sammy knew there was money, just not 'ow much, or where it come from. Once I told him what he'd be lookin' for, 'e seemed ta think 'e knew where it was—but I told 'im it wouldn't be enough. That wifout what I knew, 'e'd be barking up a tree. 'E'll be back, when 'e finds I'm right."

"So what did he not know?"

"Sonefing the Gov'ner figgered out."

"And what was that?"

But there, The Bishop drew the line. "I ain't gonna tell you that. If I did—" The old man stopped abruptly, eyes narrowing to slits. Holmes felt coldness stir within, and fought to keep it from his face. "Did Sammy tell you? 'Is part of the puzzle, I mean?"

The cold seemed to spread. "I take it Mr Hudson did not share his heart fully with you, either?"

"'E let me know 'e was hidin' somethin', just like I let 'im know I had somethin' up m'own sleeve. Did 'e tell *you* what it was? Maybe your conversation weren't really 'limited.' Maybe you and 'im 'ad a nice long talk, and maybe you and 'im thought, we can cut The Bishop out. All we gotta do is get the old man to let slip what 'e knows."

If The Bishop believed for one instant that Sherlock Holmes could point him towards the hidden treasure he had pined over for seventy years, he'd call his men in and take this amateur detective to pieces, heedless of the storm that Holmes' death would bring down. Lust of that degree was a thing Sherlock Holmes had seen often enough to recognise it, to fear it—and to know that a show of fear was what set it off.

So he locked his dread deep below the surface and crossed his legs in a display of negligence, one foot bouncing a little to illustrate the meditative process.

"You say you may have a key piece of this puzzle?" he asked at last.

The Bishop saw only a sort of scholarly interest. Slowly, he nodded, causing the chins to wobble.

"One you think Samuel Hudson will need if he is to lay hands on that two hundred fifty thousand pounds?"

Even within the folds of skin, Holmes could see The Bishop's pupils flare at the sum. "Pretty sure," he said.

"Can you just tell me—not the thing itself, but what it concerns?"

If the answer was "Clarissa Hudson," The Bishop was a dead man. But it was not.

"I know 'oo Samuel's father is."

Holmes blinked. "And knowing that might lead Samuel to the money?"

"Combined with what 'e has, I'd guess so."

"And did you tell him what it is that you know?"

"I did not."

Two criminals, each with incomplete knowledge, both wishing to get the other's information while leading him away from the goal.

Time for a risk—calculated, yes, but a risk nonetheless. Holmes put on a look of reluctant agreement, and asked, "I suppose that if the monies were found, and returned to their original investors, you would like a commission? A generous percentage, of course, by way of reward?"

The Bishop came very close to explosion, at the thought of losing what he saw as his money. But Holmes' businesslike attitude—and the word "generous"—delayed him long enough to let thought catch up with emotion: if *Sherlock Holmes* was treating this dream seriously . . .

And with thought came a voice of rationality. No one in London—certainly no London criminal—would believe that Holmes could be tempted by money, even a quarter million pounds of the stuff. Still, if the great Sherlock Holmes was offering to aid in the recovery of £250,000—The Bishop's face cleared.

"The blokes who owned it'll be long dead," he pointed out.

"Their heirs, then," Holmes said as if in agreement. "I'm sure that would be quite satisfactory. Very well. I agree to see if I can locate Mr Hudson, and act to broker whatever clues you and he might be able to put together to retrieve the Prendergast fortune. Perhaps he'll show up in Sussex. Again."

He rose, as if agreement had been reached. The Bishop wavered: letting go of Holmes had to be a mistake, but . . . *a quarter million pounds.* Even a slice of that was better than what he had now. He waved a hand with a gesture worthy of kings.

But Holmes did not breathe fully until the Radcliffe Highway was three turns behind him.

The Bishop might know who Samuel's father was. Did that possibility justify confronting Mrs Hudson with the question? Holmes was afraid that answer was yes.

Assuming the missing fortune was recovered: would The Bishop be satisfied with a cut, however generous? Not for one minute.

Would they ever be faced with that problem? About that he felt even more certain: no. The money was a pipe-dream. Jack Prendergast's cleverly defrauded fortune lay scattered across the sea bed, somewhere off the African coast. Prendergast's treasure would no doubt take on mythic weight over time, joining the fountain of youth, Prester John's kingdom, the Holy Grail, and the El Dorado gold.

So distracted was Holmes, he nearly forgot to retrieve his flowery call for help from the newsagent's shelf.

CHAPTER THIRTY-EIGHT

Because Mycroft was not in his flat that day, I could be. According to him, the Palace breakfast often merged with luncheon. After that was finished, he would make his formal handing-over of approved names to the printing offices of the *London Gazette*. And following that, with many long days behind him and several hours of booze-laced breakfast, lunch, and ritual under his belt, he planned to retire to the Diogenes Club, whose silent and soporific arms rarely let him go much before midnight.

The *London Gazette* had been *the* journal of record for government matters since 1665 (beginning in Oxford, by the way, with plague gripping London and the court of Charles II chary about contaminated reading matter). "Published by Authority," its header declared, and it took that responsibility very seriously indeed. If it was in the *Gazette*, it had better be both true and accurate, or heads would roll. Mycroft's physical presence at the ritual was a sign of its importance.

It had also been the reason behind the unwonted turmoil of his normally placid home during this past week: maddening discussions of honours list minutiae, conducted both in person with an endless series of visitors and over telephone connexions of varying degrees of clarity. The rumble of voices and ring of the bell had been nearly constant, and wore on my already raw nerves. Yet I was also grateful for his preoccupation: were it not for the birthday honours, I might have been forced into conversation, and thus a confrontation over the ethical use of power for which I did not feel ready.

At any rate, Mycroft's absence meant that Billy and I were free to set up our studies upon his dining table, our metal box making stark contrast to the table's usual sumptuous burden.

Some of the box's contents were expected: passport, cheque-book, a notebook with addresses, most of them Australian. I set that aside for the moment, and picked up the letters.

James Hudson—our Mrs Hudson's father—had been a surprisingly dedicated if marginally literate correspondent, first to his wife and later to his daughter Alicia. There were only a dozen letters here, but internal references made it clear that considerably more had filled the long gaps between these—either discarded or left behind in Australia. I sorted them by date and started reading. In minutes, Billy's forehead was resting on the table. When the snoring began, I shook him awake and ordered him home.

He blinked rapidly and scrubbed at his face, which, even with his slow-growing beard, showed bristle. "I'll just kip on the sofa."

"Billy, go home. Remind your wife who you are." I broke into the inevitable protest to address his true concern. "I give you my word, I'll telephone to you the very instant Holmes proposes to hare off to some corner of the globe."

He studied my face for deception, but in fact, I had already decided that whatever was going on here, William Mudd seemed to have some place in it. Too, between my sore arm and Holmes' years, having another hearty set of muscles might not be a bad idea.

He nodded and yawned simultaneously, nearly causing himself damage, and retrieved his coat from the back of the chair. He did pause at the door. "You swear you'll ring me?"

"Unless there's a gun to my head, I shall call."

Alone, at last, for the first time since Samuel Hudson had pulled into my drive on Wednesday morning. (Or did a car journey with a dead man count as "alone"?) I went for a quick search in Mycroft's library for the volume containing the *Gloria Scott* adventure, then arranged some pillows on his deep settee and settled in with Dr Watson's narrative, about a young man, a friendship, and the first stirring instincts of a detective.

When I had finished, I returned to the table and the Hudson letters.

James Hudson died long before I was born, so I only knew him through Dr Watson's story, and to a lesser extent, the eyes of Sherlock Holmes. Physically unsightly and morally repugnant, Hudson stood in my mind as an ageing mutineer-turned-blackmailer who had raised the ire of a fledgling detective. That Hudson might have had a life outside of those crimes and that detective seemed unimportant when compared to the direction Holmes' life had taken after—and, in part, because of—that meeting. I had, as I told Holmes, long known that our Mrs Hudson was in some way linked to the Hudson of the *Gloria Scott* case, but I had vaguely assumed that she had once been married, either to the villain or to his son.

She was instead the villain's daughter.

I had learned more about Mrs Hudson these past three days than in the previous ten years. I was also learning some uncomfortable truths about myself. Despite my affection and gratitude for this woman (once I'd satisfied myself, back in 1917, that any secrets she was hiding were no threat to Holmes), I never tried to find out more about her. As an individual, she was as much a part of my scenery as the sheep on the Downs and the basket chair in the sitting room.

I was astonished, and fascinated, and—yes—somewhat troubled by what I learned of Mrs Hudson, those days and the time that followed. But mostly, I was ashamed, that I had never even asked.

Many hours later, the key in Mycroft's door startled me from reverie. I shot a glance at the clock: ten after eleven. I'd intended to retreat to the guest room before now—but to my relief, it was the thinner of the brothers. "Hello, Holmes. I was wondering if I'd see you again today."

Holmes aimed his furled umbrella at the stand and dropped his hat on the small marble table, shrugging off his overcoat as he crossed the room.

"Been seeing your banker?" I asked. On a Saturday? The ebony suit he wore was not the one he'd started the day inside.

"*A* banker, certainly. I required a tutorial in the history of currency. Whose hand is that?" he asked with a glance at the paper on the table before me.

"James Hudson's."

He held the page up to the light—interested in the writing, rather than the words. With a grunt, he dropped it and went on into the flat. I gathered the letters and moved to the fire, adding some coal to the embers. Holmes returned wearing an old quilted smoking jacket in place of his City black. He poured a pair of brandies and handed me one.

One eyebrow went up at my eagerness. "Your arm is troubling you."

"It's just uncomfortable. What sorts of currency?"

"The tutorial was on the theory of money, not the practice. I needed to know how a man might carry £250,000 between his finger and his thumb."

"Two hundred fif—good God, Holmes," I sputtered. "Who has *that* kind of money?"

He had settled onto the chair to my right, red Morocco slippers propped on the low table. "That," he said, holding his glass up to admire the colour, "is an interesting question."

"This has to do with Samuel Hudson?"

"I cannot for the life of me believe in The Bishop's theory; however, there is no doubt that the man himself does, and that may be the only important factor."

"Explain, please."

"What do you remember of the *Gloria Scott*?"

"Only Dr Watson's account, and what you told me yesterday."

"As the story came to me, one of the convicts being transported was a man named Jack Prendergast, convicted of fraud. His partner on board, he told Trevor—my friend Victor's father—had enough money to buy the entire ship, 'right between my finger and thumb.' Now, whether that was the same as cash in a strong-box, or whether his accomplice was holding securities or the like for him, was never clear."

"But the ship blew up."

"That it did. The two convicts who later became Trevor and Beddoes had already been put into the ship's boat, along with a few sailors who drew the line at murder. After the powder barrels blew, they went back for survivors. They found only James Hudson among the wreckage. None of those convicts would have been in any position to have more than a few coins about their persons.

"And yet, one of the oldest and most vicious of criminals in London believes with all his black heart that Jack Prendergast's stolen treasure survived the destruction of the *Gloria Scott*."

"Is *that* what Samuel Hudson was after?"

"So it would appear."

"Why? I mean, why would he think ..." that it survived? That Mrs Hudson had it? That my abduction could lead him to it?

"Do any of those letters mention The Bishop, or a moneylender?" he asked.

"Not by name, though he does say he's in debt to what he calls an 'unofficial' moneylender."

"That might have been enough. Or the name could be in another letter—or even something he was told in conversation. In any event, some four days after Samuel Hudson came to London, he went to visit

The Bishop. At the time, he was aware that his grandfather may have possessed a certain amount of money, but he did not know how much or what had become of it."

"Well, the last of James Hudson's letters," I told him, "written in October, 1879, refers to a 'goodly stash' that will let them live in comfort, once he gets to Sydney."

"What day in October?" he asked sharply.

"The second. Why?"

"Interesting. What else—"

"No, you first. I take it this black-hearted villain of yours is The Bishop? Why does he think Samuel was looking for the Prendergast money?"

"Because he would be, if he were Samuel. And once he told Samuel exactly how much was involved, it brought our Australian friend to his side very quickly."

"I imagine it would. But why kidnap me? Did they think one of us knew something?"

I'd kept my tone casual, but Holmes' face went instantly dark. "Long ago, I let it be known that to touch you would be considered an act of war."

"I see." And I did. A criminal would have to be either mad or remarkably sure of himself to go against Holmes. Which was not to say that criminals were not both.

"The Bishop may have encouraged Samuel Hudson," he said. "However, I do not believe he was directly responsible for what Samuel Hudson did."

"So you didn't pull his head off?"

"I even made him an offer of assistance," he said.

"A *criminal*?"

"I gave him to understand that I would be assisting in his hunt for the missing Prendergast monies."

"You allied with a villain like The Bishop to protect *me*? Holmes, what were you thinking!"

"It was not entirely for your benefit," he conceded. "I also required a means of extricating myself from what looked to become a warm situation."

"Oh. Good—I mean, not good that he had a gun to your head, but I'm glad we haven't picked up a business partner."

"In fact," he said, "I searched for that money back in the 'eighties. Young as I was, I cannot believe I missed anything of importance."

Was that the sound of a case approaching—one that promised to be both long and frustrating? A hunt for sunken treasure, seventy years after the fact? "Perhaps you should tell me a little more."

I waited with growing apprehension as he filled his pipe and got it going. When he had stretched his dramatic pause to its end, he continued. "The survivors, as I said, were rescued by a ship bound for Australia. After a remarkably few years there, two of the convicts, under their new names Trevor and Beddoes, returned to England with fortunes in Australian gold. They bought houses, established themselves, built strong façades of respectability. Trevor married and had the son I later befriended at University. They all lived lives of happy comfort until Hudson came creeping out of the sea in 1879 with a threat of exposure.

"I cannot say I ever questioned the source of the Trevor estate. Striking it rich in the gold fields fit what I knew about my friend's father—as did the idea that, once his youthful adventures were over, he'd had the good sense to invest and nourish his money rather than fling it about on high living.

"Only later, after his death, did I learn that he had not *gone* to Australia, he had been transported there: a young banker convicted of using a client's money to repay a debt of honour, who was caught with his hand in the proverbial till before he could make good the funds. The revelation was something of a shock, certainly for my friend, but in the end it only confirmed my judgment of Trevor as an essentially prosaic individual, who was driven to the uncharacteristic hurly-burly of life in the gold field and who, once the episode was over, happily slipped back into his natural state.

"Nothing I learned then, either from the man himself or in the written account he left for his son, suggested that the money on which their estate rested was anything but honestly achieved. Well, honest apart from the crime that had banished him in the first place. The only thing that might have caught my attention was the brevity of his description concerning the life he and Beddoes led in Australia. Something along the lines of, 'We prospered, we travelled, we came back as rich colonials to England, where we bought country estates. For more than twenty years we have led peaceful and useful lives, and hoped that our past was forever buried . . .' However, I had noted when I met him that his hands betrayed a great deal of heavy digging in his past, and that too supported his claim of a time in the gold fields."

"'Claim'?" I asked.

He paused for a moment of meditative smoke-raising, then said, "It is a striking thing, Russell, how seldom one hears an original thought from a lifelong criminal. I suppose few of them have much leisure for reflection. However inadvertently, Mr Bishop has presented me with one, namely: what if those two men's fortunes originally left England in the possession of Jack Prendergast?"

"That's a lot of guinea coins to be bobbing around a sinking ship."

"Some two tons of gold," he agreed serenely. "Hence my session with the financial gentleman, to find a less-substantial alternative. The problem being that although gold may be melted down, traded for goods, or sold outright, other forms of transaction have traditionally been less anonymous. Until, that is, the Bank of England began to issue its modern printed notes, which say merely 'pay the bearer on demand' rather than requiring a cashier to write the name of the person to whom it was issued."

"And when did that anonymity begin?"

"In 1853. Precisely one year before clever Jack Prendergast defrauded his London merchants of a quarter million pounds."

"A suggestive coincidence." I sat with my drink, picturing the smoking wreckage of the *Gloria Scott:* bodies, spars, tangled lines and canvas . . . and over it all, a snow-flurry of bank notes, beckoning to the survivors? Hardly. "What denominations were those early notes?"

"They went up to £1,000, but in fact, any sum greater than a five would have attracted scrutiny. They all had serial numbers, of course, but if one intended to spend them outside of England, the smaller notes would have been relatively safe to use."

"Five-pound notes would mean fifty thousand pieces of paper to conceal. But in fifties, it could have fit into a Gladstone bag."

"A valise would not float on the surface for more than a few minutes," he objected.

"What if it were kept in a water-tight box—or, concealed in a hogshead! A barrel would float long enough for the ship's boat to row back—"

"Hoping for provisions, and finding money in the process," Holmes cut in.

"They could have divided the notes when they reached Sydney—oh, and James Hudson was one of the active mutineers, wasn't he? He'd stayed on board when the others were put off? They could well have refused to share the takings with him. Or gave him just enough to buy his silence."

Holmes nodded slowly. "When Trevor died, he left an estate that had been cleaned by twenty years of virtuous English life. Beddoes was a different kind of man—more Prendergast than Trevor. His crime was forgery, a far cry from Trevor's idiotic but essentially innocent attempt to patch together a mistake. Forgery requires malice aforethought."

I thought about a phrase I had seen in one of those letters, suggesting that James Hudson had learned something of great importance from "Trevor."

"Then again, what if it *wasn't* barrels of bank notes, and Trevor had nothing to do with it? What if Beddoes and Prendergast were—well, not partners, I guess, since he threw Beddoes off the ship, but say they had a kind of friendship? In Dr Watson's account, Prendergast goes around telling his fellow convicts that there's about to be a mutiny and encouraging them to join him. If he'd then told Beddoes what his treasure was—that thing he was holding 'between his finger and thumb'—and Beddoes told Trevor . . . Could James Hudson have learned about it from him all those years later?"

"After I confronted Beddoes in the autumn of 1879," Holmes mused, "he fled for America. For the sake of argument, say that Prendergast filled an anonymous trunk with notes or diamonds—anything compact—and left it in a London bank. Beddoes knew about it, and how to obtain access to it. When he came back from Australia, he retrieved some whenever he needed it. Then out of the blue, Hudson came to threaten him, with me on his heels. Beddoes did not dare travel to London for the rest of the trunk's contents. He might well have intended to return, once England cooled off for him, but the man died in a railway accident, some eighteen months later."

"Leaving a quarter million pounds sitting in some bank since 1855?"

"Since 1879, at least. By now, its value could be in the millions—or, it could be a stack of paper worth precisely nothing. The Bishop, however, is convinced both of its existence and its worth. He was an impressionable lad when Prendergast was arrested, and heard about the fraud—all of London was talking about it, not just the criminals. For seventy years, the man has lived with the itch of all that money lying in the dark, waiting for him to find it—*him*, where his father could not."

I looked over at his tone of voice. "Why are you smiling?"

"Because it would make for a nice irony if it turned out that all the time, James Hudson had a key piece of information that would have given the old man all that money."

"Did James Hudson and The Bishop know each other?"

"One might say that."

I waited. Then: "Is this part of the story you're not going to tell me?"

"A part that I shall no doubt tell you someday, but not tonight."

"All right, then let me ask this: did your financial man have any suggestions for how to render a fortune impervious to the waves?"

"In theory, there are several ways. I have set the investigative machinery in motion. However, it will take quite a while for answers to begin trickling in."

Holmes liked neither a slowly developing case nor one that relied on the efforts of others. As if to push away that distasteful thought, he nodded at the stack of letters I had left on the low table between our chairs. "Now," he said, "tell me what you and Billy found in Samuel Hudson's room."

"No diamonds, thousand-pound notes, or passbook with lots of zeroes, I'm afraid, but yes: his room was not without interest."

CHAPTER THIRTY-NINE

T he earliest letter in Samuel Hudson's box was written on board the *Gloria Scott* and posted, according to the second of its three post-scripts, in Gibraltar.

It had taken me several minutes to absorb the meaning of that. One might think that I, of all people, would be a touch jaded when it came to revelations about supposedly fictional events, but this felt rather like coming across a racy note in Chaucerian English dashed off by the Wife of Bath or finding oneself in conversation with David Copperfield.

In any event, James Hudson's letter it was. Between his salutation and his final affectionate signature, much of the already shaky shipboard handwriting had been rendered even more illegible by stains, the wear of frequent unfolding, and some holes in the paper. (These latter were ex-plained by the first post-script: it was sent wrapped around a doll the sailor had crafted for his yet-to-be-born child—our own Mrs Hudson!) Added to the general passage of years and the letter's considerable length, this first one took me a long time to work through.

As a detailed record of a sailor's life aboard a decrepit old boat taking thirty-eight felons to Australia, the letter was surely without parallel. Unfortunately, this sailor's life lacked somewhat when it came to drama, being heavily concerned with how much progress they made each day, what watches he had kept, and which of his fellow sailors had taken ill, broken bones, or lost a finger in the rigging. Oh, yes: and the number of maggots in his dinner.

The letter did mention Jack Prendergast, a freakishly tall and marvellously self-assured gentleman convict, but mention was all.

The second letter in Samuel Hudson's possession was by the same hand, dated three months later, on a table that remained stable during the writing. It had not been wrapped around a hand-made dolly, nor had it been read to pieces like the first.

In it lay James Hudson's version of the *Gloria Scott* sinking: how Jack Prendergast's co-conspirator, disguised as a chaplain, bought the assistance of key officers and sailors; the prisoners' violent and bloodthirsty rampage the minute they escaped their bonds; the revulsion and protest of some of the crew; the boat carrying them being loosed with little more than a chart and a barrel of water; then a short time later, the explosion, sending a plume of black smoke high into the air.

One surviving sailor, burnt and half-conscious, rescued from a floating spar.

"He white-washes the story for his wife," I told Holmes, "beginning to end. He doesn't mention that *sailors* took part in the mutiny. He implies that he was one of the objectors who were put off the ship, and leaves her to assume that the sailor they pulled from the water was another man."

Holmes made a small sound. I looked a question at him; he took a minute to reply. "James Hudson was . . . He was the second dead person I ever laid eyes on. I was eighteen. And although I knew I had to perform an examination on the body, it took me some time to work up the courage. He had old burn scars: a long one, on his back along the shoulder, and a smaller one across the palm of his right hand."

"And this episode of Hudson's death makes for a part of the apparently very long story that you are going to tell me, sooner or later?"

"It does."

I went on. "That's the last letter for years, at least among those in Samuel Hudson's box. There's one that lacks an envelope, and the letter itself only has 'Your Sister's birthday' instead of the date—but Hudson then mentions that the previous day was a Sunday. I looked in the Almanac: if Mrs Hudson's birthday is the ninth of May, that day was a Monday in 1864 and 1870, then not again until 1881."

"Hudson's wife did not die until 1866," Holmes said. "So, yes: 1870."

"That's what I thought. All the letters but the first two are written to Hudson's daughter Alicia—he calls her Allie—although two other hands also write on the pages. The first is . . . I feel odd referring to her as 'Mrs Hudson.'"

"Her name was Clarissa."

"Very well, *Clarissa's* hand, with a somewhat, er, idiosyncratic spelling. Those notes are usually at the bottom of her father's letters—comments, greetings, bits of news. The other hand on the pages seems to belong to Alicia herself. Those are all notes in the margins, correcting something he has said or, more often, expressing some bitter thought about how Clarissa is having all the fun. Most of these remarks are brief, but in a few places they spill over to the back of the page, which Hudson sometimes leaves blank. The notes were done over a long period of time, and go from a child's scrawl to the writing of a grown woman, and even what I'd have said an old woman. She must have re-read the letters countless times over the years, re-living the past and, more often than not, nursing her grudges.

"The other characteristic worth mentioning is that Hudson occasionally wrote his letters while drunk. It's easy to see the difference, not only in his hand control but in the meandering quality of his thought. I mention this because there are two places where he seems to have written something indiscreet, and either blacked out the lines himself, or had Clarissa censor him. Judging by the context, the missing lines appear to give details of illegal acts."

I raised my eyes, but Holmes did not respond. So: another item to add to my growing list of questions.

"Well, if necessary, we can look at the blacked-out portions in the laboratory. Then there's another long gap in the letters, until 1877. Hudson and Clarissa are in London, although it appears they had not told Alicia that they were going, since much of his letter takes the form of an apology for their deception and an attempt at cajoling her into forgiveness by describing in great detail a trunk of clothing being shipped to Sydney. He also points the finger of blame squarely at Clarissa, telling Alicia that it was Clarrie who insisted that they should leave Alicia behind until they had established themselves in London. At the end, Hudson makes reference to Alicia's friendship with Raymond McKenna. No doubt her future husband.

"This particular letter is almost illegible under Alicia's furious emendations—the pen nib breaks through the paper in two or three spots. Mostly she's angry about how Clarrie always got the pretty dresses, always got to do things, always was the one to travel with their father. And those notes are by no means confined to schoolgirl handwriting: in the corners, in tight little writing, she added a few gloating remarks along the lines of, 'And little good did it do her' and 'She got her just desserts.' She clearly never let go of what she saw as her father's betrayal, even after she was married.

"The next letter is from seven months later on—Hudson must have written it on receipt of Alicia's reply to his apology letter. Clipper ships took three or four months to go from Sydney to London, isn't that right?"

"A hundred days was a good time."

"That would be about right, then. Her reply must have been vicious, since this one amounts to four pages of protest that no, he didn't love Clarissa the best, that Alicia was his darling girl, that he couldn't wait to see her again. She must also have told him that she and McKenna were to be married—not asked his permission, simply informed him. He spends a maudlin few paragraphs reminiscing about her childhood, although it doesn't sound like a very happy period for any of the three, and tells her clearly that he thinks she's too young to marry. But he doesn't forbid her, and he doesn't say that he wants her to come to London. He doesn't even say that he'll come to Sydney for the wedding.

"All of which she annotates in her marginalia.

"There are just two letters after that, Holmes. They say—no, they're by far the shortest in the lot, although the second one seems to have been written while he was a bit drunk, so the writing is even more chaotic than usual. Here, take the magnifying glass—you'll need it."

CHAPTER FORTY

26 August 1878
London

Dearest Allie,

It's happened at last, your sister has lost her mind. You know how I told you she took up with some toffy Lord she met at a country house? Well, Clarrie's gone head over heels for the bloke, spends all her hours walking up and down the park hoping he'll show up.

I don't mind that she doesn't have any time for her old man, like you know, I'm happy for you girls to grow up and grow away from your Pa's loving arms, but the problem is that we owe kind of a lot of money here, and not to a bank either but a man who's kind of unofficial and not what youd call friendly, and it's hard to make it back all on my own. This is temporary I'm sure, by the sound of things her Young Lord isn't the permanent sort, if you know what I mean—not like your Raymond! (And how is married life with you, my dearie? I hope that just because youre a married woman now you'll still have time to write your old man? And no, before you ask, don't send me any of your husband's hard-earned money thow I know you'll make the offer, I expect that by the time you get this things will be easier here, I just need to make Clarrie wake up and see what she's getting herself into, is all.)

There's a new opera piece opened up here in London last month, I heard some people talking about it and thought maybe I'd take your sister (I'd rather take you, Allie dear, if only you were closer than Sydney!) and since it's said to be funny along with the music, I thought maybe once she's cheered up by it, she'll sit down and have a nice talk with her old man. It's called Pinafore, although what a girl's dress has to do with sailing I'll just have to see.

Sorry this is a short one, Allie dear, I'll write more soon. Meantime, here's a pair of earrings I made you, from some pretty silk thread that reminded me of your eyes.

Love,
Your Father

23 September 1879
Portsmouth

Darling Allie,

My dear daughter, this letter finds your father in a funny place, not so much ha ha as funny tearing out what hair he has. Last time I wrote (hope you are getting my letters—I do write all the time, promise!) I was still pretty beat up from that tramp steamer I was on for way too long, sailing is a young man's life it sure is. I had a good rest up in Norfolk with the old pal I told you about, but he died all of a sudden, weak heart I guess, so I've had to leave there. It would of been a more restful summer but his son never took to me and since the lazy lad was home doing nothing for the long vacation from University he had nothing better to do than make trouble for his father's old mate Hudson, him and this sharp-nosed friend of his with a Toff accent, two boys looking down their noses at a hard working sailor.

Anyway honey mine, I've shaken *that* dust off my boots for sure
and no thanks to them in Norfolk. However that time there proved
to be a Blessing in Disguise, ten thousand of them, because while I
was there old "Trevor" (as he called himself thow I know better) explained to me something that's been just sitting there quiet at the
back of my head for many and many a year, before you were born
even, and thow I cant go into any details at all here on paper, I can
say this here and now: DONT THROW ANYTHING OUT.
Nothing at all that either Clarrie or I left with you, don't get rid of
<u>one little thing</u>.

After I get back, things will get <u>lots</u> better. Don't know if you remember, but when you were a little mite I used to tell you stories
about secret treasures? Honest I thought they were just stories,
make-believe and only for the sorts of people who already have their
fortunes.

But old Trevor—and God Bless the man, stingy son and all—let
me know that anyone at all can have his fortune drop out of the sky.
Allie girl, your Pa has finally figured things out, and found himself a
shining temple on a hill.

<u>Just dont throw nothing</u> out, not until I get back.

And <u>theres</u> the part that's making me tear my hair—getting back
to Sydney!

I got two options, if I cant get the money off Clarrie.

First is, I got another friend—one without a son to get in the way,
far as I know. I'll see him tomorrow—I'm in Portsmouth tonight,
catching a train first thing. Portsmouth makes me think of when
your sister and I arrived from Sydney, Lo those many years ago. I
wish it was you I brought Allie, youd have stayed faithful. And Clarrie will just have to come and beg for us to forgive her.

Anyway, I'm pretty sure I can get my old pal Beddoes to stand me
the price of a ticket to Sydney, so I can get out of this stuckup country and back to my true family in Australia, where we'll live in comfort all the days of our lives. If he wont, well, I know another man,
back in London, thow he and I have a history that makes asking him

for anything a bit tricky. A kind of a moneylender among other things, like his father before him, but I already owe him, and he has the kinds of friends you don't want to get on the bad side of.

Still, asking him would be better than breaking my back on another steamer for months on end.

Honey thing, you're the only faithful daughter I know in all the world, I wish you was here in England instead of your sister. Clarrie must have had her baby by now, wonder what she had?

Allie dear I hope your well and happy. Give my respects to your husband, tell him to treat you good like youre worth, and I will write again when I am better situated to say when you can meet me at the docks.

Your Pa.

PS I know youre good at keeping mum on things—you were even when you were a little girl, like when I gave you that necklace with your birthday on it, and Clarrie never knew—but heres another thing you probably should keep tucked underneath your pretty hair.

Tantalising as the letters were, it was the notes written in the margins that drew the attention. On the earliest letter here, written in 1878, someone—one assumed their recipient, Mrs Hudson's sister, Alicia—had underlined phrases and added her notes beside them.

Next to *out of her mind* was written: *C has always been mad.* By the phrase *country house* was the note: *She spends her life at country houses, operas, and parties!* She'd noted beside *husband's hard-earned money*: *As if I'd send him money!*

But the most thorough commentary, in a bewildering tangle of interwoven and overlaid writing that spanned many years, was linked to the underlined words: *Young Lord:*

Of course it would be a LORD for Clarrie!
What does Pa mean by Lord? Anyth. short of Duke. Earl??

(Ida says "Lord" can even be peer's son—can't ask Pa, C would see it. Pa!!)
Well Pa was right about Clarrie's Lord not being the permanent sort! And
her pregnant!
When C comes, do I let her know I know this?
What is Vicount?
Viscount, not v. impt. Father an Earl? Eldest son?
Got him!
Can't see him at all in S—S looks like <u>ME</u>.

In the second letter, written by Hudson on his way to meet Beddoes, one line alone was underscored—but so many times, the bitter ink had eaten entirely through the paper, leaving nothing but a long, thin window beneath the phrase:

<u>Clarrie must have had her baby by now</u>

Holmes laid down the heavy magnifying glass and the letters, reaching again for his pipe. When it was going, he returned his heels to the table. "Those letters do indeed contain some interesting elements."

I enumerated them on my fingers. "That Clarissa Hudson was most likely Samuel's true mother, making him both illegitimate and adopted; that his grandfather had contact with criminals; that Samuel's father was a peer, who had been a viscount when Clarissa knew him; and that there was something in Alicia's possession that James Hudson thought might prove extremely valuable."

"Plus a clue towards The Bishop, and the name Beddoes, and a location near Portsmouth," Holmes added. "But how would he—"

I held out my second-to-last contribution to the puzzle.

This envelope was an oversized square, of the sort that had once held a decorated card. Inside was a full page of *The Illustrated London News*, dated 15 November, 1919. Holmes unfolded it, running his eyes over several articles concerning the one-year anniversary of Armistice, then turned it over to a page of illustrations: eight captioned photographs showing various scenes of War memorials and the laying of wreaths. Typical of *London News,* the images were clear, well lit, and crisply printed. I half rose to tap a finger on the one in the upper right quadrant.

"This man here? He looks remarkably like Samuel Hudson."

The caption read:

HUGH EDMUNDS, EARL STEADWORTH, REMEMBERS HIS
LOST SON DURING THE DEDICATION OF THE VILLAGE
WAR MEMORIAL IN HANLEIGH, BERKS.

"The Earl of Steadworth," Holmes said. "And The Bishop thought Samuel didn't know."

Time to lay my final puzzle-piece onto the table. "I looked him up in *Debrett's* and some of Mycroft's other books. The current Earl, Hugh Edmunds, was Viscount Edmunds until 1886, when his father committed suicide following some kind of financial scandal. Edmunds has a list of good deeds to his name that stretches down the page, most of them the sort of public-eye projects that engender a lot of acclaim—war orphans, soldiers' hospitals, programs sponsored by the Royal Family, that sort of thing. He served in South Africa for a brief time, where he was injured in 1878—he claimed a Zulu bullet, although there appears to have been some discussion on the matter. After that, his military service involved a lot of decorations and a very few guns: strictly red-tab stuff well behind any lines. He has several alphabets' worth of minor honorifics after his name, two living daughters, and has just turned seventy-three.

"And," I said, relishing my rare opportunity for dramatic flourish, "would you like to hear an intriguing coincidence? Hugh Edmunds' name is on the Birthday Honours list that your brother has just approved for the King."

Chapter Forty-one

At 3:40 Saturday morning, Mrs Clara Hudson stood at the bay window, watching the lights of Billy's motorcar recede down the lane. When all was dark, when the last murmur of the big engine had disappeared even from her imagination, she let the curtains fall and turned back to the room. How many times had she cleaned that floor from his muddy boots, returned those pillows to the settee after he'd used them for a nest before the fire, dusted those bookshelves after some experiment had filled the house with a noxious powder? Twenty-two years in Baker Street, then the same number here, living with a man who was ... what? Tenant and employer? Gaoler and conscience-enforcer? Friend?

That lad with the big nose and the sticking-out shirt cuffs, a lifetime ago—one lifetime, paid for a dozen times over, scrubbing on her knees.

Truth to tell, Mrs Hudson was not in the habit of scrubbing on her knees, since a woman in her seventh decade tended to hire village girls for the hard work. But that night, as the clock on the mantelpiece urged her onward and the sky crept towards morning, Clara Hudson spent some more time bent over the scrub-brush, removing all traces of the past week from her floors. She plumped the cushions, she dried and put the dishes away on their shelves, she wiped down the stove, table, and sink. As a last act, she cleaned and cooked the garden-party strawberries into preserves, leaving the cooling jars beneath a towel on the kitchen table.

When the sun was well up, Patrick let himself in the back door. He knew—unlike the constable lurking near the drive—that Mary had been found, and safe, and the knowledge restored his appetite for the Sussex ham on Mrs Hudson's sideboard.

She laid a heaping plate before him. "Now, get yourself around that while I go and dress. I think since I'm not needed here, I'll go and visit my friend Mrs Turner. But—" She affected not to notice his eyebrows coming together. "—since Mr Holmes didn't want people to know yet, that Mary's safe, I wonder if you could take me on the quiet, like? To the Eastbourne station, I think. They don't know me there as well as they do in Seaford."

His jaws began to work meditatively. When he had swallowed, doubt was gone as well. "I think that would be a fine idea. Don't you be telling anyone where you're going though, hear?"

"I'll telephone to Mr Mycroft's flat when I reach Mrs Turner's. Other than that, nobody will know."

If there was one thing Patrick enjoyed, she thought guiltily, it was to be permitted a moment of intrigue.

She left him to his breakfast, and put on a Sunday-best dress, put her feet into an old woman's shoes, settled a landlady's go-to-Town hat over her drab hair. She tucked her emergency stash of bank notes—annoying to have lost her passbook—into the very bottom of a dowdy and capacious handbag, adding a few necessities on top.

Patrick was drying his plate as she came into the kitchen. "I'll get your valise," he said.

"Oh, I'll borrow what I need from Eloise—we take the same dress size, and I'll be less noticeable without a bag. But I'm afraid Inspector Lestrade will not be happy."

"Shall I tell him where you've gone?"

"No. Although you'll have to tell him that I have gone—we wouldn't want his poor constable to discover my absence on his own."

"Leave it to me," he said, and went out to distract the constable away from the motorcar, that she might depart unnoticed.

Mrs Hudson checked the doors, arranged the dish-towel to hang more neatly before the stove, and walked firmly across her pristine floor-boards to the front door.

She waited in the roofed portico, following the progress of two men as they headed towards the back garden. As their voices faded, she listened with all her heart to the breeze in the hedgerow, the voices of the sheep, the low rhythm of wave on stone—and most of all, to the sounds of the bees working the roses that covered the portico. She gave a sigh, then turned to shut the door and drop the key through the mail slot.

She climbed into the back of the car and lay flat on the seat. In a few minutes, Patrick's feet came along the gravel. He started the car, and they continued sedately up the road to the Eastbourne station.

Mrs Hudson bought her ticket and boarded the train without having anyone recognise her. The train conductor did know her by sight, but not to speak with, so that was fine as well. And naturally, once they came to Victoria station, the huge city closed its anonymous arms around her, and she disappeared.

She had the taxi drop her two streets up from where she was going, more by habit than anything. As she walked through the Saturday morning crowds, she was a touch anxious to see if the place was still in business. Surely Jonny was getting towards retirement—but when she rounded the corner, there it was, narrow-fronted and uninformative.

The man at the desk looked up at the bell, arranging his face into a look both repressive and polite. "Madam, is there something I may help you with?" Meaning, *What could a woman like you possibly want here?*

She felt her first honest smile in days take over her face. "Oh, Jonny, you've forgotten me already?"

Startled, the little man looked more closely—and then exclaimed and hurried out from behind the desk to grab her shoulders and kiss her roundly on both cheeks.

"Clara Hudson, as I live and breathe! Oh, darling, what a treat it is to lay eyes on you. How many years has it been? Nine? Ten?"

"Surely it can't be that?" she said, returning his embrace. "You're looking marvellous, Jonny. New friend?"

"Ah, you know me too well. And you're . . . well, it's good to see you."

At that, she laughed aloud. "I'm looking horrible and grey, I know. But I need to look a little less horrible and grey, and I need it fast, so I've come to you for help."

"Oh, perfect, just let me see if I have some bubbly here, and we can lock the door and have a nice talk."

Jonny Harflinger was a dressmaker-tailor who specialised in secrets: secrets told him, secrets worn, secrets that could shatter careers and lives. If a Member of Parliament sought a negligée for the privacy of his dressing room, Jonny could make it. If that MP's wife wanted to take a special female friend to the theatre and dinner after, Jonny's evening suit would help her to move like a man. He'd got his start making theatrical costumes, but his growing reputation had led him to a specific clientèle, including one Mr Sherlock Holmes.

One or two of Mrs Hudson's special tasks for her employer had required special garments, which Jonny had been able to provide. After that, and once she'd realised that to Jonny, a secret meant to the grave, she had come to him for her own purposes: Jonny was not a couturier, but he could copy anything, and he was nothing short of brilliant at listening to a client's vague impressions of what he or she wanted and interpreting that vision into silks and fine cottons and wool.

Today, he listened with a growing frown, before leaning over and refilling their glasses with the champagne he drank from breakfast to night. "My dear thing, you're underselling yourself. Yes, you've put on a few pounds—"

"A stone," she provided.

"—but it's in all the right places, for a man with that sort of inclination, and your bones are good. Twenty years ago, that brown skin you're wearing would have been a problem, but all the best sorts wear a tan now. Although your hands . . ."

"A month of manicures won't help those," she said. "It'll have to be gloves, despite the heat. As for the other, no, I'm afraid I'm set on it. I shouldn't have come—even asking is an affront to your skills. I'll just pop up to Oxford Street and find something off the racks, but—"

"Good Lord, woman," he protested, "we can't have that. I'll make what you asked for, but you have to promise me that you'll also let me make you something proper. Something that makes you shine."

"Jonny, I'll be seventy next year, a bit late for shining."

"Never!" He was fierce about it, and he had a knack of making one feel as if he were speaking only the truth. In the end, she promised, and he sat back, satisfied, studying her body with a naked intensity that in another man would have been uncomfortable.

"Now," he said. "When you say, 'fast,' do you mean next week?"

"I mean tonight."

Fortunately, his glass was only half-full, and the carpet beneath him showed signs of being well accustomed to emphatic spills of champagne. He protested vigorously, asked if she did not realise it was a Saturday.

"Oh, Jonny, I do understand, and I wouldn't think of asking you to work late. Never mind, I'll be fine with Mr Selfridge. Thanks so for the bubbly, it cheers a girl just talking to you."

He eyed her bitterly, not fooled in the least—as indeed, she had not been trying to fool him. "You're a bitch, you know that?"

Mrs Hudson nodded her head, a bit sadly. "I do, Jonny. I really do."

"But the price will have to go up."

"Of course."

He gave a deep and dramatic sigh, and emptied his glass. "Let's look at some samples, then. Do you have a colour in mind?"

"Mauve, I think."

He winced, but the argument was gone out of him.

It took Mrs Hudson the rest of the day to finish her preparations, most of it in the hands of a woman recommended by Jonny as being not too incompetent with dye-pot, tweezers, and manicure scissors.

When she returned to Jonny's shop, his were the only lights in view. He locked the door behind her and led her to the changing room, where he stood back to examine her, head to toe. In the end, his head made a motion that was equal part understanding nod and disapproving shake, and brought out a garment that he hadn't the spirit to give his usual dramatic unveiling.

Her smile was unfeigned. "Oh, it's perfect, Jonny."

"It's not perfect, it's bloody *hideous,* pardon my French. I'll have you know that I've already started your other dress, to get the taste of this one out of my mouth. It'll be finished tomorrow, even if I am working Sunday. I expect you to come pick it up before the week is out."

"I don't—"

He glared. "You're not about to tell me you don't want it. Because you did give me a promise, my dear Mrs Hudson."

"No, no—I'm happy to have it. In fact, I'm so sure of it, let me pay you for it now rather than wait."

"You don't need to do that," he said, startled into a retreat. "What if you don't like it? What if I'm hit by a bus? What if I find God and go off to live with the Naturists?"

"Dearest, I insist. By way of apology for my complete disruption of your week-end."

"Well," he admitted, "it will help me make my own apologies to my friend, who was expecting something in the way of theatre tonight. Now, try on your dress while I get us something strong to drink."

After a while, the two of them stood, glasses in hand, to study the reflection in the three-sided mirror.

"What a horrible dress," he said.

"It's perfectly fine."

"Yes, if you don't mind looking like an aged *femme de nuit* with bad skin."

"I won't tell a soul that you made it."

"You'd better not, or I'll never dress you again."

"Think of it as a theatre costume, rather than a dress," she said.

"The phrase, 'Mutton dressed as lamb' does come to mind," Jonny grumbled.

She smoothed her free hand down her torso and over her hips, turning to look at her profile.

Once upon a time, when she had been Clarissa, she lived in front of the looking glass. More recently, her relationship with mirrors had been confined to an occasional glance when her hair was feeling awry. There beneath Jonny's unforgiving light, she took a last fortifying swallow and set down her glass, reaching into her shopping bags for the rest. She slipped on the light summer coat, its grey colour making the mauve of her dress go dull, then stepped into a pair of shiny black shoes. The hat was an uncertain cross between a cloche and a boater, and the flower pinned to it did not quite match the colour of the frock. She smoothed on a pair of delicate cotton lace gloves, settled her new black handbag over her arm, and stood back to contemplate the overall effect.

Jonny made a sound deep in his throat and rapidly drained his glass. She, however, winked at him in the mirror, and then her face underwent a change.

"Oh, who am I fooling?" she said with a sigh. "I'm an old woman; I'll never be attractive again." She reached into her handbag for a dark pencil and applied it to the grey in her eyebrows, only making matters worse.

Jonny shuddered and turned away, muttering grimly about her bringing it back with her, so he could take it into the yard and burn it.

She paid him, for both dresses, present and future. She added an apology to his friend, and kissed his cheek good-bye. When she let herself out onto the street, it would have been difficult to say which of the two seemed more downtrodden.

It was late, but it was a Saturday. The day's long warmth and the after-theatre traffic filled the streets and pavements. Those strolling along seemed unusually blind when it came to avoiding Mrs Hudson's person, with a continuous string of exclamations and apologies as she walked. Eventually, she moved towards the street, raising a tentative hand at the passing taxicabs. Half a dozen passed, unseeing, before a grey-haired driver swerved to the kerb—but as Mrs Hudson made her way towards the door, a brusque young man with a girl on his arm brushed past her to yank the door open and hand his young lady inside.

The taxi darted away, and Mrs Hudson smiled, very quietly, before turning again towards the flow of cars and putting up a somewhat more assertive glove.

This time, a cab pulled up immediately.

She gave him the address, and sat back, hands together, as the driver followed his head-lamps through the streets to the house of the man who had fathered her son.

CHAPTER FORTY-TWO

Holmes' feet slowly retracted, coming to the carpet in a sort of slow-motion counterpart to the furious working of his brain. "The Honours list?" he said. "*Mycroft* is the key to this? What is the—"

As if he had summoned his brother from the club across the road, the key sounded again in the door, and the big man himself entered.

Mycroft Holmes had shed a great deal of weight since his heart attack a year and a half earlier, but he would never be slim, and he would forever move like a man wrapped in bulk. He stopped dead as he saw our faces turned in his direction; one could see the summoning of energies.

"Hugh Edmunds." Holmes, on his feet now, threw the name across the room like a weapon.

Mycroft's fingers came up to work the buttons on his overcoat. He removed it, hung it up, closed the wardrobe door—and when he turned back, all traces of alcohol were gone from his eyes. "The Earl of Steadworth, yes. A man with sins, but most of those committed outside of England. And he has proved himself a . . . useful man in several difficult situations. So I let his name go through. Should I not have done so?"

Instead of replying to the question, Holmes asked one of his own. "Mycroft, what do you know about Mrs Hudson?"

To my astonishment, Mycroft looked discomfited. "Ah. Sherlock, it is my job to know things. Even—one might say particularly—those things that you do not care to talk about."

Holmes dropped back into his chair, snatching up his pipe. "I suppose Watson knows all the details of my past as well, and wants only to protect me!"

Mycroft came to sit down in the largest chair before the fire, waiting until Holmes raised his eyes before he spoke. "I have never made use of this knowledge, Sherlock. I merely could not risk secrets."

"Well, you missed one. Hugh Edmunds is the father of Mrs Hudson's son."

Mycroft's face underwent a series of rapid changes: an instant of surprise gave way to reflection, then his expression grew dark as his brain analysed the significance of the fact. "You think Steadworth was using Samuel Hudson as a means of manipulating me? But, I'd already approved him."

"Did he know that?"

Mycroft folded his hands over his waistcoat, his eyes losing focus as his mind reviewed the information it had been given. "He may have had doubts. I called the Earl in for a personal interview, which I seldom do. His name had been proposed for the New Year's list, but as I said, several ... misdeeds had been noted, requiring me to spend a degree more attention than I might have. One or two men regard him with distaste. I, myself, was not entirely pleased at how nakedly the man lusts after his Honour. However, neither did I think he would make any unseemly use of his position, not in public. In the end, it was decided that his sins were no more than the misdemeanours of his age and his class, and it was less important to please the fastidious than it was to acknowledge the services he had done the nation. And, frankly, His Royal Highness likes the man."

"Could Edmunds have believed you were going to refuse him?" Holmes demanded. "You personally, that is?"

"The process is only secret in theory," Mycroft admitted. "In practice, a man with the Earl's experience, and his acquaintances, generally has some idea of where he stands. Although it is not until the list goes to the *Gazette* that one may be certain."

"Are names ever withdrawn between that publication and the actual granting of the Honours?"

The older man's prodigious mental facilities worked for a time, before: "Rarely. Unless someone has died in the interim, I recall only two occasions in which the Honours list was not completed. In one of those, the man came home early from a shooting party, gun in hand, and discovered his wife with the estate manager; in the other, a newspaper reporter uncovered a series of letters suggesting a bishop had certain political sympathies with what might be called the wrong side."

"Resulting in scandals?" I asked.

"Quite."

"So if something came to light on a lesser order, such as fathering an illegitimate child, the name might be permitted to stand?"

"Once published in the *Gazette*, public forgiveness would be better than the admission of error."

"And once the Honours were actually given?"

"Retracting an Honour is a serious embarrassment. Heads would roll on the Palace staff."

"So we could say that a means of keeping information from your hands, or one that provided leverage on your decision, might be valuable?"

"Why don't you tell me what you know," Mycroft suggested gloomily. So we did.

Reiterating it to him, however, brought the fragility of the argument to light. By the end, I found myself growing more interested in Holmes' mythic £250,000. A mutineer's bounty was appealing in so many ways— and it sounded as if the *Gloria Scott* had possessed a rich assortment of financial villains to choose from, as Prendergast's partner in fraud. However, now doubts had been raised, Mycroft could not overlook Hugh Edmunds.

Mycroft glanced at the mantelpiece clock with regret: after midnight. "I might wish you had brought this to me earlier in the day."

"We did not have it earlier in the day," Holmes informed him.

Not much earlier, at any rate. "Have we any idea where the Earl is?" I asked. "Berkshire?"

"Mayfair," Mycroft replied. "He would want to be in his London house when the announcement is made."

"With the champagne already on ice," I added. "Shall we go speak with him?"

"In the morning, certainly."

"You really think we should wait until then?"

Mycroft raised one eyebrow, a look even more supercilious on him than it was on his younger brother. "Scotland Yard may be happy to break down a gentleman's door in the middle of the night, but this is a conversation, my dear, not an accusation of murder."

I heard Holmes mutter something that sounded remarkably like *Thank God,* but did not let it distract me. "If you find out that—"

Mycroft raised one hand. "If some new fact comes to light, I have until Monday noon to inform the *Gazette* of changes, without causing undue awkwardness."

"Without the newspapers catching wind of a scandal, you mean."

The big man was adamant. "I am not going to raise that sort of mid-night turmoil without good cause."

Clearly, as far as Mycroft Holmes was concerned, re-setting a few lines in the upcoming *London Gazette* was, suspicions or no, inadequate cause for storming the Earl of Steadworth's gates in the dead of night.

CHAPTER FORTY-THREE

Whether she was Clarissa or Clara, Mrs Hudson had never entirely lost sight of Hugh Edmunds. She had seen the photographs of his wedding to the Hon Virginia Walthorpe-Vane, a petite Shropshire girl with a disturbingly innocent face. She saw the announcement of his father's death, in 1886, and kept an eye on the Earl of Steadworth's progress, from the back benches to positions of growing authority, becoming a man on the inside of power—a man who, reading between the lines, was brought in for the sorts of negotiations the more squeamish shied away from.

She had studied every photograph, and wondered. In the early years, his handsome features had proclaimed honest goodwill and competence. Later, however, the lines had spoken of something else, some faint edge of cruelty and greed—although she knew it might be her own prejudice, showing her qualities that she had never suspected when the man himself stood before her.

From her first Cheat on the streets of Sydney, when the man with the gold watch-chain gave her a half sovereign coin, she had known what men were thinking. Women might escape her eyes, but few men—remarkably few. Since the attack in Ballarat, she had known that any man she was unable to read could be very dangerous indeed.

Something to remember, tonight.

The clocks were striking midnight when her cab stopped in front of Steadworth House. The ground-floor curtains of the noble building were dark, and most of the upper rooms as well. The driver peered up and said uncertainly, "You sure you want me to drop you here?"

Mrs Hudson was pleased as she counted out her coins. How much could be said with nine brief words and a tone of voice: this man knew that she did not live here as family, and knew just as positively that she was not a servant to enter at the back.

"No, it'll be fine, thank you." She waited until he had pulled away before making her way up the steps to plant her gloved finger on the button for the electrical door-bell.

Her finger was growing tired when a light came on in the depths of the house. She stood away, clasping her hands together on her cheap, shiny handbag.

By the scent that wafted out with the door's opening, she had caught the butler at a late-night glass of his master's Armagnac; his collar betrayed a rapid attempt at restoring decorum. With one glance, his butlerian attitude towards a caller at this hour—stiff disapproval mingled with polite curiosity—dismissed her person and slid into something close to outrage.

"Madam, the hour is very late."

"And getting later all the while," she retorted. "I suspect the Earl will be displeased at having to listen to that long peal on the bell."

Her confidence, so at odds with her appearance, gave him pause, though not actual retreat. "The Earl has gone to bed, Madam. Surely this can wait until morning."

"If it could wait, I would have come in the morning. Kindly tell your master that Clarissa will see him now."

His mouth worked a few times before it found words. "Madam, I cannot wake him unless it is an emergency."

"You tell him my name. Let him judge how urgent it is."

"I . . . very well, Madam. Would you please wait in here?"

She let the man usher her into a cold drawing room, switch on the electric lights, and close the door firmly behind her. If there had been a lock, she thought, he'd have turned the key.

The portraits on the walls had heavy gilt frames; the fireplace was marble; a trio of settees looked as comfortable as the table they stood around; the chandelier would take a maid an hour a week to polish. The zebra skin splayed in front of the hearth looked like a creature slow to move when a steam-roller came down the lane.

One thing to say for Mr Holmes: the man had never liked fussy decorations or dead animals.

It took eleven minutes before Hugh Edmunds came in, plenty of time to peruse the faces of previous generations, to test the hard surfaces of the seats, to peer through the diamond-shaped panes of the doors that would open on a fine evening to the narrow terrace. Through the wavy glass, colourless flowers and ghostly statues gleamed in the light from nearby streetlamps. Beyond them, the streets were silent. Then the door behind her came open, and those pale eyes of the paintings were given life. The utterly guileless gaze, the confident set of the head, yet somewhere about him—the shoulders?—there was a certain wariness, as if suspecting that the room contained a threat. The Earl had slippers on his feet, but otherwise had taken the time to get dressed, wearing suit trousers and a fresh white shirt beneath his smoking jacket: armour against importuning women.

"Good evening, Hugh."

"Clarissa Hudson, by all that's holy—I thought you must be dead long ago!"

"Not quite."

"Bit of a surprise, hearing your name. Oh, Daniels, that'll be all," he said to the butler. "I shall see Miss Hudson out."

Disapproving, and disappointed, the butler took his reluctant leave.

The door closed; footsteps retreated down the corridor outside. When he was satisfied that they were alone, Hugh began to circle the room, his eyes on her all the time. He came to a set of decorative doors and reached back to slide one side open, revealing a well-stocked drinks cabinet.

"Glass of something, old thing?"

"Thank you."

"You liked champagne, I remember, but there's no ice. Seems to be everything else."

She had no wish to follow Jonny's good bubbly with bad. "I'll have whatever you're having, Hugh."

He splashed amber liquid from a decanter into a pair of glasses, and set the decanter down. He then paused to survey the unprepossessing figure before the unlit fire. Mismatched costume, unsuitable hair, makeup that tried too hard. His guarded stance relaxed, the cock-crow aspect of his personality reasserting itself as he turned to pick up the glasses.

And to think she'd once found that charming.

He placed one drink on the low marble table in front of the fireplace, and dropped onto the scarlet settee on the table's other side. She settled obediently onto her assigned patch of brocade, and saluted him with her crystal tumbler.

Only when he had lowered his own drink and his face was in the light from the lamp at her shoulder, did she ask him, "Hugh, when did Samuel come to see you?"

His surprise looked remarkably like guilt. He drew up his leg to prop it across the knee—then caught himself. Instead, he stretched out both legs in a show of nonchalance, resting the glass on his belly. "Yes, about that. Why did I never know we had a son?"

"We didn't have a son, Hugh. I had a son."

"Come now, Clarissa—the boy's the spitting image of me at his age."

"Interesting. I've always thought he resembled my father. When did you meet Samuel?"

"He showed up here, out of the blue, a couple weeks back. The most ungodly Australian accent and a suit like something you'd bury a bank clerk in. Flourishing a handful of old letters and a photo of me from *The*

Times, along with a story I'd have thought highly unlikely if it hadn't been like looking in a mirror."

"What kind of letters?"

"From your father—who, it seems, wasn't quite as dead as you told me, all those years ago."

"Probably not. Who were the letters to?"

"Your mother and your sister. Alice?"

"Alicia. I doubt the letters said all that much. My father couldn't have mentioned your name, since he never knew it."

"No, but he knew you were having a child, and he referred to the father as a 'Lord.' Samuel seems to have grown up believing that Alice— sorry, Alicia—was his real mother, until he came across those letters. She also had a photo of me from some years back—she must've spotted it and had the same thought I did: Samuel Hudson looks a hell of a lot like Lord Steadworth.

"Oh, and he had a necklace, a half sovereign strung through a chain. Now, *that* I have a very clear memory of."

At his leer, Clara Hudson's fingers tightened on the crystal: a telegram, crumpled into his pocket before she could see it; bereft tears at the fictional loss of a mother; his face, nuzzling the front of her uncorseted gown in search of comfort. And afterwards, his fingers playing with the gold coin between her breasts.

He grinned at her blush. "Oh, Clarissa, if only my dear wife had proved as hearty as you, I might have had a more productive marriage. Instead, all I have left are two sickly girls and a son whose accent puts my teeth on edge."

"What did Samuel want from you?"

"Do you know, I think he wanted recognition, more than money— although he seems happy enough to be offered money. And I suppose revenge—on you. He went all dark and broody when he talked about you pawning him off on your sister. He seems to have found it troubling to discover as a grown man that his parents hadn't been his parents. But more immediately, he's looking for his grandfather."

"My *father*? Did he tell you Papa was still alive?" Even without a bullet, James Hudson would have been fast approaching his century mark.

"No, he claimed his grandfather had disappeared around the time he was born, and thought I might know where he'd gone. One of the letters indicated that your father had money hidden away somewhere. I believe the phrase was, 'a fortune dropping out of the sky.' Since nothing of the sort came to light after your sister died, he came here hoping that the old man might have told me about it."

"Why on earth would he think that?"

"Your father's letter said he had recently figured out something that had been puzzling him for a long time, and expected to come into a lot of money because of it—although he didn't obligingly go on to say what that might be. Were there pirates in your family, Clarissa? A map to buried treasure? Samuel thinks it might have to do with the rights to a gold mine. Your father was on his way back to Australia to retrieve whatever it was—after which, he told your sister, they would all live in comfort for ever after. I assured Samuel that not only did I have no idea about any Hudson family monies or gold mines, but the closest I'd come to your father was one night on opposite sides of an hotel door. That was he, I take it, who tried to pound down the door that night?

"I did, frankly, wonder if this was not a rather clumsy attempt to introduce the topic of money. Just in case I felt like clasping him to me and declaring him my one true heir." Edmunds shook his head, and got up to fill his empty glass. "However, it was another part of that same letter that caught my eye. Have you seen them? The letters?"

"No."

"I tried to get him to leave them here with me, but he wouldn't. Suspicious little bugger, your son—watched over me while I read them. Anyway, in one, your father says that he is on his way to see a man by name of Beddoes, down in Hampshire. Now, this was a man I met briefly, back in the late 'seventies—he was in a deal with the bank when he simply up and scarpered. Created untold confusion. And, by a fascinating coincidence, that very name was in the papers not long before Samuel showed up here. Bones found on the fellow's estate. 'The Skeleton in the Game-keeper's Garden,' I believe they called it."

Fortunately, Hugh had got up to lay a match under the laid fire, so he missed her reaction. "I remember reading about that," she said when she'd got her voice under control. "Although I'm not sure what connexion you imagined there."

He straightened, wincing like an old man. "Clarissa, I always knew you walked the line of being shady. Good girls don't spend the Christmas holidays in Monte Carlo, or keep thick packets of £20 notes at the bottom of their sponge-bag. Yes, yes, I went through your rooms when you were away. Wouldn't you? And if you're that way, it's a sure bet your father wasn't sea-green incorruptible. So when I see a letter written back in 'seventy-nine saying your father—remarkably lively for a dead man—is on his way to see this fellow Beddoes . . . well, put one criminal together with another, and come up with a man buried in the woods."

"Did Samuel know about the skeleton?"

"Not until I told him." He walked back to the settee. "I'm not sure why I did. Probably to get him out of the way for a bit, so I could think things over. It was the second time we'd met. The first time he showed up here was a Tuesday, when I have a regular lunch date with the Prime Minister, so I'd have put him off even if he hadn't been talking madness. We met again the next afternoon—not here. There's a nice anonymous restaurant I know that keeps a few muscular waiters in shouting distance, in case a customer gets out of hand. He sat there drinking a lot of expensive claret while I squinted my way through his letters. That's when I told him about the skeleton."

"I don't imagine that was the last time you saw him."

"No. He 'phoned here last Saturday, and I met him at the same place. He'd been in Hampshire, and although most people figured the bones had to be those of Beddoes himself, who'd disappeared about then, Samuel was convinced they were his grandfather's. Something on the body that the people in the village told him about. We had a long talk, and I, er, I told him he should go down and see you. Just to say hello."

Surely Hugh hadn't always been such a shockingly bad liar? Had her eyes been clouded by love back then, or had he lost the knack? Perhaps he simply could not be bothered to assemble a believable lie for such an obvious old failure as Clara Hudson?

"So you knew where I was, all the time?" she asked.

Something flickered at the back of his eyes, and he bent sharply to take a cigar from the ornate table-top humidor. He clipped the end and traded the clipper for a cigar lighter in the shape of a naked woman. Her silver head spouted flame as he warmed the length of tobacco (a masculine ceremony that had always struck her as odd, considering the cigar's resemblance to the male anatomy). Comforted by the delay, he set the lighter back on the table and spoke from a concealing cloud. "Actually, no. He'd told me where you'd been all these years, the first time he and I met. I'd no idea. Keeping house for Sherlock Holmes—imagine."

His open disdain could not hide a degree of uneasiness. Most likely it was due to the mere idea of Mr Holmes, who tended to make even the innocent a bit uneasy. She wished she could be sure. She said nothing, which encouraged him to go on.

"I suppose if I'd realised where you were, I might have looked you up. I know the man's brother, slightly. He's a, well, a professional contact, really. Not a friend—ha! Mycroft Holmes has no friends. But it never came up. And Hudson is a common enough name."

Something about Mycroft Holmes appeared to bother Hugh: he spoke the name as if picking at a sore, unable to help himself. However, she had a few more mild questions before she could begin to press.

"It was good of you to suggest that Samuel come down to see me."

"Well, a boy only has one mother. Except when he has two, I guess," he added with a bray of laughter.

"And when you told him about the skeleton, he said he might know who the bones belonged to. I'll have to let the police know that it might be my father. After all these years. I wonder what could have happened? And, what was it they found on his body, do you know? That Samuel recognised?"

"Some object made out of string, he said. Got pretty worked up about it, for some reason. And, er, that's when he said he'd go down and see you. Except that he didn't have any money. So I gave him some."

"Really?"

He shrugged, studying his cigar. "The least I could do."

"He must have been pretty broke, if he couldn't have afforded a train ticket to Sussex."

"Yes, well, it was a bit more than that. He said he'd need a motorcar. Not just to go see you, of course, but while he was in England. And I think he wanted to impress you, a little. Maybe."

"A motorcar." Some part of that was a lie, she thought.

He rubbed off the end of the cigar in the ash-tray, then looked up at her, head tilted to one side. "You're still a remarkably attractive woman, Clarissa Hudson."

She laughed. "And you haven't changed a bit, Hugh. Your face looks as if you've never had a moment's worry in your life. You look unlived-in."

Stinging words from this frumpy woman across the table startled him into a sharp reaction. "How *could* you give your baby up, Clarissa? What kind of unnatural mother were you?"

"You—" She caught herself, and turned slashing scorn into a calm interest. "Perhaps you think I should have handed him over to *you*?"

But he'd seen her reaction. "Why not? I could have given him to one of the tenants to raise, given him a job when he was grown. Too short for a footman, but maybe sub-gardener."

"That would have been generous of you." Suddenly, she was weary: weary of this man, sick of the Act. In any event, she had all the facts she needed—all but one. "Hugh, when you bought Samuel a car, did you also give him a gun?"

"I never gave—I mean, did he have a gun?"

The empty protest echoed through the room. With a sigh, and feeling every one of her years, Mrs Hudson moved her handbag from settee to lap, signalling her preparation to leave. First, however, she spoke to the man who had once been her lover: whom she had once thought she loved. "Yes, Hugh. Samuel came to my house with a gun. I think you not only knew it, you planned it. I think you and he decided that I was going to mysteriously disappear, and a ransom note would be delivered to Mr Holmes. Just . . . not for money." She waited. When no denial came, she shook her head in despair.

"I imagine you wanted to pressure Mr Holmes into doing something. That's how you work, isn't it? You find a person's weak spot and exploit it to the hilt. So you have some sort of a business deal or power play in the works, and when Samuel walked in your door, he all but handed you the means of tipping matters in your direction. I suppose the plan was that he would hold me somewhere until the deal was concluded.

"Or was he just going to shoot me and push me into a pit, like my father was? It doesn't matter. No threat to me would have bent Mr Holmes to your will. Even when he thought it was his wife you had, he was coming after you. And he will find you."

"Clarissa, I have no idea what—"

"But I wasn't at home. Instead, a young woman came out of my door. A young woman I am extremely fond of. For three days, I believed she was dead. Her husband believed she was dead. I stood back and watched him tear himself to pieces, knowing that I was to blame—that whatever took her, it was somehow due to me. But she didn't die. In fact, I believe the dear girl may have killed Samuel."

He gaped across the table at her. "Samuel is *dead*? I thought . . ."

She got to her feet. "You thought he was hiding somewhere? In a house you'd arranged for him, perhaps, with me tied up and waiting?"

He too rose, cigar forgotten in his hand. "I never! How could you think . . . !"

"I wonder if Samuel was bright enough to realise that he was condemned, the instant you sent him towards me. If he murdered me, you'd have seen that the evidence against him left you untouched. If he set me loose, once you'd got your way, you'd have been too afraid of betrayal to let him live. Either way, my son had to die. Isn't that right, Hugh? Over nothing more than a business deal." She put a twist of utter scorn on her last words, and watched him explode.

"Business deal!" he roared. "I've been working my whole bloody life for this, Clarissa. My father shot himself, my mother and wife between them made my life a living hell, I was too young for one war and too old for the other, and three times—*three times!*—I've been mooted for the Honours list and set aside. I've served my nation all my life, doing the Crown's dirty work, and I'm left as nothing but an Earl without a son. My title is going extinct, after me. Jesus, the nation owes me a Dukedom—the least it can give me is a KG!"

She could only stare at him. A son and a father, each with their own mad desires, brought together to ignite like one of Mr Holmes' experiments gone bad. This was madness—doubled. Trebled, even: her father had lighted the slow-burning fuse. Oh, the men in her life who thought their needs justified any wickedness, men for whom the world was meat and entertainment. Were it not for Mr Holmes—and Billy before him—would she have become the same?

She shuddered. "Oh, Hugh. This nation owes you nothing but a prison cell."

His face changed. His pale eyes moved, considering the flat colour of her hair, the mediocre cut of the dress she wore, the sagging skin of her ageing cleavage. She was nothing; she was less than nothing. Half a century ago, Clarissa Hudson had challenged and entertained him, and now she stood here—she *dared* to stand here—and *threaten* him?

She saw the decision come upon him: his mouth went cruel, his eyes flicked at the closed door. He noticed the cigar in his hand, and threw it at the ash-tray. With his hands free, he took a step around the corner of the table, headed towards her at last.

She retreated. He came inexorably on, moving faster now. "Hugh!" she cried, stumbling a bit on her unfamiliar shoes. And then he was on her, hands around her throat like a mockery of love remembered. His grip closed down, and the room faded around her.

CHAPTER FORTY-FOUR

Holmes and I watched Mycroft retreat to a well-deserved rest.

"He looks tired," I commented. Holmes grunted, cleaning out the day's muck from his pipe, a last act before taking to his bed. Uneasily, it occurred to me that Mycroft had looked tired before his heart attack—and that Holmes could use a rest as well.

"When did you last sleep?" I asked him.

"On the way up from Sussex this morning. Billy was driving so slowly, there was nothing to do but escape."

"So, an hour last night, less the night before."

"Oh, at least twice that."

I had not been aware until that very moment that my mind was made up. I stood. "I, however, have had more sleep than my body knows what to do with. I'm going to take a cab over to Steadworth House and make certain the Earl doesn't slip away while we're not watching. Bring me a flask of coffee when you and Mycroft come in the morning. And—would you please ring Billy before you come? I promised I wouldn't take any action without him, but I'm not going to wake his wife at this hour for the sake of watching a dark house."

Normally, Holmes would have raised an amused eyebrow and handed me my coat. Perhaps my doubts about Mycroft's infallibility were proving contagious. Or perhaps the accumulated emotional burden of the past week—my apparent death and the threat lying over Mrs Hudson—had made inroads on his usual willingness to bid me adieu. In any event, he could see I had no intention of following Mycroft's hands-off decree towards the Earl of Steadworth, and he was not willing to let me go on my own.

We resumed our coats and went to wave down a taxicab.

After I telephoned to Billy.

There were, in fact, lights on in Steadworth House: one showing through the fan window above the transom, another in the room to the left of the doorway.

When the taxi had puttered away, I asked Holmes in a quiet voice, "Do you think we should ring?"

"I'd rather know who is in that side room."

Hugh Edmunds' London home was one end of an eighteenth-century terrace block, a pair of houses joined together internally after his ancestors came into money. The narrow street down its side, little more than an access alley to the yards and stables behind, had a marked slope to it. Some Victorian-era improver had decided to tidy that side with a terrace that was scarcely wider than its collection of Grecian statuary, but tall at its back due to the slope.

The terrace, naturally, was encircled by a stone balustrade topped with spikes to discourage burglars, prank-players, and *hoi polloi* in general. The barrier did not discourage us, although we did retreat a distance down the dark alley before Holmes boosted me up, so I in turn could pull him over.

We padded on silent feet down the terrace stones, circling the urns and statues towards the shaft of light that spilled from a pair of tall, diamond-paned doors. We were still well short of the light when a muffled cry reached our ears. We exchanged a startled glance, then leapt forward as one, to press our noses to the glass.

The curtains were parted, but the diamond panes broke the room beyond into a million pieces of light. There was a lamp in there, and a fire burning, but other than that, it could have been empty or filled with a silent crowd.

I put my mouth near Holmes' ear. "I did hear something."

He nodded, but we held back, hoping for more. A cry comes from passion—but of that, there are many flavours. It would be rather embarrassing to break in and discover the aged Earl in flagrante with his housemaid. On the other hand . . .

Holmes put his head next to mine. "If all proves innocent, run."

He was bending down for a marble dryad when two other sounds broke the still night. The first was a motorcar engine, moving fast, that pulled up in the street. The din its brakes made nearly obscured a noise from the doors: a sound like a muffled gunshot. We looked at each other, then lifted the dryad and threw.

Glass diamonds exploded into the room, followed by Holmes and me—just in time to see two people collapse on the other side of a red settee, the man's hands around the woman's throat.

Even when we pulled the man away, it took my astonished eyes some time to identify the woman on the floor beneath him as my own Mrs Hudson.

CHAPTER FORTY-FIVE

Sussex that night—rather, Monday's early hours—was a place of mourning, for the best and wisest woman I have ever known.

"What about the funeral?" I asked my husband. Dawn was more than an hour away, following another sleepless night, and we were sitting at the kitchen table where Mrs Hudson had reigned. "Do you think we should go?"

Holmes made a rude noise.

"You're probably right," I said. "Our presence could be misconstrued." I sighed, my mind re-creating yet again the figure sprawled across the Steadworth House floor, a woman unmistakeably familiar, yet completely unknown. "I cannot get over what she looked like. That hair—and those clothes! I still don't understand. Not just her appearance, but why she didn't come to us for help."

"As herself—or at any rate, as Mrs Hudson—she'd not have got inside the door. And if the Earl had seen her as his old lover Clarissa, he'd have been on his guard. But a pathetic, half-deluded old woman who was clearly not only down on her luck, but had spent most of her life there?

As for bringing us in, I don't suppose she wanted that conversation over-heard. Too many sins to be forgiven, every day over the tea tray."

"There's nothing to forgive, only to understand. Oh, Holmes. I don't know what I'm going to do without her!"

"Your time would be better spent hunting for a new housekeeper. I do agree: how the devil we're ever to do without her, I can't—"

"Holmes! Mrs Hudson spent the better part of fifty years caring for you—I'd think you could spare her just a *bit* of sympathy."

"She should at least have brought *me* in earlier. I already knew her secrets. Then she'd never have had to pull that idiotic little revolver of hers."

"And if you'd shared your information with her over the telephone," I retorted, furious, "she'd never have had to set off on her own!"

Had any of us known Wednesday what we did now . . .

I sighed. Sitting here was our first moment of stillness since I'd walked away from Mycroft's fire, twenty-seven hours earlier. Holmes and I had sent Billy away from Steadworth House with Mrs Hudson, leaving us to scrub any sign of her from the Earl's drawing room.

The butler, blessedly, had slept on, and we'd done our best with the crime scene: rinsing her glass and checking the sofa for any giveaway hairs; wiping her fingerprints from the little gun and placing it in Hugh Edmunds' hand; propping him up on the sofa as if he'd committed sui-cide with a shot to the heart. The broken door-glass argued against the scenario, but we'd removed a few of the gaudier knick-knacks to give a suggestion that some passing burglar had heard the shot and gone to see . . .

Short of surgery, nothing could be done about the bullet itself: the tiny bullet that would match the one from a skeleton in Hampshire. And short of murder, nothing could be done about the butler's memory of an older woman by name of Hudson, who had called at a peculiar hour.

Lestrade was clever enough to put it all together.

Upon our return to Sussex, Holmes and I had embarked on a similar task of obfuscation, to suggest that Mrs Hudson *could* have spent the key hours of the Earl's death right here—that, tiring of her constabulary watch-dog, she and Patrick *could* have conspired to "vanish" her to Mrs Turner's to regain her privacy. We could not make it a sure thing, but enough to cast doubts on the matter. When we were satisfied—dinner things in the draining rack, damp towel in her bath-room—we set off onto the Downs. As we walked the close-cropped grass, Holmes told me at last about Mrs Hudson's convoluted history: her crimes, her father's death, his own willingness to compound a felony for her—as he was doing again now, to protect her. Clarissa the thief: Billy the pickpocket. Good Lord.

Only after Billy's car pulled into the drive, well after darkness had fallen, did it occur to me that Holmes had been keeping my hands busy and my mind occupied, so I would not dwell on what I had done to her son, or berate myself over how things might have been. How we should have told her what we knew before she left here on Saturday morning.

"You may be right," he said finally, to my surprise. He dropped his elbows onto Mrs Hudson's soft-scrubbed kitchen table, sinking his fingers in his hair. "That bloody pistol. I should have buried it along with her accursed father. Or taken it to the smithy and had Bertram melt it down."

I shook my head sadly, a portion of me agreeing with him. Without that decorative little gun, would Mrs Hudson have dared go after Hugh Edmunds on her own? Never. She'd at least have taken Billy. Only chance, and my own eagerness to stand up against an English Earl (and against Mycroft Holmes) had brought us to Steadworth House while she was still there.

And yet—

A voice from the doorway broke into our dark thoughts. "Look, you two: the point of a whistling-kettle is lost if one neglects to put on its whistle." She turned off the flame below the furiously boiling tea-kettle—and instead of taking down the teapot, she came to the table and looked down at us. "Both of you will have to take care. Kindly don't burn the place down as soon as I'm gone."

We would both, I think, have willingly sat there forever and listened to her scold us. She looked from one woebegone face to the other, and made a *tsk* noise. "You do realise that most housekeepers retire sooner or later, even without having the police after them?"

Until that day, I'd have said I knew my housekeeper—my surrogate mother—as I knew few others. But this woman, with her still-brown hair and manicured nails? "Mrs Hudson, I . . . I honestly do not know what to say."

The skin around her eyes crinkled and for a moment, she inhabited her face. Then she was gone, and the woman who pulled out the old wooden chair was a stranger: a person in a perfectly cut dress, made from a fabric that emphasised the gleam of her eyes and the lines of the body beneath. Mrs Hudson, with dark hair—and a figure! She even moved differently, with a sort of arthritic femininity and life-long sophistication. As if this rural setting, that smooth-worn chair, the scrubbed deal table were being seen for the first time, by a woman too polite to reveal her opinion of them. It was all very unsettling.

Then she reached across the table to take my hand between hers, and my Mrs Hudson was there again, warmth and sadness shining from her dark eyes. Before today, I had never understood the sadness.

"Mary, for heaven's sake, it's still me."

"Is it?"

"Just because most people's lives run in a single line, beginning to end, does not mean that is the only way. Or even the best. When I was a child, I was one thing; after my mother died, I became another. When . . . when I took over Baker Street, I was a different person yet, and again when I chose to move to Sussex. Each has been *me*. With certain, shall we say, shifts in emphasis."

"You've been living a . . ." I stopped, to change the word into something less accusatory. "An act."

She smiled, as if the word had hidden meaning. "For a lie to become truth, the past need only be rewritten. When Mr Holmes and I came here, we put my past behind us—and to be fair, a great deal of his as well. By the time you walked through that door twelve years later, the history he and I invented had long since become the truth. A truth that—had either of us given you reason to doubt it—would have unravelled and left us adrift. He and I had a long talk that first evening after you left. We agreed that dead history did not serve your needs in the least.

"But let us be clear about one thing: my affection for you, my considerable respect, has never held the least particle of deceit."

To save us from melting down into maudlin tears—we simply did not have the time—I pressed my attack. "It wouldn't have changed matters. I even knew some of it, from early on. You could have . . . I could have learned so much from you. Pretending to be someone else that thoroughly, it's not easy."

"Oh, my dear, I've never pretended—not since I was very young, at any rate. Pretence is deliberate, and I am a mediocre actress. What I do is instinctive: I read someone's needs and take on the appropriate shape. Asking me to teach you that would be like a chameleon teaching camouflage to a starling."

"So what shape were you taking on, there in London? Why go to Steadworth House looking like—like *that*?"

She chuckled. "Like a once-beautiful woman fighting a losing battle with age, do you mean? Powder, paint, hair-dye, and corsetry, in a dress too young in style and too old-fashioned in colour, with a degree of cleavage that was at the same time sad and stimulating?

"I looked that way because for a short time, Hugh Edmunds knew me very well indeed. Hugh is—Hugh *was* what I might have been, under other circumstances. A master of understanding with no trace of empathy. Someone who divides the world into taker and taken. Hugh knew I'd owned a gun—and he remembered. When he walked into the room last night, he went immediately to a desk which, to judge by how he stood, held some kind of weapon. He hovered there until I convinced him I was harmless, at which point he came back, sat down, and answered my questions. I wanted him to look at me and see only a victim. To see what he believed he had turned me into: a sad, old failure, the very furthest thing from dangerous. I had to be, literally, disarming."

"And that's the sort of thing you simply . . . know?" This was both utterly fascinating and deeply disturbing—and not only because it made me suspect my entire relationship with her. Beyond that discomfort lurked the question: What forces had shaped the shape-shifter? How did one turn a little girl into a looking glass?

"Yes. I suppose I learned early that people are more likely to give you things, and less likely to hit, if they see themselves in you. As I grew older, I learned to do it deliberately, and more or less permanently."

"How utterly exhausting!"

She laughed. "In fact, it's exhilarating. The challenge of building an Act, and the joy when one hits it spot-on—it's the closest I will ever come to a musician's flawless performance."

"Addictive," Holmes remarked.

"Sadly, yes," she agreed. "Although it became more difficult after I began to feel sorry for people."

"But in 1880, you chose to return to London and . . . put on a mask." I found it hard to imagine, a lifetime of artifice.

"Everyone wears a mask to the world. Some are thin and comfortable, others harsh and impenetrable. But in fact, the one I put on in the autumn of 1880 lay very close to the skin. That's because Mr Holmes is one of the handful of people who could always see straight through me. Him, and that brother of his."

A housekeeper and her employer, as with a landlady and her tenant, do not need to be compatible. However, as noted already, Mrs Hudson was far more than a housekeeper. And the idea of Holmes taking on the rôle of gaoler made me nearly as uncomfortable as the fact of his brother as the world's puppet-master.

She read the discomfort on my face—of course she did—and reached again for my hand. "Mary, I murdered my father. No, it's true: I took my gun with me that day, as I took it last night, knowing I might use it. Both times I believed I was protecting others, and yet both times, it was I who put us all in that situation. And both times, your husband would have been right to give me to the police. He trusts me in a way I doubt I've ever trusted myself. I personally believe that without his intervention, I'd have continued along the very path that had led me to murder. Crime is so easy: a wide road smoothed by the knowledge that one can only cheat the greedy. Without innocent victims, I felt, there could be no guilt. Your husband learned at a young age that this was not true. It took him a while to teach me."

Holmes stirred. "I did not teach you ethical behaviour, although I may have reminded you. Your mother was a woman of unflinching determination and upright, if somewhat creative, morals. A childhood under her laid a foundation that your father's tutoring could obscure but not overturn. I merely needed to isolate you, and provide you the time and the tools to chip his influence away."

Four and a half decades of chipping away, trapped together under one roof: him never slackening his attentions lest she slip, her never free of his iron rule. "I find it extraordinary that in forty-five years, neither of you killed the other."

"Oh, it did not take nearly that long," Holmes said lightly. "My Reichenbach disappearance came ten years after we began, and she did fine without me. But I should not want you to think it was only a matter of my will over hers." He was no longer speaking to me. "You know how much Dr Watson helped me understand my fellow man. Mrs Hudson has done the same. Although perhaps for different reasons."

She broke in, to jab a stopper into the spilling emotion. "And during those early years you are right: I did take comfort in knowing that poison would go unnoticed in my recipe for curry."

The two of them laughed heartily; me less so.

"Forty-five years ago—forty-six, come September," she reflected. "And fourteen years before that. Do you know, this may be the first time I have ever just been myself?"

"Whoever that might be," Holmes muttered. "Are you ready, then? You and Billy need to be gone before it's light."

"I am as packed and ready as I need to be."

I had managed to sponge the blood-stains from her bank passbook, and slipped it into her desk when we returned. And although I could not help noticing that the accumulated savings were substantial, I nonetheless ventured an offer. "Can I—that is, would a cheque . . . ?"

"Oh, my dear, the thought is kind, but I am sufficiently funded."

"You need only ask," I told her, rather more vehemently than I'd intended. "But where will you go? What will you do?"

"Well, wherever I end up, I'm probably finished with scrubbing floors. Oh, don't blush, dear heart! A clean house can be a remarkably satisfying achievement."

Any response I may have had was interrupted by a rap at the door. Holmes stood to let Billy in, his stocky figure bundled in a great-coat and bringing in a waft of Downland air.

He shot Mrs Hudson an amused sideways glance, and told me, "That man of yours gave a flick on his torch, like you said. Nobody's stirred out there all night. I'll go warm up the motor."

Patrick—that man of mine—had climbed the old smuggler's path behind the village at sundown, laden with thermos, electric torch, and a great-coat of his own, to spend the night watching for motorcar headlamps or the beams of approaching hand-torches. However, just because the police hadn't arrived yet did not mean they weren't on their way.

Holmes picked up the suit-case and followed Billy to the door. I bent for the small valise, thinking, *Such little baggage to show for a lifetime*—then stopped when her arms went around me. She embraced me, long and hard; I in turn clung to her.

"Mary, Mary," she said. "Thank you for making my life such a joy."

With that, the tears burst forth. "I am sorry." I'd said it to her earlier; she had merely nodded. "Oh, God, I'm *so* sorry! When he came—I didn't mean—I was only trying to protect you, but I should have—"

She jerked back, eyes blazing, her fingers digging into my shoulders. "*You* did not do this," she declared fiercely. "Samuel's death is on his head alone. If anyone is to blame, it is me. I knew, when my sister's husband died, that it was wrong to leave Samuel with her, but I did. You paid for my mistake. My son came here intending to cause any hurt he could: never doubt that. What you did saved me, and your husband, and heaven only knows who else."

She studied my face, and continued in a quieter voice. "When things settle, you're going to drag yourself over the coals, fretting on what you might have done differently. Know this: you had no choice. Samuel took any choice from you when he came here. He surrendered to greed, then let himself be manipulated by two men hungry for money and for power. He was dead the minute he motored away from London.

"I should be the one to say I am sorry, to you. I *am* sorry, that you were forced into the burden of taking a life. That will be with you all your days. It will haunt your nights, it will ride your shoulders. It may even slow your hand, if—God forbid—a time ever comes when you find yourself facing a similar choice.

"But know this: only one small portion of the burden belongs to you. What you did feels like murder. But it was not."

She said *you*, but she was talking about herself—and not of her son's death, but her father's. She watched my face until she saw the doubt mingling with gratitude, then embraced me again, until we heard a loud clearing of the throat from the front door.

She kissed me and stood away. I swiped my eyes beneath my spectacles, and picked up her valise.

The sky was black and clear, the smoke from Billy's motor streaming across the light that spilled from the portico. Mrs Hudson pulled her gloves from her pocket. As she worked them on, she spoke to Holmes. "If Mr Lestrade seems to be on the verge of making an arrest—any arrest—let him know that he is to speak to me first. I will return, if you need me."

"But where are you *going*?" I pleaded, sounding like a child. "France? Australia? How will we find you again?"

The three of us paused as Mrs Hudson worked the buttons on her gloves. When her head came up, she looked young—almost young enough for that brown hair.

"Do you know," she said, "I've always been fond of Monte Carlo."

VI

CLARISSA HUDSON

CHAPTER FORTY-SIX

As Billy's motor crested the road out of East Dean, Mrs Hudson spoke. "You'll take care of them for me, won't you?"

"I will," her old friend promised.

"This will wear on Mary's mind."

"But not on yours?"

"Oh, Billy, it'll have to find room with all my other sins."

Halfway to Newhaven, the sky began to grow light. When it was bright enough to see, Billy pulled out his watch, then tucked it away and put his foot more firmly onto the accelerator pedal.

"The boat will wait for me," Mrs Hudson reassured him.

"I know that. I just want to get you on board before the harbour inspectors come on duty."

"It'll be fine, Billy. Unless we get into an accident on the way."

He eased his foot back a fraction.

"What am I going to do without you?" he lamented.

"Ah, Billy, we've had such a good run of it, haven't we? Who'd have guessed, that day at The Bishop's den, where the two of us would end up?"

"It's not over," he insisted. "Things'll die down, you can come back. This is just a holiday."

"I don't think things are going to fade, my dear. If it was just Hugh, perhaps: a struggle, the gun going off accidentally. But the police have the earlier bullet. The one from my father. And Mr Lestrade is a very clever copper."

"We might be able to disappear one or the other of 'em," he suggested.

"That would only make matters worse. No, Billy, I think I'm finished with England. You'll just have to bring the family over for holidays."

His hand shot out to seize her fingers and lift them to his mouth. He kissed her hand, long and hard, then gave it a squeeze and let it go.

"You were always a sweet boy, William Mudd," she said, not far from tears. *If only,* she thought. *Oh, Samuel . . .*

But Billy's fingers had felt something when he took her hand. "What've you got there?"

She held the thing up, and he glanced briefly away from the road for a look. "A dolly?" An ancient and much-chewed dolly.

"My father made it, on board the *Gloria Scott,* when my mother was pregnant with me. He posted it from Gibraltar, and told Mother that she could make a dress for it if I was a girl, or a sailor suit if I was a boy. My sister, Alicia, took it over when she was young. As she took over most of my things. After she died, Samuel included it with a load of what he regarded as rubbish. Something in one of my father's letters yesterday brought it to mind." As she spoke, she had been digging through her handbag, and now came up with a pair of nail-scissors. She bent over the misshapen, dirt-coloured manikin, snipping with care.

As the stitches holding the doll's spine together parted, kapok welled, and she made a sound of irritation. "May I borrow your handkerchief?"

He kept a clean one in his breast pocket. She arranged it across her skirt, and began to dig at the packed kapok with a finger-nail.

It did not take long to come across something that was not fibre.

It looked like an oversized commercial cigarette, a tight roll of cream-coloured paper some five inches long with a length of fine linen string around it. Mrs Hudson worked the cord off, then spread open the near-rigid paper.

Billy caught a glimpse of ornate writing—then the roll snapped shut, shooting kapok fibre in all directions. She made the sound again, and pulled off her other glove to separate the roll's outer layer.

In the end, one cylinder turned into five somewhat looser spirals. She picked one up and stretched it between her hands. Billy took his eyes off the road for a glance, which went on . . .

Deliberately, slowly, Billy steered into a nearby farm lane, shut down the engine, and took a shaky breath.

When he looked again at the object in her hands, he felt as if he were still headed for a tree.

"What the bloody hell is—Sorry," he said. "What is *that*?"

Clara Hudson cleared her own none-too-certain throat. "That, my dear friend, is what they call a bearer bond. Designed to be paid out to whoever holds it."

"Fifty—that can't be real."

"I think it may actually be."

"Fifty *thousand* pounds?"

The second was identical, and the third. At the fourth, Billy let out the breath he'd been holding, and reached out tentatively for one of the water-stained, long-furled pieces of official paper. Gingerly, he stretched it open, trying to make sense of the ornate writing.

"These are old," he said.

"A bit older than I am," she told him. "Which means they are either worthless, or they have decades of interest accrued on top of their face value."

The fifth piece of paper was a different size and texture. No official document, this, but a letter, undated, from a hand she knew well—from, most recently, the letters Mary had found in Samuel's hotel room. In this

case, the writing was tiny, the paper onionskin. It was dated two days
before she and her father had left Sydney for London.

My dearest Allie,

I hope this surprises you one day, or if it dont, it comes as something I show you in person. I'm leaving it hidden here until I can figure out if these mean anything at all. Knowing my luck, they
probably wont. But once upon a time they were the work of a very
clever man, and thow even now just looking at them reminds me of
some things Id rather not remember, and makes me feel a little sick,
I've always thought there was just a chance they'd be worth something. But I never wanted to get arrested for trying to hand them
over.

I came across them fair enough, the day the ship that I was on
going to Sydney went down. Her name was the Gloria Scott. On
board was a cove named Jack Prendergast who pulled a bank dodge
in London and stole a whole stack of money. He had a partner on
the old boat, and when she went down that day and I was waiting to
drown, I kept my mind off the sharks under my feet and the bodies
of all those men—mates, they were, men I'd worked with and played
cards with for weeks—by talking to anyone who floated by and going
through their pockets. Sounds mad, I know, but I think talking to
dead men kept me from just letting go of the spar I was hanging to.
Anyway, I found some letters that I mailed later on, and not much
cash or anything, but when the so-called chaplain's body floated by, I
found a waterproof pouch around his neck, and put it around mine.

Later, when I looked, I found these. I'm not sure just what they
are, and I never quite nerved myself up to trying to cash one in.
What happened on that ship, well, I never done nothing wrong,
Allie, I promise—but if anyone got wind of your father being on that
ship, I'd hang for sure. But just in case, when Clarrie and I are in
London, I'll see if I can find somebody to tell me about these things.
If I do, and if I can be sure it's safe, I'll send for you (and the dolly!)
and we'll all do London in a big way then.

Nobody knows about this but you, Allie dear, not even your sister. Let it be our surprise.

Your Loving Pa

She handed the letter over to Billy, who read it twice.

"The Bishop was right," he said in awe. "The money didn't end up nibbled by fishes."

"So it would appear."

"But these couldn't possibly be good anymore, could they? Do bonds expire?"

"That remains to be seen." She fitted the five pages together, and began to re-roll them into their tight cylinder.

"Don't *you* get arrested over them."

"No."

"Would you like me to take them to Mr Holmes?"

She did not reply. His head came around. He bent down to stare into her face. "You . . ." He studied her expression, a look of mischief that he hadn't seen since—when? Since he was a child, and she had rescued him. Long enough to forget she was capable of looking like that. He shook his head in wonder, and felt his mouth begin to lose control. "You're not going to tell him, are you? Oh, you wicked woman."

She tore her gaze from his and concentrated on returning the roll to its manikin exterior, her own lips wearing a demure smile. "You know, when it comes to women, Mr Holmes has always been just the teensiest bit naïve."

"Ha!" Billy pounded his fist on the wheel, grinning hugely. He slapped the car back into gear and pulled merrily out, chuckling like a cooling percolator. Clara Hudson, meanwhile, took the little sewing kit from her handbag and set to work closing up the doll.

Yes, she thought. Monte Carlo would do nicely, to begin with.

NOTES

The chronology of the Conan Doyle stories makes for a perpetually
delightful conundrum, keeping generations of Sherlock Holmes
scholars occupied. The story at the root of this current volume,
"The Adventure of the *Gloria Scott*," contains few internal dates, and
those it does have are often contradictory: the sailing of the *Gloria Scott*
is firmly stated as 1855; however, the following years of gold fields and
settled life in England are more than a touch slippery. Conan Doyle
furthermore failed to enlighten the reader as to the precise year when
Holmes himself was introduced to the story. According to Mary Russell's memoirs, that took place in the summer of 1879, with Dr Watson
being introduced to the young detective eighteen months later, in January, 1881. Many will disagree with her.

Similar problems occur with names: nowhere does Conan Doyle suggest that the sailor Hudson of the *Gloria Scott* case is related in any way
to the Baker Street landlady (nor, indeed, the Hudson mentioned in
"Five Orange Pips," or even Morse Hudson of the "Six Napoleons"). Nor
is there the merest hint that Billy the page might be the same person as
Wiggins, the "dirty little lieutenant" of Holmes' Irregulars, much less
that there were two separate boys named Billy in the life of Baker Street.

Some might take these problems as proof that Miss Russell's memoirs
are fiction. Certainly, her stories can be problematic. However, the same
may be said of the Conan Doyle canon itself: Dr Watson could be a remarkably unreliable chronicler of life in Baker Street.

ACKNOWLEDGMENTS

I owe eternal gratitude to my editor, Kate Miciak, and her omni-competent and long-suffering right hand, Julia Maguire. And to the rest of my own personal team of Random House improvers—Libby McGuire, Jennifer Hershey, Lindsey Kennedy, Allison Schuster, Kim Hovey, Scott Shannon, Matt Schwartz, Kelly Chian, and Carlos Beltrán—you people are nothing short of amazing, time and again. If you, dear Reader, are looking at these words now, it's thanks to them.

Thanks also to the community that loves me, lends a hand, and urges me on with verbal whips even when I threaten their beloved characters with murder: my agents, Zoë Elkaim, Mary Alice Kier, and Anna Cottle; my conjuror of everyday magic, Robert Difley; and my Devoted Readers Alice Wright, Merrily Taylor, Vicki Van Valkenburgh, Erin Bright, and John Bychowski. The staff of the McHenry Library continue to work wonders, and Linda Allen continues to nurture my career. As for the details of Sherlockian life, Leslie S. Klinger and Lyndsay Faye caught some of my mistakes, and can't really be blamed for anything I've got wrong herein.

IF YOU ENJOYED

THE MURDER OF MARY RUSSELL

READ ON FOR AN EXCITING PREVIEW OF

LOCKDOWN

THE THRILLING NEW SUSPENSE NOVEL

FROM BESTSELLING AUTHOR

Laurie R. King

CAREER DAY

GUADALUPE MIDDLE SCHOOL

THE DARK HOURS

12:31 A.M.

LINDA

S leep was proving every bit as elusive as Linda had feared. She'd thought about pills, but decided chemical grogginess would be worse than mere fatigue tomorrow. So she stared up at the dim ceiling, letting her thoughts toss and turn instead of her body.

Paper cups will be fine—nobody expects proper cups and glasses. At least lunch will be off real plates. Wait: did I warn the speakers against gang colors? Like that substitute who'd turned up in a blouse made of red bandannas and—oh, yes: that made it into the letter, after talking to Mrs. Hopkins about the Taco Alvarez trial.

What about that typo in the flyer—she'd corrected it, right? Her leg twitched with the impulse to get up and check—but no. Mrs. Hopkins had caught it, too.

Praise the heavens for school secretaries! And for the teachers (most of them) and the volunteers that Señora Rodriguez (*I do wish I could like that woman more*) had commandeered to help with Career Day. And the Social Studies department, for the grant they'd gotten, and the old hippie who'd finished restoring the school mural just in time—and not to

forget "Tío" (was he actually anyone's "uncle"?) because, oh, what a difference a good janitor made in a school's life. (Ridiculous to be suspicious of the man: He lived to keep Guadalupe running smoothly.)

But—the loose button on her white blouse! The blessed thing was *sure*
to pop off at the worst possible moment. Like during school assembly,
fifty minutes that already filled her with cold dread, and not only because
of her speech. A gym full of adolescents on the brink of boiling over into
impatience, mockery, and even the violence that was never far away.
Seven hundred-plus fuses waiting to be lit by a perceived insult or a slip
of the tongue—or a display of their principal's bra.

Do not forget to wear the blue blouse tomorrow!

Linda would bet Olivia Mendez never went to work with a loose button. Ever-competent Sergeant Mendez of the San Felipe Police Department, watching Gordon walk across the distant playing field the other
day, that too-intelligent, endlessly speculative gaze of hers . . .

As if she'd said it aloud, Gordon shifted on his pillow. "You're not
sleeping."

"Sorry, love, I didn't mean to wake you. I'll go make myself some tea."

"Worried about tomorrow?"

"You could say that. I can't help thinking I've set us all up for a . . . a
catastrophe." She didn't even like to say the word aloud. "There must be
something I'm overlooking."

"Linda, I cannot imagine you've overlooked *anything*."

Her laugh was forced. "Compulsive, right? Like when I was a child,
I used to lie awake and invent horrible things that might happen. My
parents dying, the neighbor's dog biting me. I must've heard someone
say it was always the unexpected that crept up you, and I thought if I
could imagine a thing, at least I'd be safe from *that*."

"Linda, you have it all under control. You're prepared to the hilt, with
good help, competent volunteers, a responsible team of guests. There's
nothing to worry about. Tomorrow will go fine."

His calm voice almost made Linda . . . believe. *There's no restlessness in
him, is there? You've been imagining problems, like you always do. This is*

Gordon, the most trustworthy man you know. There's no reason whatsoever to imagine—

His arm came out then, to stroke warm fingers up and down her arm. Up and down. Wordless and hypnotic. Before long, her nerves ceased their rattling. Paper cups and loose buttons, gang members and school secretaries, bulldog police sergeants and too-efficient janitors, and all the rest gathered together in a narrow stream, circled around a hole, and poured away into the darkness.

12:40 A.M.

SOFIA

This little time between taking the pill and falling into it was the best. A melting time, warm and dark and comforting.

At school, Sofia stuck to half-pills. They softened the edges without making her groggy. But at night, after everyone went to bed, she could let go. Here, in these slow minutes as the pill worked its way into her, there was no murdered sister, no Alvarez brothers looking hate at her, no pressures for grades or looks from Mina or presence of boys or . . . nothing.

Just the melting, rich and warm and delicious, tingling along the ends of your nerves, making the world soft and deep.

Some nights—not always—she was aware of a last, juddering breath, sucked into her chest just before she tipped into the dreams. Like a relieved infant in its mother's arms. Safe.

2:23 A.M.

THOMAS

Tom Atcheson looked up at the ceiling. Brendan?

Maybe he should have gone in and dragged the boy out of bed when he went to check on him two hours ago. Control was such a tenuous thing, whether with a company in turmoil or a rebellious son. At least the boy was set for the academy next September: that would straighten him out.

But depending on others to solve the problem wasn't a sign of weakness or cowardice. Was it?

No: A man *had* to prioritize. He'd been right to shut the door and walk away.

This time.

True control—with work, with family—sometimes required an *appearance* of weakness. Vulnerability could be the leaves covering a trap.

Tom picked up his pen again.

He wasn't entirely happy with his plan for the 9:00 a.m. board meeting, but he had to admit there wasn't much more he could do about it now—other than fire the entire board, of course, which according to his useless lawyers, he was no longer in a position to do. Sleep might help, but he could tell that wasn't going to happen. Instead, he turned to his notes for the talk at Brendan's school. "Career Day." What an exercise in futility! Urging ill-trained children to become entrepreneurs was like telling finger-painters to aim for the Sistine Chapel: those with drive required no encouragement.

But the boy's principal had asked, and when Thomas Atcheson made a commitment, he kept it, no matter how pressed his day had become or how pointless the exercise might be.

Advice for young people? Obviously he had advice—for people of any age.

Don't trust your partners.

Don't marry a harpy with lawyers in her family.

Don't have a son who fights you at every turn.

And never, ever let people screw you into a corner.

2:45 A.M.

CHACO

Chaco put his head around the outside corner of A Wing, filled with ... what was the word? *Foreboding*. Yeah, so the janitor made him nervous. Gave Chaco *misgivings*.

Scared the shit out of him.

Far as Chaco knew, *Tío* wasn't nobody's *uncle*, wasn't even from Mexico like everybody Chaco knew. Sure he talked Spanish, but his accent was, like, *exotic*—from somewhere else. Nicaragua, maybe? El Salvador? Tío was just the limpiador, walking up and down in his dirt-colored uniform and cleaning the floors. Big thrill for the old guy was the day he got to shut off the water in the girl's *baño*, stopped it from running all over the floor. Real hero, man.

Maybe the reason Tío made him nervous was 'cause the dude was so *pinche* quiet. He talked quiet, he didn't turn on a radio the minute the bell rang—even his cart with all the mops and brooms, the same one the last janitor used, didn't rattle and squeak so much. And, like, last week when one of the substitutes shouted some question down the breezeway at him? Tío didn't just shout back an answer. Instead, he put away his broom and walked over, all polite, to see what the guy wanted.

Funny thing was, the teacher looked a little . . . not *embarrassed*. More like he thought maybe Tío coming at him so quiet (*like Angel*) meant the old guy had a knife. *Edgy*, maybe? Wanting to *edge* away?

Anyway, yeah, Chaco felt a little *edgy* tonight himself, crouching in back of A Wing away from the all-night floods, a can of spray paint in his hand. He really, *really* didn't want to turn around and find the old guy looking at him.

Which was stupid. Or—what was that word he'd found the other day?—*ludicrous*. (Chaco had a private collection of perfect words—words he'd never, ever use out loud.) Tío didn't spend the night at school, and no way could he just guess who'd done a tag. Chaco knew all about crime labs and *forensic science* and stuff, so he was wearing a set of his uncle's overalls that he'd fished out of the trash and his most beat-up pair of shoes, and he'd dump it all on his way home. He'd take a shower in the morning so he wouldn't smell like paint. How would Tío know?

Besides, there wasn't really much choice. He was almost thirteen— and he was family to Taco Alvarez.

So now, at near to three in the morning, Chaco the Tagger crept down the A Wing breezeway, the old rubber on his shoes making a kissing sound against the smooth concrete. Nothing moved, no cars went by. Under the main breezeway, into the entrance arch—and there it was, all shiny and new-looking, hundreds of little chips and tiles with pictures of school things and people on them. He hesitated, just a little, 'cause really, it was kind of cool. *Intricate*, like. And a man didn't tag someone else's art unless it was enemy action. But this was a school, and in the end he had to prove himself to Taco—and to Angel. And maybe to Sofia Rivas, though she'd probably just give him one of her looks, all *arrogant*, or maybe *condescending*.

Chaco's arm went up to shake the can, making the little ball inside *ting* back and forth five, six times. He chose his spot with care, right there on the face of the school secretary for the first letter, and—

And as if the pressure of his finger had triggered a lot more than paint, the universe exploded into a blinding glare of floodlight, outlining every tile, giving texture to the grout, showing the cheerful expressions on a crowd of pieced-together figures.

The can bounced and skittered across the walkway as Chaco fled into the night.

5:17 A.M.

GORDON

Gordon ran beneath the waning moon, fighting the need to circle the park.

The fight lay not in the running, but the circling back—although granted, three and a half years ago when he'd first made this circuit, he'd thought his lungs would explode. He'd been old: washed up, worn out, ready for the knacker's gun. But not *put out to pasture*. Men like Gordon Hugh-Kendrick were not generally granted a placid retirement. Men like him ran until they were brought down.

To his astonishment, it turned out he'd merely been tired: bloody tired and older than his years. Thank God he'd been wretched enough to make one last mad, whimsical, despairing lunge for shelter—because he'd hit pure gold. Instead of a farewell tour, he found haven, and comfort, and a degree of purpose. The affection of a good woman.

Forty-four months later, Gordon was . . . if not at the top of his form, certainly better than he could have dreamed. And surely the low cunning of age counted for more than the dumb muscle mass of youth?

Which would be fine (he reflected, circling a fallen milk crate) but for two problems. One was specific: He'd gotten sloppy, and let his name appear where it should not. He couldn't even blame Linda, not entirely. After thirty years of habit, he'd become complacent, failing to check the list she handed to the police department. That was five months ago, and though he appeared to have dodged the bullet this time, he couldn't risk a second mistake.

The other problem was more general. With a fit body and faint return of optimism had come restlessness. The familiar itch of being in one place for too long; the inborn need for challenge—his kind of challenge, which was thin on the ground in a sleepy farm community of California's Central coast. Hence the hard joy of running a little too fast through a hazard-strewn park, and the temptation to keep going.

But not today.

He'd been honest with Linda from the beginning—well, more honest than he'd been with anyone for many a year. And since she'd lived up to his terms (apart from that one slip), she deserved his loyalty. Gordon would cut his own throat before letting her down. Not forever—maybe not even for much longer, but today? Today was important to Linda.

So this morning he would circle the park and turn back. He would polish his shoes, shave his face, and don the appearance of an ordinary man, to spend the day walking amongst the unsuspecting.

5:34 A.M.

OLIVIA

The early morning air had just taken on the oddly rich smell of celery when the figure dashed across the road at the limits of Olivia's headlights. Her hand snapped out to trigger the cruiser's lights and siren—then her front-brain caught up, cancelling the cop's chase-impulse. No predawn burglar, this, but the same gray-haired Englishman in khaki shorts she saw pretty much every time she was out this early. Linda's husband Gordon . . . something. Not McDonald. Olivia had only met the man a couple times, but she'd seen him all over: Safeway, library, coming out of the martial arts dojo, pushing a mower across his front lawn. Once, weirdly enough, up at the homeless encampment near the levee, squatting beneath the drifting smoke of their illegal cook-fire like some gung ho anthropologist with a primitive tribe.

So what's your story, Gordon not-McDonald?

Back in September, she'd had the excuse to run a background check on him—a legitimate excuse, since his name was right there on Linda's list of volunteers. His hyphenated name . . . ah: Hugh-Kendrick, that was it, although he went by just Kendrick. Gordon Hugh-Kendrick, could you get any more English than that?

He and Linda made for an odd couple—the twenty-some-year difference in their ages; his thin/gray/British and her round/blonde/Midwest—but they fit like pieces in a jigsaw puzzle. Even if Gordon's piece seemed to belong to a different picture altogether.

Still, everyone was entitled to their privacy, and although Gordon Hugh-Kendrick might rouse Olivia's nosiness (honestly, was there anything that *didn't?*) his record was clean as can be, and as a cop she had no right to pry further. Even if she'd wondered, back in September, just what a wider background search might reveal. Wider as in international . . .

Not. Her. Business.

Because even if she didn't get caught and fired—even if Sergeant Olivia Mendez wasn't reprimanded for a search with dubious probable cause—whatever she learned from it would stand between her and Linda, forever and ever. And Linda McDonald was on her way to becoming a friend—a rare enough thing for a cop to have.

So: no snooping beyond that of any normally inquisitive civilian.

She expected to see him today—Linda had mentioned that he'd be helping out for Career Day, and Olivia was due to speak about The Joys of Being a Cop. Assuming she hadn't been buried under an avalanche of paperwork, or summoned to an urgent felony, or (God help us) dragged back to the Taco Alvarez trial.

She'd already wasted a full day listening to the two lawyers squabble over her right to testify against a man she'd been arresting since he was fourteen. And then yesterday . . . that gesture Taco made. Should she tell the judge? No one else noticed. Taco's attorney would claim she was trying to sway the jury. But there it was, a message from Mr. Taco Alvarez: his hand on the table shaping a gun, thumb coming down like the hammer.

Threat, pure and clear.

If her boss was around, Olivia would ask his advice, but the chief was back East, leaving Olivia Mendez to wear not only her usual two hats—

uniformed Sergeant and plainclothes Detective—but also that of acting Chief. Didn't matter. Taco Alvarez wasn't going anywhere.

The celery aroma faded, replaced by the vinegary smell from the apple-juice plant, and Olivia slowed to take the pulse of San Felipe. The Kwik Mart was doing its usual early-morning business, men in suits ordering pricey coffee drinks for the pleasure of an insult from its tattooed barista. (And talk about stories: the pierced, inked, muscular ex-gang member was married to a nerdy accountant, with two little girls she dressed in pink.) Olivia stopped to look down the adjoining alley (a place she knew a little too well for a girl who grew up to be a cop), but that light the city got the owner to install remained unbroken, and the space was empty.

She crossed Main Street at the signal, looping around for a survey of the industrial area near the tracks. All quiet here, the air smelling of fresh sawdust from the lumberyard. The sandwich place hadn't fixed their dangling sign yet, and Olivia made a mental note to have one of the men go by with a deadline. A glance down the street beside the lumberyard— and her foot stamped on the brake, her hand slapping the cruiser's gear shift into Reverse.

But it was only Señora Rodriguez, self-proclaimed community activist and widely recognized pain in the ass. One of the Señora's designated Causes must live down here. Olivia put the cruiser back in Drive and continued on.

It being February, spring planting was just starting up, and work was slack at the cannery. The guy who ran her favorite burrito truck hadn't got back from Mexico City yet, and the paleta man—the old guy who went everywhere, saw everything, and who she suspected of sending a couple anonymous tips that led to arrests—wouldn't sell much ice cream until later in the year.

But old Tío had a job now, didn't he? Janitor at Linda's school. She wondered if he'd show up again in June, selling the kids frozen goodies from his pushcart, or if that shifty fellow with the blaring ice cream truck would move into Tío's territory.

She waved to the manager of the sprinkler supply business and turned up Main Street, past the burned-toast smell from the coffee roaster and the sad windows of the Goodwill and the line forming outside the church's soup kitchen. She doubled back around the anonymous women's shelter, went by the secondhand furniture shop, the barber, the theater— then again, up at the limits of the cruiser's headlights, a lean figure in khaki shorts flashed across the street.

For an old guy, Linda's husband sure could run.

5:45 A.M.

LINDA

inda's clock was so old-fashioned, it gave a little wheeze before its alarm went off. As usual, she hit the button before the ring started—although this morning she was nowhere near sleep when it wheezed. She had managed a few hours of unconsciousness after Gordon's soothing, but when he got up for his run, the whirring of her mind (which, equally old-fashioned, seemed to have gears instead of silicon chips) started up again.

Career Day? What was she *thinking*? Just a year ago, her life had been so easy! The nearby elementary school where she'd been principal had its problems, sure, but at least it had an experienced staff, community support, and children that her memory tinted as sweetly innocent.

And then the city's Busybody-in-Chief, Señora Rodriguez, walked through her office door and pronounced the words Guadalupe Middle School. Linda had cowered behind her desk—as if anything short of a loaded gun could be an effective defense against Señora Rodriguez.

Guadalupe was the Señora's most recent Good Cause, a school in desperate need of ... yes: a principal. Seven hundred and twelve students, ages eleven to fourteen. Half child, half adult, all hormones and passion—an age group Linda found problematic as individuals and a horror en masse. Even the best of middle schools were places to fence in the dangerously adolescent. And the bad ones, those that suffered an indifferent staff, poor choices, and school board neglect?

Schools like Guadalupe?

Better to bulldoze it and turn it into an apple orchard.

But no one Linda knew had ever managed to put off Señora Rodriguez when she had the bit in her teeth. So she'd sighed, and let the woman drag her off to a school with a history of bad grades and violence, a school with an alarming turnover of newly fledged teachers, a school whose buildings were a mix of the rundown (library, cafeteria, most of the classrooms) and the ridiculously elaborate (the gym). A school splintered into gangs and cliques, whose corridors would be filled with the hunched shoulders of the beaten, most of whose teachers would have prescriptions for mood suppressants. A school whose last principal had been driven to suicide.

A school that last May had sidled up and murmured sweet nothings in Linda's ear.

She'd held herself aloof during the Señora's tour, nodding and asking few questions, until she somehow found herself standing alone in the arched entranceway.

Its tiled walls had once been a mosaic. Under the years of filth, felt pens, and chewing gum lay a mural somebody had spent a lot of time on. Up at the top (beyond student reach) was a row of surprisingly ornate hand-painted tiles—a sort of picture frame, wrapped around a sky as blue as the afternoon beyond the archway.

Linda studied the brutalized surface, trying to pick out the design. The tiles themselves were a mix of tidy rectangles and anarchic shards: a long rectangle evoked the school's façade; in the blue sky, a spatter of chips made for an Impressionistic, breeze-stirred flag; ten thin triangles shaped the circle of a wheelchair. Some of the tiles were painted, rather than pieced: a woman's face here, obscured by felt-pen beard and horns; a cluster of high-top shoes there; a brown hand sinking a basketball.

Linda stepped closer, her attention caught by that face: a woman with an expression of authority, captured in a few deft lines. Wasn't that the school secretary?

Bemused, she let the Señora drive her back to the elementary school, and set about composing her refusal, polite but firm.

The job would be thankless. If Guadalupe's new principal managed to get test scores up five points, the school board would demand to know why it wasn't ten. If absenteeism and violence fell a notch, why not two? Playground bloodshed, drugs, and student pregnancy would be daily concerns. It would be terrifying and exhilarating and the mere thought of it made Linda want to take to her bed.

But that night, she had a dream of using her thumbnail to scrape the felt pen from that tile face. The next morning, Gordon asked why her sleep had been restless. The next day at school, her thoughts kept going back to that mosaic. And when the final bell had rung, Linda picked up the phone and called the district office with her demands—a lot of demands.

Over the summer break, Guadalupe was turned inside-out: classrooms to teachers; sports equipment to art lab; math curriculum to the school's policies on cellphones, parent communication, and bullying.

The school year started the third Wednesday in August. By that Friday night, she loved Guadalupe with the ferocity of an elderly cat-lady nurturing 712 runt kittens. Six months on, she felt more like a mother watching her child climb the ladder to the high-dive.

"Today will go fine," she said aloud into the dark bedroom. Once upon a time, it would have been a prayer. Today, all Linda felt entitled to ask of the universe was that Gordon had left some coffee in the pot.

5:50 A.M.

CHACO

Chaco woke up to the smell of coffee and the sound of his mother's shoes, scuffling across the old floor. *Weariness,* his mind offered. *Retribution.*

He'd got, what? Two hours of sleep? Out the kitchen door at 2:15 and back an hour later, freezing cold. Then just when his feet had got warm and he'd started to drift away, a little voice in his ear said, *You think that light mighta been hooked up to a camera?* His heart pounded so loud he thought it might wake up his little brother until he forced himself to *think,* like cousin Taco. *The light was at your back, right? And you didn't turn to look, did you?* So what if a camera took his picture? All it would show was some kid wearing too-big overalls and dirty shoes. Just a kid.

Still, it took Chaco a while to warm up again, and what felt like five minutes later, Mamá came in with the cup of mostly milk coffee and the gentle shake on his shoulder. The coffee was her way of saying he was doing a man's work. The shake told him it had to be now.

He threw back the covers and put his bare feet on the floor—harder to fall asleep if you were sitting up. *Vigilant,* that was him. When his mother looked in a few minutes later, he wasn't exactly awake, but the mug was still in his hands. She crossed the room to give him a kiss, and to whisper that there were some eggs if he wanted to cook those, but not to put cheese in his sister's until they found out what was causing her stomach problems. When he didn't answer, she asked if he was all right.

He grumbled he was fine and stood up to prove it. They both heard the car door slam, two doors down, which meant her ride would be outside in a minute. He made a little wave toward the hallway, then followed her down the cold linoleum to the kitchen. It was the only room they kept warm in the winter.

She looked up from buttoning her coat. "I nearly forgot. They called last night and asked if I could work Saturday. I said yes."

"Oh, Ma."

"I know, I told you I wouldn't, but it's time and a half, and I thought I could ask Angel to—"

"No!"

"He can borrow a car seat for your sister, and—"

"No, Mamá, promise me you won't ask him. Angel is . . ." Angel is what? Crazy? Dangerous? *Malignant?* "Angel's got things to do. The little ones like the swings in the park. We can walk down there."

"He said he didn't mind. That maybe he'd meet some of your friends there. Oh, *mijo,* you're shivering—go stand near the heater!"

It wasn't the temperature that made Chaco shudder, it was the idea of Angel around his friends. "We don't need Angel! We'll be fine."

Headlights flared across the window, and Chaco's mother picked up her lunch bag. "I have to go. If you're sure, about Saturday? I'll take the little ones in with me Saturday night so Sunday you can sleep late. You have a good day, *mijo.*"

"You too, Mamá."

"Make sure your brother wears his coat."

"I will, Mamá."

She rested her lips against his forehead. "My big man," she murmured. "I'm sorry I have to work so much."

"It's okay, I don't mind. You better go."

Cold air reached through the doorway, then she was gone. Chaco warmed his shins in front of the heater's red bars for a minute, drinking the last of his milk coffee, before turning down the expensive electricity.

Maybe he'd meet some of your friends. Yeah, right. Angel was sending him a message. *Friends* could only mean Sofia Rivas. *Meet* meant delivering a threat. If Chaco didn't want Angel to confront Sofia directly, he'd have to do it himself. Let her know what would happen if she and the kid, Danny, testified against Taco.

The idea of Angel 'fronting Sofia made Chaco's worry over the paint can feel pretty stupid. Though it was a good thing nobody'd seen him running away like some . . . some *invertebrate.*

Any chance of getting respect from Taco or Angel after that would've gone right out the door.

5:52 A.M.

TÍO

Jaime Ygnacio Rivera Cruz—*Tío* to the residents of San Felipe and the students of Guadalupe Middle School—watched yesterday's coffee rise up the woven threads of his clean rag. He squeezed it, then slid his left hand into the shoe and began to rub the cloth around and around, his father's trick to bring up a gleam on aged leather.

Perhaps it was time to buy a new pair. He had money now, more than he could have anticipated just a short time ago . . .

But discarding these would feel like an admission of defeat. And Señora Rodriguez had told him of a reliable shoe repair shop, at the other end of the county. He had doubts: This was not a generation of repairers. Still, he had bought these shoes for his wedding. They were on his feet the proud day he was hired for his first real job, and on the Sunday morning his son was baptized. He had worn them on the rainy afternoon that son was lowered into a hastily dug grave, and again two weeks later when his wife was buried at the boy's side. The shoes had gone with Tío across the border and through the desert to America. They were comrades who deserved preservation.

When the shine was to his satisfaction, he set them aside, washed his hands, and finished dressing. The rest of his clothing was equally respectable: the brown janitor's shirt was freshly ironed, as were the trousers, every button and fold in place. No necktie, though. Tío still did not feel properly dressed without a necktie, but appearance was all, especially when it came to the fragile sensibilities of adolescents.

The first day, he had worn a tie and the students had mocked it. The second day, he had let his collar go bare, for the sake of invisibility. The tie would remain in the drawer until such a time that he could reclaim his dignity.

He studied his reflection in the cracked mirror. Of the various faces he had worn in his life, this might be the most deceptive. And to think he had hesitated to put on this uniform. He had nearly turned it down entirely.

Little did he anticipate the doors that would open to a lowly school custodian. *Limpiador* simply meant one who cleaned, but his old English dictionary told him that *janitor* had to do with doors. The janitor was a doorkeeper. And the word *custodian*? In either tongue, that had to do with custody, with possession. With guarding.

The word made him the possessor of Guadalupe Middle School and all its persons. To guard the place as he saw fit.

And surely the triangle of crisp white undershirt at the neck bore the same function as a necktie?

Yes: on such a day as this, it was better to show the uniform than the man inside.

Although perhaps not when it came to young Mr. Santiago Cabrera—who called himself "Chaco" as an emulation of his dangerous cousin, the man with dreams of drug cartels in his heart. Chaco Cabrera needed to see past the surface of his school's janitor, just a little.

Because Tío had plans for Chaco. Plans that did not include permitting the boy to follow his gang-banger cousin "Taco" into a courtroom on a charge of murdering a young woman.

6:02 A.M.

#SPEAKFORBEE

Bylines beat coffee any day. They beat pills and powders (not that she'd tried the really hard stuff) and even sex (most of it).

Not that a *Clarion* byline meant a whole lot, but a girl had to start somewhere, and if they wouldn't let her have the Taco Alvarez trial, she'd make her own damn stories. Like this one. There was potential in this school. Something big under the surface, she could just smell it. What had started as a filler piece far from the trial action—Career Day? Give me a break!—ended up setting her reporter's nose to twitching. She'd give them a *human interest* story, all right.

Half the old farts working for *The Clarion* didn't know what a hashtag was. For them, #speakforbee would be one of those things kids got up to. Like they'd think *viral* meant a disease, not a thought that spread through minds.

The future Pulitzer winner wrestled open the desk drawer and took out the folder labeled #speakforbee. When she flipped back the cover, the first thing she'd found grinned up at her: the local Ford dealer, Charlie Cuomo, in a picture from an ad campaign a few weeks after his daughter disappeared—cheerful features overlaid with Hannibal Lechter's leather mask and given the hashtag.

The effect was so disturbing, any potential customer who came across it would think twice about a Ford.

She shoved the day's article into the back of the folder and tucked it at the bottom of the drawer, then went to see if the *Clarion* had a long-lensed camera that actually worked.

GUADALUPE MIDDLE SCHOOL
TO HOLD CAREER DAY

Guadalupe Middle School will hold its annual Career Day today, with a stellar list of guests. The school's principal, Linda McDonald, has invited local residents from a variety of backgrounds to speak to the students about jobs ranging from law enforcement to weaving. She has also given this year's Career Day a theme: "Unexpected Threads."

As Ms. McDonald says, "Many of us come to our careers by an indirect route: we train for archaeology and end up in computer science, or plan to teach and become actors instead. This school, in this California farm community, is linked to the wider world by a million unexpected threads, any of which can be grasped by a Guadalupe student. School is a time to learn, but it is also a time to explore.

"This Career Day celebrates the discoveries our speakers made in their own lives. By telling us their stories, letting us see how they came to be here, I'm hoping that these members of our Guadalupe community not only encourage our students to dream large, but to show them the cold, hard tools they'll need to succeed."

Shortly after Ms. McDonald was hired last May, the school board discussed cancelling the event. During last year's Guadalupe Middle School Career Day, one of the key speakers, District Attorney Raymond Crosby, was assaulted by an alleged fellow gang member of Thomas "Taco" Alvarez, after charges were filed against Alvarez for the shooting death of sixteen-year-old Gloria Rivas (a former Guadalupe student) and the attempted murder of Sergeant Olivia Mendez. The Alvarez trial is currently under way. This year, Principal McDonald says the presence of Sergeant Mendez among the guests should help quiet any unrest.

Other Career Day speakers include the aptly named Suze Weaver, an internationally famous fiber artist; local family therapist Dr. Cassandra Henry; Allison Kitagawa, a university professor of Japanese history, whose niece Bee Cuomo was a Guadalupe Middle School sixth grader before her still-unsolved disappearance last October; and high-tech entrepreneur Thomas Atcheson, whose son, Brendan, is a star player on the Guadalupe basketball team.

6:55 A.M.

GUADALUPE MIDDLE SCHOOL

Dawn, and sunlight finds the low spots in the hills to the east of San Felipe.

Half a mile overhead in a cloudless sky, a businessman on descent to San Jose International rests his bleary eyes on the fingers of light across a multicolored tapestry: rich brown soil readied for planting, dark maroon lettuce seedlings, myriad shades of green from celery to kale. An east-west curve of river dips under a north-south stream of highway. Near that crossroads, the sun touches a sprawl of low buildings, the sorts of huge rooftops and industrial-sized lots that suggest raw materials rather than finished products. Traffic builds on the freeway's asphalt tributaries.

To the north, where suburban rooftops give way to plowed fields, sunlight flares against glass: the clerestory windows atop the cafeteria of Guadalupe Middle School. Grades six through eight: 712 adolescents between the ages of eleven and fourteen; forty-eight teachers, full- and part-time; and twenty-one administrators and staff, principal to janitor, part-time nurse to the three lunch ladies. Today, the number of souls at

Guadalupe will hit 820, although beyond those threads (as Principal McDonald has so colorfully told the local paper) lie a million others that weave the students into the fabric of their community: the warp of teachers and staff, the weft of visitors and volunteers, binding experiences, passions, and ideas into a tapestry of life, both light and dark.

A part of today's population are twenty-three outsiders, bearing with them twenty-three stories of childhood, training, decisions, and work— all the events that brought these adults out of Indiana and India, Australia and Austin, England and New England, and set them down at Career Day in Guadalupe Middle School.

The growing dawn finds a few cars already in the staff lot. Lights go on in the cafeteria, where low-income students will soon gather for government-subsidized breakfasts. The jet-lagged passenger overhead hears the flight attendant's recitation, and pulls his gaze from the placid landscape to search for his shoes. He does not see the long, white-topped buses emerging from the district lot. In forty minutes, the first of them will deliver its load of noisy adolescents to Guadalupe Middle School.

The morning will pass, devoted to dreams. The visitor's lot will fill, guests will be welcomed and introduced, then escorted to their respective classrooms.

By the time lunch hour comes, the school will be exploding with energy as young hearts whirl around the sheer *possibilities* of the lifetime stretching out before them. More prosaically, the guests will be fed, before their stories resume.

The firefighter will speak not only of heroism, but of injuries and insurance premiums. The forensic technician will balance the satisfaction of figuring things out and locking bad guys away against the boredom of testimony, the paperwork, and the sense of being a small part of a large team. The game designer will describe how difficult it is to make a profit out of those thrilling red splashes on a screen. The weaver will make no effort to conceal her dependence on luck, and the propensity of artists to starve. Students will be given the raw material for their life's plan, and shown the means to turn it into their life's tapestry.

All that is, at least, the plan.

But today, the weaving of dreams will unravel long before the final bell.

A long white van will drive onto the school grounds. A dark figure will get out. Carrying a heavy nylon bag, he will walk calmly into the school from the side road. The door to classroom B18 will open, and not quite shut again. Minutes later, the first *pop-pop* will echo across the quads and fields.

Adult voices will stutter into silence; adolescent heads will snap up; farm workers in the field across the road will straighten, looking at each other in wide-eyed disbelief. At the next *pop-pop-pop*, a wave of fear will crash across the school. A woman walking through the playing fields will drop her bag and break into a run; another woman in the school office will scramble from her chair. Before the two come together, the midday sun will be sparkling off a thread of blood oozing down the center of the concrete quad.

Career Day at Guadalupe Middle School.

ABOUT THE AUTHOR

LAURIE R. KING is the *New York Times* bestselling author of fifteen Mary Russell mysteries, the Stuyvesant & Grey historical mysteries, and five contemporary novels featuring Kate Martinelli, as well as the acclaimed novels *A Darker Place*, *Folly*, and *Keeping Watch*. She lives in Northern California.

LaurieRKing.com

Facebook.com/LaurieRKing

Twitter: @LaurieRKing

Twitter: @Mary_Russell

ABOUT THE TYPE

This book was set in Caslon, a typeface first designed in 1722 by William Caslon (1692–1766). Its widespread use by most English printers in the early eighteenth century soon supplanted the Dutch typefaces that had formerly prevailed. The roman is considered a "workhorse" typeface due to its pleasant, open appearance, while the italic is exceedingly decorative.